The BrimTier Chronicles

Part 1

Life of a BrimTier Pirate

By: Lisa J. Comstock

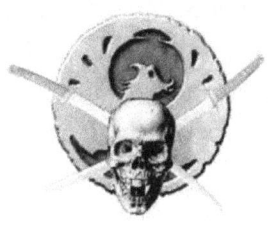

2018

Softcover ISBN: 978-0692193877
PUBLISHED BY ENCLAVE PRODUCTIONS, LLC
USA

Printed in the United States of America

Look for all The BrimTier Chronicles
at your local bookstore
if you don't see it on the shelf, ask for it!

Check out them all at

www.brimtierchronicles.com

This book is dedicated to my father, Royce A. Witham.

Sadly, I lost him before he got to hold it in his hands but his love, encouragement and support meant the world to me. He is, and will always be, remembered with love!

There are far too many people I would like to thank for their time, patience, encouragement and support than I can feasibly list on this page; without whom this book would still be nothing but a pipedream.

I want to say a special thank you to Steve Comstock, Jane Witham and Nina Liv Witham for their love and support, for lending me their ears and for helping me make this dream come alive.

Articles of Phoenix Enclave

- All aboard must obey civil command; the captain has final say in all matters.

- Any caught attempting to desert will be marooned on the first dead planet with one bottle of water, one laser pistol and one magazine of charges.

- Any found deliberately keeping secrets or lying will suffer marooning as previous item.

- Any caught stealing from the ship or fellow shipmates shall spend up to four days in the brig, suffer the gauntlet or flogging before crew, depending on item of theft.

- Any who lays hands on a superior officer shall receive flogging.

- Any found not ready for battle, and not under doctors orders to remain so, shall receive flogging and forfeit their shares of next haul.

- Any who attempts to meddle with another without his or her consent shall suffer death.

- Any who refuses to follow an order given by a superior shall suffer one or more of the following, depending on the outcome of refusal: Forfeiture of shares of one or more hauls, up to four days in brig, flogging, gauntlet or marooning.

- Any attempting mutiny shall be spaced.

The Space Frontier

"We progress by reaching towards
what has yet to be done."
– Confederational Regime mission Statement

My name is Iain Daniel Bryce, pronounced <Ī-yăn>, and I am a pirate but not in every sense of the word. I've done my share of swashbuckling and do indeed steal, and I won't deny that I've occasionally pillaged, sometimes burned, from time to time wantonly destroyed many a thing in my day and, yeah, I've killed, but only when I was forced to, and truly took no pleasure in doing so. One thing I will adamantly deny, and dare anyone to say otherwise, is *I've never, nor do I allow my men to rape*! I'll admit I *am* guilty of being a menace to society and imagine someday I will have to pay for the crimes I have committed, but not today!

I been called the Robin Hood pirate by some, which I don't particularly like, I say leave the man to his own story and legend, I wanna make one of my own, but 'cause I steal from them that's got and give to them that don't, I guess that's an accurate appellation. Some say I'm a hero and I guess to some I am, but not to anyone that really matters. I been called a god by some 'cause I seem to be immortal and I guess to some it would seem that way as well, but believe me that's far from the truth. I am just a man. I bleed red, I love and I hate like all them others. I can die, and someday will, hopefully of old age, but my life will most likely end in a far more bloody way. Difference between me and some of them others is I believe in something that's bigger than me and that belief has helped me make it out of some right tight scraps, is all.

Before you is the first of my journals, hopefully one of many more; these chronicles are not meant as a declaration of my guilt, quite the contrary, they are intended to be a true account of my exploits as a BrimTier pirate aboard the diamond class star vessel Phoenix. Some of these stories will be rough in language and a bit graphic in content but then what would a pirate story be without? I haven't changed the names to protect the innocent, partly because I don't think there are any and partly because I believe in giving credit where credit is due. No doubt I will long be dust by the time anyone that could do anything to me for these pages reads them.

Nor have I inflated, embellished or lessened a story to make it any more or less enjoyable. Everything you read between these covers will be exactly as it happened with the feelings and emotions of the people at the time. Even my own shortcomings will be laid out for all to see. Yeah, I got a fair few! And don't worry – after you get past this introduction the rest of this tome will be far more exciting, or at least a little less droll, perhaps.

I suppose the best way to begin is to give you some backstory to explain why I chose this way of life, since it was a conscious choice. First let me explain how the BrimTiers came to be then I'll tell you a bit of my world.

The word BrimTier is a synonym for the space frontier – the last true frontier. We never found proof of aliens, though some still look – it's a big frontier. By 2160, Earth had become the utopia everyone prayed for, disease and war becoming only brief passages in medical and history books, but this paradise lasted for only about fifty years then the truth of the situation became too much to dispute. It was finally admitted, though it caused more than a fair few tribulations, that this paradise hid an acrimonious side; without disease and war the death rates dropped while the birth rates continued to climb, at an alarming rate, meaning a great population boom.

By the year 2215 the increased population had all but depleted Earth's already strained resources, forcing extreme measures. This did act as a jumpstart to the space program, which had been all but spinning its wheels for close to a hundred years; this jumpstart was more necessity than advance in true science, though some of the latter was achieved in the offing. Now, in 2261, we have people all over the known universe.

How exactly was this achieved, you ask? Earth's scientists, under pressure from the Confederational Regime, our current government, came up with a rapid way to make some of the moons and planets of known space more Earthlike by a process called terraforming. This creates a livable atmosphere on a celestial body, be it an actual planet or manmade, by mimicking Earth's atmospheric climate. This is achieved by regulating the atmosphere, finding or making water available and bringing ultraviolet and cosmic radiation to within manageable levels. By satisfying these four conditions an ecopeosis, there's my ten-letter word for the day, or rather nine, but you get the gist, can be achieved.

When optimal conditions are reached: plants, animals and insects are introduced the people move in, creating the circle of life. Some moons and planets took well to this process; some it destroyed – causing horrific weather conditions. The planets that were not able to terraformed were peraterraformed. A mini ecopiosis is created using biospheres with cities, forests, gardens, rivers and lakes are constructed and systems allowing reproduction of any weather condition wanted.

By using these processes we've moved outward from Earth. This seemed a new version of paradise but it didn't take long for the colonies on Venus, Earth's moon, Mars, Jupiter's moons: Europa and Callisto, Saturn's moons: Mimas and Rhea, and two space stations: one between Jupiter and Saturn and one just beyond the mini planet, Pluto, to fill to capacity as well. This pushed us out farther and farther.

The colonies within our original solar system are called the Inner Tier, fifty lightyears out from that is the First BrimTier, the next twenty-five lightyears out is the Second BrimTier and all after that is uncharted space. The tiers are separated by more than just blackness of space; all the advances have done nothing to change the public's perspective of social orders, more than ever a person's name and birthplace is all that matters.

The Inner Tier is mostly old money and gets the best supplies, middle class families and blue-collar laborers, the ones that had the resources and money, were able to purchase spots in the First BrimTier which is adequately supplied. The rest: the ones without wealth or influence, and the criminals, were sent to the last, the Second BrimTier. This tier barely sees any supplies at all.

That's where me and mine come in; we try to help the people of this forsaken tier. What my crew and I do won't make their lives more likable but I hope we do make them livable. Our task isn't an easy one though, we must contend with less benevolent pirates and the CRF. I'll tell you of each, beginning with the latter, since they are currently the bigger thorn in our side.

The CRF is the police for the CR, which is an acronym for the Confederational Regime, rolls off the tongue, don't it? That's why most of us call 'em simply the CR. This is our current government. Did you notice I didn't say elected? In spite of all the scientific, technological and medical advances the political arena has reverted back to feudalism. The position of leader of the people is now passed down from father to son in the same family. The president is like a king, in many ways: having power over all beneath him; he has his lords: the CRP, his army: the CRF, and his subjects: the rest of us. Most of us think he's a bumbling oaf, but he's the final authority on all things so then he must be respected, right – NOT!

The president's name is Thomas Nason and he's my nemesis. He knows there are people that aren't getting the supplies they need and I don't think he particularly cares; least he never seems to anyway. He knows too that there are pirates robbing the cargo and supply vessels, and though this bothers him, I'm sure, they are no more than nuisances, a little like bothersome flies to be swatted. When he learned one of them pirates wasn't only robbing his ships but giving the goods to the uncared for colonies, that irritated him.

See, I think he'd rather forgot there is a problem at all, my being around makes him and others see it and that paints him in a right bad light. In order to send them aid he'd have to first acknowledge there was a problem, then make changes to rectify it – that would mean shaking up the status quo and we all know how much politicians like doing that!

That's how he learned who I was and why he'll stop at nothing to see my neck stretched. You'll learn far more than you wanna know about him in the coming pages, believe you me.

Though the president isn't my biggest fan and will prove to be a right royal pain in my ass, his second in command, Gerard Nikolas, is far worse. He has the proud distinction of being my arch nemesis. He plays a major role in my tomes and you'll learn all about him as well. The main thing you need to know about Mr. Nikolas is that he hates me more than any other pirates, though he hates them all as well, but I'm special – see. And I'm not talking the kind of hate that you feel for someone you don't like being around; I'm talking true hatred, as in wants to erase me from the very fabric of life. Gives you a right warm and fuzzy, don't it? I've heard he is a cruel bastard and enjoys torturing any he captures so I hope never to let him catch me. He's a very unforgiving and obsessed man and no doubt dreams of nothing but putting me in my place and I imagine he'll get his chance one day but not for many years to come, if I can help it.

Mr. Nikolas is also the fleet admiral, or high commander of the CRF: Confederational Regime Forces, and head of the lesser known CRIA: Confederational Regime Intelligence Agency. He, just a right bit, enjoys using both of these to irritate me as much and as often as he can.

The CRF has one star admirals, vice admirals, rear admirals, colonels, leftenant commanders, sergeants and ensigns like the Navy of the past but instead of patrolling the high seas in battleships; they sections of space on battlecruisers. There's several dozen cruisers patrolling the Tiers but I'm only concerned with the few I have had regular run-ins with – all of whom you will learn plenty of soon enough.

The CRP: Confederational Regime Parliament is the senatorial body of government: a representative from each of the colonies in the Inner and First Tiers and a total of five that represent the more than fifty colonies of the Second. They act as judge and jury and have tagged most BrimTier pirate captain and their enclaves with prizes of capture. Mine's currently set at one million creds as of this penning – impressive, ay?

It's not the highest of bounties but it will climb before I am finished. It's enough to cause me a right bit of bother. Other pirates and Mr. Joe Public have tried to capture me for this bounty over the years, the greedy bastards, but luckily, I have allies that consider me a bigger asset free to do my pirating. My allies will be described throughout, as will other BrimTier pirates.

Where we differ from other BrimTier Pirates, and how we got the Robin Hood pirates moniker, is that we give three full shares of our hauls to the colonists we help, the rest is split between me, my officers and crew, with any leftovers going into a slush fund.

Speaking of shares brings me to the real reason we all become pirates to begin with; the booty, plunder, treasure, spoils, cache, horde, haul or whatever you want to call the overall prize. We typically keep any weapons, ammo, liquor and ship parts, we sell off any trinkets, jewelry and such, give the colonists any clothing and technological innovations and we split any food, medical supplies, fuel and livestock with the colonies.

Though there's more than fifty planets and moons colonized in the Second BrimTier we only help about fifteen of them; we call 'em Phoenix colonies. Some need more help than others and some have natural resources we can use for ourselves or to help other colonies. We don't ask for any payment in return for this help, per se, but we do take advantage of their gratitude by using them to hide us away when the need arises. Most of the time they don't mind doing this because most of them consider us friends. Describing each of them would take up way too much paper as well. They will be described in various stories, as needed.

My enclave consists of upwards of forty. Of these are nine officers and me, the rest are the grunts. We're a lot pickier than most enclaves with who we take on as crew: anyone who can't be entertained by books, music, a right good game of cards or well stocked bar won't be allowed to crew my ship; hence there will be no need for a holodeck.

The grunts are just that, the worker bees. I won't describe each of them separately as they come and go so frequently. Specific ones will be described as needed in each story. My officers, on the other hand, are important to all my stories; they are my eyes, ears, and at times, arms and legs, the ones I rely on and the ones that rely on me. I trust each and every one of them with my life, would die for any one of them and believe they'd for me as well; a theory that will be tested more than once in the coming pages, I expect. I will describe each of them in detail and in order of seniority.

Jaimes Aaron Cable, or Jaime <Jāy-mē>, is my quartermaster, my first officer, second in command, and is answerable only to me. He stands six foot five, has shoulder length medium brown hair, brown eyes and a dark complexion. He handles all the aspects of the daily operations and crew rosters as well as acting as captain when I'm off-ship, whether by my own accord or against my will, often takes the off-ship missions to meet with our fencers and is the first on site for a siege.

Jaime's like a brother and, not to sound mushy or queer, I love him. I've known him since I was seventeen and he eighteen, and trust nobody more. He knows how to handle me, even in my worst mood, and I give him *a lot* of practice. I allow him far more liberty to speak out and he acts as my conscience at times, since I've a tendency to ignore mine. He never wanted to be anything but a soldier so he don't mind me being captain, he trusts me and he knows I'll listen to him if he thinks my commands are too harsh – most of the time.

My second officer, and third in command, is the weapons master, Hayden Paul Fabris, pronounced Fabry. He is six foot eight and is built like a tank, he prefers his keeps his hair short, crew cut, and his square jaw always has a 5 o'clock shadow. His primary duty is to keep my ship and its crew in weapons and ammunition and directs the guns team – six grunts that man Phoenix's laser cannons and the fore and aft laser batteries. He gets one and a half shares for this position and is very stingy with them, often refusing to spend any unless absolutely necessary and refuses to tell any of us what he's saving for. Though, I would be right willing to bet my security master knows, since the two are lovers.

Now, don't go and have a conniption; I've no special dislike of people that've chosen the alternative lifestyles, other than it ain't for me, my security master is a woman.

Like Jaime, she defected from the CRF. As my security master, Evelyn Marie Oakley, Eve for short, is five foot nine, has an athletic build and keeps her brown hair braided most of the time. She takes care of all aspects of security, on and off my ship. She screens the replacement grunts, trains and keeps them fighting trim, and acts as bodyguard to any of us when we are off the ship. She too gets a share and a half of our hauls and, like Hayden, for the most part, banks hers away.

Our health master, Robyn Ann Carter, has long wavy blonde hair and is well turned. She is very good at her job and we give her plenty of practice at it. She also defected from the CRF but hers was for reasons of the heart – me.

She manages a staff of two, a nurse and an intern of sorts that acts as nurse, assistant or surgeon when needed. Her staff was handpicked by her and has been by her side for most of the ten years she's been with us. She more than earns her one and a quarter shares but unlike my weapons and security masters, she loves to spend it on anything she thinks is pretty.

My procurement master, Mitchum Wayne Gordon, is near as round as he is tall and has short chubby fingers, but he manages to keep all our business affairs in a semblance of order. Mitch is our banker, purchasing agent, accountant and brains. He acts as buyer and fencer for the supplies and articles we need bought or sold, doles out the shares and handles the ship's coffer monies. He has set us up a rather complex banking system that allows our shipmates to put their shares into a holding account and has issued loans and advances on pending hauls when the need is great. My only complaint with him is he likes his spirits and casinos a bit too much. He spends most of his one full share on one or both pastimes, most times both at once. I won't complain about it though; it's far less than he would earn in a legitimate position, and because he rarely does.

My chief-cook and bottle washer is Samuel John Yardley, or just plain Yard. Yard is our ship steward, or more formally: galley master. In this capacity, he manages all the aspects of the galley, the mess, the aft lounge and cleaning staff with a staff of eight grunts. He keeps his brown hair spiked most of the time, when it isn't covered with a doo rag. He is surprisingly thin for one who works with food all day, and is a right excellent cook; in point of fact he could make a pile of shit taste delicious. No joke, I have seen it and tasted it! Yard works closely with Mitch to pick out the ship's food stores and has been known to add some of his own one full share to the food budget to get exactly what he wants for his galley.

My ship mechanic, the engine master, is Grant Edward Taylan, or Digger. He has bright red hair that is never brushed, and wears thick, coke-bottle glasses. He is a grease monkey if ever there was one. He eats, sleeps, breaths, and some think, makes-love to engines. He knows Phoenix's engines and electrical systems inside and out, forward and back. As long as she works he can do whatever he pleases to her. Unlike most other pirate mechanics, who are lucky to get half a share, he gets one full share – and he is well worth it!

My navigation masters are twins, Kassie and Kyle Cambridge. They are the only people of color currently aboard my ship. They compete at near everything they do; especially how tight they can make my ship go. I've seen them both do things with this ship that would make your hair turn white. Kassie flies better than anyone I've seen behind the helm but both make it look easy. There are no better pilots out there in my book, pardon the pun. They each get three quarters of a share but they pool their money, saving most of it hoping to buy their parents out of slavery.

As for the captain of this crew. How do I describe myself, as I look in the mirror across from me, without sounding modest or conceited? I try not to let my dirty blond hair get beyond my shoulders, because it gets right annoyingly curly, and often have a scruff on my chin. I'm considered young, at thirty-two, to be a ship captain but over the years I've proven my worth and have earned the respect of my crew, which is all I truly care about. I understand the value of a good shipmate and try to give them a good captain to lead 'em. It's taken me ten years to make a name for us in the pirating world but I can proudly say we have rightly earned our place in them history books.

I was born on Beta Four, one of the farthest out colonies in the Second BrimTier, on the very edge of known space; one of the planets that didn't take well to terraforming, and wasn't considered important enough to be peraterraformed. It's a dry husk of a planet with little natural atmosphere and even less vegetation but whole lots of dust and its fair share of crime; the only thing this planet ever grew well was its criminals; look at me. Some say I take our "cause" a little too personally but you see I've lived the life of a forgotten colonist and felt I was forced into a life of crime in order to survive – so it is personal. I ain't trying to get rich at this life; I only give myself two and a half shares.

The final, and arguable most important, member of my crew is my ship, Phoenix. She is a diamond class star vessel named partly for the color of her exterior: a mix of red, black, silver and gold; she looks a bit like she's on fire, soaring gracefully through the blackness of space. She isn't the fastest or the best gunned ship out there but she is, by far, the best manned. As far as I'm concerned that goes a long way toward the first. She is very maneuverable, thanks in part to my pilots and mechanic, and has outrun many attacks. She can support a crew of fifty but I find more than forty to be crowded.

Phoenix operates primarily on plasma fuel engines; she has two main engines that can be used for either quick bursts of speed or a sustained burst thrust for jumping to hyperspace. She also has spacesail technology for between jumps, to conserve on the precious and expensive fuel. They look impressive when fully open, like the wings of her namesake. Her defenses include six laser cannons, fore and aft repeating laser batteries, a full bank of stealth torpedoes, an enshroud device that makes us invisible, and fully encompassing deflector shields, that keeps us from sustaining too much damage in battle.

The last two systems were decommissioned years ago by the CRF for flaws but Digger has found ways to get them to work. We also have something that is in much demand but is exclusive to Phoenix. It's a Digger Taylan special: a micro vascular membrane system. MVS for short. This system is like a nervous system on the outer hull of my ship, a second skin, with veins that bleed an adhesive epoxy and polymers that cure to a hard coating, filling in the breached area, in essence healing herself. Just one of Digger's more brilliant ideas, he comes up with some right nutters, which is why I value him so much.

So now you know who we are and where we call home – now onward.

Though we are criminals, we will never deny that, we're not completely amoral. Our cause *is* just, for all it's camouflaged as crime. Life in the Second BrimTier is complicated, it's not black and white, there are many subtle layers and shadows of grayness. we live our lives in the gray areas. It's cold and harsh out here in the black but we try to make a life at it 'cause we know nothing else. When you can't find food or shelter you turn to whatever you can, sometimes that means taking from others. I s'pose I do the crime so they don't have to. I know it sounds ass-backwards for a petty thief to say he is in the right, but we are.

As my first journal, and your voyage into the darkness that is me begins; you'll learn why, more than ever, Thomas Nason won't be happy until he has my head and body in one of these cases. He thought he detested me when all I was doing was robbing from his supply ships, now he's got an even deeper hatred for me, because I have messed with one of his own.

So, now let us begin. Welcome to life in the big black!

Love Thy Enemy

"Love thy enemy – it'll drive 'em
crazy trying to figure out what you
are up to."
—   Anonymous

"We've got to get moving!" said Hayden, rather pointedly.

"Tell us something we don't already know, Weapons master," Jaime snapped back sarcastically.

"*This is not...* helping..." started Mitch, squeaking slightly and quickly losing his nerve.

"ENOUGH!" said a deep voice from the darkness of the hall. The grumbles all quickly stopped as their captain, Iain Daniel Bryce, stepped through the hatch into the conference room. His always slightly mussed up hair made him look angrier than he was, "We know what we *must* do, let us figure out *how*."

Phoenix was anchored, rather precariously, to a chunk of FSD – floating space debris, at the moment.

This chunk of what was likely once a planet or moon may yet prove her deathbed. The crew was unhappy about this condition since it was the beginning of the second week of it. They were attempting to hit a convoy of three supply ships when a blast from a CRF starling managed to pierce an opening in the starboard shield and punch a hole in her primary fuel tank. Digger's micro vascular membrane system works quite well for smaller fractures and dings from FSD's, but not large gaping holes. In the time it took the MVS to seal the breached area they'd leaked most of their raw plasma stores; which is how they wound up where they currently were, with barely the fuel to keep the environmentals running.

"Now, what is our highest priority?" asked Captain Bryce. He sat down at the head of the table and took a drink from the cup of coffee waiting for him.

"We need water," said Yard.

"We don't have fuel to go anywhere to get any, the first burst will finish us," grumbled Digger. He'd spent most of the last week repairing the hull and wasn't in the best of moods.

"We can survive several more weeks on what we have of fuel but we need to replenish our water supply or we could have a medical crisis on our hands," said Yard more adamantly, looking to Dr. Carter for agreement.

"He's right, Captain. The water reintegration filters are all but spent. They aren't purifying the recaptured water, meaning we aren't getting all the contaminants out. That will cause bacteria levels to rise and kill us," said the doctor, ignoring the evil looks from Digger and Hayden.

Digger started again, "We *cannot* filter the water unless we have the fuel to..."

"This we already know, Digger, tell us something new," interrupted the captain. He was getting tired of going over the same issues every day. He too was frustrated, and he too knew the dangers if they didn't do something soon, but no one seemed to have a solution.

"We should take what can be spared of the fuel in a sandpiper and go after more," said Jaime pointedly. He'd offered this same option three other times already but had been shot down each time previous.

"Is there enough?" the captain asked Digger.

"I think just, sir."

"I volunteer," said Jaime, standing up.

Before the captain had a chance to accept, Kyle's voice came over the ship's intercom. "Go."

"We have a ship on the radar, sir. It's about three clicks off our aft."

They all rose quickly and left the room, making their way to the bridge.

Captain Bryce, who was in the rear. He pushed his way through them and stepped into the helm room. "What class, Kyle?"

"It's a transport class, Sir, a bluejay."

Captain Bryce looked to his mechanic for a breakdown of this class of vessels.

"They're a type of space bus. They'd have good fuel stores for the backtrip. We should be able to siphon the tanks; that'll get us up and moving, at the very least. The food stores should be good as well, but there won't likely be much cargo for resale."

"What's it doing out here in the middle of nothing and nowhere?" asked the captain. There were no resort planets for about ten lightyears.

"She's submitting a general distress call to all channels," Kyle offered as possible explanation.

"Damage?"

Digger studied the scanning array and said, "Her hyperdrive is offline, Sir."

"Weapons?"

"None usually," said Digger, sounding confused, "they usually have a CRF escort though."

"Is there any other ships in the vicinity?" asked the quartermaster.

Digger shook his head and said "They could be hanging back, but it would take them time to reach us."

"Is it coming this way?" asked Jaime.

"They'll come within a quarter click."

"Do we have the fuel to intercept her and get back if we meet trouble?" asked Captain Bryce. He wanted this hit as much as any of them, but he had to look at the bigger picture.

"No," answered Digger dejectedly; the collective sigh completed the simple answer well.

"Then we modify the quartermaster's plan. Jaime, put the CRF insignias on a starling and go to them as if you're responding to their distress call and lead them this way. How close does she need to be to grapple her?"

"Within a tenth of a click, Sir."

"Alright, Kyle, keep an eye on the radar for siege crashers. When she's within a quarter click, engage the shroud then hook her and bring her in. Go to it, Jaime."

"Aye, aye, Captain," Jaime and Kyle said in unison then Jaime ran to the hanger deck.

The first stages of siege getting all their adrenaline flowing, the captain told Hayden to ready the grunts with weapons, the doctor to fill a bag with medical supplies, in case of injuries, Yard to raid their kitchens for anything worth taking, Digger to retrieve any fuel he could and strip the vessel of any usable parts and Mitch to be ready to record the haul and went to dress himself more appropriately for the siege on the bluejay.

"All the mischiefs in the world may be put down to the general, indiscriminate veneration of old laws, old customs, and old religion."
– George Christoph Lichtenberg

Iain felt the first viewing of Phoenix Enclave was an important ceremony, in homage of sorts to their pirate forefathers. His simple dress of tan linen trousers and white button up shirt was fine for regular ship wears but he felt he had an image to uphold so he changed the linen pants for a silk pair with wide red and black stripes and the plain shirt for a black silk tunic with puffy sleeves. A purple bandana was now tied over his head, leaving the sides and bottom of his hair loose and curling wildly, the simple silver stud earring in his left earlobe was swapped with a fake finger bone, dangling from a golden chain, and his regular brown leather boots were replaced with a pair of black leather boots that came up to his knees and folded over, completing the look. He glanced at himself in his full-length mirror and smiled at how outlandish he looked; it was an important impression to make, so it was endured.

As he turned to leave, Kyle's voice announced the bluejay was within a quarter click and the shroud was being engaged. He smiled wickedly as he grabbed the black leather belt that held the holsters for his laser side arms and ran towards the hanger bay.

Captain Iain Bryce, seven officers and fifteen grunts walked through the docking tunnel and stepped through the opening that had been cut in the other ship's hull. The first thing they saw was a large billboard that made them all laugh heartily and set the mood appropriately. The sign told the passengers of the bluejay what they should do in case of a hijacking and hinted that any who cooperated would be all but considered accomplices to the crime.

Once they all got over the initial joke, the captain said enthusiastically, "Let us begin. *The siege is on!*"

Yard and his men went immediately to the galley and began to inventory the food stores, Digger went to move the fuel tanks to Phoenix, Hayden and five grunts went through the ship, herding the occupants and crew into the dining hall, and Captain Bryce, Jaime, Eve, Dr.

Carter, Mitch and the balance of the grunts went there to wait.

It wasn't long before the passengers and crew began to flood into the room; all stopping dead at the sight of their captors, who were standing on a catwalk that went around the room, like a terrace above the assemblage.

The lights from below, streaming up through the open grid work grating, made them all look quite impressive but they made Iain Bryce look superhuman. The way they flickered made his mussed up hair look like it was being blown by some unfelt wind and the smile, that normally looked quite warm and friendly, look very sinister. It made more than a few passengers forget how to breathe for a moment.

Captain Bryce looked down on the passengers of the bluejay before him and smiled, they all seemed appropriately frightened. The first thing he needed to do was weed out any that might try to cause unneeded hassle. Before him was an unusual mix for a resort transport, not many looked to be vacationers, but he didn't linger on the thought. Most of them, including the ship's crew, were ignored at once, not worth worrying about. Seven CRF officers, the highest rank a lieutenant commander, three men dressed in business suites, a young couple hanging on to each other for dear life, and a very portly lady, being comforted by what was possibly the most beautiful woman Iain had ever seen, and took all his effort to look away from: held his interest. Iain nodded to the quartermaster.

Jaime's strong, steady voice carried easily across the room. "Eyes forward, ears open, mouths shut!" It took only one attempt to fulfill the request, even the fat lady quieted. He nodded to the captain.

Iain took up his most imposing stance and said, in his deep, commanding voice, "You are under siege of Phoenix Enclave, as long as no one attempts anything foolhardy none of you will come to harm. I am Captain Iain Bryce and this..."

"You're the Robin Hood pirate," interrupted one of the bluejay's crew with a snigger. This sent grumbles of disappointment and mockery through the crowd.

"Aye, and these are my *merry men*!" snapped the captain as ten pirates stepped out from behind him, aimed laser rifles at them and, in unison, charged the guns up with a loud and overt tweak of energy.

They all fell silent and the fat lady swooned.

The pirate captain stood quietly as he waited for his men to report on the condition of the ship. He was trying to build the prisoners' anxiety, nervous people tended to do as they were told better. Though he would harm any of that fought him, he didn't want to. The problem was he was getting anxious himself. Digger should haved commed by now. He was about to send someone to find out the man's status when his voice finally came over the badge on his lapel.

"Go, Digger," answered the captain.

"The hyperdrive is extremely unstable. If we bleed it dry it could explode. I've siphoned all I dare, Sir."

"How much did you get?" asked Iain, trying to hide his anxiety.

"Enough, Sir," answered Digger.

"Any idea what they're doing out here alone?"

"It looks like the drive failed while they were in jump and it dumped them here; their escort is most likely lightyears from here," answered Digger.

"Can you repair it?" asked the captain.

"It's fried; it will cost more than she's worth to even try." The frustration in Digger's voice was very thick, he hated when he had to admit he couldn't fix an engine; it really bothered his pride.

"Your suggestion?" asked Captain Bryce.

"We scuttle her, Captain."

"Alright, finish up and get back to Phoenix."

"Aye, aye, Sir," finished the mechanic.

That wasn't good news; these vessels rarely had much of worth beyond their resale value. Hopefully at least one passenger would prove worth ransoming.

"As I was saying before, no harm will come to you, long as you cooperate," said the captain as he once more addressed the prisoners. He paused to see if he got any dissension before continuing. "First, is there any here that require medical attention? Any with weak tickers, or the like?" There was some chatter then a unified no. "Good, you can return to our ship, Doctor."

Dr. Carter nodded and started to leave the gangway. She stopped when a voice called out.

"You're the one that will need a doctor."

Eve quickly brought her laser rifle up, which prompted the grunts to do the same, looking for who had spoken. It had come from one of the suits.

Undeterred by the number of rifles now aimed at him – or just plain stupid – the man continued, "Release us immediately or you will receive no mercy."

"Excuse me, did I give you leave to speak?" growled Captain Bryce.

"I'll see you hanged for this," said the suit.

"My neck's just long enough, thank you, but *you* will need my doctor to sew your tongue back on if you don't hold it."

The man looked ready to continue but one of the CRF officers put a hand on his shoulder and slowly shook his head.

Iain looked down at Mitch, who had come from the purser's office during the exchange holding about a ream of paper. "How many aboard, Master Gordon?"

"Thirty-one, Sir," Mitch quickly counted the heads before him, "Captain, I see only thirty."

The captain looked over the heads before him and came up with the same. He was about to tell Eve to search the ship again when the mousy man, part of the clingy couple in the back, raised his hand.

"Sir… excuse me, Pirate, Sir? My son is passenger number thirty-one."

Captain Bryce motioned the couple forward. The woman was holding a bundle of cloth in front of her; both jumped a foot when the captain twisted his hand in the air, motioning for them to drop the cloth. The woman hesitated then complied, revealing the head of a baby. Iain kneeled before them, bringing him eye level to the man and asked, just loud enough for the three to hear, "Boy or girl?"

"B… boy, S… sir," the man was shaking so bad it sounded like he was stuttering.

"How old?"

"Si… six… mo… months, sir. You… you *are*…the pirate… who gives to the poor… aren't you?"

"I am," said Captain Bryce proudly.

"We will do… noth… nothing to cause you any… any trouble, I pro… promise."

"That's good to hear," said Iain just as Yard stepped from the hatch below, carrying ten bags, his grunts each had ten bags in their arms also. Iain acknowledged his galley master then turned to the bluejay captain, "How many lifepods is this vessel equipped with?"

"Ten."

"And, they each can hold how many?"

"Six each."

"Plenty," said Iain. He looked back to the young couple. "Might you have an ident card on you?"

"Yes, Sir." The man stepped forward, passed his tattered billfold up to the pirate captain and stepped back.

Iain opened it and pulled out at an ident card that had seen better days. The holograph was definitely the man standing before him. It listed him as a resident of Bangor, a planet in the First Tier, with an occupation of coalminer, meaning he had no monetary connections. There was thirty credits inside the billfold, which he passed to Jaime, then he handed the wallet back to the man. "Thank you," said the captain. "Yard, take two bags, add some extra milk and water, just in case, and escort them to a pod, if you please."

"Sir?" asked the coalminer, confused.

"The bags hold a week worth of provisions. The beacon in the pods is more effective than the distress signal of this ship. You should be found by a CRF cruiser within three days, we will be back through in four. If you're still here we'll collect you and take you to the closest colony," answered the pirate captain.

"Thank you, Sir," said the man through tears.

"Bless you and your men," said the woman as two grunts escorted them and their baby from the room.

Captain Bryce waited for them to be gone before he stood and turned his attention to the rest of the travelers. "Now, let us see if any of you is worth keeping?" Grumbles erupted but quickly stopped when he held up his laser again, "Form a neat line before me and kindly have your ident cards ready, if you please."

The first of the three men in the suits, was a lowly banker; nobody would pay for his safe return. He only had fifty credits and nothing else of worth. The next five passengers proved to be of little value either, except they had three hundred fifty credits between them. The bluejay crew might fetch a little from their company but not enough to be worth the effort. They would hold the CRF men for ransom. One of the two other men in suits was the head of a conglomerate of farms on Jones Province within the Inner Tier; he was taken immediately to Phoenix's brig for ransoming. The final suited man, the one that had heckled them, stepped up then.

Iain drew in a breath. "Right bloody brilliant! Please pardon me, ladies and gentlemen, we are in the presence of none other than the most dishonorable, oh, pardon me, that should be honorable, shouldn't it? The second in command of our *fine* government, Vice President Gerard Nikolas," said Iain in fake reverence. He put his hand over his heart like he couldn't contain the excitement then quickly spit on the deck at the man's feet. "Tell me, Mr. Nikolas, what is the likes of you doing aboard such a public vessel?"

"That's none of your business, you despicable rogue," snarled Vice President Nikolas.

Captain Bryce acted momentarily affronted then smiled and said, "It matters not. You'll fetch a right pretty pent, I expect."

"The president will pay you nothing."

"You'd better hope he does, 'cause I've got no other use for ya and I wouldn't consider submitting any of these fine folk to the torture of being stuck with you in a pod for even a day!" Iain turned away from him as if he were any other man.

This was an insult the man took personally, "You arrogant bastard, I'll kill you myself!" Mr. Nikolas grabbed Iain's silk shirt, drawing the captain's attention back to him.

Iain looked down at that hand, then back up and raised an eyebrow as he said, through clenched teeth, "Remove your hand, now!"

The man did release the cloth and took a step back, his face turning white for a moment.

Iain almost wished the vice president did try to hit him and was disappointed when he didn't. He motioned two of the grunts over and said, disdainfully, "Take this piece of shit from my sight at once."

That left only the two women.

The fat lady had cried herself dry but was still whimpering hysterically. She looked to be about fifty but there were no gray in her almost jet black hair. It was pulled back severely in a bun on the top of her head. Her face was round and her cheeks were bright red though not due to makeup. She had dull gray eyes and very thin, almost colorless, lips that didn't look like they had smiled in many years. She was dressed in a plain brown dress with no waist to it, which only made her look fatter.

The other woman had an impudent look on her face, though she was trembling a little. He had thought she was beautiful from the catwalk, she was even more breathtaking up close. Blonde hair fell in loose curls to just past her shoulders, her deep brown eyes had a defiant sparkle to them, she had a well-shaped nose that had just a bit of an upturn to the end and was wearing just enough makeup to look natural. She had an air about her that was very refined and was trying, very hard, not to show how afraid she was.

Iain almost felt sorry for them, they likely had an idea what most pirates would do to them. He couldn't tell them that they didn't have to worry about that from his crew because their anxiety was essential. Neither of them had ident cards on them, which was odd. When he asked why the girl only put a hand up to quiet the fat woman and shook her head. "At least tell me where you were heading?" An innocent smile was now on the captain's face.

The girl said nothing.

"I cannot get you home if you don't, Lady," said the captain patiently.

Still, the girl said nothing.

"No matter. I dare say a few days in my brig will right loosen up your tongues," said Iain. He was about to wave them away when the fat woman burst.

"You can't do that, she can't be harmed, she is…"

"Moira!" the girl shouted then stamped her foot, upset that she had been made to speak.

"You do have a voice to go with that beautiful face," said Iain, hoping to charm her into speaking more. She blushed a little but had already regained her self-control. He turned back to the heavy-set lady, obviously the weaker link, and asked, "Why can't I harm her?"

The woman was back to only whimpering.

He shrugged, turned away from them, climbed the stairs back up to the gangway and took up position in the center of his men.

The pirate captain held his hand out to his quartermaster. His second handed him a decorated scroll case. He slowly, dramatically, unrolled the scroll inside it, looked up to be sure he had all their attention then cleared his throat and began, "Per the articles of Phoenix Enclave, you are hereby offered the chance to renounce all your former alliances and join me and my crew as free BrimTier pirates. First, I will read you my requirements, then you choose to agree to them or refuse my offer."

"What if they refuse?" asked the girl.

"The CRF officers, the farm boss, the vice president and you two will be ransomed and released, the rest of you will be set up in escape pods with enough provisions to survive, as I did the couple with child."

The girl seemed unconvinced, and a bit amused, but only nodded for the captain to continue.

Captain Bryce thought about asking her why she was so concerned for everyone's safety but he didn't want to lose his momentum. He began to read the articles of Phoenix Enclave. He paused halfway through and looked over the crowd to be sure all were still paying attention, they were, the girl looking a little green. He glanced up at the girl again as he said the line about meddling with another results in death, this was said with absolute sincerity, and the line about mutineers getting spaced was said almost in anger.

Once he had finished, the captain rolled the scroll back up, handed it to Jaime to put back into its case then leaned forward on the railing with a bit of amusement on his face. He looked down on the passengers and bluejay crew before him as they spoke amongst themselves. He wasn't surprised none took the option; he rarely got any that did; he felt it was only right to give them the choice.

He ordered the ladies and CRF officers be taken to the brig and the rest to be loaded, three to a pod, those pods released, the rest of the ship stripped of anything of value then, as Digger suggested, to scuttle the ship.

Back aboard Phoenix, Iain went immediately to his office. He set his computer to find any information on the vice president. While it was searching he stepped through the door that opened into his cabin to get back into his normal ship wear. He tossed the discarded pieces into a pile in the corner. He stopped before the mirror across from his bed and ran his fingers through his hair to muss up the matted portion that had been covered by the bandana. When he stepped back into his office he poured himself a fresh cup of coffee and stepped behind his desk, smiling as he found fifty-six documents relating to Mr. Nikolas waiting for him.

It took him nearly an hour to sort through all the articles; most were of appearances made throughout the first two Tiers and were quickly discarded. A brief piece on his current business holdings gave him potential sources if the president did refuse to pay but one article caught his eye and made him smile.

It actually wasn't the article so much as the photo with it that stopped him. It showed the first and second families before the capital building on Earth, on the left was the vice president with his wife and son and on the right was the president with his wife and son on each side of him and his daughter in front of him. It looked to be from about five years ago but the resemblance was unmistakable. Iain left his office, feeling better than he had in months, to meet with his officers and find out how lucrative the haul had been.

Yard set a mug of steaming coffee before the captain and took his seat at the long conference room table, still in a bit of a snit.

"It's only until we have received some of the ransoms, Master Yardley" said the captain, the initial amusement having waned now.

"But, no meat, sir?"

"We don't have enough fuel to run the coolers, Yard," said Digger, more than irritated already, having gone over the same subject three times before.

"The first ransom credits we receive are yours, Galley Master, you may purchase and slaughter as many beasts as you like. In fact, throw a right freakin' huge barbeque if you like," said the captain.

Yard harrumphed but remained silent.

Captain Bryce turned his attention to Mitch and asked him the question the rest had been waiting for.

"We knew it would be slight at best," said the procurement master. He brought out a digital tablet and punched the numbers on the calculator before looking up at the expectant faces, "Six hundred fifty credits between all the crew, passengers and cabins, the ship wielded trinkets that should fetch near two thousand and miscellaneous parts and equipment another five hundred or so. Some crates of fresh vegetables and fruits, two-dozen live hens and two barrels of fuel." He pausing to take a breath and added, "I don't believe there is enough in this haul to be worth giving to a colony so I put forth we use this to replenish our own supplies?" He looked at the others for consensus.

"I don't see as we've much choice. I'll forfeit my share of the first ransom we receive to purchase supplies for them and make up for the small haul," said Iain.

The others said the burden should be shared equally, so it was decided they would each give a share.

Iain smiled and nodded proudly at his officers then they began to make plans for ransoming their prisoners and adjourned the meeting.

The captain had asked the pilot before they started the meeting to get a comlink through to Earth, which meant relaying the signal through several stations and then all the levels of staff on the planet to speak directly to the president himself, knowing it would likely take many hours to finally get connected to him. He was standing at the counter across the back of his office, setting up the coffeemaker for a fresh pot, when Kyle's voice spoke from the combadge pinned on the right side of his shirt. He pushed the skull shaped button to open the channel and said, "Go, Kyle."

"Captain, I have the president on com for you."

"That was quick. Patch him through."

Iain sat down and turned the monitor on to find the very irate face of the president looking back at him. He flashed his trademark smile and said, "Good Day, Mr. Nason, or is it evening there? Well no matter, it seems we have some business to transact. I am Captain Iain Bryce of Phoenix Encla…"

"I know who you are. Let's dispense with the pleasantries, I've no need for such with the likes of you."

"Now, now, no point getting put off before we even begin." said the captain, more than a little amused.

"I've received a report that you're holding the vice president and my daughter hostage, before I say anything more, what proof do you have to show me?"

"Let's get right to the point," said Iain, smiling wickedly. He reached behind him, removed two items from a glass case and held them up to the monitor. He watched the man's eyes move from one to the other and the color drain from it as he recognized them. One was a golden locket with the scrolling letters CJN engraved in the center, dangling on a golden chain; the other a signet ring with the Confederational Regime seal set into a black onyx stone, still on the finger that had worn it. Iain smiled, knowing the president had gotten the message, and waited for the official to speak.

"Wh… what do you want?"

"Let's see, I think Vice President Nikolas ought to be worth… one hundred thousand creds. Your daughter should be worth more, I think. I'll take another hundred thou for her, plus twenty head of cattle, six being virile males, twenty ton of grain and twenty barrels of drinkable water. I'll throw in her retinue for nothing."

"That's too much!" spat the president.

"For your second in command, and your very own flesh and blood? No, I think not. Your answer will be required in seventy two hours."

"What then?"

"If you accept my terms, we'll make arrangements for the ransom delivery and prisoner drops, if you refuse, you'll receive a piece of each every week until you have them all back."

"You wouldn't dare," said the president.

"I wouldn't? Would you like this to be the first piece of Mr. Nikolas or would you prefer something a touch fresher?" asked the captain darkly, showing him the sliced off digit with the ring on it again, "Now, exactly why wouldn't I do this?"

"If you harm my... *I will hunt you down and destroy you.*"

"I have enjoyed my life so far, *Mr. President*, if my ticket is up, so be it," said the pirate smugly.

"You arrogant bastard, I'll..."

"Mr. President, please don't provoke him," said a voice somewhere beyond the monitor.

"Listen to your advisor, *Tommy boy*. I'll be waiting for your ans..." the screen went black.

Kyle's face appeared moments later, "The connection was severed Earthside, sir."

"Thank you, Kyle." Iain stared at the piece of finger with the ring on it for a moment. He turned back to the case, pulled the ring off the severed digit and placed it into the case then tossed the finger into the rubbish incinerator across the room. He smiled sickly as it ground in the tines. It wasn't really the vice president's finger; it wasn't even a real finger. As yet the man was unharmed but the pirate had to present a front that he *was* willing to harm them. He lifted the locket from his desk and started to put it in the case. He stopped and smiled as he held it up to the light, watching it sparkle as it twirled. He closed his hand over it, closed the lid on the case, and left the office.

Iain walked down the corridor leading to the cells that made up the brig. The first cell on the right had three CRF officers and the businessman, the one opposite had four other officers and the next held Mr. Nikolas by himself. The vice president sneered at him as he walked by. He thought about stopping to taunt him for a moment but was in too good a mood to let him spoil it. He continued on to the last cell, which was around the corner, by itself, holding the two ladies.

The heavy-set woman, Moira, was sitting on the cot across the back of the cell, looking extremely distraught, and the young lady was pacing back and forth across the center. Hearing footsteps approaching, the girl turned toward the opening and crossed her arms defiantly over her chest.

The captain smiled at her and was pleased to see a touch of red color her cheeks. "Is the cell to your liking, ladies? Please be sure to let me know if there's anything I can do to make your stay more… enjoyable," said Iain.

"You can let us go," said the girl.

"I don't think you right want us to release you just now since we're in the middle of space and it gets right cold out in the black," said Iain, a smirk on his face.

Moira jumped up and stepped in front of the girl, "Do not harm the girl have your way with me instead!"

Iain fought the urge to laugh, partly at the thought that he would even consider touching a woman like her. He put what he hoped was an innocent look on his face and said, "I would never consider having my way with either of you, against your will."

"Don't you play your games with me, Pirate," spat the fat woman.

The captain smiled, the woman might not be attractive but she had spirit; he knew she was honest in her desire to protect the girl.

"Moira, enough," said the girl, rolling and then closing her eyes and shaking her head in obvious annoyance. She turned her attention to the pirate captain, locking her brown eyes on his blue-gray ones and asked quite boldly, "What do you want, Captain *Bunce*?" emphasizing the intentional mispronunciation.

Iain didn't react to the insult, except to smile even wider. "I wanted to return this." He pulled the necklace with the locket dangling from it out of his pocket and passed it through the laser bars to her.

The girl didn't say anything at first, suspicious of his intentions, when he shrugged and started to return the chain to his pocket, she quickly said, "Thank you," and reached for it. Their hands touched briefly and another spot of pink tinged her cheeks briefly.

Iain couldn't speak for a moment and his heart felt like it had forgot how to beat. He coughed quickly and said, "I was wondering if you would care to take a turn about my ship?"

"Lady, no!" cried the fat lady quickly.

Without even looking at her retinue, the girl quickly said yes.

The pirate captain smiled as he punched the button to shut off the laser bars and put his hand out to the girl. She took it with a bit of the same glimmer of defiance she had when he first saw her on the bluejay.

They walked through the hanger bay and cargo hold in silence. They rode the lift up to the central deck where Iain slowly walked her past many doors, but didn't open any of them, only telling her that they were the crew quarters. He did let her see into the sickbay briefly, where he got a displeased look from the doctor, so he didn't linger. He pointed out the doors at the end of the hall, in the rear of the ship, and told her those were his rooms. He had a feeling she wanted to see inside them but he didn't show her, partly because they were a mess just then and partly because he could tell it bothered her that he hadn't. He motioned that they would be climbing the ladder just outside his cabin to the upper deck.

Iain climbed up first and offered her a hand to help her off the last rung. Once she was on the walkway he asked her name; he wasn't surprised when she lied.

"Ca... Cathy, Mr.... Captain Bryce."

"Okay, *Cathy*, you may call me Iain if you like."

"Iain... what *are* you planning to do with me?"

"Once your ransom has been met you may be taken anywhere you like, *Cathy*."

The girl tensed again and quickly said, "But we are poor, I thought you helped the poor," starting out shy and ending sarcastically.

Iain smiled and motioned her around the corner.

They stepped into a large room with lots of tables; some had people sitting at them but most were empty. The sound of pots and pans rattling and the smell of cooking coming from behind a set of double doors at the end of the room told her this was the dining hall.

"This is our mess hall," confirmed the captain. He motioned her on. He made her jump as he said, "You know you don't lie very well, Ma'am."

"I'm... I'm not lying..." she said shakily.

Iain pointed out the day room and the conference room. "First, your clothes are wrong for someone poor."

"It's second hand," she said cheekily.

He skipped the next door and took her to the observation deck. "Secondly," he continued, undaunted, "That necklace I just returned to you could be swapped for enough to feed a colony for a week. Third, I know of no poor girls whose parents can afford a retinue; that is what Moira is, if I'm not mistaken." The girl started to say something else, Iain quickly continued. "And lastly, your looks are far too soft and beautiful for one with a hard life of poverty."

She blushed again, in spite of herself.

The captain showed her the aft lounge next, which wasn't near as clean as he'd have expected, or liked, a couple empty beer bottles and dirty ashtrays were still on one of the tables, this made both of them frown for different reasons. She gave him a disapproving look, like she would have expected no less on a pirate ship so he didn't linger there. He motioned her back to the door he'd passed over, where he wanted the tour to end. The girl started to say something when the door opened to the arboretum and hydroponics bay. Her quick intake of breath told him he had made the impression he'd intended, which made him smile.

Before her was a room filled with foliage in many shades of green, white and yellow and flowers of every color. The sound of water trickling somewhere out of view, butterflies flitting between flowers and real bird calls made her want to go explore the many pathways but instead she closed her eyes, laid her head back and let the warmth of the overhead lights, which felt very much like real sunlight, wash over her. Though her lips said, "This is beautiful." The look on the girl's face said, 'Why would pirates have a garden?'

"We're not all uncivilized, Ma'am. Though, I give you, most pirates are criminals, crooks and rogues, please, I beg you, don't lump us all together."

The girl sat down on a marble bench and played with a leaf hanging over her shoulder for a moment. She looked up and said, "I… I know what you're going to do to me… if I don't fight will… will you leave me alive?"

Iain was taken aback by the question; he had been trying to put her at ease. He asked her delicately, "May I ask what you think I'm gonna do with you?"

"Moira says you will beat us, torture us, take turns raping us and either kill us or leave us on a distant planet to die," answered the girl, her voice shaky with tears.

He wasn't sure what to say at first, some pirates would likely have done just exactly that, though not necessary in that order, how could he reassure her she didn't have to worry about that aboard his ship? "As I said on the bluejay, I don't allow unwanted meddling of any captives on my ship. That rule applies to me as well as my crew. I give you my promise no harm will come to you, in any way, while you are aboard my ship," said Iain as sincerely as he could, placing his hand over his heart.

"Your articles also state you don't allow lying," said the girl, big tears now coming to her eyes, "You're right, I'm not poor… I'm…"

"Caitlyn Nason, the CR president's daughter."

"You knew? How?"

"I'll admit it was mostly by accident, I was reading up on our… illustrious vice president and came across a holograph of you and your family." She gave him a look that implied she was surprised he could read, which bothered Iain. "Not all pirates are uneducated either, Ms. Nason," he added a little curtly.

Caitlyn looked properly chastised then she got a quizzical look on her face. "Do you really give to the poor colonies?"

"We do," answered the captain proudly.

"My father says you are a phony, that you only give enough to make yourself out a hero, he says you *are* no different than other pirates. He says there are no poor, only less fortunates," the girl said this all extremely fast, as if saying it quickly would make it truer.

Iain closed his eyes and shook his head. "There are some among your government would like you to believe this. They don't want it known there are people living in refuse, that there are mothers starving themselves to feed their children, who don't live much longer anyway because it's far too late by the time they get any food, that there are people dying from drinking polluted water because they never got the filter units to cleanse it properly…"

"These must be isolated cases, Daddy would surely see all this if what you say is true," she said quickly.

"Maybe if he left his fu… right comfy office Earthside once in a while, he just might," snapped the pirate. "*I*'ve seen people living in shipping crates because they never got supplies to build anything more substantial. *I've* seen people having to live off roots and dirt because they didn't receive the amendments to make the soil fertile enough to grow anything edible and I have seen people dying from diseases the doctors of Earth had cured long before you and I were ever even thought of because they didn't get the medical supplies or the doctor trained to administer them. I, for one, couldn't stand by knowing they don't have to live this way. What I do might be wrong, on the surface, but they all need someone to help them and I don't see anyone else right *stepping up to do it*."

The girl was still unconvinced, "Why don't they appeal to my father, surely if all you say was true he would send them additional supplies."

"Believe me they all have, to no avail."

"But you steal for profit too?"

"I'm not getting rich at this, Lady," Captain Bryce said pensively.

The captain knew his words were falling on deaf ears; the girl had been raised to believe her father was the end all and be all; he was the center of her world. And, no doubt she had been told all pirates are nothing but evil heathens who maim and kill everything they come in contact with. That was true for most pirate enclaves. How could the likes of him, one of the evil pirates, hope to make her see what he said about the Second BrimTier conditions were true and her father was lying, unless she actually saw it for herself. A thought came to Iain then, but did he dare?

"Come with me to the planet Dvorak? Soon as we receive the first ransom we'll be taking them supplies. You can ask the colonists yourself, see if they agree."

Caitlyn looked panicked, then her shoulders stiffened and she said, "Yes."

"Very good. I will fetch you when we arrive then."

"Captain… Iain, may I stay a little longer?"

Iain was about to say no because he had things he had to see to, when Robyn and her intern, Harris Adams, stepped into the bay. He called Harris over and asked him to stay with the girl and return her to her cell in about an hour then followed the doctor up the path.

"You're quite taken with her, aren't you?" asked Robyn when they were out of earshot.

"She is merely a prisoner whose education is more beneficial to us than most, Dr. Carter. If she can see our cause for what it is, she could, perhaps, convince her father and make our lives a right sight easier," said Iain.

Robyn acted as if she hadn't heard anything Iain had just said, watching the girl. "You have her intrigued as well, yes, I do believe she is just as taken with you." A slight smile was coming to the doctor's well-formed lips.

Iain pulled the doctor to him and kissed her very passionately, stopping her from saying anything else for a moment. When they separated he had a mischievous smile on his face. "I'm right taken with you, Ms. Carter. Tell me, would you be busy just now, I'm coming down with something, or rather up, that needs to be looked at?"

The sparkle in his eyes was more than obvious; Robyn smiled, "I'm free at the moment, captain."

"Marvelous!" said Captain Bryce. He motioned her to lead the way. He didn't follow immediately, he looked over his shoulder at the girl who was blushing brighter than the pink rose beside her; telling him she had been watching. Smiling cunningly at his personal triumph, Iain followed the doctor to his cabin.

"The possibility of failure ought not to deter us from the support of a cause we believe to be just."
–   *Pastor Maxwell Bryce*

Captain Bryce set the sandpiper down gracefully in a large meadow, surrounded by giant trees. He locked the landing gear, dropped the loading ramp and motioned for Caitlyn girl to follow. He asked her to wait just outside the shuttle then went back up the ramp, reappearing moments later on a four wheel ATV with a trailer hitched on the back. Once he was clear of the ramp he helped the girl climb on the seat behind him and told her to hold on as he gunned it, heading up a dirt path that went into the huge trees.

Caitlyn looked into the trailer and saw a small pile of buff colored gunny sacks marked grain and rice, three large blue barrels of what she guessed was water, by the sloshing sounds she heard coming from them, several small boxes marked with the medical symbol, three cages full of live chickens and several other nondescript boxes of varying sizes. She wondered if the pirate was so arrogant that he was willing to give up these supplies just to impart his view on her. She wasn't sure what she was about to be shown but she guessed he'd contacted these people and told them to act grateful when they arrived. After all, he couldn't possibly be telling the truth, could he? She didn't want to believe anything Captain Bryce showed her, she wanted to believe her father, that he was right; she was quite tense with that desire, but the pirate's sureness that he was the one in the right was quickly making her very uncertain of it.

The ride to wherever the captain was taking her wasn't enjoyable in the least, except for being close to him. A part of her had to admit he was a very handsome man and his sureness, his presence, was unquestionable; there was something so strong and real about him, something so striking in his overall demeanor. He was nothing like she had read about. A part of her, a small part, was intrigued by the conviction of his statements of the ailing colonists; if he was lying he did a very good job of it. She'd seen true caring in his eyes. And those eyes, those blue-gray eyes – eyes that seemed to look through you, to your very core. Those gorgeous eyes, that she longed to have looking at her now…

She couldn't let the pirate trick her; he was the enemy. It was only the rebel in her talking; the part that wanted to prove to her father that she could make it in the world without him. The smell of his hair blowing in her face was agreeable to her nose, mildly fruity, and the feel of his muscles as he moved with the vehicle under the thin gauzy tunic was pleasant to her fingers, but that was where her delight ended, or at least where she would admit to.

The road was muddy, the thick, foul smelling, black stuff was splashing onto her white shoes and the bottom of her dress. A part of her wondered if he was hitting every wet spot he could find on purpose. She was about to ask him to try to miss a few, and when they would be wherever he was taking her, when they dropped over a rise in the terrain and their destination was before them.

He slowed them to a crawl.

She guessed so she would get a good view of the whole city, except she couldn't call it a city, more a group of buildings, except she couldn't exactly call them buildings either. "Is that it?" Caitlyn asked. She realized how snobbish that had sounded even before the pirate gave her the indignant look.

"Welcome to Pioneer Town, *Princess*."

Caitlyn had expected to see skyscrapers, malls and lots of bright lights, used to seeing hovercraft buzzing around in air lanes and hearing noises of busy city life. What she saw instead was about two dozen canvas and mud huts with bits and pieces of shipping crates, paneling and even rusty parts of ships as roofs and walls and all she heard was the wind whipping through holes in those structures and the chickens cooing in the crate behind her. A small fenced off vegetable garden, not nearly enough to feed the number of people she saw moments later, was behind the farthest row of huts. The only building that looked even remotely uplifting was a dingy little church at the far end of the road.

She saw a head peer out from behind a curtain hanging in one of the church windows and then a bunch of people, ranging in age from elderly to mere infants, filed out, standing just off the road. They cheered loudly, some jumping up and down. Captain Bryce waved back at them and stopped the ATV near a stone wellhead. She gagged as she was hit with a horrendous smell. "What is that?" she asked, holding her nose.

Iain pointed to that well, "Water's not drinkable."

A middle-aged man, that looked like his skin was meant for a man twice his size, hobbled over to them and stuck his hand out to the captain. His smile was more than warm, but the state of his teeth made Caitlyn turn away. Out of the corner of her eye, she watched the pirate shake the man's hand willingly.

"Hello, Gibb, it's been too long. We hit a right bit of a snag but came as quick as we could," said Iain.

"We rationed your last deliveries, Captain Bryce, so we have been okay. Still, we are very glad to see you today. Please allow us to prepare you some dinner," said Gibb. He motioned to some other colonists who quickly started toward the garden.

"No, Gibb, we cannot stay." The captain waved the scattering colonists to stop and come back to him.

Caitlyn saw real relief on the man's face and was struck with sick realization this was because they *did not* have enough to spare. She felt like crying then but knew that would be an insult to them. She was about to turn away from all the dirty faces, so they wouldn't see this, needing a moment to catch her breath. She jumped when something touched her hand. She looked down and found a young girl, of maybe eight, looking up at her. At first she was going to pull away from the dirty child but the blue, saucer like, eyes drew her in. "What is it?" she asked sweetly.

"My mum had hair like yours," said the little girl.

The word *had* seemed to scream at Caitlyn.

Iain leaned over and whispered, "Her mum, Meg, died of influenza last year, and her father died while helping dig the well three years before."

She didn't know what to say; tears did well up in her eyes and she no longer struggled to fight them.

Iain bent down, so he was about the girl's height and, winking up at Caitlyn, said, "My dear, Marissa, I've got something special for you, go look in the blue box," pointing to a box near the front of the trailer.

The girl kissed his cheek and rubbed it with her tiny fingers, as if to set it permanently. Her dirty face broke into a huge smile as she called out to the other children then ran to the trailer, giggling with excitement.

By her reaction Caitlyn guessed the captain had brought boxes like that before. She found herself giggling when she watched Marissa pass out balls, kites, stuffed animals and hoops; the girl kept a small blond doll for herself. Each child came up to her and Iain after and thanked them, many giving the captain hugs and kisses, all he happily returned.

"You're very good with them," said Caitlyn as she watched two boys tossing a ball back and forth.

"They get it the worst so we try to give them a little something whenever we can," said Iain as the ball bounced over to them. He picked it up and tossed it back.

"Do you have any… any of your own?" she asked, finding it hard to hide her anxiousness.

"Nope. And, I don't have a woman in every port, either."

"Oh," she said quickly, blushing a little.

Iain watched Caitlyn as he helped Marissa change the dress on the doll, and smiled. No matter how much she might try to deny it, he had made an impression.

By the time the supplies were unloaded and put away the sky was starting to darken. Iain said they had to go, which brought several cries of whoa. Caitlyn watched him shake many dirty hands and hug many dirty bodies with no prejudice and smiled, he somehow seemed even more handsome among these weathered people.

Iain patted Gibb on the shoulder, and said, "We'll bring more supplies as soon as we can."

"Thank you so much, Captain," said Gibb ardently. He said goodbye to Caitlyn then stepped back to give them room.

Once they were well into the trees, Caitlyn asked, "What do you get for helping them?"

Iain smiled; she was still her father's daughter. "Mean besides the thank-yous?"

"Although they are a heart-lifter, you must be profiting somehow."

The girl wasn't stupid, "These people are willing to hide us if we ever need to disappear for a bit."

She nodded as if that was partly what she had expected. "You really are good with the children."

"Been told that's about my maturity level," said Iain, smiling as he felt her giggling behind him.

They fell silent as they boarded the ship and didn't say anything the hour-long trip back to Phoenix.

Iain spent much of the next morning hold up in his office, partly because he wanted to be alone and partly because he was waiting for an answer to come from Earth on the last prisoners. A reply was supposed to have come yesterday. He wasn't happy with the president's apparent lack of concern. He was about to contact the vice president's family directly to see if they might care for his return, not sure what that would mean for the girl, when his com buzzed, making him jump a little. He turned on the monitor before him and was pleased to see it was Nason. The look his face told him he wasn't going to like what the man had to say.

"I have one hundred thousand credits for you. Where do you wish the exchange?" said the man with no emotion whatsoever.

"That covers Nikolas…" started Captain Bryce.

"That's correct," said the president as if that was the only issue at hand.

"What of the girl?"

"I'll expect Mr. Nikolas' immediate release," said the man, ignoring the question.

Iain was stunned but he hid it well. "Drop the credits in a probe just beyond the final buoy in sector three seven five. *If* we are able to retrieve it without incident we will send you the location of Mr. Nikolas."

"It'll take a few days to get a probe to that sector."

"We will begin to scan for the signal in three, if we haven't received it by the sixth, you'll get the vice president back in a right tiny little box," said the captain plainly, imitating the size of said box with his fingers. The look that came over the president's face told him he had gotten the point. He looked ready to say more but this time Iain cut the connection before he could.

As soon as the monitor went black Iain said, "That son of a bitch!" He slammed his empty coffee cup on the desk, making the pens and rulers scattered over it jump up and shift positions. It sickened him that Nason was willing to pay for Nikolas but not his own daughter. If he could have gotten near the man he would have strangled him with his bare hands then; not only because the credits would have more than replenished their stock, and could have helped several colonies, but for the girl. Now he had to figure out what to do with her. He was supposed to have dinner with her in a little more than an hour. What would he say if she asked about her father and the ransom? Part of him wanted to tell her that her father was an asshole, but he knew that would hurt her, not her father.

Iain picked up the cup he had just abused, checked it wasn't cracked and poured himself another cup of coffee. He sat back down behind the desk, sighed and put his hands over his eyes. He rubbed them hard for a moment then picked up the digital newspaper he'd been intending to read all week.

He had just begun an article about the horrific weather conditions terraformers had caused on Phelps, the latest moon the CR was attempting to colonize in the Second Tier, when the com buzzed loudly making him jump near out of his skin. His sudden movement caused some of the hot coffee to spill over onto the corner of the digital board in his lap. "Shit!"

He shrugged and slurped it off the board just as the com buzzed again. He pushed it on and found a blue screen with the presidential seal. The captain smiled, thinking the president had changed his mind. He set the cup and tablet aside and attempted to straighten his hair while he waited. The face that appeared wasn't the president. This man didn't look a day over twenty-five and was nervous. Iain knew him from somewhere, but couldn't place where at first.

"Are you the pirate holding Miss Caitlyn Nason?" asked the man. He was obviously disguising his voice, forcing it to be deeper than it normally was.

"Yes, and you are?"

"Who I am isn't important," said the man, looking around quickly as if making sure no one was coming, "Is Cait... Miss Nason still alive?"

Iain realized this was Caitlyn's brother, Dylan. He tried to hide his smile as he answered, "She is."

"No doubt, my fa... the president has told you he won't pay the girl's ransom?"

Iain nodded, trying not to appear amused.

"Is she still with you, now, unharmed?" Dylan asked, forgetting to disguise his voice.

"As of now, yes."

"Good, it's not too late then," said Dylan, he stiffened again and said, again in the disguised voice, "*I* wish to meet the girl's ransom."

"How do I know you are good for it, I don't know you from Adam," the captain teased. He felt only a slight pang of guilt for toying with the man.

Dylan snapped, "Just tell me if you will accept payment from me, and how I can get my... her back."

"I'll transmit the coordinates for where to send the supply ship. When we have it secured you will be given the location of Miss Nason and her retinue," said Iain, "I'll allow you one CRF speedster for protection, wouldn't want another pirate getting the goods, would we? I will scan the speedster and if I find her weapons hot the drop is off."

"How long do I have to get the items together?"

"I can allow you... two days," said Iain, trying to sound like he was being generous.

"Two days... I can do that," Dylan replied in his real voice, then, in the deeper voice, said, "I will contact you when the supply vessel is ready," and was gone.

Iain smiled, and sighed. He wished he could have told Dylan his sister was alright, the fact he cared enough for her spoke volumes for him, in Iain's eyes; his parentage not-withstanding. He finished the last bit of his coffee and left his office to let the officers know the ransoms for both were going to be met.

Iain walked to the galley slowly, trying to decide what to have prepared for his dinner with Caitlyn. Hearing the loud, obnoxious noises of the chickens made up his mind. He knew it would please Yard greatly to be rid of two more of the foul fowls. Samuel Yardley is a meat and potatoes man, beef, pork and lamb not poultry or fish, if it don't walk on four legs he don't want no part of it. They hadn't gotten enough fuel to bring the coolers back online so they still didn't have any meat, but the noisy birds would fill the men's bellies well enough.

He swung one of the galley doors open and found Yard chasing one of the hated birds around with a rolling pin. Laughing heartily at the spectacle, and the look on the man's face, the captain asked him, when he caught the thing, to roast it and have two plates with fixings and a chilled bottle of the white wine from Sunnen brought to the observation deck about six o'clock. He made a threatening and graphic gesture to stop the flippant comment the galley master was about to utter.

At quarter to six, the captain walked to the cells to fetch Caitlyn for their dinner date. He was so engrossed in thoughts of subjects they could discuss that he jumped when the vice president's hand grabbed his arm. Without even thinking, he grabbed it and twisted it backward. The man cried out in pain but Iain continued to hold it in the bent position. "I'd right recommend you not do that again if you value the use of your hand!" After a few more seconds he released his grip, just before the bones broke.

Nikolas snapped, "How much longer am I to be held?" as he massaged his hand.

"That depends largely on your boss, don't it?"

"You think you're hunted now, Pirate, if you don't release me..."

"Do I look worried?" asked the captain, wishing now he *had* broken the man's hand.

"I know what you are doing with the president's daughter. If you soil her you will know no rest."

"Think you should worry about yourself, Nikolas."

"*I* care nothing for the girl, I too have thought of tasting her fruits, but she is the president's daughter."
"Keep your foul thoughts and opinions to yourself or I *will* remove your tongue and feed it to you between two pieces of moldy bread. Understand?" growled the captain. If he weren't so valuable, Iain would have spaced the man then and there. He'd find a way to teach him his place before they removed him from the ship.

Iain stopped just beyond the cell and leaned on the wall, waiting for his temper to subside. Part of him knew he shouldn't be messing with the girl and he shouldn't let it get personal, but he couldn't help it. It had started as a fun game, turn the president's daughter against the man as an ultimate slap in the face, but now he was beginning to… what? Fall for her? No.

As his breathing slowed he realized the ladies were talking. He moved close enough to hear without being said and listened.

"You don't know what he's capable of, Miss Nason. I know his type, they're all sugar and honey," Moira said loudly.

"He promised no one will hurt us."

"Unless he doesn't get what he wants."

"Daddy will meet the ransom, don't worry."

"There are things he could do, Caitlyn, and will do to you, before the ransom can be paid. As long as you're returned, still breathing, he'll consider his bargain kept," berated the women.

"He has been nothing but a gentleman with me, Moira. He hasn't even tried to touch me inappropriately. Not once," said the girl.

"Then he's only biding his time, waiting until your guard is down. He is playing mind games with you."

"He promised no harm will come to us."

"Have you ever heard of a pirate that told the truth, unless it benefited him?"

The girl didn't say anything.

"Your father didn't want you to go to Tarnis Prime, remember? What if he doesn't pay, Miss Nason? Do you think the *pirate* will be so accommodating then?" challenged the woman.

"I am sure he will still release me unharmed."

"And what of me?" squawked the woman shrilly.

"I will make sure Iain lets you go as well."

"Iain? *Iain*? Not Captain Bryce? You truly think you have that much influence on him?"

"You should've seen him on Dvorak, Moira. He truly cares for those people."

"I don't believe this, you're falling for him, aren't you?" said the heavy woman forcefully.

"Don't be ridiculous, Moira," Caitlyn's voice was getting irritated now.

Iain faked a cough and slid around the corner. He pretended he hadn't heard their exchange, as he asked, "Are you well this Eve, Ms. Moira."

The heavy-set woman's mouth was open and her face was about three shades of red, all the way down to her neck. She shut her mouth so quick her teeth snapped as they came together, sniffed at him loudly, strode to the

The BrimTier Chronicles

cot and sat down hard, making the edges of the thin mattress fold up from her weight.

Captain Bryce tried hard not to laugh, hiding it in a cough. Smiling satisfactorily he said, "Your dinner this evening is roasted chicken, I hope that will be agreeable to your pallet?"

The fat woman didn't respond, too busy staring arrows at her ward.

Undeterred, and still smiling, the captain looked at Caitlyn and asked, "Are you ready?" When she nodded, he punched the button to release the laser bars and put his arm out to her.

Iain popped the cork on the bottle of wine with ease and held it between his teeth as he poured them each a glass, then pushed the stopper back in and set the bottle aside. "This is from the vineyards of Sunnen, bottled in 2226, so it should be excellent. I've no way to judge this, I typically don't drink wine."

"Thank you," said the girl. She took sip and said. "It's very good."

Iain smiled, happy that he had pleased her.

"This ship belongs to you?" asked Caitlyn.

"She does."

"Did you steal it?" the girl said, partly in jest.

"Yes and no," said Iain with a sly smile.

Caitlyn couldn't help but smile back, "What do you mean?"

"I actually *won* her in a poker game," answered Iain, raising one eyebrow. "It's previous owner thinks otherwise."

Caitlyn shook her head in feigned reproach then said, "She flies smoothly. I usually can' eat on trips because of space sickness. Your pilot is very good."

"She'll be right pleased to hear that."

"She?" Caitlyn was unable to hide her surprise.

"Yeah, there ain't none better than her. I have two pilots, twins, brother and sister, each has their better skills, hers is smooth flying, so she takes the nightshift."

"Are all the colonies like the one on Dvorak?" asked the girl, a little quietly.

"No, not all. Some took better to the terraforming process. Some are a lot like any planet in the Inner or First BrimTier but far too many are exactly like Dvorak."

"I really didn't know," she said, choking a little on a piece of chicken.

Iain waited for her to catch her breath and said, "Your father wouldn't likely have had the kind of information just lying about for you to learn."

"He really isn't a bad man, Iain, he just has a lot of responsibilities. I think if he saw what you showed me you would find him more than willing to help."

"Mmmm," said Iain, not entirely convinced, but not wanting to argue her father's worth just then either. He got a serious look on his face and asked, "Will you tell me where you were heading?"

"The university on Tarnis Prime, it's a finishing school. My father didn't want me to go to it but it was always a dream of my mother's."

"You say that as if she's dead. Haven't I seen her in recent pictures?" asked Iain as he took a drink of the wine to wash down a dryer bit of the chicken.

"That's my stepmother, my mom died when I was eleven," said Caitlyn with a sad look.

"I'm sorry to hear that," said Iain truthfully.

"Do your parents approve of your lifestyle?"

"They's long dust by now, and, I right well expect they'd've found fault in me even if I's the president," said Iain bitterly. He pushed his only about half eaten plate away from him having suddenly lost his appetite.

"I'm sorry," said Caitlyn. She noticed he tended to sound a little uneducated when he was upset. This more intrigued her than turned her off, it only seemed another of the facets that made up the unusual man before her.

"Don't be. I's a right sight better off without 'em, believe me." Iain's hand unconsciously went to the scar below his right eye and lingered there a moment.

"What does the tattoo on your neck mean?" asked Caitlyn, hoping to keep him talking.

He pulled his collar back to give her a clear shot of it and said, "It's a Celtic symbol for love, life and loyalty, the three things I value most in my crew."

"And that one?" She pointed at his right wrist.

Iain twisted his wrist to show her the red Celtic cross on the top of his wrist and the black thorn covered vines that were twisted around it, spelling out his initials as it continuing around to the back side, and said, "I s'pose it represents my faith more than anything else… full of thorns." He lifted his left sleeve then and said, "And, of course, that's my pirate crest."

Caitlyn stared at it for a moment, and smiled, then pointed to the braised skin on his left forearm and said, "Was there another there once?"

Iain looked at her funny, thinking she knew, the innocent look in her eyes made him relax a little. He rubbed at it and said, "Yeah it was, had it removed long time ago, though." Not giving her anymore explanation than that.

Caitlyn could see that one apparently bothered him so she didn't ask anything more on it. She was happy to see him pull his plate back to him and begin to eat again.

They fell silent as they finished their meal.

When they had eaten all they were going to, Iain asked the girl if she wanted to go for a walk.

"Once the ransom has been met, will you take us back to Earth?" asked Caitlin, sounding afraid that was to be the case.

"No, I'll take you to Tarnis Prime."

"What about the vice president? He was supposed to be escorting me; will you take him there as well?"

"That depends. I know what I'd right *like* to do to him," Iain answered with a sly smile.

"That would be?"

"I'd right like to maroon his bony ass on a distant planet and eventually send your father his location, I think," teased the captain.

Caitlyn, who wasn't a fan of Mr. Nikolas either, smiled in spite of herself. It took her a moment to realize they weren't heading for the lower deck and the cell she'd been sharing with Moira. She stopped quickly and looked at Iain with fright in her eyes; remembering the hall they were walking down led to his cabin. "Iain, I…" He stopped her at a door diagonally across the hall from his, put a key card into a slot on the wall and stepped aside so the girl could see inside. She was surprised to find it was a guestroom with two beds, a bureau, a vanity table and two chairs. She looked at him.

"This is your new cell," said Iain, handing her the card. "You may come and go as you please. I'll have your retinue brought up presently… unless you'd rather I left her below?"

Caitlyn got a bit of a sly smile on her face then she said, "You had better bring her up, for all our sakes."

Iain started to walk away, her hand on his arm stopped him. He turned back to see what she wanted.

Caitlyn went up on tiptoes and kissed him on the cheek then disappeared into the room.

"Force is all-conquering, but its victories are short lived."
    –   Abraham Lincoln

Three days later they received the signal from the probe with the vice president's ransom and Jaime went to get it. He returned about two hours later with a black leather bag, the credits inside. Once they'd confirmed it had the correct amount, Iain, Eve and Hayden went down to get the vice president.

He was in his usual condescending mood. "I see you disposed of the women. Did you all have your way with them first? The fat one wasn't the most attractive, but I'm sure *some* of you would have enjoyed that," said the man, looking down his long nose at Hayden.

"No, I'm saving myself for you, Sugar," said Hayden. He puckered up and made kissing noises as he dropped the laser bars and used the rifle barrel to direct the man out.

"Where are you taking me?"

"You'll see, soon enough," taunted Captain Bryce. He enjoyed the look that this brought. He smiled and winked at the other two then started up the hall.

The captain walked in front of and Hayden and Eve stayed behind Mr. Nikolas. All went well until they came to the hanger bay. Thinking they intended to space him, Nikolas thrust himself backward. He knocked Eve into the bulkhead and rammed a fist into her face. He brought his arm back to hit her again as Hayden hit him between the shoulder blades with the butt end of his rifle. The man started to swing for the side of his head, which no doubt would have ended him then and there, but the captain caught his wrist.

Iain released Hayden's arm only when he was sure the man wouldn't lash out again, and put his hand out to help his security master up, "You okay?"

Eve wiped blood from the corner of her mouth and winced as she touched the bridge of her nose. She used her sleeve to stop the blood that was gushing out of it. "Think it's broken, sir."

Iain pushed the vice president against the wall. He set the crook of his elbow against the man's throat and the end of his pistol against his cheek, poking deep into it. "Master Oakley, what punishment do you wish given for this crime?"

She spit more blood out then smiled wickedly and said, "I think we should strip him, sir."

"Brilliant," said Captain Bryce, smiling wickedly.

"Strip me, what does that mean?" asked the man in trepidation.

"I suggest ya keep your mouth shut or I'll exercise my authority and choose my own penalty, one I *promise* will be much more painful," said the captain, malice thick in the words.

The vice president did as he was told until they reached the airlock door then he started to fight again, "You can't space me…"

"If only!" said Captain Bryce with a shake of the head and a look of longing. He punched the button and the ramp slowly began to descend, showing Phoenix was settled on solid ground. The scene the ramp opened to could've been any of the deserts on Earth; sand dunes in all directions and no shade, plant life or cover to speak of, except that two suns were blazing overhead.

The captain picked up a green canvas bag and tossed it to the man. "You've got about a two day supply of food, maybe more, if you portion it right, two gallons of water, a thermal blanket, for shelter in the day and warmth at night, and a laser pistol with one charge. You may not need it, but who knows?"

"You can't leave me here, I'm not dressed for this environment."

"You are correct. Now comes your punishment. Remove all your clothes now, if you please," said the pirate captain, trying hard to keep from laughing.

"You're joking?" the vice president.

"No, I most certainly ain't. That is the punishment my security master has requested for your crime against her body. You can do it now or I can have someone do it for you? I've no doubt I will have no trouble finding volunteers, though they will likely be using some right sharp and over enthusiastic knives to do it," said Iain a little amused as one appeared in his own hand and he began to use the very tip of it to clean under his nails.

While the pirate was talking most of the crew had filed in the back of the hanger to witness the marooning, and Caitlyn appeared in the doorway opposite him.

The vice president looked around at all the eyes upon him and stopped on the president's daughter. He grumbled quietly, "I refuse to do this."

The captain made a quick gesture and most every grunt in the hanger drew their pistols, charged them and aimed them at the vice president. Iain spread out his hands, the knife still held in his right hand and said, "You can be marooned alive or dead, your choice, Nikolas, we have your ransom already, so I care not."

"I will destroy you for this, Bryce!"

"I look forward to you trying. Now kindly comply, we're on a tight schedule."

The vice president took a moment, weighing his options. Deciding he had none, he began to remove his clothing. He stopped when he reached his underwear. The pirate captain motioned with his knife that they had to be removed also. His eyes shifted to the president's daughter and he saw a look of disgust on her face, this made him want to kill the pirate even more. He picked up the bag, took out the laser pistol, charged it fully, aimed it at the pirate's head and smiled triumphantly.

"That's your only charge, Nikolas, you right may find you'll need it to defend yourself while you wait for rescue," said the captain calmly, not looking up or with an ounce of worry, using the knife to clean under the nails of his other hand now.

Mr. Nikolas looked around and saw thirty pistols aimed at him. He lowered it and slowly walked down the ramp with no more fight.

Iain kicked the pile of discarded clothing toward Hayden and said, "Have these burned, I don't want his *funk* stinking up my ship," just as the vice president stepped off the ramp.

Nickolas stopped at the bottom of the ramp and looking back at the captain so scathingly that some of the grunts brought their guns up again, thinking he might use that only charge. They didn't relax their grip until the ramp was completely closed.

Caitlyn followed Iain back to his cabin, once inside she asked, "Why did you do that?"

"Because he is an asshole!"

"That was humiliating!" She was all but in tears.

"And?" asked Iain, as he opened the door between his cabin and his office.

"I thought…"

He turned back to face her and barked, "He broke my security master's nose, Caitlyn, his punishment could have been, and right well should'a been, far worse." He didn't know why her disapproval was making him so angry, or didn't want to admit why was more to the point. "This is my life, Caitlyn, I will not fucking apologize for it. It was this before you and will be long after. What do you know of it, you've had everything right fucking handed to you!"

"I'm sorry, Iain…" Caitlyn said quickly, not liking how mad he was, she had never heard him swear before.

"Tell me, Cailtyn, have you ever had to fucking live off dirt and cockroaches before… or … or… the drips of water off a goddamn rusty plumbing pipe?"

"I understand about the coloni…"

"No, I ain't talking 'bout the fucking colonists, I's talking 'bout me… Me! That waste of human flesh is part of why I had to do that. If him, his fat ass staff, and *your father*, gave two shits about the people…*Their* people…"

"I'm sorry, Iain… it just… took me by surprise; you have been so gentle with me."

Iain felt like he was going to be anything but gentle with her right then and knew he had to make a break now. "Then it's about right fucking time you learned pirate and gentle do not go together, *Princess*," said Iain very callously, as he removed the belt that held his pistol holsters.

"Wha… what? What do you mean?" said Caitlyn, backing up a little. Tears were building in her eyes, thinking he was about to turn into the man the reports said he was.

"I think it's time you left," said Iain, reading the look in her eyes correctly. He slammed the belt down on his bed and turned away from her. Even with all the kindness he had shown her she still thought he would be capable of raping her. He knew he would never be anything more than a scumbag pirate to her.

"But you said you would take me to…"

"You're gonna be taken to the school tomorrow," said Iain, stepping into his office.

"You got my ransom then?" asked the girl.

"Not yet but I think it's best. I wouldn't want you seeing anything else *humiliating* for you!" he said as he turned his angry gaze on her.

"Will we be having dinner together tonight?" She suddenly wasn't sure she wanted to, his usually beautiful eyes looked very dreadful at that moment.

"No, I have too many plans to make. I will try to see you in the morning, before you leave."

"Okay, I will see you later," said the girl.

The captain turned his back on her and pretended to be looking over the starcharts spread out on his desk. He didn't breathe again until he heard the door of his bedchamber close and was sure she was gone.

Iain paced his office for several minutes, chastising himself for letting Caitlyn get so far under his skin then he went into his cabin and began to pace that. He knew getting her away from him was the right thing to do; they had been spending far too much time together and the affects were starting to show. At first it had been a good game but he realized he *was* beginning to have real feelings for her. That *could not* be allowed to happen.

He started toward the door, intent on leaving his cabin to walk the decks, when his door alarm buzzed, making him jump. He said enter, reluctantly, expecting it to be Caitlyn coming to say she was sorry. He relaxed a little when he saw it was Robyn.

"Hello, Iain, God, you look tense."

"Ya think?" retorted Iain gruffly.

"Is it the girl? I saw how disappointed she looked in the hanger," said the doctor.

"I don't know what to do with her."

"Or more know you can't," chided the doctor.

"Don't terry with me tonight, Robyn, I'm not in the fucking mood."

The fact that he was swearing told Robyn just how upset the girl had made him, she knew her worries were right; he was falling for her. "That's bullshit, Iain. What did you expect, I mean honestly? You know you can be very disarming when you want to be, we both know you poured it on pretty thick for the girl, got her to fall in record time, but you can also be cruel and brutal when you want to be. By the looks of you I'd guess you gave it to her pretty hard, hoping to break the ties quickly."

It still surprised Iain how well Robyn knew him, he wasn't ready to stop being mad yet. "Goddamn it, Robyn, our fucking way of life is cruel!" He slammed his fist into the door casing, then took a deep breath and added, "Anyway, she is better off hating me."

"She is, or you are?"

"*Robyn*," he said shaking his head menacingly.

"I don't want to fight, Iain. You want me to go?"

"No. I really don't wanna be alone just now," said Iain, turning on his charm. "I would very much like it if you would stay, my dear."

Several hours later Iain worked his way out from under Robyn, slowly. He smiled down at her as he pulled the blanket over her naked body. Their spirited activity had made him hungry; reminding him he hadn't had dinner. He also remembered that he hadn't sent the CRF the vice president's location yet.

He flipped the coffeemaker on and started to his closet to get dressed when the door alarm sounded. He said, "Enter," without giving it any thought. He was only a little surprised to see it was Caitlyn.

The sight before Caitlyn shocked her but she didn't look away. The pirate captain's dirty blond hair was mussed up even more than usual and he was completely naked. He turned to face her but did nothing to cover himself up. Her eyes quickly traced the length of his well-formed body twice, lingering on the scars that looked like a roadmap in places on his stomach and upper thighs. She wondered how he had gotten them, they almost looked like whip marks but wasn't a person normally whipped on the back? She forced herself to keep her eyes on the tattoo on his left triceps, of the enclave symbol, as she said, "I'm sorry about last…"

"Mmmm, Iain? Is it morning already?" asked a musky voice from the corner.

Caitlyn jumped and turned to see Robyn sitting naked on Iain's bed. There was no denying what had happened between them. "Oh, I… excuse me… I'm… sorry," said Caitlyn despondently. She turned and ran from the room.

Iain pulled on the pants he had just taken from the closet, poured two cups of coffee and handed one to Robyn without saying anything.

She took the cup from him with a perturbed look on her face, "That wasn't very nice."

Iain set his down without drinking any, grabbed a maroon t-shirt, pulled it on and said, "Yeah, s'pose I should go after her."

Iain found Caitlyn sitting on the bench in the arboretum. "Been looking all over for you. You a'right?" He could see she had been crying when she looked up, for all she tried to hide it.

"I'm fine," she lied, "You said you would take me to the school today?"

"Actually, my quartermaster will be taking you. I need to go to the supply ship carrying your ransom."

"But... I was hoping..." she started, "Mr. Nikolas said my father wouldn't pay."

"Your father didn't, your brother, Dylan, is," said Iain matter-of-factly.

"Dylan?" said the girl, clearly surprised.

"I *am* sorry for how upset last night made you, Caitlyn, but that is my world; given, it was something you shouldn't have had to witness, and this morning..."

"Don't be, I was being foolish... I just... I thought we... had something." Caitlyn started to cry again.

"I *cannot* have feelings for you."

"Because you're in love with the doctor?"

"No. Robyn and I... we have an understanding... she and I... well, we enjoy each other's company... nothing more... It's complicated." Iain realized how silly it sounded even as he said it, but it was true.

"Then why?" Caitlyn was even more confused.

"You're the president's daughter," Iain answered, as if that was all that needed to be said.

It was. Caitlyn nodded and thanked the captain for being so kind to her.

Iain started to reach for her shoulder then pulled back, remembering his knuckles were scabbed over from meeting the door casing.

Caitlyn grabbed his hand. "What did you do?"

He pulled his hand away from her and stuffed it in his pocket, "Just an argument with a door casing. I think it might be best you and Moira stay in your cabin until Jaime is ready to leave."

"People with courage and character
always seem sinister to the rest."
–   Anonymous

Two days later Phoenix reached the coordinates for the ransom pick up. Iain was pleased to see the supply ship, Calypso, waiting for them, and the CRF ship accompanying it didn't have its weapons charged, as was the agreement. He told Kyle to send a message to the ship to have their hanger open and ready to accept them and went to meet Hayden, who'd be piloting the shuttle since Jaime hadn't returned from taking the girl and her retinue to Tarnis Prime yet.

"I'm Captain Jeffery Scott," said the man who met them at the hanger door. "Captain Bryce?" he asked, looking from Hayden to Iain.

Iain waved.

"Mr. Nason is waiting to speak to you in the conference room. He has instructed me to offer the use of my men to assist with loading the supplies."

"Very good," said Iain, he looked at Hayden and added, "Stay and supervise."

Iain found Dylan pacing the conference room; he was taller than he had expected, Caitlyn was only about five foot four and the picture he had seen that had first told him who she was showed him as not much taller, he had apparently had a growing spurt since the photo was taken. The man standing before him today was closer to six feet tall, his hair was short, curly and sandy blond and he had brown eyes, though not as striking as his sister's. He looked worried off his pins and jumped when he heard his name called from the doorway.

"Captain Bryce?"

"Thank you for honoring the agreement," said the pirate plainly.

"My sister?" asked Dylan.

"Is safely at school."

"Mind if I confirm that?" asked a skeptical Dylan.

"I would'a been right surprised if you hadn't," said the pirate with a knowing smile.

Dylan went to the combox on the table, called up to the pilot and asked him to contact the administration office on Tarnis Prime. As he waited he watched Captain

Bryce intently. The pirate was leaning against the wall in the corner. He could tell the man was uncomfortable, which made him nervous and uncomfortable. He wasn't acting nearly as smug as he had the day they had spoken on the com about his sister.

The man before him didn't look anything like Dylan had imagined a pirate would. The stories of old always portrayed them as old men with long wild black hair, thick coarse beards and mustaches, and teeth that were blackened or all but gone. Captain Bryce was younger than he expected, had dirty blond hair, was clean-shaven, well dressed, though a bit plainly, appeared to have all his teeth, which were straight and white, and looked quite friendly. He looked more like someone he might see, and be friends with, at the university he attended. He found himself more than a little fascinated.

The com before him buzzed loudly then, making him jump a little. He looked down at the monitor to see the school's headmaster looking back at him. He quickly said, "Hello, Headmaster Albus."

"Mr. Nason," said the man with a genuine smile.

"I wanted to make sure my sister arrived safely?"

"Yes, Ms. Caitlyn arrived yesterday, along with her retinue. She missed first term, but with some hard work, I believe she will be able to make up the missed assignments," said the grandfatherly man.

"May I speak to her?"

"Of course, give my assistant a moment to fetch her," said the headmaster. "How is your father?"

"He is well. Your wife and daughter?"

"Quite well. Is your stepmother feeling better?"

Dylan surmised Caitlyn had used their stepmother being sick to explain her tardiness. Keeping up the front, he answered, "She's doing much better, thank you." He heard his sister announce herself and said, "Could we speak alone for a bit? Family business."

"Certainly, Mr. Nason."

"Thank you. Good day, Headmaster Albus." When Caitlyn nodded he was gone, Dylan asked, "You well?"

"I am, Dyl. Iain said you paid my ransom…"

"Iain?"

"Captain Bryce. Daddy wouldn't then?"

"You know Dad's stand on such, Caitlyn. Were you… were you treated well?"

"Yes, Iain… Captain Bryce, all of his crew, were nice. They really are helping the poor, Dylan. Daddy doesn't understand…"

"Dad won't listen to that from you, me, and certainly not him, Sis, you know that." Dylan was a little surprised she was being so blunt. It felt weird speaking of the man as if he weren't standing in the corner across from him. He could tell he was trying to pretend he wasn't there and that he got stiff every time his sister mentioned his name.

"I know but there are colonists that do need help, and if this is the only way…"

He saw the pirate smiling a little at that comment and wanted to ask him why but stayed focused on his sister. "I don't want to debate, Sister, I only wanted to be sure you're safe," said Dylan, knowing if he didn't cut her off then he'd be listening to her recount every minute on the pirate ship. He did want to hear but not right then.

"I am. When you see Captain Bryce's men, can you ask them … to… to give him… a message?"

Dylan looked up at captain, who was now tense.

"Please tell him… I understand… and… it doesn't change my feelings any," said Caitlyn, a slight quiver shook the bottom of her lip.

Dylan gave his sister a look to say he didn't understand the cryptic message.

She smiled and said, "He'll understand."

"Alright, I will," he said, still looking a bit unsure.

"I have to get back to class now, Dyl."

"Okay. Call if you need anything."

"I will. Love you," Caitlyn disappeared.

Dylan looked up at Captain Bryce. "What did she mean?"

"Just a misunderstanding," said the man a bit too quick.

Dylan could hear the strain in the pirate's voice and thought he just might understand; Captain Iain Bryce was just the type his sister would fall for. "So, what now?" he asked.

"It's customary for me to offer the crew of a siege vessel a chance to join my enclave."

"Very well," said Dylan. He called up to Captain Scott and asked him to arrange for the assembly then turned back to the pirate and asked, "Do you really use the supplies you take for Second BrimTier colonists?"

"Not all of them. We replenish our stock and I pay my crew first, the rest goes to various colonies."

"My dad doesn't like your kind, you most of all."

"*I* don't like most of my kind, Mr. Nason," said the captain candidly.

"Caitlyn apparently thinks you're better as well."

"Yeah, well, as you told your sister, I don't have time to debate on that just now, Mr. Nason," said Iain, dismissing the subject of the girl.

Captain Bryce and Dylan were both surprised that ten of the Calypso's crew did want to join him. Iain was pleased since he needed eight to replace some that had left his service recently and a couple of these new recruits had very useful skills.

Iain was in his office again, his feet up on the desk, his eyes closed, holding a half full cup of coffee – finally feeling like things were getting back to normal. Having the vice president, Caitlyn and her retinue, Moira, on Phoenix for nearly two weeks had put a strain on the crew and their already diminished supplies.

With a deep sigh, he drank the last bit of his coffee in one fast swallow and rose from his desk, ready to head for the hanger. Jaime should be arriving at any moment. He thought he would waylay his friend into a nice game of friendly poker. He started out the office door just as Kyle's voice came over the com. "Go," said Iain.

"Captain, we've reached the rendezvous point but the sandpiper isn't here," said Kyle.

Iain watched the pilot's face scrunching up as he said this, in anticipation of his reaction. Not one to disappoint, Iain shouted, "Son of a bitch!" as he smashed the cup, which, this time did shatter into many pieces, along with all his feelings of things finally going good.

Odynia

"A gem cannot be polished without friction, nor a man perfected without trials."
— Anonymous

"The minister will be down to inform you of your crimes and tell you your punishment shortly," said the guard, spitting out blood along with a tooth, as he shoved the men into the holding cell.

Phoenix's quartermaster sank slowly onto the lumpy cot, making a painful looking face and holding his bruised ribs, as he thought, *this is just great!*

Jaime and two grunts, Evan and Miles, had left Caitlyn on Tarnis Prime then made a side trip to Berem to sell off the trinkets from the raid on the bluejay when all hell broke loose. They had gone to meet with Tiki Blone, one of their most reliable fencers; Captain Bryce didn't care for the smarmy little man but he always got them top credits. This day he was acting especially odd; nervous and noncommittal about making any exchange. When Jaime asked what was wrong the man had suddenly announced he was getting out of the business and said what sounded like, "Oh dear," then stood up, knocking his chair into the back of a burly fellow behind him and all but ran out of the side door. The burly fellow had taken offense to this and a fight had ensued, nearly all the patrons quickly joining in.

Not wanting them to get arrested with the rest of the rabble, the quartermaster headed for his shipmates, sitting together at the bar, intent on making a beeline for the exit as well. A chair crashing into his back stopped him in mid step. Before he could let the perpetrator know he did not want to fight his face was colliding with a large fist. The stunned pirate never threw a punch but the Berem patrols took everyone in, intending to sort the details later.

Jaime had no idea how long they were going to be detained. They had already missed the rendezvous with Phoenix by five hours. They couldn't contact the ship to let them know the reason even if the guard hadn't taken their comlinks because they were lightyears from them.

He couldn't remember anything after the punch to his face but his injuries implied being unconscious hadn't stopped the bar's patrons from continuing to strike him. He wasn't a doctor but he knew at least two of his ribs were cracked, a gash in his right shoulder, held together by a crudely tied bar towel, needed stitches and his nose wasn't broken but the spongy feeling of his cheek bones suggested there might be some tiny fractures.

Evan and Miles couldn't remember throwing any punches either, just being struck from behind. They were in worse condition than him. Miles had a broken shoulder and left collarbone yet seemed to be in good spirits. A welt on the back of Evan's head made Jaime nervous, one of his pupils was dilated and he was slurring his words, implying he may have a concussion. Jaime told Miles to make sure he didn't fall asleep.

The quartermaster spent the next two hours calling for a guard to come to them. Finally one appeared; the same one that had so kindly helped them into the cell.

He had a smirk on his still swollen face. "Yes?"

"We need medical attention, if you please?"

"And?"

"I demand to see this minister of yours this instant. This is not legal," growled Jaime loudly, holding his ribs as he expelled the air to do it.

"And see him you shall."

Jaime had heard that voice before, though it was out of context. He closed his eyes, praying it wasn't who it sounded like. It was. That man, Allister Ashgroth, stepped from the shadows.

Jaime hoped Allister wouldn't recognize him with the blackened eye and swollen face. That hope was dashed as he saw a look of amusement played cross the man's face. The quartermaster wanted to sink into the cracks in the slate tiles he was standing on but he knew that wasn't possible.

"My judoka, Jaimes Cable, as I live and breathe. How long has it been, nearly eleven years, yes? Though I do think you were gone long before that even. You've let your hair grow out and look like you met with a door, or several, but all in all. Tell me your story."

Allister had been Jaime's trainer in the Dragon Troop and had taught him the martial lifestyle he lived by, semai' and semainath. His trainer had been very upset with him when he told him he was quitting the troop, to become, of all things, a pirate. He had tried to talk him out of it, saying he knew he hadn't enjoyed his first assignments but he would learn there was more to it than that, once he had seen the good the troop could do. Jaime had lost all his naiveté when he watched a soldier in his unit kill three colonists just for trying to take water from their vehicles. He had told Allister the CRIA and his idea of good wasn't the same and three years was long enough to give the enemy. He had hoped the years would dull any anger the man might've felt and someday, if they met again, he might say he understood. That dream lay in pieces before him.

Already knowing his story wasn't going to sway Allister, Jaime started to recount what he remembered, "My friends and I were at the bar having a drink when the brawl broke out. None of us even threw a punch. Next thing we're being, rather forcefully, I might add, tossed in here. There must be a vidfeed in the bar that shows this. When can we expect to be released?"

"My boy, you will not be released. Yes, there was vid in the bar but it shows *you* leveling the room. I'm pleased to see you've kept up your semainath."

How could he not remember fighting? Jaime asked his ex-sensei that very question.

Minister Ashgroth motioned the guard to release the bars and stepped aside. He swung his arm out to direct Jaime to follow him, "Let me show you."

Jaime hesitated but the curiosity was too much.

The pirate followed his former master to a large, poshly decorated office. The man he had known would have had no need for such rich decorations; his semai' beliefs alone would have forbid it. He knew then, without doubt, the Allister Ashgroth standing before him was no longer the caring man he had remembered so fondly.

The minister directed Jaime to a chair, walked over to his huge desk. He pushed a button and a panel set in the wall slid down to reveal a vid screen showing a paused image of the bar; aimed, coincidently, right at the very table Jaime and the fence had been sitting at.

The quartermaster watched Tiki Blone push his chair into the man behind him, that man's drink spilling down the front of him then the fence quickly ducking out a side door. He saw himself standing and walking towards the bar then the same man Tiki had shoved his chair into smash a chair over his shoulders and punch him in the face, giving him the black eye and bloodied nose. Finally, he saw a strange look come over his own face and watched himself go through the room, taking all out, including his own shipmates.

Jaime was completely stunned; it was as if he was watching one of the twentieth century movies he loved to collect. "I don't remember doing this. You know me. I'm not the type to fight without provocation, sir."

"The Jaimes Cable I knew, once, my former judoka, might not have been, but you're a pirate now. We all know what pirates are capable of."

"Captain Bryce doesn't allow those things," said Jaime quickly.

"Yes, yes, he is the *Robin Hood* of pirates; we've all heard the ridiculous stories."

Jaime didn't like the man's condescending tone or the feeling that he was being set up. "It sounds like I have no recourse here."

"The evidence is quite overwhelming, Mr. Cable," said the minister, "How can *you* explain this away?"

Jaime had no answer.

"While you were training in the Dragon Troop, a trigger, was worked into your psyche. A word that would make you into a killing machine, if we were ever faced with a situation that required it." said the man. He pointed to the vidfeed replaying, in slow motion, before them. "Your tablemate uttered it before he left. I am willing to testify that you were triggered unintentionally, thus your actions were involuntary. In exchange, you would have to be willing to do something for me."

Jaime had a sinking feeling, "And that would be?"

"Your captain on the end of a lasernoose," said Allister.

The look of vigor in his former mentor's eyes knocked the quartermaster for six. "NEVER!"

Jaime was taken back to the cell to find that Evan had been taken away. Miles had been patched up, but he couldn't tell Jaime where their shipmate was. His mood, sour already, was now getting violent. He was beginning to feel he didn't need a trigger to level a room.

"Miles, who attacked you?"

"I don't know, sir, I was hit from behind. I felt my arm break but nothing after."

"Son of a bitch!" shouted Jaime.

This made Miles jump. It was the first time he had ever heard the quartermaster swear in the four years he had been a grunt.

The next morning two men took Miles away.

The quartermaster was beyond frustrated. He was pacing the small cell, grumbling to himself and kicking the leg of the cot every time he walked by it when a loud "Ah um" sounded from behind him. He turned to find Allister with his arms folded in front of his chest and a very smug look on his face. "What?"

"You've lost your core," said his ex-sensei.

"I'm not in the fucking mood to be toyed with. Say what you're here to say and be done with."

"I thought it would interest you to know your sentence?" said the minister smugly.

"Without a trial?"

"There was no need. There was no way for you to defend yourself; what with the vidfeed and numerous witnesses, including your own men," said the minister.

"They told you that?"

"After a little persuasion..."

"If you've harmed them..." snarled Jaime.

"Most regrettably, it did prove too much for them. Luckily, we were able to record their statements."

"You fucking bastard!" He dove forward; stopping just short of the laser bars, close enough to feel the energy tickle the hairs on his arms and face.

"As I was saying," the minister continued, "You can still save yourself, if you…"

"I will not turn on my captain!"

"Such loyalty for the man, a pity you didn't feel the same for the CRF and the CRIA. Do you honestly think the likes of Iain Bryce would be so quick to do the same for you, if the tables were turned?" asked Ashgroth with a sparkle in his eyes.

"I know he would!" barked Jaime.

"Yes well, that's inconsequential at the moment. You're being transferred to Belgorian Prison tomorrow."

"You can't be serious?" Jaime's voice caught in his throat. Iain had barely survived that prison.

"Don't worry, I'm sure your cellmate will take good care of you," said the man wickedly.

Jaime stumbled back to the cot he'd been abusing and fell on it, hard.

"Character is what you are in the dark."
— *Allister Ashgroth*

True to the minister's word, the guards came the next day and escorted Jaime from the cell to a prison transport vessel. He was shackled around his wrists, ankles and waist, keeping him from being able to move.

The quartermaster looked around as best he could, given his immobility, hoping to see something he could use to break free. He saw was two other people on the vessel; one was sleeping; all he could see of him was the top of his head, which was bald except for a ring of black hair, like a halo, sticking out around his ears, the other looked like he belonged in prison. He was bigger even than Hayden, with a square jaw and skull and spiked hair that made his head look far too small for his body. He was staring at Jaime too. He blew Jaime a kiss.

With nothing else to keep himself occupied, Jaime found his mind replaying the last days, trying to figure out what had really happened. He was not willing to believe he had done this, trigger word or not. Allister claimed Tiki had said it; he tried to remember anything the fence uttered that could be it but came up blank. What if he got rescued and someone said it on Phoenix? Would he beat up or kill his own shipmates? He had essentially already killed two. Did he dare rejoin them?

The trip to the prison was uncomfortable, made even more so by the thoughts going through Jaime's mind. By the time they docked with the space station his head was reeling and throbbing and his legs and feet had long since fallen asleep. It took several tries to stand; the guards were anything but sympathetic, forcefully pulling him along.

He was taken to a room with no cot or chair, only four blank walls and a brightly lit ceiling panel. He hoped this wasn't his cell. He had been put through mental conditioning when he first become a Dragon Trooper, to build his defenses against torture, this room reminded him of a sensory deprivation chamber he had been left in for eight hours once. He realized this was the processing room when a voice came from nowhere.

"Remove your clothes and put them in the slot," said the voice as a panel opened in the wall beside him.

He hesitated.

As if answering his thoughts, the voice said, "Do it immediately so we can finish processing you."

Jaime did so, grudgingly. He watched his favorite jacket, one that would be hard to replace, disappear down the chute. The wall before him became a mirror then. His eyes took in all the bruises glowing like beacons of his guilt.

"Turn around slowly," said the disembodied voice.

Jaime knew then this was a two-way mirror.

"State your full name."

"Jaimes Aaron Cable."

"Your occupation?"

"I'm a BrimTier pirate," snapped Jaime.

"Your age?"

"Thirty-three."

"Any illnesses in your family history?"

"No," he said quickly. There was a pause as if waiting for him to say more, he wondered if they knew he was lying. Like his parents, he had the gene for autism. It was supposed to have been wiped out decades ago but some still had it in repressed form. He was born healthy so his parents didn't think it was an issue when they became pregnant again but his sister, Jenna Lyn, was born with the ailment. He couldn't imagine why the prison would need to know this; he certainly didn't intend to do anything in this facility for it to be an issue. He started to say something to that affect when the voice spoke again.

"Two hundred thirty eight pounds, six foot five, brown hair, brown eyes, medium skin tone, earring in the left earlobe and two tattoos. One on the left triceps, of a skull and crossed swords over a bird; the other on the right shoulder blade, of a rearing red dragon. No other visual tamperings."

"Excuse me, am I a piece of meat?" asked Jaime impatiently.

"In a manner of speaking. What is your sexual orientation?"

"Pardon me?" spat Jaime. He jumped as a shock shot through his feet. "What the hell?"

"As long as you cooperate, that will not happen again. Answer the question."

"Heterosexual!" he barked.

"Always?"

"YES!" Jaime just wanted this to be over.

"How many sexual partners have you had?"

"Five."

Another panel dropped down with a black box sitting on it. "Lift this box as high as you can."

He did so. He guessed it weighed about a hundred pounds as he lifted it over his head with ease.

"You may get dressed now," said the voice.

The panel with the box closed and another opened to a basket holding an orange jumpsuit, underwear, a gray t-shirt, a pair of black sneakers, a comb, a bar of soap, a bottle of shampoo, a toothbrush, a tube of toothpaste, a towel, a roll of toilet paper, a pillow and a set of gray bed sheets. Jaime put on the t-shirt then pulled on the jumpsuit. He frowned at his reflection – it wasn't the least bit flattering.

"These supplies are replenished once a month. Do not lose, trade, sell or use them for favors. You will not be given more until your next replacement time."

When he picked up the basket the door he came in through slid open. He slowly stepped toward it and found a large guard waiting outside. He had a taser wand in his hand, which he used to point down the corridor.

The guard led him down a row of cells that looked like any prison, thick metal bar doors blocking the inmate from leaving. An off-white porcelain john, a mirrored metal cabinet and a bunk bed were in each cell, along with personal items – many that turned his stomach.

There were three levels of cells; a metal grid work catwalk ran along the outside of these to allow access to and from the cells. A single set of rough tread metal stairs, at the end of each wall, barely wide enough for two average men standing side by side, serviced the entire block.

It had taken many months of planning to get Iain out of this prison, and they had someone on the inside helping them. Jaime looked around, hoping to see an alternative escape route. All he saw was huge ducting pipes for heating and plumbing, electrical conduits that ran the length of the ceiling and long fluorescent light fixtures, hanging four stories up, barely lighting the huge chamber.

He could feel eyes on him. Catcalls, whistles and graphic descriptions of sexual acts sounded from all around him. He remembered what Iain said went on here, he knew he hadn't told him everything by the strange look he would get when speaking about it. Like him, Jaime was fond of his manhood; he didn't cherish the thought of anyone attempting to violate it.

The guard pointed for the quartermaster to climb the stairs on the right and directed him to the second floor landing. He had a sick smile on his face as he smashed and zapped hands that tried to reach out and grope the newbie as he walked past. He was stopped at the eighth cell in. He hoped he would be alone but he saw a man sitting in the far corner, his face hidden in the shadows.

The guard opened the door and said, "Here's you new boyfriend."

Jaime jumped when the metal gate clanged shut behind him. He asked, "Which bunk is mine?"

"You can have the top one."

The man looked about Jaime's age but was much smaller built. He had the start of a scraggly beard and mustache, short greasy brown hair and brown eyes, set deep in his face; one split by a scar. He smiled at his new cellmate's obvious unease. "Don't worry; you're awful pretty but not my type." The man snickered, then added, "My name's Gideon Welch," as he put his hand out.

"Jaime Cable," said the quartermaster. He shook Gideon's hand then jumped up onto the top bunk.

"Wha'cha in for?"

Jaime fought to make the lumpy pillow lay the way he wanted as he said, "I apparently took out fifty people in a bar on Berem."

"That was you?" Gideon said with awe. "They showed us that vidfeed last night."

"Brilliant," said Jaime flatly.

"You were. Wouldn't surprise me if you're chosen to be a competitor," said Gideon.

"Of what?"

"To compete in fights around the Tiers and the Ky'istri Challenge. It's held every three years; this year is the thirtieth anniversary so they are looking for better fighters. You obviously can hold your own."

"I don't intend to fight anyone," said Jaime.

"You'll find they don't take kindly to being told you won't participate. There are benefits to doing it."

Before Jaime could reply a male voice came from the speakers, announcing lights out in ten seconds. The cellblock went dark. Moments later one of the inmates began to howl loudly, others answered, and others answered these, like a sick sort of song sung in the round. Squeals and screams that didn't sound pleasant or faked sounded in between these calls.

"Really don't feel like talking," said Jaime.

"Suit yourself," said the man.

Jaime put his left arm across his tightly closed eyes, hoping, without much hope, to block out where he was and what he was hearing. He found his mind drifting back to when he had last known Allister Ashgroth, when he was still his trainer, sensei, mentor and friend.

"Judoka Cable, the secret of victory lies in getting the vanguard on your adversary. First, is the eyes; second, the feet; third, motion, and last, space. The eyes are the index to the mind, where they are fixed, there the mind is concentrated and there the body will follow. If your posture is stiff and hard you can be overpowered. If you keep your motions fluid, your opponent cannot break you. Do not limit your movements or your opponent can predict your subsequent movements. Never allow your opponent to break your personal space; if they are able to breach this, the first three will be negated," explained a younger Allister Ashgroth, to a younger Jaime, as they went through the semainath routine he still did at least once a day.

Two weeks later, Jaime found himself still in the tiny cell in Belgorian Prison; stiff from trying not to roll off the thin cot each night. This morning he was awake first, which suited him fine; he really didn't need to hear any more of his cellmate's questions. Fourteen days of Gideon Welch wanting to know everything about Jaimes Cable had grated his nerves raw.

He jumped down and stretched his muscles out as best he could in the limited space. He longed to do a full semainath routine but couldn't in the tight confines so he'd have to sate himself with his meditation. He took the lumpy pillow from his cot, tried to fluff it a little, set it on the hard floor, sat down on it, crossed his legs and repeated the mantra of his beliefs in his head until his mind floating in a sea of darkness, *'In times of strife, without distraction, light in heart and light in limb, let us endeavor with full attention, to concentrate our mind within.'*

He had just reached his center, his core, found his equilibrium, when the man, whose face was only inches from his, opened his eyes and broke into a huge shit ass grin. His laughter broke all Jaime's efforts and brought the reality around him crashing back twice fold.

"You gonna start humming too?" asked Gideon through apparently a gut wrenching laugh.

Jaime gave him an irritated look as he stood up and jumped back onto his bunk without a word.

"I'm sorry, Cable," said Gideon, trying to stifle the laughs, "I didn't mean to poke fun at you. It was just the look on your face. Does the meditation work?"

"When I am allowed to complete it!"

Gideon started to say more when the lights flashed on and the metal door slid open.

The rush of inmates going to get their share of the tasteless mush that served as breakfast was like the white water of a raging river. Jaime waited until the tide had passed then stepped out, Gideon tight on his heels.

"I really am sorry, Cable. Will you teach me?" Gideon called after him over the crowd that was now pulling him along.

Jaime ignored him. He left the line and entered the lavatory. Gideon was caught too deep to follow him.

The quartermaster had learned to take his shower while the others ate breakfast. His first group shower had put three inmates, with thoughts of violating him, in the infirmary. He was like the golden egg, nearly all had vowed to *have* him. He didn't intend to let them.

He turned on the last of ten showerheads to warm up the water while he removed his jumpsuit. He set it over the half wall of the first toilet stall. He had no more than gotten himself wet when he heard the doors open behind him. He tried to ignore it, hoping if he kept to his own whoever it was would do the same. The reflection in the chrome of the faucet surround told him otherwise.

Four large men were standing behind the Charlton Williams. Charlton had tried to take Jaime on two other occasions, once in the shower and once in the breakfast line, failing both times. He was barely five foot five, had long blond hair and very feminine features, which was probably why he needed to act like such a brute. He'd like to think he ran the prison but most thought he was a joke. He wasn't joking this time.

The four men with him were each as big as Hayden. They were Charlton's muscle but he treated them like dirt under his shoes. Jaime couldn't understand why they put up with the man, unless it was because they truly had no brains of their own.

Charlton had a sick smile on his face as he eyed Jaime's body, "Such a fine form. I see you're ready for me, how considerate of you."

Jaime pretended not to hear him as he rinsed the soap off. He turned the water off and reached for his jumpsuit. The massive hand of Don grabbed it first. He took the towel from the rod instead and began to dry off.

"Rex, Grant, take his arms and bend him over," said Charlton unzipping his jumpsuit.

The two men started toward Jaime.

The quartermaster coiled the towel before him, whipped it around Rex's throat like a garrote, pulled it like a ripcord and sent the man careening into the tile wall. The man broke a circle of them to rubble with his shoulder and head. Even before Rex hit, Jaime swung around and twisted Grant over his waist and slammed him into the base of the shower. His head cracked against the raised rim of the shower stall and he lay still.

Don and Isaac came at him at the same time. One smashed his fist into his side, the other into his face.

Jaime took Isaac under the arm and by the throat and flipped him over his shoulder into the toilet stall he'd hung his jumpsuit over. He was knocked unconscious by the edge of the toilet bowl. The quartermaster grabbed Don's ponytail and yanked his head back, intending to use him as a shield to get out of the room.

While engaged in the melee, Jaime hadn't seen four more men had entered the room, each with a shank made from a spoon. They enthusiastically joined in the attempt on his body. They weren't part of Charlton's usual posse but the man said nothing to stop them from attempting to take the prize, knowing he would still get his turn.

Jaime was cornered, he still had Don's ponytail in his hand, and was still using the man as a shield. He couldn't see an escape. He was unsure what to do. For the first time since his semainath training began, his core was shattered. His mind was racing and his heart was beating so fast it was hard to breathe. He could hear Charlton laughing in the background, telling him what he was going to do to him when he was downed. He could find no way out, still he vowed that he would die trying.

Jaime pushed Don into two of the men with shanks and heard him grunt in pain as they stuck him. Those two were knocked off-guard but the other two took their place quickly, advancing on him at the same time. One's shank barely missed his throat the other plunged deep into his right bicep. He heard someone shout what sounded like 'oh dear' then the room was flooded with a light so intense he was blinded.

The room slowly came back into focus. Jaime saw the eight men in a pile at his feet, Charlton cowering under one of the sinks, babbling incoherently, and his cellmate standing by the door holding a taser wand.

Gideon grabbed the jumpsuit from the corner and tossed it to his cellmate. "Get out'a here."

Jaime pulled on the bottom half quickly and stumbled out of the room. Three prison guards appeared before him. One of them called him to stop him then, seeing the wound on his shoulder and blackening eye, told him to get to the infirmary.

It took twenty stitches to repair Jaime's bicep and the same ribs that had been bruised in the bar fight were bruised again so he was kept in the infirmary overnight. He found himself jealous of Iain, it was in this prison he had met and begun a relationship with their doctor,

Robyn Carter. His doctor was a woman but not nearly as pretty, or as attentive, as Iain's had been.

Gideon wasn't in the cell when Jaime was taken back to it the next morning. He didn't find him in the cafeteria at either of the next two meals or in the yard that afternoon either. He hoped his cellmate hadn't gotten himself into too much trouble helping him. He felt bad for how he had treated. When lights out was called he was forced to accept the man was gone. He climbed up to the top bunk and tried hard to forget where he was.

The door of the cell banged open, awakening Jaime from his troubled sleep. A bright light was shining in his eyes so he couldn't see who was entering. He was pulled from his bunk, slammed against the wall and pinned by an elbow at his throat. Images of the botched attempt on his body the day before being completed now flashed graphically before his eyes. The quartermaster grit his teeth, pinched his eyes shut and tried to ready himself as best he could for what was to come next.

"You have been selected to be a gladiator."

"Wha?" Jaime couldn't get his addled mind around the statement.

"You will begin training tomorrow."

The elbow holding his neck moved, releasing him and dropping him back to the floor, then the door banged shut again loudly.

Jaime bent over and put his hands on his knees. He took several deep breaths then held the last one for several seconds. He waited for his heartrate, which was erratic, to slow, and fought back the feeling that he was going to vomit. He had never gone through so many emotions so quick; all his semai' and semainath training and the conditioning he'd received as a Dragon Trooper had simply vanished from his mind. Imagining what his ex-sensei would've had to say if he were there made it worse. He jumped as a hand appeared before his face with a silver flask clutched in it. The cap was loose and he could smell alcohol.

"It's whiskey."

Jaime opened his eyes and saw Gideon was the one holding the flask. He took it and brought it to his mouth. He coughed as its less than smooth texture burned his throat – like Iain he was used to drinking the best. He sat on the edge of the toilet bowl sticking out of the wall and said, "Thanks, I needed that."

"Figured you might. Been a tough couple days for you, huh?" said Gideon, sitting on his cot.

"Yeah. Thanks for coming to my rescue. Normally I could've handled myself, but..." Jaime wasn't sure what he wanted to say just then.

Gideon waved him off. "You likely would have taken them. The guards weren't far behind me."

Jaime nodded but he wasn't so confident of it. "Did you get into trouble for assisting me?"

Gideon shrugged and said, "The box for twenty four hours. I have suffered through worse. Not that I was especially looking but I couldn't help noticing your tattoos. What do they signify?" asked Gideon, finding something he hadn't asked him a hundred times before.

This time the pirate didn't mind answering; it took his mind off the horrible images he was having of what might've been had Gideon not come in when he had. He laid his head back and said, "The dragon on my shoulder blade is a group I was once part of, the skull and crossed swords over the phoenix is one I'm currently with."

"You're a pirate then? What group are you in?"

"Their called enclaves. I am Phoenix Enclave." Jaime lifted his left sleeve to reveal the fiery bird with the pirating symbol over it.

"That's Captain Brince?"

"Bryce. I'm his quartermaster, or I was." Jaime closed his eyes tight as another wave of nausea hit him.

"You think he has given up on you?"

"Never. Captain Bryce believes in leaving no man behind. I'm just not entirely sure how he could find me."

"Resigned to your fate then?" challenged Gideon.

"Not likely, just have to find the right time."

"Life is a competition to be the
criminal more often than the victim."
— *Joshua Travis*

Captain Bryce was pacing back and forth behind
Kyle, making him nervous. He knew he wasn't doing
anyone any good doing this, but he had to keep moving
or he would hit something. He had already paced his
office and cabin and needed a different set of walls to
look upon. Both men were so keyed up that the com
beside them buzzing made them jerk suddenly.

Kyle chuckled a little but didn't open the link.

"WELL!" shouted Iain.

"Sorry, Captain."

"Captain Bryce?" came Hayden's voice.

Iain already knew, by the tone of it, it wasn't good
news. "Report!" he snapped.

"Jaime was taken to Belgorian Prison!"

Iain's insides felt like he'd been punched and his
heart lurched into his throat. He'd spent three years in
that Prison and had barely survived. He wasn't a trained
Dragon Trooper at the time but that wasn't a hell of a lot

of consolation at the moment. Either way, he couldn't leave Jaime there. "Did you learn which block?"

"Uh… he isn't there anymore…"

"Damn it, Man, do you know where he is *now*?"

"He was chosen to be a gladiator."

"And what the hell does that mean?" snapped the captain. He wanted to reach through the com and strangle the man on the other side, his irritation level reaching critical.

"It's a sort of fighting competition slash circus that travels around the first Tier."

"Which means they'll be moving him around a lot, so it'll be harder to find him," said Eve as she stepped in behind the captain.

"Oh, Brilliant, Eve, got anything else right fucking constructive to add?" Captain Bryce snapped.

Hayden's voice broke in before Eve could say anything back, "There are posters all over saying there's to be a challenge in two months."

"He will survive that long; they'll make sure of it. Having a well-known pirate in the contest would be a draw," said Eve.

Feeling a little better, Iain said, "Hayden, get the ship refueled. I'm gonna contact Kohzu to see about tickets and schematics to the stadium. I want you ready to leave to meet him as soon as we get word."

"Yes sir."

The captain gave Eve another perturbed look and a sneer as he stomped out of the helm room. He knew it wasn't her or Hayden's fault and he shouldn't lash out at them but he couldn't help it. He placed a foot on either side of the ladder poles just outside the bridge and slid down it quickly then all but ran to his office.

"It isn't the size of the dog in the fight, it's the size of the fight in the dog that counts."
— Anonymous

Jaime and Gideon were partnered up in several small tournaments around the Tier, against both man and beast. Both sustained injuries that put them in the infirmary many times but they did survive. During that time the two had grown comfortable with each other and had become a sort of friends. Gideon still annoyed Jaime on occasion with his seemingly endless questions, but it was a manageable annoyance now.

Jaime was glad he was no longer in the Prison but he knew moving around so much would make it all but impossible for Iain to find him. He had all but accepted this was now his life when he received a package.

Gideon was bent over Jaime's shoulder as he opened the box, teasing him that it was likely from one of the female spectators. "What did you get?"

Inside the package was two things, a poster for the Ky'istri Challenge and a long red and orange feather. Without saying a word, Jaime spun the feather and smiled. He stood up, slid the corner of the poster into the corner of the mirror on the wall, climbed up to his bunk and laid down with the feather resting on his chest.

"What is it?" asked Gideon.

"A synthetic bird's feather," said Jaime plainly, finding it amusing to tease his cellmate.

"And?"

"It represents a fiery bird," said Jaime.

"So, what does it mean?" asked Gideon, the suspense near killing him.

"It would be from a phoenix, if they were real."

"Enough already, Man…"

"Captain Bryce is coming to the challenge."

Gideon got a dark look in his eyes, "These fights will be to the death."

"I will not kill," said Jaime adamantly.

Gideon scoffed, "You'll be surprised what you're willing to do when it comes down to you or them."

Five days later, Jaime stepped onto the field of battle inside the large metal and glass structure. Rows of seats spanned the sides of the field, all the way to near the roof, which was reinforced luminescent plating, transparent in the center to expose the stars and moon beyond. Nearly every seat was filled. The rowdy cheers and jeers ringing through the air echoed loudly as they reverberated back down from the cavernous ceiling, making his ears ring painfully. His eyes shifted to the bodies of the previous fighters being taken off the field. He crossed himself and said a prayer that their souls went to whatever heaven they believed in and asked for the strength to make sure he left the field on his feet.

He scanned the audience and was assuaged when he saw several friendly faces. He also saw some not so. Eve and Hayden were sitting in the east section, looking around like this was the first of such shows for them, Digger and Yard were on the other side, acting like this was a regular outing; he knew Iain had to be there too. His eyes kept stopping on a man staring at him from the west side. He looked close to eighty, with silver stringy hair and wrinkles upon wrinkles. He was alone, an empty seat to either side of him, he was holding a crooked cane and was slightly hunched over. Jaime knew those blue-gray eyes, which were locked on him.

Iain winked and smiled at his quartermaster.

Jaime didn't react because sitting only a few seats over, was the president, vice president and Caitlyn Nason. He watched Nikolas' lean over and say something to the president while pointing at him. He guessed they were hoping to use him as bait to catch the rest of the crew of Phoenix.

The quartermaster jumped when Gideon touched his arm, bringing his attention back to the task at hand and reminding him it didn't matter his friends were here, he still had a battle ahead of him.

They were chained together at the wrists, with only about three feet of playroom. Gideon pointed out several areas of weapons spread around the arena. Jaime nodded. He wasn't able to ask which they wanted to go to first when the crowd began to stamp their feet and howl.

A huge man in full body armor was entering the field on the other side of the arena.

"Hugo Degart, the current Ky'istri champion!" said Gideon, "What an honor!"

Jaime didn't share the admiration his partner felt at their opponent. He did feel his stomach twist. He was the huge man that had blown him a kiss in the transport to the prison the first day. He was even bigger standing up.

His arms and legs would have looked normal as the columns before a Coliseum and his fists looked like sledgehammers. He would have been a challenge bare-handed but of course he wasn't. In his right hand was a huge battle-ax with a six inch spear tip on the end and a very sharp curved blade on either side of the head, in his left was a flail – a metal ball with dozens of sharp spikes around it hanging by a chain. That ball was hitting against the man's knee as he waited.

Jaime had hoped to fell his opponent quickly with his semainath skills; their opponent's size destroyed that notion. He would have to rely on his smaller, stealthier, body instead. Gideon touched his arm, startling him. His partner pointed behind them, he turned to see the master of ceremonies stepping into the main box. He was only slightly surprised to see it was Allister Ashgroth.

The man raised his hands to silence the crowd and said, "Ladies and gentleman, please allow me to present the champion, Hugo Degart, five time winner of the Ky'istri Challenge!"

The audience cheered and stamped their feet.

Hugo pumped his arms in the air while turning in a circle, the ball of the flail coming within inches of hitting his huge, square head.

"And, his challengers: one convicted of theft and murder, Gideon Welch, the other, former BrimTier pirate, Jaimes Cable."

A howl went through the crowd.

"Gladiators, the game is to the death! There are no rules except that both challengers must live for them to be considered the victors." Ashgroth looked directly at Jaime as he said the last, smiling wickedly.

If Jaime had been able to get to his old teacher at that moment he would've throttled him. He didn't get to enjoy the thought long though as Gideon pulled on the chain that went between their wrists to get his attention. He pointed to a rack of spears and swords and told him to head in that direction when the game started.

The minister signaling them to begin.

They ran to the rack and each took a weapon – Jaime a spear, Gideon a long curved sword – then moved to meet the mass at the other end of the field.

Hugo smiled savagely at them, showing teeth capped in gold. He pointed at Jaime with the tip of the battle-ax and mouthed, 'You're dead, Motherfucker!' He started moving toward him, swinging the spiked ball of the flail over his head.

Jaime tried to get out of the way of the business end of the flail but the chain between him and Gideon stopped him. The metal sphere smashed into his right shoulder blade and would've broken his bones if not for the shoulder pads he was wearing He went down hard on his left knee, from the impact. He tried to stab at the man from below but he brought the ax in his other hand down and snapped the pole of his spear in half before it connected with any flesh. Before he could form another mode of attack he was yanked backwards. Gideon pulled him out of the way just as the weapon swung back around and would have sliced him in the back. He didn't have time to thank him.

After twenty minutes of fumbling this way and that, tripping over each other, all the time choosing and discarding weapons, as they were each smashed in turn, the two men finally found a good rhythm and were able to roll and move in and out of each other's way. They even used the chain to trip the huge man a couple times. So far they'd managed to hold their own but both were showing signs of fatigue; the big man looked hardly winded. Then, Jaime saw the break he was looking for.

Gideon was lying on his back, after taking a particularly hard hit from the flail, Jaime was kneeling beside him, trying to catch his breath, and the blade of the battle-ax was coming at them at a high rate of speed. The pirate jumped over Gideon, brought the chain across his partner's chest and held it taut. The blade connected with the chain and cut it in two. Jaime shielded his eyes as a shower of sparks and chips of broken metal flew outward. The sudden release of tension on the chain made the pirate fall over, and the force of the swing rebounding off the chain made Hugo stumble backward and go down on his right knee.

The crowd went wild.

Jaime, now loose, ran toward the huge man, who was still on his knees. He took him square in the back with both feet. Hugo went down on his left side and swung out with the ax. The edge of the blade caught the quartermaster's left thigh. He screamed as blood spurted from the gash. He stumbled backward and fell into a small wooden structure.

The crowd screamed in pleasure at the sight of the blood.

Hugo, back on his feet, had a clump of Gideon's hair clutched in his right hand, the ax held in the other, the edge of the sharp blade against the smaller man's neck. He was asking the spectators if he should slice the man, who was hanging limp.

The crowd was screamed an enthusiastic yes.

Jaime's right hand had landed on the butt end of a pistol. He picked it up, pulled the charge pin, flipped it to full, and aimed it at the huge man all in one single fluid motion, then he pulled the trigger.

Hugo was about to bring the ax blade across Gideon's throat as the laser beam struck him in the left shoulder. It knocked the arm around and made him release the ax and his captive's head. He turned toward the pirate, a mix of surprise and pain on his face.

Jaime brought the barrel of the pistol to a point in the center of Hugo's head, between the eyes, and said, in a menacing voice, "Don't move, *Motherfucker*!"

The crowd was on their feet, stomping and screaming for Jaime to pull the trigger.

Jaime started to comply when a beam of light from the audience flashed in the corner of his eye. The blind rage subsided as he looked over to see Iain standing.

The captain lowered the mirror and slowly shook his disguised head.

Jaime took a deep breath and lowered the gun.

Minister Ashgroth stood up and said, "You must finish him or the game cannot end!"

The quartermaster tossed the pistol away, took the ax, that was stuck in the ground beside him, and used the handle to knock out the huge man kneeling before him.

The crowd was now screaming in disapproval.

Jaime helped Gideon to his feet and told him to stay close. The lights in the arena went out, throwing the stadium into total darkness. The shouts for blood just moments before were replaced with cries of fear and of soldiers barking orders. Within minutes he felt hands on him and heard Hayden and Eve's voices telling him to follow them. He did so, without question, grabbing a handful of Gideon's shirt and dragging him along.

The lights in the corridor were still lit so it took them a moment to get their eyes adjusted. Hayden and Eve removed the infrared goggles they were wearing and quickly secured the doors behind them. Digger and Yard were running toward them from the east wing and Captain Bryce, still disguised as the old man, so he looked foolish running toward them, came from the west, all with guns out and ready.

The captain smiled at his quartermaster, tossed him a spare pistol and said, "You put on a right good show, Quartermaster. How's the leg, need a hand?"

"I'll manage, thank you, Captain."

"That's the captain? I thought he was a lot younger than that," said Gideon quickly.

"Where's Evan and Miles?"

"Dead."

"Damn," said the captain.

"This is Gideon Welch, he would like to join our crew."

"Very good, Mr. Welch. We'll properly introduce ourselves later. Now let us get to the ship," said Iain with a thick guttural laugh, enjoying this immensely.

"Aye, aye, Sir," said Gideon with gusto.

The pirates, plus one, bolted for the hanger deck. They could hear people coming from before and after them and the alarms denoting an escape attempt in progress were now howling loudly through the corridors. They skidded to a halt just as they entered the hanger. The president, vice president and a squad of CRF troops were waiting for them in front of their sandpiper.

The CRF soldiers charged their rifles.

The pirates' guns were already charged.

"Where is Bryce?" asked the president.

Iain smiled, he had forgotten he was still disguised. He removed the wig and fake skin from his face and said, "That's *Captain* Bryce, if you please."

The president gave him an annoyed look and raised him arm to give the order to fire.

"NO!" Caitlyn came from behind her father and jumped in front of Iain, shielding him with her body.

Both the captain and her father said, "What the hell are you doing?" at the same time.

"Get out of the way, Caitlyn," shouted her father.

"No, father. I won't let you harm him," cried the girl defiantly.

"Caitlyn, don't do this," pleaded Iain.

"Caitlyn, he's a *pirate*," said President Nason, as if he didn't like the taste of the word.

"He was nothing but kind to me, Daddy. I won't let you harm him."

An odd look came over the president's face then.

Iain saw he was still about to give the signal to open fire. He brought his arm up, ready to throw the girl out of the way as soon as he saw a trigger finger moving.

The first round of spectators appeared in the opposite gangway. There was a collective gasp tinged with excitement that sounded louder in the tense air.

The vice president put his hand on the president's shoulder and shook his head, staring knives at the pirate as he did.

Murmurs sped through the throng watching the heated standoff with anticipation, many saying they were about to see the blood and death they had paid for.

The president slowly motioned the men to lower their rifles. "Caitlyn, over here now!" He pointed to a spot next to him as if calling a dog to heel.

Just loud enough for Iain to hear, Caitlyn said, "As soon as I move they *will* open fire. Take me hostage."

"No," whispered Iain. He wanted to fight her but he knew she was right. He placed the end of his pistol to the side of Caitlyn's neck and lit it up, then said, loud enough for all gathered to hear, "Out of the way or the girl gets it!"

The crowd was screaming, from excitement not fear, as they watched the pirate captain, holding a pistol to the president's daughter, and his men board their shuttle and blast out of the hanger.

Several jumps later, Iain was on the observation deck, staring out the rear window at the beautiful display of spent plasma residue with a very sullen look on his face. He knew he had made Thomas Nason an even bigger enemy today. He snorted loudly, thinking at least his bounty would go up. He jumped as he felt arms coming from behind him and a body press against his back. He didn't need to look at the reflection in the window to know who it was.

He turned in her embrace and hugged her back, then he pushed her away, "Caitlyn...I... "

"I understand why we can't be together, Iain, but it changes nothing. I'm in love with you."

"Your father is gonna be pissed at you."

"He knows I know what kind of man he is now and that I would rather be with you. That will be a tough lesson for him but I am and will always be his daughter."

Iain kissed her on the forehead and said, "What am I gonna do with you, Girl?" He meant it rhetorically. "Take me back to Tarnis Prime."

"You can tell the character of a man by what makes him go 'round the bend."
— Anonymous

"And, how much credits it takes to turn him."
— *Iain D. Bryce*

Tiki Blone was sitting alone in a bar on Berem. The same one Jaime Cable had smashed through months before; in fact, at the very same table he'd been sitting at with the pirate that day. He was smiling to himself. He still had almost half the credits the vice president had paid him for turning on the pirate, which was, even now, in his pocket. He finished the last of his ale and left the bar, intending to go to the casino and spend some of it. He was halfway across the crowded street when he looked up and saw four men walking very purposefully toward him. He started to bolt for the doorway of the casino. They reached him before his hand could grasp the handle. The two biggest each took him under an arm and together, directed him down an alley beside the building.

"Captain Bryce… Jaime, what a delight," started Tiki, as though nothing had happened.

Iain's left hand grabbed the much smaller man's shirt and used it to slam him, quite hard, against the side of the building. His right hand, holding a knife, shot out quickly and stopped just short of the man's throat, "Tell me what you did, you piece of *shit*!"

"What do you mean, Captain Bryce? Ooww," Tiki felt the knife slice into his flesh then the warm trickle of blood dripping under the collar of his shirt. "Okay, okay, the vice president offered me credits to say a word to Jaime."

"Jaime, Gideon, take up watch at the end of the alley, if you please." After Jaime was out of earshot, Iain looked back at Tiki and snarled, "What word?"

Tiki thought about lying but the deadly look in the pirate captain's eyes, and the knife at his throat, made him think better of it. All the stories of Iain Bryce being easygoing, fainthearted and weak quickly dissolved in his mind. "Odynia! Odynia! He wanted me to say Odynia to Jaime. I didn't know what it would make him do, I swear!" Real tears were flooding from his eyes and piss was running down his left leg.

Iain recognized the word immediately, from a book he had read a long time ago. It was an ancient Greek word meaning *pain*. How primitive that it would be used as the trigger to make Jaime inflict it. Keeping the knife at the man's throat but not cutting him, Iain snarled, through clenched teeth, "You cost me two right

143

good grunts and nearly an officer that's worth a hell of a lot to me. Tell me, how fucking much were my men worth to you? *How much?*"

"Five hundred thousand!"

Iain told Hayden to search him, since him heading towards a casino implied he had those credits on him.

The weapons master pulled a large stack of credits from the man's pocket. He whistled as he flipped through them, "Must be near two hundred thousand here, Sir."

"That'll right about cover the two men you lost me, Mr. Blone," snapped Captain Bryce. "I *ever* so much as *hear* you in close proximity to me and mine, I'll finish what I started here, understand?"

"Yes, yes sir, yes, never again, I swear!"

Iain lifted the front of the man's shirt and used it to wipe his knife clean then folded it back up in his face and returned it to its hiding place amongst his clothing.

Once free to move, Tiki sank to the dirty street and sat shaking in his own bodily release.

"Few things stand up to diligence, time and skill."
— *Old Semai' Proverb*

The Captain, the other officers and Gideon were waiting in the hanger as the starling set down on the deck. Jaime had been gone for five weeks having the trigger word deprogrammed.

"Keep your weapons charged," said the captain.

Several laughed, thinking he was joking, the staid look on his face told them otherwise.

The ramp lowered and Jaime strode out, smiling.

"Welcome home, Jaime," said all but Iain.

Jaime thanked them then saluted the captain and asked permission to return to the crew.

Iain said, "Odynia." He hadn't said this a sick joke; the deprogrammer's had told him to do this when Jaime returned; to be sure the trigger word had indeed been fully removed from his psyche.

A strange look came over the quartermaster's face. He took his captain's arm, flipped him over his left shoulder, then swung around quickly and caught him before he hit the deck. "You did ask for pain, didn't you, Captain?" said Jaime, winking at the others. He burst into laughter at the look on Iain's face.

"You jackass! Don't ever do that again!" spat Iain. He grabbed the hand Jaime offered him and straightened his clothing with an aggravated look on his face.

Everyone else in the room began to laugh as well.

Rather than try to stop them Captain Bryce walked from the room. He smiled in spite of himself; his crew was back together and all was as it should be.

Confronting The Past

"A ship in the harbor is safe, but that
is not what ships are built for."
  – Anonymous.

Captain Bryce was faced with a moral dilemma, one he wasn't comfortable confronting at that moment. He paced the back of the conference room listening to his officers complaining that they hadn't had a siege in nearly three weeks. There hadn't been any ships through their usual space in that time and the captain would not give the order for them to go looking for any elsewhere.

Hayden, Eve, Digger and Kyle wanted to go into a rival territory. Jaime, Yard, Mitch and Kassie were against this – the pilots rarely got involved in the votes but as this was such an important one, Iain had asked them to weigh in. He wasn't surprised they were on opposite sides. The quartermaster reminded them how they felt when rival pirates came into their territory but it didn't sway them. Robyn was abstaining. So the vote was four to four, meaning he would have to make the choice. As captain the final say was ultimately his, regardless of the vote, but he preferred there be consensus. Frustration was boiling inside Iain's stomach, giving him a wicked case of heartburn, and a headache. He needed time to think, to weigh his options; he didn't want to make a rash or hasty decision. "We will meet again after dinner. Dismissed."

Hayden didn't like the captain's lack of immediate decision. He slammed his cup onto the table, making more than one in the room jump, and spat. "We may not have time to wait," then left the room.

Iain started to call the man back to tell him off but decided to let it go, this time.

He was getting a right bit uncomfortable with his weapons master's attitude, and disrespect, of late. He wasn't sure he could count on him to do as told if a situation arose. He didn't like that.

Hayden had made it more than clear in the past that he didn't think they should be so benevolent in their choice of hits but he had never been able to sway the others to back him up.

The weapons master had been with Victor Black's enclave before joining Phoenix. Black was infamous for torturing, raping and murdering his captives. Hayden said he left his service because of this excessive cruelty. Some of the big man's reactions during heated situations had been harsh but, as yet, Iain hadn't seen anything he would've considered *excessive* cruelty in the man. Both Jaime and Mitch had warned him about offering Hayden an officer position so fast after joining the crew. He had dismissed them as being unnecessarily cautious then; the last few weeks were making him question this appraisal. He had a sinking feeling it was only going to get worse.

Captain Bryce studied the starcharts in his office until the tiny shapes marking off the territories on the charts were floating before his eyes like fake balloons. The pirate counsel was still in its infancy so no one was truly enforcing the boundaries; it was more an unspoken concord between pirate enclaves. Iain considered them binding, but, they needed supplies. If he planned it carefully they might be able to hit a ship and get back to their own territory without anyone being any the wiser.

Butch Herrick mostly hunted the sectors to the right of theirs, on the Kingfisher. Captain Herrick was as close to an ally as a rival pirate could be; invading his territory could put a strain on that relationship. Dirk Riley's enclave, aboard the Gray Hawk, patrolled the sectors to the left of theirs. Captain Riley wasn't the worst pirate captain, that would be Black, but he was nasty in his own right and not a friend either. Running across him could bring up rough memories for Eve. The man, known as the Gray Pirate, had killed Eve's mother.

Iain wasn't willing to cause her unneeded pain just to keep Hayden from an impeding irruption. Inactivity and having to further ration the supplies wasn't good for any of his crew but starting a pirate war would be worse. He guessed he had made his decision.

Iain started to leave his office, resigned to his decision, when the combox on the corner of his desk bleeped. He hesitatingly said, "Go."

Kassie said, "I have a call for you, Captain."

"Who from?"

"It's private, sir?"

Iain stepped behind his desk to see the girl shake her head slowly and give a strange look over her shoulder at Eve. His curiosity was heightened now. "I am alone. Connect it." He was barely able to hide his surprise when he found Markus Oakley, Eve's father, staring at him.

"Good day, Captain Bryce," said the man with obvious distrust.

Iain wasn't sure just what to say, this was a feat not many could say they had accomplished. Why would Markus be calling him? As far as he knew Eve hadn't spoken to her father since she quit the CRF and joined his crew eight years ago. The last time he and Markus had spoken heated words and threats were exchanged. "Senator Oakley," said Iain quickly, with a puzzled nod. "Did you want your daughter?"

"No, I wanted you, Captain Bryce. I know you and I have had… disagreements in the past, but I'm hoping we can put those aside. I have a… a situation that needs to be… handled delicately, and I believe you are the best man for the job."

"I'm listening," said Iain, curious why the man was trying to charm him.

"We're having problems getting supplies to the new colony on our moon. To date, three supply convoys have been attacked. I am hoping you can help…"

"A right bit of what comes around…" started the captain sarcastically.

"Captain Bryce, please don't make me beg."

Iain was shocked silent. He couldn't imagine Markus Oakley pleading for anything, like Eve, his pride ran deep. Could this be an elaborate trap? He asked the man that very and wasn't sure if the look of innocence should make him feel at ease or sick. Reminding himself this was Eve's father, he hoped for the first. "Give me details," said Iain.

"As I said, we have lost three convoys. Colum Province doesn't have enough resources to support the more than three hundred people. They are starving. Eve told me that your enclave steals… ah… helps… helps colonists in such situations."

"You asking me to supply them stolen goods, Senator? Won't that make you as much criminal as I?"

"No, I don't want that... I don't want that... I was hoping... hoping you could escort, and offer protection to, the next convoy?"

"Ain't that what the CRFers are for? You are a member of the parliament, why do you need me to get involved?"

"I'd prefer not to discuss this on an open comlink. I'll come to your ship if it will put you more at ease?"

Iain hesitated, then said, "I will send a shuttle to meet you by Ryger. You try anything, Eve or no, they will have permission to shoot, understand?"

"I do."

The captain's mind was reeling now as he stepped through the door of the conference room. All of the officers, except Kyle, who was at the helm listening, were present and looking to him for his answer. He leaned against the casing and said, "I am not voting for or against any move at this time. Something else has come up that needs to be decided before we can discuss anything else." He turned and left, not even giving them a chance to ask him details.

"Don't ever be first, don't ever be last and don't *EVER* volunteer for anything."

– Anonymous

The door alarm buzzed about half an hour later. Iain ignored it, hoping whoever it was would go away. When the door slid open he knew it was either Jaime or Robyn, the only two who had the override code to open it when he had locked it out. It was Jaime that stepped in.

"Iain, what's going on?"

"I'm not at liberty to say, Jaime."

"You know I will stand by you and will defend any choice you make, but leaving the choice unmade entirely is not going over well," said Jaime.

Iain was about to tell the quartermaster he didn't care if it went over like a lead balloon but instead he said, "Eve's father is en route to us as we speak."

"Markus Oakley? Why?"

"He says three convoys of supplies for the new colony on their moon have been taken by pirates and he wants us to escort the next to make sure it arrives safely."

"That's deep in the Inner Tier. I didn't think any pirates hit that far in-space. Where's the CRF?"

"I don't know. Sounds a right bit queer to me as well. He wouldn't give a reason, said he'd prefer to speak in person," said Iain, handing Jaime a cup of coffee.

"You think it's a trap?" asked Jaime, blowing over the top of the steaming cup.

"I don't wanna think that, Jay... for Eve's sake, more than ours, but I think maybe we should approach it as if," said Iain dryly.

"Does Eve know?"

"Not yet. I don't need Hayden mad at me for that as well," said Iain, throwing his arms up in surrender.

"I want to say he's just restless."

"I fear whatever it is will become a right bit more if I don't get to the root of it quick. I can't let him continue to question me like this. In front of the officers is one thing, you know what we have to deal with and can understand frustrations boiling over at times, but he starts up in front of the grunts... who may already be the brink of mutiny. What do your Semai' teachings say?"

"Confront the issue."

Confront the issue, was Jaime's suggestion, he wished he had been a bit more descriptive. He punched fast at the speed bag hanging from the ceiling in the quartermaster's dojo, trying to relieve some of his growing stress and anxiety but it was only making him feel worse. He realized he was picturing Markus and Hayden's faces on that bag. Iain had no idea what to do about Hayden; with Markus not more than three hours from arriving, he knew it needed to be soon. He decided he had to buck up and get it over with. He stopped the swinging bag and grabbed a towel to dry off just as the very man stepped into the room.

"Sorry, I didn't know you were here," said Hayden, turning to leave.

"Hayden, stop. We need to talk."

The big man stopped but he was looking out the door like he wanted to run away.

"Is it that time of the month?" asked Iain, trying to make a joke as he put on his t-shirt.

Hayden didn't laugh. He sat down on the bench across from the captain and looked at the ceiling grates.

"You seem to have a hair crossed up your ass lately, and it seems aimed at me. Anything we need to talk about?"

"Eve is pregnant."

"Brilliant!" said Iain, excited for them, "By the look on your face, I say not so?"

Hayden looked halfway between anger and tears. "Not now."

"You love kids, I've seen…"

"Not now! We're not ready, not here… Too much at stake," Hayden spat. He stood and started to leave the room. Iain's hand on his arm stopped him.

"So, why are you so up in arms at me?"

"I have been a bit of a git to you lately, haven't I? I really dunno, I guess you're just the easiest target."

"Thanks, I think. What are you gonna do?" asked Iain stepping behind the body bag so Hayden could hit it without it swinging back.

"She didn't wanna go to Robyn 'cause she might tell you..."

"Robyn's a doctor, she'd never tell me anything any of you told her... unless..."

"Unless it would affect her ability to perform."

Iain nodded. "Well, now I know and I'm not upset, so she can go to Robyn and discuss options."

"Truth is one of the few things that
doesn't taste better sugarcoated."
      — Samuel "Yard" Yardley

Captain Bryce was standing in the hanger waiting for the sandpiper transporting Markus to arrive. He could feel his stomach twisting and his throat getting tighter with each minute that passed. It *was* a good thing, Eve being pregnant, wasn't it? Should he tell Markus about this turn of events; he was, after all, her father. No, it wasn't his place. A cramp shot up through his chest suddenly. He pressed on the center of his breastbone. He didn't like this one bit.

He stood still as the ship entered the bay, settled onto the hanger deck. The landing gear locks engaged, the vents blew out the oxygen to regulate the ship and the exit ramp slowly lowered before him. He could see the senator standing in the opening as it got larger; first the peppered hair, short and spiked, preferred by his rank, then his face, with a well-trimmed beard and mustache, and sour expression, and finally his large body, dressed in full parliamental regalia; a deep burgundy suit with silver embroidery and a thick gold sash, covered with the medals and markings of his status, spanning his chest.

The Confederational Regime Senator would have been an intimidating sight to anyone that didn't know him but few intimidated Iain Bryce. He locked his shoulders put what he hoped was an intimidating look on his own face and waiting for the man to speak first.

Markus wasn't sure what he was walking into. He knew Eve trusted this pirate enough to leave him, her friends and her career but she had never been able to tell him just exactly why. He really didn't hate Iain Bryce but he really didn't like him either. He was a crook, in all technical terms, but he knew he was a man of integrity as well, which was an oxymoron. Bryce's ideals may well be just but in all point of fact he was still a criminal and he'd made his daughter a criminal. Markus knew he was taking a big chance by asking him for help but he truly didn't know where else to turn.

He expected to see a group of the pirates with weapons on him when he stepped from the ship but found only the captain standing before him. The men that piloted the shuttle quickly left the hanger and, after a salute to Bryce, none looked back. He certainly had a handle on his men; Eve must appreciate that security. He was feeling very insecure though, something he wasn't used to.

Captain Iain Bryce cut a very imposing image for one so young. He stood before Markus with his feet spread to the distance of his shoulders, his hands clasped behind his back, under the lower half of his brown suede and leather knee length coat, exposing the side arms, in holsters on his hips – both uncharged. He was wearing a white shirt and brown pants, which fit well, ending in the cuffs of brown leather boots. He had shaved the five o'clock shadow he had when they had spoken earlier, clearly showing pursed lips and a set jaw. The look in his blue-gray eyes was one of high confidence – obviously comfortable in his skin. CRF reports said he was a handsome man, he thought those eyes played a big part in that. The pirate was a striking character indeed – except his hair. The dirty blond locks were curling around the bottoms and the layered top was going in every direction, all mussed up, as if he'd just stepped in from a stiff wind. The pirate captain didn't intimidate Markus but he was uncertain of him, so he wouldn't let his guard down yet.

"Captain Bryce, thank you again for allowing this meeting," said Markus, putting out his hand in greeting.

The captain ignored it and said, "Let's just get on with, we have places to be." This was a lie but Iain didn't want the man to know of their current state.

"Is there somewhere, more intimate, that we can speak?" asked Markus, not liking how his voice echoed in the large chamber.

"This way."

The pirate turned and walked out of the bay with his back to him. Markus wasn't sure if this was out of arrogance or ignorance; was the captain that certain he wasn't a threat?

The senator was taken to a very tight office at the back of the ship. It was dimly light and the dark brown wood paneling and dark colored desk didn't help. That desk was cluttered with starcharts, rulers, markers, a digital tablet and five coffee cups, and was set off-center. Two ratty looking orange chairs, the tweed-like fabric pulling apart at the seams, one set before the desk and one behind, took up most of the room's floor space. A glass display case was behind the desk with what he guessed was items Bryce had stolen through the years. He could see old leather bound books, empty bottles, rusty weapons and the signet ring he'd likely taken from the vice president when he had him held hostage prominently displayed on the center shelf, as if a trophy. A shelf across the back had an antique looking coffee machine, a tin of coffee, a dish labeled sugar; several more coffee cups, all stacked up crookedly, and four mismatched crystal decanters of what was probably liquor. A silk flag, with a right facing skull that appeared to be sneering rather than the full grin their recognized crest was, likely a precursor to it, with two swords crossed behind it embroidered over a rendition of the mythical bird their ship was named after, hung between the two windows. The view from the windows was of blue, purple, orange and yellow, with a jet of red streaking through every now and again, exhaust streams from the rear plasma engines. They made for a beautiful display behind the ship. He thought it was just the place a man like Iain Bryce would be at home.

The captain took the chair behind the desk and motioned Markus to take the other as he piled up the charts. He set his digital tablet on this and made another pile with the coffee cups, rulers and markers on the other side then leaned on the cleared area on his elbows, his fingers steepled in front of his face. He waited a few seconds and asked, "You're now in person, and in a more intimate location, what's this all about?"

"Can I be frank with you, Bryce?" the senator's eyes were looking everywhere but at the pirate's face.

"I think it best, given the circumstances."

"As I said, we believe a pirate is attacking the convoys… The moon took well to terraforming but the fields haven't been able to produce enough crops to support the colonist between supply drops. With no drops in close to a month, they are nearing dire-straights… and I was hoping you and your crew would escort the next."

"Skip to the end, please," said Bryce impatiently.

"I believe it's Riley. You know of my connection to him?"

Iain didn't know the whole story, but he knew enough of it. He now understood some of the man's angst, "Yeah, Eve doesn't talk much about it… I ain't an assassin, Oakley."

"No, no… of course, I couldn't… not…"

Iain had a feeling that was likely just what Markus had been hoping he would do, but no matter the senator's or Eve's, or even his own, ill feelings toward the awful pirate captain, Iain wasn't a murderer. "So why ain't you asking the CRF; that's what they're for, ain't it?"

"I have asked for a CRF escort but the president refused. He says if he helps this colony others will expect it." Markus knew this statement would only add more fuel to the fire that already burned inside the pirate.

"That sounds like Tommy boy."

"Our need is true," said Markus.

"We don't venture into the Inner Tier, it's too well-guarded. How is it this other pirate, whether Riley or not, has been able to without getting caught?"

"The patrols have been moved to other sectors, mine is no longer well-guarded."

It looked like that bit of information hurt coming out. Iain smiled slyly and asked, "Why might that be?"

"My pull in recent years has greatly diminished. They know my daughter is with you… Some think that makes me a pirate sympathizer."

"So, you think you can capture me and make right again?" asked Iain, has hand instinctively going to his laser pistol.

"NO!"

This was said with such intensity Iain found he believed him. Still, something was off, "We don't have the fuel, or, as long as we're being frank, the funds."

"We'll pay you… whatever you request, within reason."

"Eve will have to know what we're doing," said Iain. He hoped having to face his daughter would compel the man to tell the truth if he wasn't being completely forthright.

Markus only nodded.

Captain Bryce called a meeting of all the crew, which surprised more than a few of them, he usually only called these kinds of meetings when someone was to be set in front of the crew for breaking an article or when there was to be a major change in course for them. They only had two rooms big enough for such, the mess hall and the hold, the latter being where punishments were usually given, and both were tight. This meeting was in the mess so no one was particularly worried.

The captain stepped up onto an empty table, so all could see him, and motioned the quartermaster to call for attention.

"Eyes forward, mouths shut, ears open," Jaime's deep voice said clearly.

"We have a request to help a colony that hasn't had supplies in three months."

The room erupted with names of colonies it could be.

"Quiet down," shouted Jaime.

"We haven't helped this one before, and it will be at great peril to us to do so..."

Gideon called out from the back of the room, "That's what we do, isn't it?"

"Yes, Mr. Welch, that is indeed what we do. This colony is on the moon of Colum." Not surprising to Iain, most of them didn't know where the planet was, having never been into that Tier. All of his officers, especially Eve, recognized it and the men that had joined from the Calypso, but he was a little surprised Gideon did as well.

"That's in the First Tier!" Gideon shouted.

"Their convoys are being hit by another pirate enclave. They have been deprived of three shipments of supplies already and are on the brink of starvation. We have a request to escort the next supply convoy…"

Eve stood up slowly and asked, through clenched teeth, just loud enough for the officers closest to hear her, "Captain, whom did this request come from?"

"Eve…" said Iain, "not now."

She stormed from the room.

Hayden, giving Iain an irate look, left behind her.

Iain, Robyn and Jaime found Eve and Hayden on the observation deck. She was sitting on a bench along the wall, crying – something no one, except maybe Hayden, had ever seen her do. He was standing beside her, a hand on her shoulder.

Iain motioned Jaime and Robyn to hold back as he slowly walked over. He looked up at Hayden, who was clearly displeased with him, and nodded for him to step away. The big man hesitated, but did. Iain went down on his right knee before Eve and said, "I'm sorry…"

"How dare... how dare he?"

Iain was confused by the question, "What?"

"It's a trap, Iain," she said with such surety.

"No. I don't think so."

"He has a way of making you believe what he wants," said Eve fervently.

"I saw true worry in his eyes and posture," said Iain, thinking how strange it was defending the man.

"Is he's here?" she asked quickly, looking like she wanted to run again.

"Yeah, in my office," said the captain, holding his breath that she wouldn't explode.

"Does he know?"

"I didn't feel it my place to say. Do you wanna see him?" Iain wasn't surprised that she immediately said no.

After a moment she dried her face and said, "Bring him here, please."

The captain stood and said, "I'll send him in, the rest of us will go about our business."

"Will you come back, and can Jaime stay?"

Iain nodded.

Hayden started to go back to her side also but she shook her head to him. He didn't look especially happy but slowly walked out of the room.

Iain found Markus looking at holographs of him, his officers and the crew from the most recent leisure excursion to Ryger; staring, most intently, at one of his daughter in Hayden's arms. He jumped and dropped the picture as the door slid open then stood and squared his shoulders. "What's your decision?"

"Eve has requested to see you."

The same look Eve had on hearing her father was aboard came over his face but he stood and followed the pirate captain out the door to the observation deck.

Iain motioned Markus in then waved Jaime to follow him to the window in the far corner; both were trying to be supportive without listening.

"Dad…" Eve stiffened and said, "Senator Oakley."

"Evie, please?" He stepped closer to his daughter.

"If you're leading us into a trap I will… I will…"

"Evie, believe me, the thought of taking Bryce to President Nason has been a dream for many years…" He looked over to the captain. The man's eyes were squinted and his jaw was clenched, but he didn't say anything. "I swear, that's not what I'm here about."

Eve shook her head and said, "Why us?"

"Dirk Riley had been attacking our convoys, Eve. I was hoping…"

Eve jumped at hearing the name of the pirate that had killed her mother, right in front of her, when she was five. "You were hoping what? Be honest," she screamed.

"I was hoping Captain Bryce might kill him."

"So there are no colonists in need?"

"Yes there are. The colonists *do* truly need help," Markus turned to the captain and repeated this to him.

Iain walked over, put a hand on Eve's shoulder and said, "We will save the next convoy and *capture* Riley, *alive*."

"The wise learn many things from their foes."

—   Aristophanes

The trip through the First Tier and into the Inner Tier was uneventful; Markus knew the routes of the CRF patrols so they were able to avoid them. Colum was half-way between the two tiers, It couldn't be terraformed because it didn't have a natural water source, but it was along a major trade route so it was deemed profitable enough to be peraterraformed. It had three biospheres, each the size of a large city, connected by tunnels.

The building Markus directed the pirates to was stark white. The parliamental seal, a rolled up scroll over an olive branch, was carved into the cement lentils of each window. Three gold capped spires jutted up from a circular roof like giant mushrooms, the tip of each tower coming to a point. The purple-blue lines of the security grid over the main dome was mirrored in each roof tile. It was a touch gaudy but it suited the senator.

A squadron of CRF officers were stationed before the building. Markus stepped from the hoverlimo first, followed by Jaime, Hayden, Eve and then Iain. A man with the insignia of leftenant commander clearly displayed on each shoulder brought his gun down, not expecting the senator to have guests. "Stand down, they're with me," said Markus.

The leftenant hesitated then released the charge on his rifle and waved his men to do the same. He didn't relax his grip though. His eyes grew wide when he got a clear view of who was behind the senator. "Leftenant Commander Oakley?" asked the man breathlessly. He stood erect quickly and saluted her.

"Hello, Leftenant Commander Way," said Eve, waving his hand down. "I'm no longer an officer."

"This is my security chief, Leftenant Commander Jared Way. I introduce Captain Iain Bryce, his quartermaster, Jaime Cable, weapons master, Hayden Fabris and Eve, you already know, is his security master. They're here to help us with the colony convoys."

"But they're pirates… How do we know it wasn't them…"

"Because they were deep in the Second Tier when I went to see them, three days ago."

Even Jared couldn't explain how they could have possibly been able to hit the convoy six days ago and return to that Tier without some new, and unheard of, faster-than-light technology. "Still, can they be trusted, Senator?" he asked.

"They can. I know this goes against everything you've been taught but these particular pirates are not what President Nason has made them out to be."

The pirate captain looked sideways at Markus, more than a little surprised; he sounded like he actually believed that. He stepped forward, gracefully bowed, extended his hand in greeting and, in a poised voice, said, "Pleased to meet you, Leftenant Commander Way."

The man looked at the pirate captain uncertainly, ready to run him through with the tip of his rifle. He shouldered it, finally, and took his hand. Both men's grips were firm but neither tried to out squeeze the other. Senator Oakley surprised Officer Way again when he asked him to join them in his office to discuss options and decide on the best course of actions.

Senator Oakley's office wasn't dark, cramped or cluttered like Captain Bryce's; his was spacious and had white washed walls and large windows showing views of the lush gardens beyond and an azure lake in the distance. Beautiful landscape art hung on the walls and abstract sculptures stood on marble platforms around the room. Three black overstuffed chairs were situated before a clear glass desk, which was centered between the windows, the chair pushed under it was transparent as well. A black combox was on only thing on the desk. There wasn't a spot of dust or a fingerprint anywhere and no personal items at all, no photos of Eve, plaques of CRP or of CRF service awards. The formality of it made Iain uncomfortable but Eve seemed to find it normal; telling him at least this wasn't because of their personal distance.

Markus stepped behind the desk, pushed a button on the combox and asked to have the starcharts showing the last routes the convoys had attempted brought in. He then went to one of the larger pieces of artwork, swung it into the room to expose a bar set into the wall and asked if anyone wanted drinks. Only Hayden accepted. While he was pouring the drink a soldier came in with the charts. Markus handed the glass to Hayden as he passed him then motioned them to step up as he unrolled the charts and spread them out on top of the desk.

Leftenant Commander Way was uneasy with the people in the room. He wanted to scream at Markus that he shouldn't be discussing this with pirates but he was his superior so he had no say. He remembered he had always scoffed at the reports of Iain Bryce's supposed extraordinary indoctrination abilities, he had always thought them just hype to increase the men's desires to see Bryce taken down, now he was all but sure he was seeing them first hand. How else could he have gotten a man like Markus Oakley to agree to this? The pirate had influenced the man's mind, no doubt by nefarious means. He vowed he wouldn't let that happen to him.

He tried to watch them all, to be sure none of them tried anything, his hand was on his pistol just in case, but found himself watching the captain most, quite intently, trying to figure out why he didn't seem at all like the pirate he had learned so much about. He found he was very curious about him.

Iain Bryce was reported to be uneducated and an amateurish captain with thoughts of heroic grandeur, capable of doing near anything to get his way. The man before Jared seemed nothing like that. This man seemed quite confident in who and what he was, was calculating and methodical, spoke softly and eloquently and seemed to have strong convictions. The members of his crew didn't seem remotely unsure of him either. Eve, whom Jared was still a bit enthralled with, even though he hadn't seen her in twelve years, seemed very comfortable with him. She was one of the strongest willed people he knew. Either this man was really good at brainwashing or he wasn't the evil conniving criminal he had been led to believe. A voice inside his head was shouting he was being indoctrinated as he listened to the man's steady, confident voice, but he didn't hear it for long.

Despite his apprehension, he was impressed by the captain's thought process as he and the one named Jaime stood and began to move pens around on the chart to act as the convoy, their ship and the enemy pirate ship, debating where the other pirate might be hiding, what routes they might try taking and how they might be able to sneak up and take them by surprise.

Their plan sounded plausible but... before Jared realized it he was asking out loud, "How will you attack them and not be seen yourselves?" He immediately clammed up, thinking they wouldn't take kindly to being questioned. He wasn't sure if the pirate's reactions made him feel better or worse. Worse, he'd expected to be ridiculed and would've known how to react to that.

Captain Bryce turned around, sat down on the corner of the desk and said, quite calmly, "We have our ways, Master Way," then he flashed him his trademark sly smile.

Iain continued to watch the leftenant commander as Jaime and Hayden spoke. The man was only five foot eleven but was squarely built. His short-cropped brown hair fit the shape of his head and set off his face that ended in a cleft chin well. He was stiff with eagerness and an obvious deep sense of duty; his dark blue eyes seemed to look everywhere at once. He couldn't put his finger on the man's perception of him yet because he guessed the man wasn't sure of it himself yet.

Jared smiled back at the pirate, in spite of himself, feeling a strange mix of edginess and well-being under that steady gaze. Again a part of him wondered if that was Bryce working his power on him, but again, the thought didn't stay long. He finally let himself relax a bit with the overall friendliness in the room, asking other questions and even offering suggestions of his own. He was feeling quite encouraged by their willingness to listen to his thoughts without prejudice. He was thrown off-guard again when Senator Oakley announced he and a squad of CRF soldiers was to accompany the pirates. He started to protest, realizing he wouldn't be safe if he did that, but the pirate stopped him.

"Master Way, we have no way of knowing how many single fighters Riley has, but we only have two and two shuttles and not enough experienced pilots to fly them all into battle successfully. I realize this'll be a right bit uncomfortable; we won't exactly enjoy exposing ourselves to you either. I'm willing to open my ship and crew to you if you're willing to open yourself up to us." said Captain Bryce.

"Keep your friends close and your enemies closer."
— *Michael Coreleone,*
character from the movie "Godfather II"

Captain Bryce spent the first hour of the CRF occupation of his ship presenting them the articles then he had Eve give them a tour of the ship, minus the areas that were off-limits – weapons storage, the array room, any officer's quarters, unless invited, the engine room and the gun areas, he didn't need any of them getting the idea this would be the perfect opportunity to take him out, then he asked Leftenant Commander Way to join them in a meeting.

Iain was listening to Hayden and Jaime discussing the best travel route for the convoy but he was studying the CRF officer, who was studying each of them as if trying to permanently etch them in his mind. The look on the man's face when his eyes came to Iain and found him looking back was priceless. "So, tell us, Leftenant Commander, does this sound a viable plan?"

Jared took a moment to answer, still recovering from being caught studying them all. "No. I still say their plan is flawed. The other pirate hit our convoys at different places and in different ways each time, how can you know for sure this will be the route they'll choose?"

The captain looked at his quartermaster.

Jaime nodded and motioned the CRF man over. He pointed out the cluster of asteroids that rimmed the space just before the planet and moon of Bangor, "That's perfect cover for a hidden ship, given where the previous hits were. It is likely he's using it. It's dangerous even with deflector shields, the asteroids shift when the planet is in close orbit, due to gravitational pull. If we have the convoy take this route," said the quartermaster, pointing out a trajectory that would take them within three clicks of the outermost chunks, "Riley will be too tempted to pass it up."

"If Riley is using the cluster, how will we?"

"We won't," answered Jaime.

"You see, Leftenant Commander, as I said on the planet, we have our ways," said Captain Bryce, curling one side of his lips into a smile and raising one eyebrow.

"Which you won't divulge."

"We'll be hidden in the convoy's wake."

"You mean you have an enshrouder? Those were decommissioned years ago because they aren't reliable."

"They are if you're lucky enough to have a right brilliant master mechanic who can make near anything work, which we luckily do," said Iain, nodding toward Digger who saluted and nodded back, with a proud smile. "Are we in agreement then?" after all, including Jared, had nodded, the captain added, "Dismissed."

The captain slowly walked to his office wondering what Jared Way really thought of all of them now that he was before them for real, not just reading the black and white CRF propaganda. He was only a little surprised when the man himself came jogging up behind him.

"Captain Bryce, might I have a word?"

"Yes, Mr. Way, you might. I'm on my way to a cup of coffee, care to join me?"

"I can't stomach the synthetic stuff."

"That stuff don't deserve to be called *coffee* by any stretch of the imagination."

"You have real coffee?"

"Yup," the captain said, smiling at the disbelief in the man's eyes. "Just one of the, if you will pardon the pun, perks of my job!"

"I have a feeling you will never cease to amaze me," said Jared quietly.

Iain motioned the leftenant commander to take a seat, started a fresh pot of the precious black gold, took a seat behind the desk and said, "What word would you like, Master Way?"

"I want you to know, I believe this is a just cause and my men and I won't jeopardize it but I am, first and foremost, a CRF officer, so when this is done I feel it is my duty to take you into custody."

"I figured you would try and I truly wish you the best of luck in that endeavor," said Iain candidly, "As long as you realize I and mine will, in the same way, do all in our power to stop you; feeling it is our duty to keep out of your custody."

"Why did you allow us on board, you aren't afraid we now have knowledge that could help capture you?"

Iain smiled as he stood, walked to the coffee pot and poured two cups. He motioning to Jared for sugar and cream. He handed the cup to the CRF officer and stepped back behind the desk, taking a sip of his own before he answered, "As I once told your president, I've had a right good run, if it ends tomorrow, so be it."

"You are arrogant though, Captain Bryce," said Jared, unable to stop smiling.

"I've been called worse," said Iain, with a smile. "If we both know our end goal, our relationship can be a much healthier one."

"You thrive on the prospect of capture, you get a thrill from it, don't you?" observed Jared, absolutely astounded.

"Some have said I enjoy the adrenaline rush a right bit too much, and they are likely right," said the pirate captain. He held his cup up in a mock toast then he took another healthy gulp of it. "You're finding yourself liking me despite your better judgment, aren't you?"

Jared shrugged and nodded "You are nothing like the reports, I'll give you," said Jared, taking another sip of coffee, "And you make one hell of a cup of coffee."

"I've always wondered what those reports say."

"First, that you only made it through eight years of school, yet you sound well educated."

"I was… released, let's say, from school when I was about thirteen… for a much more… educational facility," said Iain, with a dark look entering his eyes.

"The penal colony on Benwick?"

"Yeah, right good education there," this was said with sarcasm. "Between that, a good library I had access to shortly after, and my officers," he paused, and said a little more like he imagined the leftenant commander had expected him to sound, "I right learnt teacherin' me-self a right sight lots of loads be'er."

Jared smiled at the man's mocking, held up his coffee cup in a feigned salute and said, "You're also much more commanding than some reports claim. You don't seem to rule by threat or force."

"I respect my crew and expect the same," said Iain.

"And you seem to get it. The fact that you have former CRF among your higher crew says a great deal. How is it you and Master Cable can just look at each other and know what the other is thinking?" asked Jared, obviously captivated.

"Years of knowing each other, and being of the same mind. Maybe we are twins, separated at birth?" said Iain, shrugging.

"Doesn't it worry you one of your crew might turn on you for the bounty?"

"As I said previous, so be it."

"Why did you choose this life then?" asked Jared.

"I think it more chose me... I don't especially like crime but it's the only thing I know. I don't especially like the label but I do suppose I am a Robin Hood of sorts as well. Yeah, I steal for profit, and yeah, I right enjoy the excitement of the hunt and siege. I won't deny that. I truly do it more for them. I grew up as on Beta Four so I know a right lot what they are going through. I can't ignore them now, when I know I can help. Without us most of 'em would as likely die. Take your colony's situation, should they be left to die?" asked Iain tilting up his cup to get the last drops.

"I have friends in the colony so, no, I would prefer they not be." Jared couldn't help but admire the man's innate honesty. Iain Bryce knew what he was and was not. Jared realized he liked the man. "And you make a point, Captain Bryce, President Nason does have a way of handily forgetting about the outer Tier planets."

"Careful, Leftenant, you're beginning to sound like one of us!" said Iain with a sneaky smile. "Seeing as you now know so much about me, mind if I ask what it is about the CRF that is so much better?"

"Well... uh... they enforce the laws..." said Jared. He was suddenly finding it hard to come up with a good reason to be with them.

"As you heard from my articles, we have our own set of laws; do you agree they are just as sound?"

"Yeah, many are similar to the CRF."

"Should be, Jaime wrote most of 'em. So, tell me, why did you choose your path?" asked Iain. He stood and poured himself another cup of coffee and topped off the man's cup.

"My father mostly, he was career military. I was in my second year of university, Science Major, when he got ill. It was his dying wish that I join the forces. He used his life savings, my inheritance, to purchase me a commission. I kind of felt I owed it to him, I guess."

Iain was about to sarcastically recount the virtues of having overbearing parents but he wasn't sure Jared felt his had been yet. "You and Eve know each other... from before. Take it there was something once?" Iain wasn't trying to pry, he already knew the answer. Eve had spoken in confidence to he and Jaime, nervous

Hayden might react bad if he learned of their past relationship. He was testing the CRF officer to see how much the man trusted him.

"Once. Yeah. We went through boot camp on Calista together." Jared stood and began to pace the back of the office.

Iain nodded. After a few seconds of silence, Iain smiled and said, "I promise I won't attempt to take you hostage and hold you for ransom, 'long as you promise not to kill us in our sleep. Deal?"

"Deal," said Jared.

"Now, I am late for a poker game. Tell me, Master Way, are you a gambling man?"

"A man who steals from others should
not complain if he is stolen from."
    –   *Kohzu Wu*

The trip to Bangor was as uneventful as the trip to Colum had been, since the leftenant commander knew where the CRF patrols ran in this space as well. They entered orbit over the planet the day before the convoy was set to leave it and took up a position in the last ship's wake, enshrouded, when it did. They had decided not to advise the convoy of their presence so they wouldn't give them away with a stupid move. Now it was just a matter of sitting and waiting.

While they waited Jared and his men found themselves integrating into the ship nicely. He, himself, attended all the meetings, played poker with, and ate most of his meals with Iain and Jaime; the other officers joining them occasionally. He would've never believed it, but life on the pirate ship was really quite comfortable and safe feeling.

He only found himself uncomfortable once, as he was following the captain and quartermaster to another friendly game of cards. A shipmate he hadn't seen before stepped from the dayroom as they were walking by and called out to Jaime. He had stopped in his tracks. He knew this man, not from reading reports of pirates and criminals, but, for the life of him, he couldn't remember where.

"Get the game started, I'll be right along," said Jaime as he followed the man back up the corridor.

"I've seen that man before," said Jared. "How long has he been on your crew?"

"About two months, I would guess. Why?" asked the captain.

"I know him from somewhere…"

"He was a gladiator in the Ky'istri Challenge, maybe you saw him on a poster?"

"Yeah, I am sure that was it."

Iain gave the leftenant commander a sideways glance, seeing he was still trying to work it out in his mind. He thought then maybe he would do some digging into the odd crewman himself.

When the convoy reached the cluster all hands were ordered to take up positions. Jared, three of his CRF officers, Hayden, Jaime and Iain were sitting in starlings waiting for the signal to launch. It began to seem Jaime's thoughts *had* been wrong as time grew longer and they got closer to the asteroid field with no sign of any other ships. The captain was about to order them to stand down when Kassie's exasperated voice came over the com.

"Captain Bryce, the lead ship just got hit with a torpedo from the asteroids." They waited again for what seemed like forever before Kassie's voice came over the com again. "The Gray Hawk just left the cluster and is in full view, bearing down on the convoy."

"Launch!" shouted Iain, punching the engines.

Phoenix appeared behind the last ship in the convoy in a fiery glow, surprising them and the other pirate ship, which had to adjust its course or hit them. Kassie called to the convoy to follow her to safety as six starlings burst from Phoenix's belly and swarmed the other pirate ship, hitting its port side in tandem attacks.

Three falcon fighters came from the Gray Hawk's hanger bay.

Captain Bryce asked Jared to lead his men in an attack on them while his stayed on the main ship.

Two of the CRF starlings were taken out quickly; one exploded in place, the other took a hit to the larboard wing, which sent it careening into the cluster. It collided with a clump of rock and disintegrated into nothing but chunks.

Iain ordered Hayden to keep on the ship while he and Jaime joined Jared's dogfight. One of the falcons was destroyed shortly after, hit by torpedoes from both Jared and Jaime. The second falcon spun out of control with its larboard engine destroyed moments later, it didn't explode but the ship was useless, drifting away at an odd angle. The final falcon put up a good chase before it rammed into the rear of the Gray Hawk taking out half its hanger deck.

A grizzled voice came over the com moments, "Who is this attacking me?"

Iain opened his comlink and answered, "Captain Bryce of Phoenix Enclave. Do you surrender, Riley?"

"Aren't you jumping the wrong ship, Bryce?"

"I think not. Do you surrender?" Captain Bryce said again. He was ready to attack the Gray Hawk again if he didn't get the response he wanted.

There was no answer.

Iain swung his starling around to make another pass at the now unprotected aft hull of the rival pirate ship, avoiding the beams of the laser cannons with ease. He struck the larboard side with a direct hit and the ship's atmosphere exploded out in a cloud of gas and debris.

"Very well, Bryce," growled Riley's voice.

Captain Bryce told the remaining starlings to stand down and called for Kassie to release the shuttles. He and Jared remained outside in case the crew of the Gray Hawk thought to put up a fight or run. When they got the call from Jaime that all was set, the captain and Jared boarded.

"Once you open a can of worms, the only way to re-can them is to use a bigger can."
   –   Anonymous

Jared was waiting for Iain when he set down in the hanger bay, together they walked to the Gray Hawk's mess, where the quartermaster had Riley's crew gathered. The conditions inside the ship were beyond atrocious, the walls were covered in rust and grime, the floors were sticky and littered with refuse and the windows were black with muck and grease and neither of them wanted to think about what they might be breathing in.

It wasn't hard to pick Dirk Riley out of the group, for all he wasn't exactly a prize specimen himself. He was a short stalky man of about fifty-five, with greasy black hair, streaked with three different shades of gray that hung like curtains along his face, past his shoulders and down over his back. He was wearing tall brown boots, burgundy pants, a gray tunic and a black velvet cape, which was draped over his right shoulder. All were soiled and wrinkled as if they hadn't been changed in many days. His face was unshaven and dirty and his teeth were yellowish brown and thick with plaque.

Riley's beady black eyes looked like those of a mad man, darting to and fro, never alighting on anything for long, until they locked on the blue-gray eyes of Iain Bryce. "Cap'n Bryce, are you gettin' so needy that ya now attack yer own compatriots?"

"You're no compatriot of mine, Riley!" spat Iain.

"Them supplies could buy us both loads of liquor and whores, Bryce," said Riley, laughing wildly.

"That's not my idea of a good time, thank you. Those supplies are for the Colum colony. You've already deprived them of three convoys; another and they won't survive."

"So be it. Yer goddamn self-righteous cause, ya make us all sick, you're a fuckin' disgrace to this profession," barked Riley. He spit a glob of black chewing tobacco on the deck as an insult. The soggy globule landed on Captain Bryce's left boot. This made the man smile and break into raucous laughter. Many of his crew joined in. He, and they, stopped when he, they, saw the huge laser rifle aimed at him.

"You're the fucking disgrace!" shouted Eve. She stepped from behind Captain Bryce with that laser rifle held tight in her arms. The red light on it denoted it was fully charged.

Iain spun around, unable to hide his surprise, he said, "I ordered you to stay on Phoenix, Oakley."

She ignored the captain. "You killed my mother!"

Riley looked at her like she was crazy, "I 'ave killed a lot loads of mothers, Girl!" A funny look came over his face, a look of recognition, followed by an ugly smile. "He said Oakley, ay? I 'member yer muver. A right young pretty thing, from Colum, yes?"

"You sick bastard!"

"She was right pleasin', for 'bout a minute. After she died... then the real jollity began."

"No, don't... *don't*..." Eve shook her head and backed up a couple steps.

Captain Riley ran his purplish tongue over his lips and closed his eyes in feigned ecstasy, "I 'member 'er beggin' me not to 'urt 'er daughter as I ran me 'ands over 'er tight lil body." He cackled wildy, "Even after havin' 'er three times, and in three different 'oles, said she'd do anythin' I asked, just not to 'urt 'er wee lil girl."

"No... no... no," said Eve, stepping closer.

"She gave a right good fight, she did though, made 'er hips wriggle even more an' get me off right good, she did, almost 'ated havin' to slit 'er throat, she mighta' been a keeper, but in the end I was just too much for 'er. I gave 'er me hot juice and she couldna' take the pleasure a' it, I think," he said, stroking his crotch and licking his lips. "The girl was 'bout five, I reckon. Think she too woulda' been a right great loads of hilarifying for 'bout a minute, coulda' taught 'er right how ta please a man from the start, make 'er ready for the future, know what I mean? I is bettin' it woulda' been right tight, being' all that young, ya know? Never got to do 'er nothing... Had ta clear out quick 'cause the dumb girl's daddy brought the cops down on us." Realization lit in the crazy man's eyes and they cleared in a flash, "Ooh, that girl musta' been you? Come to make an offer of yourself ta me, 'ave ya?" Hee started to make like he was unbuckling his belt.

Iain had hoped by leaving Eve on Phoenix they could avoid opening this can of worms. He was sickened by Riley's recount of Eve's mother's death. He knew the man wasn't exaggerating by the look in her eyes. He could see she was reliving it as Riley was describing it. He knew he had to make a move now, before she did something she would regret. He started forward to stop her but it was too late, she was already too far gone.

Eve screamed, "NO!" at the top of her lungs as she ran past them, bringing the barrel of the rifle up, ready to shoot.

Iain and Jaime both lunged forward, trying to stop her, but she was too quick. Iain landed hard on the decking, with a harrumph of painfully exhaled air. Jaime landed a little softer with using the captain as a cushion. Both of them and Hayden shouted, "Eve, stop!" at the same time, but she was beyond hearing them. Jared was just plain stunned, frozen in place, just watching the scene before him.

Jaime rolled off the captain and began to rise. At the same time, Iain came up on his knee. Both men pulled their laser pistols, unsure just what to do, watching in horror as their worst nightmares became real.

Riley saw the woman coming at him and quickly pulled a knife he had well hidden. The rusty weapon collided with the barrel of the rifle throwing off his aim so it sliced her across her belly instead of plunging into it. Warm blood spurted from her middle, covering the front of the pirate, startling even him for a moment.

Eve released the rifle, which clanged loudly as it hit the floor in the dead silent room, and fell forward into the man.

He held her a moment, laughing, then ran his tongue along her neck and cheek.

She moaned in disgust and pain as her eyes rolled back and she fell unconscious.

Riley dropped her to the deck like unwanted rubbish.

Jared, Jaime, Hayden and Iain all screamed, "NO!" in unison and the orange yellow blast of a laser pistol lit up the room.

The blast took Riley dead center of his chest and knocked him back a few feet. Somehow he remained standing. The evil pirate looked down as if unsure why he had a hole in him, then up to the man who shot him. "Right good show, now you're one of us! Right good sh…" His eyes rolled back and his body slumped to the floor like unwanted rubbish, twitched once and went still.

All eyes turned to the source of the laser blast, none believing what they'd just witnessed.

Iain was still on one knee. A stream of smoke was rising from the barrel of the pistol he still had aimed in the direction of where the other pirate captain had just been standing. His eyes were red, his cheeks were wet with tears, and his jaw was clenched so tight it looked like he was trying to bite through his own gums.

Hayden looked at the captain in disbelief briefly then stumbling over to see if Eve was still alive. Jaime slowly stepped up to Iain and took hold of the still hot pistol. Iain was holding it so tight that an imprint of the gun was left in his hand when he finally did. Jared stood shocked and dumbfounded, looking from Iain and Jaime, to Eve and Hayden, to the dead pirate captain, to the dead pirate captain's crew and back to Iain and Jaime, not sure what to do. He started toward Iain and Jaime, to see if he could help. Just as he got there Iain stood.

Captain Bryce said dryly, "Space Riley's body and lock the crew in the brig. Leftenant Commander Way, please gather your men and take this ship and her crew to Senator Oakley." He turned then, walked from the mess to the hanger and boarded his starling. He opened a jump window just after leaving the bay and disappeared.

Captain Riley's rusty knife had sliced deep into Eve's middle, making it hard to stop the bleeding. All aboard Phoenix now knew of her condition. Most of the grunts were hold up in the mess, praying for her. Jaime and Hayden were pacing outside sickbay doors. Jared, Digger, Yard and Mitch were on the observation deck. Kyle and Kassie were on the bridge. No one was sure just where Captain Bryce was.

"Should someone go look for him?" asked Jared.

"He'll be back when he is ready," said Mitch.

"He was so flat as he gave his last order."

Jaime stepped into the room just as Jared made this comment. "Captain Bryce has never shot a man in cold blood before."

"But, he was jailed for murder…"

"Being jailed for a thing and actually doing it are two entirely different things. Iain killed his father in self-defense. I was there," said the quartermaster.

"*Is* he going to be alright?" asked Jared.

"I don't know," answered Jaime, shaking his head, "I truly don't," as he turned and left.

It was well into the next morning before Dr. Carter finally came through the door into the observation deck. Everyone came to attention and more than one looked ready to cry at the sight of all the blood covering the front of the doctor's smock. Robyn motioned Hayden over and whispered into his ear. The man's eyes grew large and his hand went to his mouth as he ran from the room. She looked after him for a moment then turned to the rest of them and said, "Eve is stabilized."

A collective sigh went through the room. The look she gave them told them that wasn't the whole of it.

"She… lost the baby… the knife sliced through the wall of her uterus… killing her baby instantly… and… destroyed one of her ovaries. She'll likely never be able to conceive again." The room began to spin as the last words left the doctor's mouth.

Jaime took the distance between him and Robyn in one large step and pulled her into his arms. She was exhausted, beyond tears. He helped her to a chair and told Mitch to get her a glass of water.

She thanked him but didn't drink any; she looked around and said, "Where's Iain?"

To Know Thy Self

"I wasn't lost, I just didn't know
where I was."
— *Iain D. Bryce*

The starling had run out of fuel two days ago but its occupant no longer cared. The ship had dropped out of jump so fast the pilot was thrust into the windshield, knocking him out. His head, just below his hairline, was split open and bleeding profusely, and he was coming in and out of awareness. Just long enough to realize he needed help, but not long enough to do anything about it. Luckily, the ship was equipped with a distress beacon that activated when the empty fuel tank light lit, and luckily it was within range to be received by the space station orbiting Sunnen. A shuttle was dispatched, the drifting starling was picked up, and its injured occupant was taken to the hospital on the planet.

Three days later, when the man finally awoke, not only did he not know where he was, he didn't know who he was. His left hand went to his the side of his head and found it wrapped with gauze, his right arm wouldn't respond. He looked down and found it in a cast from mid-bicep to wrist. His left leg was also in a cast, from mid-thigh to his toes, and was inclined on a stack of pillows. More bandages covered his chest. One inch round pads were spread around his torso and each temple, each attached to wire leads connected to a monitor beside the bed. The steady beeping in his left ear told him his heart was still beating at least. He looked around, as best as he could, but could see no identifying features; other than obviously a hospital room. Two things he did know was the lights were very bright and his throat was very dry.

He tried to sit up and yelped as a painful hitch pinched his left side. Just as he was lying back down the door opened to a woman dressed as a nurse.

"Well, hello," said the nurse then she shouted, "Doctor, he's awake," to someone in the hall. She walked over, checked the pads on his chest and asked, "Is there anything I can get you?"

"Water?" said a voice he guessed must be his.

The nurse disappeared and returned with a pitcher and a cup. She poured some water into the cup and held it to his mouth. She pulled it back when he began to cough. "Must be full," she teased.

He smiled at the joke and tried again to rise, "What happened to me?"

"I'll let the doctor explain that." She held him down and added, "No, don't get up, you'll hurt yourself."

A man who looked to be about forty, with black peppered hair and a well-trimmed beard and mustache, stepped into the room and said jovially, "Hello, sir, you gave us quite a scare. I'll be your doctor during your stay with us, Dr. Daniel Jacobs, in case you've need to ask for me. And, you are?"

"I... don't... know?" said the man in the bed.

"Nurse Stocker, could you get the mirror?" asked the doctor. The nurse picked up a hand held mirror from the table beside the bed and handed it to the doctor. Dr. Jacobs held the small mirror up to the man in the bed so he could see himself, and said, "Sometimes, this'll help bring things back."

The face staring back at the man in the bed was swollen, a black and purple patch of bruises covered his right cheek and eye, the left eye was puffy but the color was blue-gray. What he could see of the hair, spraying out from under the bandages, was dirty blond and was a tangled mess. It wasn't a face he knew, or particularly liked. The man groaned and dropped the mirror.

"You have a lot of healing to do. You have a broken tibia," pointing to left his leg, "a fracture of the ulna," pointing to his right arm, "and three broken ribs, on the left side, and you struck your head and fractured your frontal bone. We found no bone fragmentation but there is some inner cranial swelling. The amnesia you are suffering will likely go away with that. We found no ident card on you but you do have some interesting tattoos and significant scarring, which we may be able to use for identification," said the doctor, pointing to his left triceps, neck, wrist and stomach.

The man on the bed lifted and twisted his left arm. He saw a strange looking bird with a set of crossed swords and grinning skull over it and used the mirror to look at the black scrolling line that had what looked like a heart and cross worked into the motif on his neck, and at a red cross entwined in a black thorny vine on his wrist of his casted arm, he found a letter B also as he twisted it around as far as he could. then he looked at the scars the doctor had pointed out that crisscrossing his stomach. He gave the doctor a strange look and shook his head that he didn't remember getting them.

"You kids today, all so obsessed with pirates," said the doctor. "We don't know your name but we must call you something. He looks like a Curtis, doesn't he?" the doctor asked the nurse.

"Yes, I think Curtis is just fine," said Nurse Stocker smiling pleasantly.

"Curtis? Curtis," he said as if testing it, "Guess it's good as any." The man shrugged and looked again at his reflection, feeling very anxious.

By his second week at the hospital the bruises on Curtis' face had healed and most of the cranial swelling had gone down, at least enough to take him off the monitors. This allowed him to get up and wander once in a while. The cast on his right arm was replaced with an ace bandage that only covered his forearm and the cast on his left leg was shortened to below his knee. He couldn't put weight on it yet but he could walk with the help of crutches. The bandages around his head were replaced with a small butterfly bandage and, though he still got hitches whenever he moved wrong, or breathed deep, his ribs had healed enough to remove the bandages around his middle. Dr. Jacobs still visited on a regular basis. He assured him the lingering amnesia was normal for an injury such as his but he was getting frustrated as the days stretched on. He stared at his reflection, for hours at times, hoping something, some tiny bit of recognition, would jump out at him but so far nothing had.

The dirty blond brown hair on his head was down to his shoulders and was wildly curly, especially around his ears and neck, both of his eyes were blue-gray and his face was well-formed, or at least balanced. He had a V shaped scar on his right cheek, just below his eye, that looked like it happened long before this current incident, he could now clearly see the tattoo with the heart and ankh symbol on the right side of his neck, where the collar of the hospital gown began. The tattoo on his right wrist, with the thorny vine and a red cross, went all the way around his wrist and actually had the letters I, D and B, worked into it. Those could have been explained away as just decorations but the skull and crossed swords over a thunderbird on his left triceps wasn't so easily. He noticed a patch of brazed skin on the inside of his left forearm that Nurse Stocker said could have once been another tattoo that had been removed. Nothing came to him of their significance, other than he must apparently enjoy pain to have endured sitting for each of them. None of the above listed items evoked anything, except for curiosity.

Dr. Jacobs suggested he might be a CRF soldier. He did have an image of holding a pistol and a Leftenant Commander patch, but he wasn't sure it was real. The fact that he had been found piloting a CRF style ship did seem to suggest this. He thought the tattoo of the pirate symbol could be in mockery of the enemy. About a week into his stay Dr. Jacobs contacted them to check the dockets but so far no one had come looking for him.

Though Curtis was physically capable of taking care of himself, Dr. Jacobs wasn't ready to release him; still concerned about the lingering amnesia. He wanted him to be close in case he had a sudden flashback or his memory returned in a rush that caused debilitating stress. To satisfy his growing need to be moving, he wandered the hospital halls or the garden, when the weather was warm enough, for exercise.

He was walking down the halls one particular day, because it was storming horrendously outside, when he got a wave of dizziness. Luckily this particular time he was beside the visitors lounge. He stepped into the room that had several tables and slowly sank into one of the cold hard chairs around them. He laid his head back and took several long, deep breaths, until the lightheadedness went away.

His heart had finally slowed its speed when a voice spoke behind him, making it and him jump. He turned quickly but no one was there. He closed his eyes tight, feeling like he was going to be sick. He wondered if he was losing what he had left of his mind. He was just about ready to call for help when he heard the voice again. He realized, with a nervous laugh, it was the DTV in the corner. The volume was turned down so low that only louder snippets of conversations, here and there, could be heard.

He grabbed the remote beside him and turned it up to hear the newscaster giving the latest headlines. She was telling of a pirate attack on a supply convoy in the middle of the First BrimTier near a planet called Ryger. She was standing next to a man, who kept fidgeting with his clothes, saying she was about to begin an interview with an eyewitness. Curtis brought his legs around in the chair and turned the volume up a touch more just as Nurse Stocker came in.

"There you are, Curtis. It's time for your meds."

He didn't want to stop watching the DTV but he knew she wouldn't leave him alone until he took the pills so he downed them quickly. She looked pleased but she wouldn't go until he said he was alright. By the time he looked back at the screen the interview was over and the reporter was finishing the story.

"...the witness says it was the Robin Hood pirates of Phoenix Enclave. He said they were all very courteous and pleasant and didn't harm anyone. It makes me wonder two things; first, if these *Robin Hood pirates* are to be believed, and, second, why so many of their so-called *victims* don't consider themselves such. If the pirate captain is listening now," said the pretty reporter, the name below her image said Ashley Tyler, with a flirtatious smile, "I would be interested in a personal interview."

Nurse Stocker's voice came from behind Curtis then, making him jump again, "You know, my brother was aboard a ship that pirate, Captain Bryce, hit once. He said the same thing. He, his wife and their baby boy were on vacation when they got hit. He said they only took what credits they had and set them in an escape pod. Guess, maybe, they really are kind of heroes, in a way."

Curtis had nothing to say, he didn't know this Captain Bryce or his pirate reputation from Adam, but for some reason he found himself unable to stop thinking about the bit the pretty newscaster had said. "Excuse me, Nurse Stocker, is there a digital tablet around?"

"There should be one on the cabinet in the corner."

"Blessed is the person who is too busy to worry in the daytime and too sleepy to worry at night."
      –   Unknown

Jaime was just getting up from the captain's desk after exhausting all possibilities, when the combox beside him buzzed. "Yes?" he said curtly.

"Any word?" asked Robyn's voice.

No, Doctor. Nothing."

I t had been three weeks since the captain had disappeared. The starling he took shouldn't have had enough fuel to make it out of the Tier, even in full jump but he could've stopped anywhere and refueled. The quartermaster had spent most of that time contacting every colony and port he could think the captain might have gone to and had so far come up empty; making more than one of the contacts just as anxious as they were. All of them promised to contact Phoenix if he turned up. The only person Jaime had not yet contacted was Caitlyn. He didn't know how things were left with them and he didn't want to upset her needlessly. Something told him he wouldn't have gone there anyway, and that he wasn't staying away because he wanted to. One thing he did know was Iain hadn't been captured by the CRF. That would have been all over the DTV. So, then, where was he?

They hadn't wanted to leave the Tier, but a delegation from Earth was set to arrive, including the president himself. Jaime didn't want to chance them getting caught, so they have called off the physical search after two weeks. Before they left, Leftenant Commander

Way told them to com him if he could be any assistance. Jaime had asked him to monitor the CRF docket for anything sounding like Iain.

Meanwhile, back in their own territory, they had continued their quest, hitting a supply ship just inside the First Tier, had taken on two new shipmates and were now docked on Ryger, unloading the unneeded merchandise and reloading supplies for their next search attempt.

Everyone on Phoenix was on edge, jumping down each other's throat for little or nothing. Eve was battling a severe case of depression, not only from losing the baby but because she felt whatever might have happened to the captain was her fault. Jaime doubted she would be better until he was back on board. He doubted any of them would be. Hayden was being even more belligerent than before, saying the captain was only looking for attention. He was ready to write Iain off and swear Jaime in as captain, which only made Jaime more anxious.

The quartermaster didn't want to be captain, even temporarily, and was upset with Iain, himself, for disappearing and thrusting this on him. He knew why Iain had left as he had, he was not a violent man, unless he was forced to be, and unless it was justified. Killing Riley, as he had, had gone against a lot of his core values. In the past, he would go into a funk for days when he had felt forced down to that level. This was beyond just being in a funk though; this could be seen as deserting. He would've smacked his best friend if he knew where he was.

Jaime was walking toward the mess hall, realizing he hadn't had anything to east since dinner the night before, when Kyle's hurried voice broke through his building funk. He punched the comlink on his jacket and said a gruff, "Yes?"

"I have Leftenant Commander Way on link, Sir." The quartermaster ran to the ladder just beyond the mess hall, slid down and went into his cabin, which was just under the bridge, "Send it to my cabin, Kyle." In his haste to get behind the desk he banged his knee on the corner of it. "Ouch, FUCKEN A!" he shouted.

"No thanks, Master Cable," said a voice from the combox.

Jaime held a middle finger up to the smirking face of Jared and said, "I caught my knee on the corner of the desk. "

"When did you start swearing?"

"When the situation warrants it, I do. What news Leftenant Commander?" asked Jaime; rubbing the spot in an attempt to keep it from bruising.

"I found a report of a starling found near sector six three, in distress. One man aboard with head injuries. The description sounds like your captain. Do you want me to check it out?"

"Very much. This won't get you into trouble?"

"The man is reported to have amnesia and is thought to be a CRF officer. If I show up with intentions of identifying him it will look perfectly normal."

"Good. How soon?" asked Jaime trying not to sound too overly excited but having a hard time not, this was the first possible trace in weeks.

"I'll leave within the hour. It'll take me two days to reach there, how close are you, just in case?"

"We can get there in three. Keep in contact and stay safe."

"Same to you, Jaime. Way out," said Jared as he cut the connection.

Jaime sat back and sighed all the way from his boot heels.

"Sometimes I think I have a clue…
then I wake up!"
   —   *Iain D. Bryce*

The bright white yellow flash of a laser pistol discharge temporarily blinded him. The pain in his chest felt like a dull knife was being plunging deep into it and twisting upward. He couldn't breathe or cry out. His tongue was dry and his mouth was metallic tasting. Everything around him was blurry, dull and gray. He could hear voices but couldn't make out the words. He jumped as he felt someone touch his hand. He realized his hand hurt and it was him holding the pistol. He felt another hand on his shoulder, shaking him and calling him a name he didn't recognize.

"Curtis? Curtis, are you okay?"

"Wha... what?" the man opened his eyes to find Nurse Stocker bent over him, holding him still. "What?"

"You were screaming. You must have been having a bad dream?"

"I... I don't remember," said Curtis as the nurse stood and helped straighten the sheets he had kicked off himself in his thrashing. He was covered with sweat and his mouth was dry.

Nurse stocker handed him a towel to dry off.

He sat up, flinching from the twinge in his still tender ribs, "How long was I screaming."

"Only a few seconds. You were shouting no and it sounded like Eve? She a girlfriend, maybe?" she asked, sounding a little jealous.

"Eve? Doesn't ring any bells," said Curtis, and he hadn't lied, it didn't.

Dr. Jacobs stepped into the room and asked, "Do you remember any of the dream?"

"No. Just a right lot of noise and pain."

"That could have been your last moments before your injury. They are usually the first to return. Was this you first dream?" asked the doctor.

"I don't remember."

"So nothing has come back at all?" asked the doctor, obviously trying hard to hide his disappointment.

"Glimpses once and a while, nothing concrete…"

"I'm afraid we have done all we can for you here, Curtis. You are healthy in body, at least. The hospital board isn't ready to release you entirely, just yet though, so you're being transferred to our rehab and convalescent center this afternoon."

Nurse Stocker looked on the verge of tears as she reached into a cabinet next to the bed and handed Curtis a stack of clothing, neatly folded, and a pair of boots then left the room with the doctor so he could get dressed.

Curtis stared at the clothes. They didn't look like what he would have expected a CRF officer to wear. He was holding a knee length black leather jacket, light brown linen slacks, a maroon tunic and a pair of black leather boots. He laid the jacket across his lap and checked the pockets. The doctor said they didn't find an ident card on him but he hoped they might've missed something.

His hand closed on an object in the stitching of the right wrist cuff almost immediately. He rolled it up and found a pocket with a small tube. He removed the tiny screw top and opened it, inside was a bunch of tiny metal tube-like needles, some with flattened scoop heads. He stared at these for a moment, unsure what they might be then shrugged, shook his head and put it back. Behind the left lapel was a tiny filing tool which puzzled him as well and several other small, well-hidden pockets that looked about the right size for a folded up pocket knife. He also found a pin on the right lapel, a small metal sword with a skull on its hilt. The skull was a button but he heard only static when he pushed it. Feeling even more confused now, he set the jacket aside and began to get dressed. He draped the long leather and suede coat over the ace bandage still wrapped around his right arm and slowly walked out of the only place, at this point, that he knew.

"Amazing never ceases to be."
   –   *Jared W. Way*

Curtis didn't care much for the rehab center, only partly because the nurses treated him like he was stupid. He wondered if his reaction was from something that had happened before his accident – had someone questioned his level of intelligence before?

He spent the most part of his days alone, hold up in his room, pouring through new storied on the digital tablet Nurse Stocker had given him, hoping to find anything that might help trigger his still lost memory and tell him who he was. He was having what Dr. Jacobs called recollection flashbacks on a regular basis now, sometimes in dreams, sometimes just bursting out as he was walking the halls, showering, eating and even going to the bathroom. He wasn't enjoying them in the least. None of them made any sense or helped figure out who or what he was. The doctor said they were likely not in any true or particular order, just pieces of random memories, and not to dwell on them but he couldn't help it; most all of them were of a violent nature.

He saw himself standing over dead bodies, people cowering and crying before him, fighting other men, sometimes with laser pistols, sometimes in hand to hand combat, and sometimes in ship to ship dogfights, and around safes full of credits and jewels. The recollection that bothered him the most was of himself shooting a man that was unarmed and was only standing before him. He was awakening again, in a cold sweat, from a recurring dream of that last memory when he felt a hand on his shoulder, making him jump and scream.

"Curtis? Are you alright?" asked a familiar voice.

"Robyn?" The man opened his eyes and grimaced. Where had that name come from?

"It's Nurse Stocker. Who's Robyn?"

"I don't know." He was tired of saying names and not knowing how, why or where he knew them from.

"You were having another bad dream, I think." The nurse picked up the digital paper from his lap and tisked. "No wonder, you shouldn't be reading this stuff."

The article on the front of the holographic paper showed a misshapen mass that had once been a man. An ore surveying crew had fished it out of the asteroid cluster between the planets Bangor and Colum three day ago. The story said it was the pirate captain, Dirk Riley, who had been missing for about a month; his cause of death was a laser blast to the chest. Nurse Stocker set the digital paper back down on the bed beside him and said, "Let's get some air."

Nurse Stocker had come to visit him as often as her schedule would allow. She was a little too attentive for his liking but she was the only person, aside from Dr. Jacobs, who treated him normal, so he didn't discourage her attention either. The two were walking the paths that crisscrossed the grounds of the compound, like they often did when she came, talking about her life.

A man was walking toward them. This, in and of itself, was not unusual; other residents and their visitors also used the paths. This man wasn't a resident or a visitor and he was wearing the uniform of a CRF leftenant commander. Curtis' legs suddenly went weak; he felt himself falling but he never felt himself hit the ground. It felt like he was caught in a giant black hole, the world around him spinning and getting darker and disappearing. The name Jared Way burst through the darkness then all was gone.

Curtis woke with a start to find himself back in his bed in the tiny nondescript room at the rehab center. He reached up, wiped sweat from his forehead and cheeks and took several deep breaths trying to slow his heart down. He was trying to tell himself it was only another nightmare. The sound of the chair shifting beside him made told him he wasn't alone. He turned his head to find Nurse Stocker sitting beside him. She smiled at him but it looked more than a little forced. "Sorry, did I faint?"

The nurse nodded. "Leftenant Commander Way helped me get you back here."

"Who?" asked Curtis, his pulse suddenly jumped to near double speed.

A voice from the corner said, "Hello, Captain."

Curtis went up on his elbows to see the man from what he had thought was a nightmare standing at the bottom of the bed. "Who are you?"

"He says he knows you, Curtis," said the nurse.

"Can I have a moment alone with him, Nurse?"

Nurse Stocker looked afraid to leave his side, and Curtis wasn't sure it was a good idea either. Something about the glint in the man's eye made him nervous, but he wanted to know who he was and if this man had the answers he wanted them. "I'll be okay."

"I'll be just down the hall, getting a cup of coffee, if you need me," said the nurse.

As soon as the door closed, the soldier said, "You haven't lost your touch with the fairer sex, I see," in what sounded like admiration.

"Who are you and who am I?" grumbled Curtis.

"So, this amnesia thing is real then?"

Getting very frustrated, Curtis said gruffly, through clenched teeth, "Tell me what you know or leave!"

Jared sat down in the chair the nurse had vacated and pointed to the pin on the stand beside the bed. "Know what that is?"

"No, should I?"

"It's a comlink to your ship. Do you remember anything at all?" asked Jared, getting serious now.

"Bits and pieces," said Curtis. He put his fingers to his temples and rubbed them in a circular motion, trying to relieve the headache that was beginning to build.

"How much do you want me to tell you? I don't want you to digress further."

"I know I'm a right foul person; my dreams have shown me that well enough. I'm guessing you're here to take me for my punishment."

"For what?"

"For killing him!" spat Curtis, throwing the tablet at Jared.

"Well, yeah, you did *technically* kill him, but you didn't murder him." The look on the face of the man before him was so distressed he couldn't bring himself to joke anymore, "Your name is Iain Bryce and you're the captain of the pirate ship Phoenix."

The man who had been called Curtis for more than two months would have fallen over if he wasn't already lying down. It felt like a huge chasm had just opened beneath the bed and he and it were falling to their doom. He was shaking his head forcefully as he said, "What!? I can't be... The news said Iain Bryce and his crew hit a ship just a week ago, lightyears from here."

"That was your quartermaster, Jaime Cable. He used your name so no one would know you weren't with them."

The man in the bed twisted his right wrist to see the IDB in the vines. Could they be his initials? "I am Iain Bryce and I'm a pirate?" Those words were strange and hollow sounding to him, as if coming from someone else's mouth. Bright lights suddenly burst in front of his eyes and he was hit with a severe pain in the back of his skull so intense it made him scream.

Curtis slowly opened his eyes. He found himself on the cold floor beside the bed. He took a deep breath and shook his head as he tried to pull himself up. It was less than graceful because of the cast on his arm and the still tender ribs. He thought he'd had another bad dream, a very vivid bad dream, when a noise from the corner of the room made him jump. He pulled himself up the last bit onto the bed and looked sideways at the man he had thought was part of that dream. The man's right eye was turning bluish purple and his nose was bleeding. "Did I do that to you?"

"It was my fault," said Jared. "I'm just gonna push on here at risk of further injury to us both. I *am* a CRF officer but I'm not here to arrest you. I am… an ally, I guess you could say. Jaime asked me to keep an eye on the dockets for any reports, when I saw one he asked me to check into it. Yes, you shot Dirk Riley, the man from that article, but only because you thought he had killed your security master, Eve, you are not a cold-blooded murderer."

"Eve?" He remembered Nurse Stocker said he had called out that name once.

"Yes, Eve Oakley. You thought Riley had killed her. You were distraught after you killed him and took off in a starling. Jaime says you've always been sensitive about that sort of thing."

"Isn't that what pirates do?"

"Not yours. You help the poor and oppressed. Anyway, I'm not the only CRF here. I passed a squadron on the way here. By a lucky bit of chance they went to the hospital first. By now, they will have learned you were transferred here. So, we need to get you out."

As Jared was talking, the last few weeks before arriving on the planet replayed in Curtis' – correction – Iain's, mind. It was like a switch was thrown and it all was back. He only half listened as Jared prattled on. He finally interrupted him before he started to repeat every report he'd ever read on Iain Bryce. "Enough, Master Way, right get on with."

Jared looked stunned for a moment then he smiled and said, "It's about bloody time!" as he opened the door and motioned Iain out.

Twenty-one men in CRF uniforms were walking up the hall toward them. The one in front, a three star admiral, was someone Iain wished he couldn't remember.

Admiral Walter Flint called out to the CRF officer with the pirate, "You there, hold that man!"

Jared wasn't sure just what to do; it was one thing to help a pirate when no one of weight knew of it, it was entirely another to willingly jeopardize his career for one. He looked at the pirate captain, about to say he was sorry. He saw a strange look come to the pirate's eyes.

Iain pulled Jared around, grabbed his sidearm, wrapped his right arm, with the soft cast on it, around his neck, squeezed slightly, held the gun to his temple and said, "Don't move!"

The admiral froze and motioned his men to hold off. "This isn't the answer, Bryce."

Iain shouted, "*Back off*, unless you want the wall redecorated with this man's brains!"

"No need to add killing a CRF officer to your rap sheet."

"Pirate... CRF officer... Admiral... what's the difference? Either way, I'm gonna swing," said Iain, in a very evil sounding voice. He charged the pistol to full.

Jared didn't have to fake being afraid, the man holding the pistol on him hadn't known who he was just minutes before and *had* shot a man the last time he had seen him. He really didn't know Iain Bryce well enough to know whether he'd shoot him in order to save himself.

"Relax, Leftenant Commander, the pirate isn't going to shoot you, are you, Mr. Bryce?" said Admiral Flint as if speaking to a child.

"Try me!" said Iain in a truly desperate sounding voice, looking around for any exit.

The admiral motioned to his men and they began to advance again.

Jared felt the pirate's body tense up and realized he was about to make a move.

Flint apparently thought the same as he signaled his men to take aim. Twenty laser rifles came down to bear on Jared and Iain then.

Jared felt the muscles in Iain's wrist, which were resting against his shoulder, twitch, about to pull the trigger, and shouted, "NO!"

Iain did pull the trigger. He felt Jared's body go limp in his arms and dropped him to the floor. He laughed wildly and brought the pistol back up toward the admiral, who had frozen. He aimed the barrel between the man's eyes. A part of him wanted, very badly, to pull the trigger again. He did but he brought the gun barrel up quickly and shot one of the chains holding a fluorescent light fixture to the ceiling above the CRF troop instead. The unit swung down, throwing sparks around the hall, and blocking Flint and his men from advancing.

Iain could hear Flint telling his men to find a way around the blockade and knew he didn't have a lot of time to waste. He checked Jared's neck for a pulse then ran down the hall.

"Men of genius are admired, men of wealth are envied, men of power are feared; but only men of character are trusted."

– Unknown

Nurse Stocker was checking the heart monitor just as her patient opened his eyes. She said, "Hello," sweetly then called for the doctor.

The doctor entered the room reading a medical chart, which he set down on the edge of the bed. He smiled at the patient and began to remove the bandages wrapped around his head. "I'm Daniel Jacobs. I'll be your doctor while you're with us. Have you experienced any headaches or loss of memory?"

"No," answered the man in the bed before them. "How much damage is there?"

"We were able to graft some fresh cells we took from your upper thigh so, aside from a slight pinkness around the wound and a little spot tenderness for a couple weeks. You should not have any lasting scars, Leftenant Commander Way. We will keep you for another day, just for observation then you will be released into Admiral Flint's care, to be returned to your base on Colum Province. You are very lucky he was such a bad shot."

"Believe me, Iain Bryce is an excellent shot." Jared knew Iain had intended to only graze him so he could escape and allow him to keep his name in the CRF.

"Was that really Captain Iain Bryce?" asked the doctor incredulously.

"That was," said Jared. He touched the new skin on his temple.

"He seems nothing like the reports." the doctor had read up on the man he had been calling Curtis.

"He's absolutely nothing like the reports. Iain Bryce is one of the best men I know."

Enemy Among Us

"Better to have a thousand enemies
outside the house than one inside it."
–   Anonymous

Captain Bryce knew he expected a lot of his crew, and loyalty was at the top of that long list. His meaning of the word loyalty was faithfulness to him, their fellow shipmates, their cause, and to their ideals. He would like to think the definition was the same for all onboard his ship but he knew, realistically, that was too much to ask. His officers had proven themselves loyal many times over so he would never doubt any of them. The rest of his crew, the grunts, came and went so frequently that the meaning of loyalty to some of them was synonymous with the amount of loot they received. He had heard grumblings from time to time about an order they didn't agree with but none had ever openly acted against him – until now.

They had almost been caught three times before they realized their location was being conveyed to the CRF. Usually, when CRFers were on their tail, they would hide out for a few weeks on one of their colonies. They didn't dare to this time. They couldn't risk the mole knowing any of their locations. The colonists would suffer ill treatment if found harboring pirates. So, instead, they were anchored to the side of an asteroid while they tried to figure out where their leak was.

They had intercepted four scrambled messages. They were each sent from a different station so they hadn't been able pin down anyone. They'd had to replace nearly a third of the grunts in as many months, so odds were it was one of them. Common sense said it was one of the supply ship additions, having come from the CR; they could've easily planted a spy among them. The trick was to figure out who before they got caught?

The captain was pacing his usual path around the conference room table, half listening to his officers discussion of who they thought the leak could be as he was running names through his own mind.

The clues all seemed to point to Norris Kinden, a short mousy man with a wiry mustache and stringy black hair. He had been engineer of communications on the supply ship Calypso. That was the ship the president's son, Dylan, had used to bring them the ransom for his sister's safe release. He had eagerly told the captain of his radio experience when they were going over the best placement for him on Phoenix. Iain had to admit he did look the part. and two of the messages were sent from a station near his, just outside the engine room. He doubted the man would have been quite so obvious. It all fit a little too well; like someone was trying to make them think it was him. Unless he thought being so obvious a mole would keep him from suspicion.

"I say we name someone, we know isn't, as the mole and use them as bait," offered Yard, for the third time.

"If Mr. Kinden is the real culprit, perhaps he will slip up," agreed Mitch, nodding.

"I don't believe it was Norris," chimed Digger. He had been working with the man in the engine room for several months and felt he knew him pretty well. "If it were him, why wouldn't he just disable the ship?"

"How do we know he hasn't?" asked Hayden.

"I would know," grumbled Digger.

"If he can hide his communications, he could hide sabotage…"

"I have looked over every nut, bolt, conduit and circuit on this ship, I know fucking well *there is no sabotage*," said Digger, starting to rise from his seat in anger.

"THIS IS NOT HELPING!" shouted Captain Bryce, stopping at the head of the table and slamming his fists down. "If you two got no right helpful suggestions, I suggest you both get out now."

"Sorry," grumbled Hayden.

"Sorry, Captain," said Digger at the same time, lowering himself back into his chair.

"If we do what Yard is suggesting, how *can* we trap *whoever* it is?" asked the captain.

"I could rig the communications array to send all outgoing messages to the terminal on the bridge but we'll be without sending capabilities," offered Digger.

"A right constructive suggestion there. Do we have need for outside communications?"

"We're awaiting an answer from Kohzu on the belite crystals," answered Mitch.

Iain had taken the belite crystals from Calypso's safe. The ship's captain had tried to hide them, hoping the pirates would only be interested in the stock they were delivering. Iain had decided not to miss out on the opportunity to take any other potential prizes as well. They had scored two thousand credits, two barrels of plasma fuel and the belite crystals, and surprisingly, the approval of Dylan Nason, who said it was a small price to pay for his sister being safe, so it was worth it.

The CRF had been taking the crystals to the power station on the planet, Sigpri, being as they would be only a short jump from it. Belite crystals produce an enormous amount of energy, without a converter and a reactor they were nothing but lumps of ugly rock. Kohzu had found them a buyer and they had planned to make the exchange in two days, Now they weren't so comfortable making the switch. They had few enough reliable fencers left and didn't need to put any of them at risk for the sake of credits.

Iain pressed the com button on his lapel and said, "Kyle, send Kohzu the message we spoke about earlier."

"How do we get the bad information to the mole?" asked Hayden.

"Digger, set up the array then you and Hayden discuss this meeting in the mess tonight. The mole will have to send a message right quick to get the CRF to the location in time."

"Aye, aye, sir," said Digger, saluting quickly then stood to leave. He gasped as two recent recruits nearly fell through it. "Uh, sorry, Sir. I was looking for the observation deck?" said Eric.

"It's the next door down," said Digger.

"I was looking for Master Yardley, it's the trash incinerator again," said Thomas.

"Not again," spat Yard, rolling his eyes. "It hasn't worked right since we had to shut it down from lack of fuel!" He looked to be sure he was released.

Just as Yard stepped out, Gideon stepped in. He looked at Jaime, "Still on for training?"

Jaime looked to the captain also before answering.

Captain Bryce nodded and mumbled dismissed as he motioned Mitch over.

Once the others were out of the room, the captain said, "I'm with Digger, Master Gordon; I don't believe it is Mr. Kinden either."

"You sound like you think you might know who it is?" said Mitch curiously.

"I do, and I don't like it," answered Iain flatly. He stood and looked out the window at the darkness of space around them as he told Mitch whom he suspected.

The procurement master's face lost three shades of color. "How sure are you?"

"I'd be willing to bet my share of our next haul on it, Old Man," said Captain Bryce as he tapped his fist onto the table twice in frustration.

"What do you want me to do?" asked Mitch, wringing his hands.

"Leave it to me."

Gideon lit the candles set around the room that resembled a twentieth century dojo and sat down on one of the pillows on the floor. "What now?" he asked, barely over a whisper.

Jaime was already sitting with his legs crossed and eyes closed, "We cleanse our souls of all worldly desires and evil thoughts."

Gideon got his own legs crossed and was about to ask another question when the doors slid open and Eve Oakley's face peered in, "Am I too late?"

"No," said Jaime, "We're just getting started."

Gideon was surprised to see the security master, being slightly intimidated by her. He relaxed a little as he asked, "You're still in training with Jaime?"

"Not in semai', but I still find the relaxation techniques of semainath' comforting."

"*I* would find it more comforting if you two would shut up," said Jaime rather pointedly.

The three sat in a triangle meditating for close to an hour before Jaime rose and asked them to take their stances. As if in a ballet, the three bodies began to move as one through the many poses, with fluid-like motion.

About halfway through their routine, Eve asked, "You still taking out a sandpiper when we're done?"

"I am," answered the quartermaster.

"For the sale of the belite crystals?" asked Gideon.

Eve ignored Gideon's question and said, "We'll be waiting on Ryger for you."

"They should bring us a fair haul, yes?" asked Gideon, the sparkle in his eye more than obvious.

"Not bad," said Jaime offhand, "Want to join me?"

"Yeah. *Ooww!*" cried Gideon as he bent over in pain. "Let me get some pain meds, I think I pulled something important." He stumbled out with a weird look on his face.

"Can we finish the rest of the routine in silence?"

"Yes, Sensei," said Eve smiling at him.

The captain played the recording, which sounded like just a bunch of crackly static, over and over again. He was sure the breaks in the static were words being jammed but no matter how hard he tried he couldn't make them out. This was the first of four messages they had intercepted; the other three were also on disks before him. He wondered how many others had been sent out before they had realized it?

He waited for it to end then punched the button on the combox on the corner of his desk. He called down to Digger and asked him to send his assistant to his office. As he waited, he poured himself a fifth, or was it sixth, cup of coffee. He smirked at what Robyn would say about his consumption for the day.

All of Norris Kinden was covered in grease except his hands; Digger had had him greasing the bearings of the turbines but he had, most courteously, wiped his hands off before arriving so he wouldn't get the captain dirty when he shook his hand. "Captain Bryce, pl... please, let me say again how... how very pleased I am to be... to be a member of your crew."

"I'm sure the colonists will thank you a right lot more than I ever could," Iain answered dully.

"Aye, aye, Sir," said Norris, standing up straighter.

"You said before you were a radio expert?"

"Yes, Sir."

"I have some recordings that have gotten messed up. You think you can clear them up some?"

"I would be willing... willing to give it a try, Sir," said Norris. He took the captain's place behind the desk. He played the first recording through once and looked up quizzically. He started biting his lip and asked, "Any idea what caused the distortion?"

"Not a clue," answered Captain Bryce.

Norris played the disk a second time, then a third; his ear held up to the speaker after each play through. During the fourth he started to turn knobs on the player.

Iain sat down opposite him and watched intently; the man was clearly good at this. After the fifth listen through Norris smiled up at the him. The static slowly became the garbled words he was sure had been hidden. They sounded too robotic to be able to match them to a crewman but at least the captain now knew what message had been sent.

"Report."
"They are planning to... days in..."
"You have... that?"
"... is not that large, you should be able..."
"Very well. I will make... to your... as promised."
"I must go, I am being watched."

"I might be able to get it a little clearer, with time, Sir," said Norris, unconsciously wiping the back of his hand across his forehead, streaking the grease there.

"Can you rerecord it after you've cleaned it up the best you can?

"I can, with some of my equipment."

"Does Digger expect you back?"

"No, sir, he told me to cut out for the night."

"I got three more feeds like that, you game to clean them up and rerecord them as well?" asked the captain. The man before him nodded quickly. "Alright, bring the equipment up here and do what you can. I'll be in the mess when you are done." He stood to leave.

"Thank you, Sir."

Iain stopped and asked, "For what?"

"My parent's... they were colonists on Tirnta. They... died in the outbreak of flu there two years back. The CR could have helped... I should have... Now I can make good on their deaths."

Captain Bryce nodded to the man then left him in his office and walked up to the bridge where Mitch and Robyn were waiting.

"So?" asked Robyn as Iain bent down to step through the opening to the bridge.

"He got the first one cleaned up enough to hear some of what was being said but I can't match the voice to anyone. He didn't act familiar with the conversation, so he's either well-trained or he's not the mole. Where's Jaime?"

"He's in the shuttle waiting for Gideon," answered Mitch.

"I have two messages going out, Sir," said Kassie quickly, "both are scrambled!"

"Record both and check the cameras," said Iain.

Kassie brought up the surveillance cameras and scanned the ship for unusual activity. Norris was still sitting at Iain's desk, fooling with the knobs on a unit he had in his lap, Thomas was bent over the sink in the galley, Eric was standing at a data terminal just outside the day room, Gideon was standing in an odd position just outside the sandpiper, with his back to the camera, and Jaime was sitting in the pilot seat of the shuttle, also with his back to the camera.

There was no way Norris could be sending the messages and Iain highly doubted Thomas was. His eyes squinted as he looked at the image of the man he was now all but certain was the mole. He wanted indisputable proof before he would take action on his suspicions though.

"Have the disks brought to Mr. Kinden and ask him to attempt to unscramble them as well."

"When water and fire wage war,
water will always be the victor."
—   Anonymous

The sandpiper was drifting quietly and calmly in the endless darkness of space, neither of its occupants seemed eager to disturb the silence.

The quartermaster shifted his position and turned to his passenger. In almost a whisper, he asked, "What do you think of our world?"

"Not as profitable as I had imagined," said Gideon flatly, looking out the window beside him at the stream of heated plasma residue escaping the starboard engine.

"Yeah, we seem to have hit a bit of a snag lately."

"How so?" asked Gideon.

"What do you think of the captain?" Jaime asked suddenly.

"What... do you mean?" Gideon's voice sounded strained.

"Nothing, just thinking out loud," replied Jaime cryptically. He moved the throttle slightly to fix the ship's course and compensate for drift. "Just, a lot has changed since my return, not all of it good... I guess I've changed a bit as well."

"Do you still believe in the cause?" asked Gideon.

"I still think it has merits. There are a lot of people starving and dying for no good reason, I just wonder if we're really helping?" said Jaime.

"Do you think the president would help more if not for your meddling?" asked Gideon.

"I think we make it difficult for him."

"Because you draw attention to the issue," Gideon added matter-of-factly.

Jaime nodded then hitched himself up in his seat as a ship, about the same size as theirs, dropped from jump about a click before them.

Its bow lights blinked once and it shot its thrusters, sending it toward the moon they were orbiting. Jaime blinked the lights in his own ship twice then brought the engines up and followed it down.

The shuttlecrafts landed about thirty feet apart and their respective occupants exited them with re-breathers on. Jaime and Gideon followed the other man into an old looking bunker. Once the doors were sealed off, Jaime set the airlock to exchange the moon's thick atmosphere for oxygen. When the red light turned green he nodded that they could safely remove their helmets.

"Good, you were able to slip away," Jaime said to the other ship's pilot.

"I told them I needed to think on things awhile."

Gideon drew a quick breath as he saw the person opposite him, "I thought we were meeting Kohzu Wu?"

"We don't meet him for another couple days, this is a meeting of a different sort," said Hayden cryptically. He turned to Jaime and asked, "What do ya' think?"

"I think he's primed," answered Jaime.

"Primed? For what?" asked Gideon, backing away.

"We want to overthrow the captain," said Jaime bluntly.

"You mean mutiny? But... I thought you were all like best friends?"

"Friends don't sell you out for a piece of ass!" spat Hayden.

"What do you mean?"

"A few months back we hit a passenger vessel that had the president's daughter on it. He took a liking to her. I think he may have aspirations of them being together," said Jaime.

"That's where me and Eve think Bryce went after he killed Riley. He wasn't in any hospital with amnesia, he was playing house and making nice with the president and his daughter," said Hayden.

Jaime shrugged. "All I know is he's been different with me since my deprogramming. I don't think he trusts me anymore." Jaime was leaned against the airlock door, playing with the straps of his helmet.

"How do you mean?" asked Gideon, unsure how to take this sudden change. He remembered how ardently the man spoken of the captain when they shared a cell in Belgorian Prison and over the months as partners in the challenges after.

Hayden started to say something but Jaime jumped in over him.

"I'm beginning to think you and Eve might be right, Hayden. He was a little too chummy with Jared Way. They spent a lot of time alone. I think the two of them may have hatched a plan. How else do you explain a highly decorated officer just letting us get away without once trying to take us in capture? They don't get paid that well, believe me. The bounty for capturing the notorious crew of Phoenix Enclave would be substantial, even if he were planning to split it with Bryce, and he would likely get a promotion for it. Incentive enough to play along and allow Bryce to trick us into capture."

"I bet he's the one that sent the messages," barked Hayden. He picked up and threw a loose chunk of flooring into the corner of the bunker. It clinked loudly and fell to the floor.

"Yeah, he wants out and is gonna give all of us up to get it," offered Gideon, getting really excited now.

"Who better knows Phoenix's com system and the best way to scramble 'em?" spat Hayden.

"Hey, wasn't that guy, Norris, a radio expert or something?" asked Gideon.

"Yeah, what about it?" asked Jaime.

"He near knocked me over running with some radio equipment earlier. I followed him, figuring to offer him a hand... I saw him go into the captain's office with it. You think he's helping?"

"Perhaps..." said Hayden as he began to pace.

"So what do we do?" asked Gideon, eager to help.

"We need to set a fucking trap of our own," said Hayden.

"Chances are he's told them when we are to meet the fence... but he never goes off-ship for such... which means it will be me they catch," said Jaime snidely.

Gideon started pacing the room, the index finger on his right hand extended and that hand moving up and down as he walked, "What if... what if... If we could make him go in your place? Tell him you're unable? Then, they would get him and we would be rid of him."

"That would make me captain. Could you swear your allegiance to me?" asked Jaime.

"I would!" said Gideon with excitement.

"I can speak for Eve, we are yours," said Hayden.

"Well alright then, we've got work to do, don't we?" said Jaime excitedly. He turned around, put his helmet back on, waited for the others to get theirs secured before he punched the air lock release button and opened the door.

Captain Bryce was sitting in the mess with most of the night crew when Jaime came in, followed closely by

Gideon. Hayden and Eve came in shortly, they sat at a table in the corner with their heads together, whispering quietly to each other.

Jaime looked around the room once, then walked over to the captain. Gideon was hot on his heels. He waved for him to go away and waited to be sure he was gone before continuing to Iain's table. "We need to talk," said Jaime, as if expecting Iain to rise and follow him then and there.

"Sir? My captain? Captain Bryce?" said Iain. He set the digital tablet he had been reading down and put a finger to his forehead, to emphasize the required titles and gesture, then added gruffly, "When I'm finished with my drink," rattling the ice in his glass of whiskey.

"When you are done with that, *Captain Bryce*, Sir, *we need to talk*," spat Jaime emphatically, using his middle finger to make the salute.

The captain ignored Jaime's obvious irritation, and listened to him sigh, grumble, and shift his feet, for several minutes. Finally, he drained the last swallow from his glass and stood up, as if leaving were his idea. Several eyes followed them from the room, and confused whispers followed that; they had never fought before, at least not in public. Norris physically followed them. Gideon followed him.

"A doubtful friend is worse than a
certain enemy. Let a man be one
or the other, and we then know
how to meet them."
— Aesop

Captain Bryce was clearly put out the day of the rendezvous with Kohzu came. He stormed into the mess, screaming for the quartermaster. Jaime wasn't there but the crew that was quickly moved out of his way in case he thought to take his frustration out on them. Gideon was sitting in the corner, Thomas was coming from the kitchen, Norris was behind the captain and Mitch was entering from the door opposite.

Mitch went up to the captain and said something through clenched teeth, just loud enough for him to hear.

"The fuck? WHO DOES HE THINK HE IS?"

"Please sir, not here," said Mitch with obvious discomfort. Many eyes turned to them, not being used to hearing the captain shouting or swearing. Mitch tried again to get him to follow but he pulled his arm out of his grip, almost knocking the man on his ass.

"No! *This is my ship*. MY FUCKING SHIP! That asshole thinks he can… ever since he … He will do as *I* command or face the gauntlet!" shouted the captain.

Digger and Yard came in then, as if drawn by the shouting. They both looked around to see if anyone was watching. Most eyes quickly looked away.

"Captain, please step into the conference room with us," pleaded Digger.

Iain looked ready to argue more but instead he threw the digital tablet he'd been holding on the table hard enough to crack the tempered glass screen, threw his arms up in the air, turned and left with the three men flanking him on all sides.

Norris waited a moment, then followed behind.

Gideon waited a moment longer and left as well.

Jaime and Eve were sitting on cushions opposite each other when Gideon came into the dojo.

"The engine, galley and procurement masters just had it out with Bryce in the mess." He took a deep breath and held it for a minute then continued, "They shuffled him off to the conference room before much could be heard but he was obviously pissed off. Norris Kinden was right on his heels."

"I told him I couldn't meet the fence today."

"He doesn't like anyone questioning his orders," said Eve slowly, as if she had firsthand experience.

"Bryce spoke of the gauntlet, what is that?"

"The crew lines up on either side of the main hall, each with laser whips, the accused is led down the line at sword point, barebacked. Each strike him with their whip as hard as they can as he passes," said Eve dryly.

"Any seen not striking for all they're worth will go through next," added Jaime.

"That sounds like fun… makes the Ky'istri seem like child's play."

"To this day, Bryce has never issued punishment to an officer. I doubt he has the nerve to. He knows the crew is divided, that might be enough to tip the sides." Eve looked at her watch and added, "He'll have to leave within the hour to make the meeting."

"We'll make our move while he's gone. Gideon, go to the observation deck and signal me when Bryce's starling has departed," said Jaime. He handed the man a comlink in the shape of a dragon's claw. "Bryce is in for a very rude awakening, I fear."

"Aye, aye, sir," said Gideon. He ran from the room, forgetting to close the door.

Gideon's heart was beating fast and he was having a hard time standing still with the excitement. He was looking forward to seeing Captain Bryce get what was coming to him, and was pleased Jaime was letting him assist in that castigation. He had liked the quartermaster from the start; he knew they were alike in ways neither knew yet; perhaps he could recruit Jaime as he had recruited him when this was done. He didn't have long to think on it though because the ship he had been waiting for slowly moved away from Phoenix. He punched the com in his hand and said, "He's gone."

"Good, stay there and make sure he doesn't return. I will call when I'm ready," said a calm sounding Jaime.

"Very good, sir," said Gideon.

It was nearly three hours before Jaime's voice spoke to Gideon again. He had started to doze off. He cleared his throat before responding by a simple, "Yes."

Jaime said, "Bryce hasn't returned yet; he was due back more than an hour ago. We need someone to go and see what's become of him and you're the only one I trust just now, Gideon. I want you to take out the other starling and go to his last coordinates."

Gideon dashed out of the room, ran to the hanger and was off within seconds.

"I always wondered – what exactly does a rat smell like, anyway?"
—   *Iain D. Bryce*

Gideon reached the coordinates for where the captain was supposed to be meeting the fence about an hour later. He slowed the ship and scanned for Bryce's starling; he found no sign of it. He did, however, find a CRF battlecruiser, Archimedes, and a squad of starlings about ten clicks in front of him.

He wondered then if Bryce really was conspiring with the CRF. A little baffled, he scanned for any radio signals. He stopped when he heard a voice he recognized, that of Vice Admiral Anton Anders.

"What have you got?" asked the vice admiral.

"A small vessel is off your larboard side. Appears to be a starling, but it's not one of ours. It appears adrift, Commander,"

"Are there any life signs?"

"One, sir, and the weapons are empty."

"What is the meaning of this?" asked Anders.

"Unknown, sir. The pirate was supposed to be in a starling though. What are your orders?"

"Escort it inside."

Gideon scratched his head. What were they so afraid of; if Bryce's ship had no weapons then he was no threat. He punched the button to fire his thrusters to move closer; the helm wasn't responding. The proximity alarm was still working though, telling him the CRF starlings were approaching his ship. They took up formation around him and a voice came through his com.

"Surrender or we'll destroy you."

Gideon realized they were speaking about him. He opened a channel to Archimedes, and said, "This is Confederational Regime Intelligence agent four twelve. I was tracking Iain Bryce? Have you found his ship?"

"We are guessing we are looking at it."

"Yeah, he *is* in a starling also, but not this one," said Gideon, starting to smell a rat.

"We received a report that he was in a ship with the same ident number as is printed on the side of yours."

"I was onboard Phoenix with the pirates of the Phoenix Enclave on orders of Vice President Nikolas. I request permission to come aboard."

"We will escort your vessel in."

Gideon climbed out of the starling with a superior look on his face, holding his ident card – the real one, naming him an agent of the CRIA, not the one he had shown Jaime. He found himself facing twenty men, all with a laser rifles pointed at his chest. One of them stepped forward with a shock collar. Knowing arguing with them would do him no good, he put up his hands, allowed them to put the collar on him and lead him to a cell.

It was twenty minutes before Vice Admiral Anders appeared, walking smugly up to the cell. "Hello, Captain Bryce, I've been hoping for this day for a long time. I'll get a promotion for this, I think."

"What? No. I'm not Captain Bryce? I am Gideon Brody, a member of the Red Squad of the CRIA."

"We have eyewitness descriptions of you, Pirate," spat the vice admiral.

"This is ridiculous!" Gideon guffawed. How had Bryce managed this one? He apparently hadn't given the man as much credit as he should have.

"It is that. There is far more honor in admitting who you are. But then, pirates have no honor, do they?"

"I'm not lying. I was tracking Iain Bryce, who was supposed to be meeting with a fence at this location to hock the belite crystals he stole from the Calypso about three months ago."

"You mean these?" asked the vice admiral holding up a velvet bag. He opened it and showed him the rocks in question, "We took them from your ship."

"I've been framed!" shouted Gideon.

"We'll see. Calypso's communication master, Mr. Kinden, is here to give a formal identification."

A man appeared at the end of the hall wearing the uniform of the supply ship. Gideon's expression soured as he waited for the man to come closer. Instead of the mousy Norris Kinden, it was the real Iain Bryce walking toward him, with a sly smile on his face.

Iain winked at Gideon then went into a convincing imitation of the real Norris Kinden. "Yes, that's… Ca… Captain Iain Bryce, sir. I watched him kill three men right in… right in front of me, sir. They did nothin' to him, nothin'. Only… only refused to join his cr… crew. Keep an eye on him, s… sir, he's right dodgy, he is."

"We know, Crewman Kinden, thank you."

"What? No! Vice Admiral Anders, THAT is Iain Bryce!" shouted Gideon, pointing to the bent over man beside the vice admiral.

"Wha… me?" asked Iain in the mousy voice, shriveling under the caged man's stare, "I have never… never even held a gun."

"I WANT TO SPEAK TO VICE PRESIDENT NIKOLAS, NOW!"

"No worries, you'll be speaking to him very soon. He and the president are looking forward to seeing you," said the vice admiral, quite pleased with himself.

Gideon started to speak again when Captain Bryce said, "You're not a very nice man, Mr. Pirate. I hope you get your comeuppance!"

Gideon realized then that he no longer had a voice.

The vice admiral smiled and said, "The collar around your neck is emitting a sonic pulse, it will prevent you from spewing any more lies, until your meeting with the president and vice president."

Gideon wanted to scream he knew what the collar do, having used them on prisoners before himself, instead he thrust his fist into the wall.

Vice Admiral Anders gave the man in the cell a satisfied nod then turned to leave the hallway.

Gideon heard Anders tell the guard at the end of the hall to allow no one near the cell from then on.

Captain Bryce held back a moment. "Jaime sends his regards, and regrets, Mr. *Brody*. He said to say he wished things coulda' been different. He thought you and he had a connection but then he can be a right sap. I don't think they could be – leopards and spots and all," Iain shrugged then glanced up the hall to be sure he was still okay to speak, when he turned back he had a wicked glint in his eye. "I see you again and you'll find out how true my spots are. No one squeals on me and mine, Mr. Welch, *no one*. When you see your friend, Vice President Nikolas, tell him I won this round. The score is now two to nothing."

"Don't taunt the prisoner, Mr, Kinden," the vice admiral called out.

Iain went back into the mousy impression, "Yes, sir, thank you, sir. Not so scary behind bars, is he, sir?" said Iain, he glanced back and winked at Gideon.

"Man is the only animal whose desires
increase as they are fed; and the only
animal that is never satisfied."
   –   Amy Lowell

President Nason and Vice President Nikolas were both pacing the reception room of the president's cabin aboard their battleskip, CR One, waiting impatiently for Vice Admiral Anders' battlecruiser to arrive. Both men were more than pleased to finally have the hated pirate in custody, though for different reasons.

The president was going to enjoy putting Iain Bryce to death to finally break the hold the man had on his daughter, and was attempting to have on his son. He knew Caitlyn would hate him for killing Bryce but she already hated him, at least now it would be for a good reason, and Dylan needed to see that pirates aren't what he needs to associate with if he is to be the next president.

The vice president was relishing the chance to torture and humiliate Iain Bryce, before his neck was stretched. He still had blisters on his back and chest from being left naked on the desert planet Proxis for three days, and an image of the president's daughter staring at him with disgust and pity. Both still haunted him. If the CRF hadn't arrived when they did he might have died of dehydration.

Both men jumped when a voice came over the combox on the wall, announcing the vice admiral's ship was in view. They smiled at each other and quickly walked to the docking bay.

After pleasantries were exchanged, the president asked Anders to bring Bryce before them. The vice admiral punched his badge and within moments two CRF soldiers appeared, escorting the prisoner. He had been beaten and was being dragged between them. The president and vice president both were smiling, until one of the soldiers took hold of a handful of hair and pulled the man's head up.

"WHAT IS THIS?" shouted the president.

"My men had a bit of sport is all, Mr. President." Vice Admiral Anders hoped he wouldn't get into too much trouble for having a bit of fun with the pirate before turning him over.

"*That is* not *Iain Bryce!*" spat Vice President Nikolas. "That is one of our agents, Gideon Brody!"

The beaten man spit a globe of blood onto the vice admiral's boot and said, "I tried to tell you, Dickhead."

"Our greatest glories come not from never failing, but in rising every time we fall."
— *Old Semai' Proverb*

"Enter," said Captain Bryce. He set aside the star-chart he had been studying as the door slid open.

Jaime stepped in, sank into the spare chair and sighed as if his whole life was over. "I feel like such a fool, Iain."

"Why, because you gave him a chance?"

"I think I knew, from the start, something wasn't right about him. He was too ingratiating, too smarmy. I was hoping I was wrong. How did you know?"

"It was the little things. You said he was interested in every little thing about you, and then us, which seemed right bit queer. Jared said he knew him from somewhere but couldn't say why. Gideon told you he had been in prison for six years; I highly doubt Jared saw him there. Gideon knew where the new colony of Colum Province, most in his supposed status in life would not. And, for your cellmate to be, right conveniently, going to the challenge as well, and as your partner. It was all a right little too well-situated. I contacted Kohzu and asked him to do a background check for me. He found no Gideon Welch in the public records. It all added up to something right nefarious," said Iain. "Kohzu was able to find a lot on Gideon Brody, who is a highly decorated CRIA Red Squad agent."

"The are some of the best the CRIA have," said Jaime. Knowing this helped ease his conscience a little. "I just don't know how you do it."

"What?" asked Iain. He didn't like how unsettled the usually calm quartermaster was.

"Judge people so quickly and correctly. I'd never make a good captain."

"You would make a right excellent captain, if you wanted to be, Jay. Not all us are meant for that, though. As you say, I'm a right excellent judge of character and yours is impeccable. You have a good heart, my friend, you want to see the good in people. That is an admirable quality. You are my other half. You continue your rosy view and let me be the cynical one."

"I guess we owe Kohzu, and Jared, don't we."

"Kohzu always comes through for us. We ought to think about upping his cut, or giving him a bonus... And, if I may remind you, you were the one who got us that particular contact."

Jaime wondered why Iain was ignoring the equally helpful participation of Jared. Had he judged him wrong too? "Jared went above and beyond to help us find you, is he not an equally good ally?"

Iain got a dark look in his eyes. "He might right well have been, if I hadn't shot him."

"You what?" asked Jaime, in disbelief.

"Just grazed his temple. Shouldn't have caused any lasting damage. It was the only thing I could think of to get away from Flint. I haven't plucked up the courage to com and apologize yet. I mean, what do you say to that?"

"Pity. Waste of a good ally there."

"Who knows, maybe I just knocked some sense into him," said Iain smiling.

Jaime nodded and said, "You realize Nason and Nikolas are gonna hate you even more now. You'll be lucky to live a second if they get their hands on you."

"Yeah, thought of that too. I suppose my head will be kept in one of them cases in one of their offices now instead of a museum at least."

Jaime chuckled a little at the thought then he got a serious look on his face. "No hard feelings for being so horrible to you in the mess? Most of the crew had no idea what we were up to; half of them still expect you'll be ordering me through the gauntlet."

"Don't push it, I still could," sniggered Iain with a wicked smile. "Hayden and Eve have been around to apologize as well. We, all of us, played our parts well 'cause we knew what was at stake. Now I've had right near enough of this, if you don't stop acting like a child I will take you over my knee."

Jaime pushed his sleeves up and said, "Go ahead and try."

Iain stood and started toward his quartermaster but instead ran out the door and bolted for the ladder to the upper deck. Jaime was out the door moments later, right on his tail.

Fête Interruptus

"If you let fear of consequence stop
you from following your instinct your
life will be long but extremely boring."
–   *Jaimes A. Cable*

"Iain, we just received a com from Magistrate Ty. The festival has been cancelled," said Robyn as she sat down beside him at the table in the mess hall.

"That's too bad; I was looking forward to it, too. Did he give a reason?" asked the captain, over the top of the tipped up cup of coffee.

"No, just said to stay away. I don't like it, Iain."

He was concerned by the sudden termination of the holiday too. He set the empty cup down, looked into the worried eyes of the doctor, and said, "Don't worry; we'll see what's the matter."

In the eight years they had been bringing Ansi supplies Captain Bryce had never known Ty Northrup, the magistrate, to cancel a festival. In fact, two years ago they had held it even though they were being hit with solar storms worse than any in previous history. It was hard to keep the tents down and many of the activities had been called off but they had still held the festival. The solar storms weren't expected to return for three years, when the planet's orbit brought them close to their sun, so it couldn't be that. The Ansians had always welcomed Phoenix, whether for supply drops or just to stretch muscles, why would canceling the celebration have changed that?

He wondered if the CRF had stuck their foul noses in and found Ansi guilty of harboring criminals and had forced them to see the error of their ways. It wouldn't be the first time, or likely the last, in the CRF's attempts to send him a message. They wouldn't write Ansi off until he had heard it from them. Despite the ominous message, and, since they were only two days from it, they wouldn't alter course.

Iain was in his cabin getting dressed when Kyle's voice came through the com.

"Sir, we're in view of the planet."

"Scan for CRF and ask the quartermaster to meet me up there," said Iain as he buttoned his shirt up.

He found Jaime waiting for him at the bottom of the ladder just in front of his cabins with a look that closely mirrored his own, telling him he too was worried about the colonists' sudden change of heart.

"What'd you find?" asked the captain stepping through the portal to the helm room.

"Nothing, sir, we're the only ship in orbit of the planet and I scanned for unusual weather conditions and found none; it looks to be a perfect day over New Essex," said Kyle, perplexed.

"Set us down in the usual, Pilot," said Iain then he punched his badge and said, "Hayden, Eve, get outfitted and meet me and Jaime in the hanger."

Ansi was one of the first planets of the Second BrimTier to be colonized and was one of few that the terraforming had taken well on. The colonists had been able to make a good life for themselves with just the first drop of supplies; except for the solar storms, it was paradise. The planet had more natural resources than most did so their lives had started a lot easier than most in the Second BrimTier. The hills provided an abundance of limestone and coal and the thick forests thrived through selective foresting, providing them plenty of building material. Enough to allow Phoenix Enclave to use the overstock for trade and exchange. Ansi really only needed their help when the storms hit and killed their livestock. At which times, they made more regular visits, in the off seasons they checked in on them from time to time, just to keep the good rapport they had built with the planet's magistrate. That relationship had afforded Phoenix safe harbor on more than one occasion. That was only one of the things Iain would be very upset to lose.

If Ansi had been visited by CRF and they were no longer willing to risk association with pirates he would honor their wishes but he wanted to be sure they were certain of it, and that they understood they wouldn't be easily accepted back if this was their decision.

The planet the colonists had named Ansi wasn't large, but it served the peoples' needs. It had two main landmasses and hundreds of tiny islands spread through three bodies of water. Two of the oceans were sulfuric and undrinkable but the water near the cities wasn't bad, once it was filtered. There were two main cities, ten smaller villages and near a dozen farms spread out on the larger continent but most of the second continent and the islands were unexplored. The planet had only one sun, not nearly as strong as Earth's, but it was enough to allow a good agriculture, which was more than most in the Second BrimTier could say.

What they were coming for would have been in three days. Coloné Fête, or Colonization Day, was to commemorate the day the colonists first step foot on the planet. It was heaven compared to the majority of planets the CR had dumped others on. The Ansians had started this tradition of music, food, theater and games about ten years ago to give thanks for this.

Captain Bryce thought on all these points as he and his officers walked up the road to the main city, growing tenser with each step closer.

They were on the main road to the city of New Essex, even if the party was no longer to be there should have been carts bringing goods and people to and from the smaller cities for normal commerce. Today it was empty and full of debris, as if it hadn't been used in several days.

They found New Essex obscured by a thick, hazy fog. Ordinarily this wouldn't have been anything strange; the sun wasn't fully up so it simply hadn't had a chance to burn it off yet, this day it made the city look quite foreboding. That and large red crosses, hastily painted, on the front door of some of the smaller homes just inside the gate, made Iain more than a little edgy. The captain had seen markings like that before and it hadn't been for anything good then.

The lack of colonists along the road into town could've been explained away with a little effort but the lack of people within the usually quite active city was unheard of. He looked at his crew and saw they were just as frustrated and anxious as he, not making him feel any better. He was about to turn them back to get more men, fearing something tragic had befallen the colonists, when a man came running toward them from the center of town.

A cloth was tied over the man's nose and mouth and his arms were spread in front of him as if expecting to hit something. They couldn't see a weapon on him but Iain, Jaime and Eve's hands went instinctively to their pistols and Hayden brought his laser rifle down from its usual resting place on his shoulder.

The masked man waved his arms for them to halt then stopped himself, about twenty feet away from them. The captain thought it looked like John Stearns, a local grain miller. He got his answer when he heard the man's voice. "Didn't you get the message to stay away?"

"What is the meaning of this, John?" asked Iain. He took a step closer and saw the man panicking.

"No, please, don't come any closer..." said the man as he backed further away.

"What is happened?" asked the pirate captain more forcefully, "Where is Ty?"

"We've been hit with an epidemic; Ty is at the hospital with his family."

"Let me fetch Dr. Carter," said Iain.

"No, please, we don't want it to spread."

Iain told Eve to get their doctor and informed John they wouldn't leave until they had seen Magistrate Ty.

The man looked around but found no one to offer him help in the decision, his shoulders deflated as he nodded. He told them to wait by the gazebo in the gardens and went to get the magistrate.

The gardens were empty but Jaime and Hayden still refused to relax, constantly looking over their shoulders. Iain didn't notice their anxiety though; he was too busy thinking on what he might've just done. *An epidemic*, John had said. Could they have contracted the virus themselves entering the city? Had he just sent an infected Eve back to the ship with it? He punched his combadge and said, "Eve, do not enter the ship," then commed the doctor. "Robyn, inoculate yourself for any known viruses and meet Eve outside the ship with the same for all us; and bring as much as you can spare to the city with you."

It was close to half an hour before Magistrate Tyson Northrup came around the corner at a fast jog. He didn't have a mask on but he had the same look of horror in his eyes as the miller had had. "You shouldn't have come; you should have heeded our com. You have put yourselves in grave danger!"

"Calm down and tell us what happened so we can help you, Ty," said Iain quickly.

"You cannot help, we're all going to die," cried the man, looking over his shoulder as if the virus was a physical being that might have followed him.

"Ty, MAGISTRATE TYSON!" The captain shook the man. He was about ready to slap him if he needed to. "Please, tell me what has happened."

"Some children came down with what we took as just summer colds but when they didn't diminish after a couple weeks... and no medicine would relieve them... Soon adults became ill. We've lost near a third of our number... at this rate we'll be all but wiped out in mere days."

"Have you been able to isolate the cause of the virus yet?" asked Dr. Carter's voice from behind them. She was wearing a mask and had two bags over her shoulder, Eve, also in a mask, had a third bag over hers.

"No, but we think we know who brought it here."

"Adapt or perish,"
– Anonymous

The magistrate took them to his office and offered them a drink, which they all refused. "Two weeks ago, a group of students left for the land beyond the great mountain, to scout it out. We're in need of new field space. About a week ago, Master Clive, the school director, came stumbling into town with the most horrible of blisters. He collapsed into a coma just as he came through the city gates so we couldn't question him. We thought he'd been burned. We put salves on him but it only made them worse. Some broke open, then this illness spread throughout. We can only guess that the two are connected.

"Some, like me, got severely sick but then we suddenly got better. Now we seem to be immune. Others weren't so lucky. Their deaths were… painful… it's been hard to watch," The look in the man's eyes told them far more than any verbal explanation. "We've tried several forms of healing but nothing has been successful yet."

"Were any sent to learn the fate of the others?" asked Dr. Carter.

The magistrate got tense and a panicked look came over his face.

"I can't help find a cure until I know what caused this. It could've been a plant, fungus or berry, or maybe an insect or animal bite? Did the director have any obvious puncture wounds?"

"Not that we could see but most of his body was all scabs and sores," said the magistrate, beginning to pace and wring his hands nervously.

"Have you disposed of his body?"

"Yes, we burned it, hoping it would stop the spread," answered Ty as if that should have been the obvious solution.

"It must be an airborne virus then," said Robyn, looking pointedly at the captain.

Iain took her cue and quickly commed Kyle. "Are the ship's ventilators open?"

"No, sir."

"Good. Take an orbit above the planet."

"Captain, what's going on?" begged Kyle; not liking the gravity in the captain's words.

"The colonists' seem to have a viral outbreak on their hands, Master Cambridge. The five of us are being quarantined until further notice," said the captain, ending the link. He looked at each of his officers to be sure they understood what he'd said then turned to Ty, "Alright, me, Hayden, and Jaime are gonna see what we can find of the students' fate. Dr. Carter, Eve, see if you can offer help at the hospital."

"Captain, I should be with you in case you find anyone alive…" started Robyn.

"If we do we will bring them back with us. We cannot risk you falling ill, Doctor." She opened her mouth to argue but Iain stopped her. "No arguments."

Robyn tried to make good use of her time trapped in the city by doing just what Iain had said, going directly to the hospital. She met with the doctors to find out what they'd tried and if anything had any effect. She was frustrated with their answers.

"There is a range of symptoms: severe fatigue, heavy and persistent cough, headache, fever, chills, nausea, and vomiting. Within a week of becoming sick the sores appear, harden into scabs then the scabs break open and a thick puss empties from them. We believe the initial illness was from this puss. In the final stage most all the patients fall into convulsions but in all cases they die in agony," said Dr. Nicks, matter-of-factly.

"Sounds like it could be a bacterial infection, have you tried antibiotics?"

"We thought the same. We only have Penicillin. It seemed to help at first, but fails in the end. Our supply is all but depleted. It's like we are fighting two or three different viruses."

"It's possible you are. I have Amoxicillin and Streptomycin. One of them might work, or a combination of them. Have you taken samples of the blood or puss?"

"No, we don't have equipment to analyze it."

"I do, aboard our ship." Robyn took the combadge from her pocket and called up to Phoenix. Kassie's voice answered moments later. Robyn asked her to patch her to sickbay and waited for her nurse, Bethany, to answer. She told her to pack the lab equipment and all they had of the antibiotics, have them loaded on a sandpiper and ask the pilot to direct it to the planet. Bethany wanted to come with the equipment but Robyn reminded her of the captain's orders.

Once Dr. Carter got the lab equipment set up, she went to drawing blood and samples of puss from the sick colonists, from those that hadn't gotten sick and those that had survived and now seemed immune. She knew it wouldn't be an easy task, without knowing what caused the infection in the first place, but she had to try. She found it hard to concentrate though, worry for Iain and her crewmates lingered just near the surface of her thoughts.

"The time to relax is when you
don't have time to relax."
 —   Sydney J. Harris

The three pirates were walking a path that had been created by feet, but there was no way to know whether human or animal. The captain would have preferred to split them up, to cover more territory, but he couldn't risk one of them getting lost so they continued on in single file, trying to keep their eyes on the ground before them, the sky above them and the plant life all around them, unsure where the threat might be.

"What if we get sick as well?" grumbled Hayden.

"Let's hope Dr. Carter finds a cure before we do," said Jaime, he looked back at Iain and rolled his eyes.

"Fuck of a lot it'll do us way out here in the middle of fucking and nowhere. We don't even know what we're looking for," groused the guns master.

"If you look with your eyes instead of your mouth, maybe we would find it a right lot faster!" snapped Iain.

"Sorry, Captain," said Hayden, "But we *are* on a fucking wild goose chase."

"We're already too far to turn back so we might as well go on, yes?" Iain knew it did no good to bark at Hayden, they really didn't know what they were looking for; all the magistrate could give them was that they headed west. He too was feeling frustrated and wanted to call it quits but he'd never be able to face Ty again if he did, so the thought was moot.

The captain was about to call the search off and formulate a new plan when they found the first body. They couldn't have said whether it was male or female, its face was a mass of blackened scabs, the nose was swollen to near flat and the lips were bloated and purple. Not wanting to come into contact with the scabs, The captain reached for the wrist, the only part that didn't have any, to check for a pulse. He let out a quick breath and they all jumped back as the body turned to a jelly-like substance before their eyes. "What do you make of that?" The captain shook himself and wiped his hands on the front of his pants, even though he hadn't touched it. He told them to stay away from it, without really needing to, and to look for anything that might be the cause.

Jaime returned with a vial holding a few red berries and a plastic bag with a mushroom like fungus in it. Hayden found nothing. Knowing this wasn't going to be enough, and now curious about the fate of the other nine students, they continued on.

About one hundred feet further they found five more bodies in near the same condition as the first. It was getting dark when they found the last four. Three were long since dead, the fourth, a girl, was still alive, sores just beginning to appear on the her arms. The girl's eyes fluttered open as they stepped closer to her.

Iain tried to smile as he bent down in front of her, "I'm Iain, this is Jaime and that there's Hayden; we're from the pirate ship, Phoenix. Magistrate Ty sent us to find you. Can you talk?"

At first nothing came out of the girl's mouth except a painful sounding moan; then she managed to whisper, "Water?"

Iain sacrificed his canteen to give the girl some.

She drank it too quickly and began to cough, spitting most of it back up. The loud barks echoed through the darkness. She tried to sit up straighter; Iain and Jaime both moved to help her but both hesitated, remembering what had happened to the first body they found. "I'm Christie Dillon."

"Hi, Christie," said the captain; smiling at her like nothing was the matter.

"I'm gonna die like them, aren't I?" she asked him matter-of-factly, looking around at the other bodies in the clearing.

"Not if we got anything to say about it. Do you know what might have done this?" asked Iain, trying not to frighten her.

"Spiders," said the girl bluntly. She tried to drink more water and went into another coughing fit; the deep dry hacks echoed loudly through the darkening forest, making the pirates very much aware just how defenseless they were at that moment.

"*Spiders?*" asked Jaime, there wasn't much he was afraid of but he hated spiders.

"What did they look like?" asked Hayden.

"They're about the size of a rat with hairy orangish bodies and long brown legs," said the girl when she got her voice back.

"Where did you see them?" asked the captain.

"They came from the trees," said the girl as she closed her eyes and fell silent.

Iain gently touched her neck and sighed when he found a pulse. He motioned the others to step away with him. They walked back up the trail to the last body free clearing. "Alright, we gotta get her back to Robyn but we also gotta bring one of these spiders back. What can we use for that?" Jaime pulled a blanket from out of his pack and made as if covering up something. The captain

nodded and said they'd try to find one in the morning.
The clearing they were standing in wasn't ideal for a camp but it would have to do, it was too dark to look for another. He told Hayden to go back with him to get the girl and Jaime to start a fire. They set up a watch for the night. The captain took the last and longest shift.

Iain had no trouble staying awake; he never slept well off-ship anyway; between Hayden's snores and the girl's labored breathing, he would've found it hard to get comfortable even if he could have. He wished there was something he could do to make the girl more comfortable but was at a loss. They had covered her with a damp blanket, which did seem to make her fever better. Her breathing had worsening, now coming in shallow and quick gulps. They needed her to live, at least until they got her back to town, so she could tell Robyn what she knew. He tried to com Robyn, and Phoenix, several times with not luck, meaning they were out of range.

Just as the sun broke the tops of the trees he went to his shipmates and woke them. Both had sore muscles, but were also more than ready to be on the move again. "I came to a decision while you slept. we have got to get the girl back to Dr. Carter, if she is to have any chance of surviving this. Giving your dislike of spiders, Jay, it's gonna be you."

"You have no idea if it's really spiders though, the girl may be delusional…" started the quartermaster. He could see it was pointless to protest, it was decided.

"I've thought of that as well. The fact remains she needs to be in the hospital and you are physically the best option for getting her there fast. Try your best to keep the scabs from touching you, okay?"

"I'll return…"

"No! I see your face outside of New Essex I'll send you through the gauntlet, Jay."

"Iain…" started Jaime, knowing he was only joking but serious at the same time. "Okay."

"Tell Robyn that Hayden and I will be returning with at least one of these spiders, possibly a live one, so she should be ready."

Jaime nodded and wished them good luck.

"Nerves and butterflies are fine – they are a physical sign that you are mentally ready and eager. The trick is to get the butterflies to fly in formation."
  –   Steve Bull

Jaime reached New Essex just as the sun was going down. Ty and the miller, John, had been watching the gate, waiting for signs of them. They ran over when they saw the lumbering form appear in the empty road.

"Master Cable, let me help you," said John, seeing the strain on the pirate's face. He gave Ty a worried look as he took the girl; who was nothing but skin and bone.

The magistrate took the cue and placed his arm under Jaime's, the man collapsed as soon as his weight was off his feet.

Robyn started to put the fresh slide under the microscope when a sudden ruckus outside the office she'd taken over as her laboratory startled her. She jumped, sliding the sample too far forward and smearing it. She swore loudly and started for the door to see whom she needed to scream at for this. Just as she reached them, Ty burst through.

"Dr. Carter, come quickly, it's Master Cable," was all he got out before he was gone.

It took Robyn a minute to register what the man had said then she grabbed her bag and ran to catch up to him. "Where are they?"

"He returned with one of the students from the expedition. She's in the final stages. He collapsed after we took her from him. We don't know if it's the sickness or exhaustion."

"Captain Bryce and Master Fabris?" she asked, trying to keep her voice steady.

"They weren't with him," said the magistrate.

"Take me to Jaime."

Jaime was shaking so violently that it took two men to hold him still so Robyn could take a sample of his blood. His eyes were dilated and cloudy, his temperature was close to 104°, he was pale, only half conscious and was mumbling incoherently. She set up an I.V. with a chilled saline solution for his fever and dehydration, gave him a sedative to calm him down and the first dose of the drug regime that seemed to be helping the others then stepped back and watched him until he stopped shaking and fell into a deep sleep. With a heartfelt sigh, she pulled the blankets he kept kicking off in his shudders back over him then left to find the girl he'd brought in.

Ty was standing outside the door with a very distraught look on his face. He shook his head and looked at the floor. "I think she had been dead a while."

"DAMN IT! Where is Iain?"

Robyn and Eve were pacing at the base of the bed the quartermaster was in. Neither was speaking because neither knew what to say. Robyn had tried to com Iain and Hayden all morning, and had Kyle try from orbit; so far they hadn't gotten any answer. Eve wanted to send more to find them but Robyn didn't dare risk it; with Jaime already and possibly the captain incapacitated, the medical emergency supplanted Eve's higher rank. She had to hope they were still alive. Her immediate worry was Jaime.

He seemed to be responding to the medicine, or at least his fever was down, to just above 101°, but he hadn't awakened in more than eight hours. Robyn was about to say she was going to go back to the lab, needing to feel like she was amounting to something, when a mournful moan came from Jaime's lips.

Eve and the doctor were across the room in one quick step.

Jaime's eyes slowly opened but he seemed unable to focus them; looking from Eve to Robyn and back with no apparent recognition.

Robyn asked, "Do you know who you are?"

"Jay… Jaime," whispered the quartermaster. He smacked the roof of his mouth with his tongue as if he had peanut butter on it and tried to sit up.

Robyn gently held him down and pointed to a pitcher of water beside Eve. The security master poured out a cup and held it to Jaime's parched lips. He drank it thirstily then closed his eyes. They flew back open, startling the woman. He said loudly and clearly, "Iain?"

"You were found with only one of the students, was

the captain and Hayden with you, Jaime?" asked Robyn, trying to hide the anxiety in her voice.

"No... stayed... Look for... ders."

"Ders? What are ders?" asked Eve.

"Captain... looking... for sders..." said Jaime, with a look that said there was no reason why they shouldn't understand him. "Looking for sders..." He was getting agitated that they couldn't understand him. He tried to rise again, "I gotta go back for them."

The doctor tried to hold him down but he was still surprisingly strong, considering the illness ravaging his body. She called for help. The same two that had helped hold him down before came in. She pulled a needle with a sedative in it out of her pocket and quickly injected it into the quartermaster's arm. His eyes glazed over and his limbs when limp.

"I can't take the chance that Iain and Hayden are in this condition out there. If they haven't returned by morning we'll send a shuttle to try to find them."

"I volunteer to fly it," said Eve quickly.

"I figured you would but I have another task for you. I'm out of medicine. I need you to go to the clinic on Deco-Fye and purchase more."

"Deco-Fye is a CRF outpost," said Eve.

"I know, *I know,* but they're the closest. Have Ty write up a request for aide; you will go in the guise of a colonist just making the pickup." She could see Eve was about to argue. She quickly added, "This is an order."

Eve nodded and went to find the magistrate.

"Our devils are never quite what we
expect when we meet face to face."
  —   Nelson DeMille

Captain Bryce and Hayden had found lots of normal spiders, some of which were quite large and scary looking, but none that matched the girl's description. They had no idea if these giant spiders even existed; the girl might have been delusional. This, and not knowing if Jaime had made it back to town safely, was weighing heavy on them.

They stopped for a rest and to have a bite to eat as the sun reached its pinnacle. Hayden rummaged through his pack and found some hard bread, cheese and jerky. It wouldn't be the best meal but it would sustain them. They had thought they would find plenty to hunt; the planet had wild deer, rabbits, boars, pheasants and quail – any of which would have made a good meal, All they had seen was a few song birds and a lot of bloodsucking insects – none of which would be particularly tasty.

The captain found a good spot to sit and took a couple of pieces of the jerky out of the bag the weapons master passed him. He started to take a bite of one of the strips when he felt something prick his arm.

Iain opened his eyes and squinted from the bright glare. He was surprised to see the sky directly above him, bright and blue, with wispy clouds moving about lazily. He realized he was lying on the ground, on his back. He couldn't remember how he'd gotten that way. He slowly rolled his head to the side and saw Hayden lying on his back across from him. He looked like he was asleep, a white blanket tucked tightly around him. He started to get up and found he was partially covered in a blanket too. He tried to kick it off but it didn't move. He looked down and saw it wasn't a blanket at all, it was webbing.

The fibers were sticky and wrapped tightly around his legs up to his knees. He followed a thin thread to the rear end of what appeared to be one of the spiders the girl had described. He pulled his laser pistol and aimed it at the spider's head. With a quick burst of orange light the thing exploded. Screeches sounded from the trees above him. He looked up to find three more arachnids hovering from the branches above him. Not taking his eyes off them, he pulled a knife and sliced through the webbing around his legs. When he was free, he shot and killed them. He cringed at the sound they made as they fell to the ground. He looked around for any more. He didn't see any so he ran to the weapons master.

Hayden was unconscious and stiff, his eyes frozen open and blank. Iain didn't have time to check if he was alive. Sounds in the trees overhead and in the shrubbery around them told him more spiders were coming. Even dead, he wouldn't leave his friend to them. He grabbed a handful of the sticky web and began to drag Hayden's body into the center of the clearing.

Within minutes there was about a dozen of the things, some the size of rats, others only large mice, around the clearing. The captain released the spent laser cartridge and was just getting another slammed in as one of the spiders reached the weapons master's feet. He blasted it away then froze as he heard another sound above his head. He looked up and saw the hull of a sandpiper drop out of the clouds. The heated blast of air from its engines sent the spiders scurrying for a moment.

"Want a lift?" Digger's voice asked through the com on the captain's lapel.

Iain punched the badge and said, "Thank you, you beautiful man!" He grabbed the web around Hayden's body and dragged him closer to the edge so Digger could land the ship. Once the ramp was low enough he hoisted Hayden over his shoulder and ran for it. He passed the stunned man to the grunt, Todd, grabbed an empty crate from the deck and jumped off the ramp. Conveniently, a small spider landed right before him; he scooped it up, fell backward onto the rising ramp and slid headfirst into the ship's belly. He covered the crate with a blanket and set another crate, full of supplies, on top of it, so the things couldn't get out, and then helped Todd cut Hayden free.

What did you find?" Robyn asked the captain, as he stepped from the shuttle ramp, holding a crate at arm's length before him.

"This," said Iain as he passed one of the colonists the squirming box. "It's a spider. The girl Jaime brought back said it was the cause."

"Sders!" Dr. Carter said suddenly, making the captain jump. She laughed and explained the strange word as they made their way back to town. She started to apologize for disobeying him when he held up his hand.

"You're excused, this time, but I *will* have to punish you later," Iain said with a sly smile.

The doctor smiled and nodded, very happy to take his intended punishment. She told him she had also sent Eve to Deco-Fye to get more medicine as her and the colonists stocks were all but out and there were still many that needed treatment. They weren't curing the infection just holding them in check but now, with the spider; she hoped to be able to find an antidote.

Iain wasn't comfortable knowing Eve had walked into a CRF outpost but he knew Robyn wouldn't have sent her unless the need was great. He just hoped it wouldn't be regretted. He tried to smile reassuringly at her as he said, "Take me to my quartermaster."

"When someone tells you it's an easy job, laugh in their face."
–   *Iain D. Bryce*

Three days came and went with no sign of Eve and the colonists that had gone to the CRF space station to replenish the stock of medicine. It should have been an easy in and out transaction, but they had obviously met with a problem. On the beginning of the fourth day, Iain decided he couldn't wait any longer. He was just about to board the sandpiper when Kyle called down to relay a message from the very outpost.

"Rear admiral Anton Anders says he has Master Oakley in custody. He says he wants to exchange her for you."

"Shit!" This wasn't good news on many fronts; *Rear Admiral* Anders had been a vice admiral and the commander of a battlecruiser when Iain last saw him. He was sure he was largely the reason for that demotion and apparent reassignment to the outpost. No doubt, Nickolas had been upset with Anders for bringing him his own man, Gideon, instead of the pirate captain. He knew he would be in for a whole lot of pain if he agreed to turn himself in but the Ansians had to have medicine and he couldn't leave Eve and the colonists there.

The captain's ship was hit with a force net as he reached the station and the now rear admiral's voice broke the silence of his cockpit. "Hello, Captain Bryce, at last we will meet, for real," said the man in a satisfied tone.

Iain smiled; at least he'd get to enjoy the look on Anders' face when he realized he had had the actual Captain Bryce in his mitts and hadn't even known it. That was little consolation just now, though. "Do you still hold my security master?" asked Captain Bryce.

"We do. She is awaiting your company in our brig," said Anders.

"What of the Ansian colonists that accompanied her?" asked the captain.

"I know nothing of any colonists, only the other shipmates taken with Ms. Oakley. They were attempting to rob our clinic."

"*They were not.* They were on your station to purchase medicine to treat an infection that is killing the colonists on Ansi," said Iain pointedly.

"Yes, we have heard the story already. We tried to contact Ansi but have been unable to reach anyone. I'm guessing you have killed them all already in some form of sick pirate sport."

"They can't answer because most of 'em are in the hospital fighting for their lives or are already dead from the infection Ms. Oakley was trying to get medicine for," said a frustrated captain. A wave of dizziness washed over him and the equipment before him went out of focus. He rubbed his eyes and remembered he hadn't slept in two days. He cursed himself for his stupidity, he needed to be at his best at this time if never before.

"Why don't we continue this conversation once you are aboard," said the now rear admiral, smugly.

Iain started to say more but the connection had already been cut. He felt a bit of a lurch as the tractor beam hit his ship, then he was being drawn toward the hanger on the outpost. There was nothing he could do so he sat back, closed his eyes and waited.

Twenty officers were waiting in the bay for the captain when he stepped from the ship. He pulled his pistols, handed them over and allowed them to frisk him for other weapons. They found two throwing knives, a folding pocketknife and four magazines of charges but missed a fourth knife and his lock pick set; he, of course, didn't mention their oversight. He doubted the hall they were leading him down went to the brig, so he guessed he was being taken directly to the rear admiral.

The door they stopped him at slid open to an office overlooking the moon the station was orbiting. One of the guards shoved him through the door then punched the button to close it.

The pirate captain walked around the perimeter of the room twice then stopped in front of a glass case. One shelf held plaques and medals Anders had been awarded over the years – there was a lot of them, telling Iain the man had been going places before the incident with Gideon. He didn't linger on them, feeling a little guilty. The next shelf had several holographs, which did hold his attention for a moment. The first appeared to be the man and his family from many years before, on vacation, by their casual dress. He didn't recognize the large canyon in the background but the red and brown of the rock layers were impressive. Another showed him with former President Timothy Nason, the current president's father, holding fishing poles on a fishing boat, in a lake some-where, both men smiling and shaking hands. The last was Anders with his former squad, the one Iain had caused him to lose; he didn't linger on that one either. The final shelf had knickknacks, none of which looked expensive, nothing worth pocketing there. The pirate captain stepped away from the case and walked to the desk.

On the corner of the desk was a small globe showing the continents and oceans of Earth. Iain spun it unconsciously as he walked by and stepped behind the piece of furniture. A highly carved oak humidor, holding very expensive cigars, sat beside the globe. He helped himself to a handful of them, stuffing them into his jacket pocket. A matching lighter for the previous sat in the center back of the desk, far too large to pocket, and a combox, in a matching wood box, was on the right corner of the desk. A burgundy velvet blotter filled the middle of the desk surface. Several tiny slips of paper with writing on them were stuck under the corner of this. A large leather chair was pushed under the desk but there were no other chairs in the room. The captain sat on the corner of the desk for several minutes then shrugged and sat down at the desk.

He oohed at how comfortable the man's chair was. He leaned back in it and sighed. He seriously thought about putting his feet up and lighting a cigar while he waited but decided it was best not to antagonize the now rear admiral, at least not before he was certain there was no chance of making him see that Eve and the colonists were not on the station to cause trouble.

"Bored now," said Iain as he pulled out the stack of notes before him.

Most were simple reminders to the man the office belonged to of various tasks that needed seeing to. He was smiling at a requisition slip for a state-of-the-art coffeemaker just as the door slid open to the rear admiral.

The man stood imposingly in the doorway for several seconds. The captain thought he looked more weathered than when he had last seen him; demotion apparently didn't suit him. He looked irritated that the pirate was behind his desk. Iain, again, fought the urge to put his feet up. Instead, he put an apologetic look on his face and stood up.

Anton expected to see the pirate standing in the center of his office, waiting for him, instead he found him sitting at his desk, rifling through his personal notes. He could feel his blood pressure and temper rising. He reminded himself he was the better man. He was about to order the pirate away when the man did so on his own.

The pirate wasn't wearing any disguise this time. He had the same crooked half smile on his face as he had in the photos the Fleet Admiral had made him study – so he wouldn't be fooled again. His hair was flatter and matted and his face was drawn and a lot more gaunt than they had been in the photos, but there was no doubt it was the real Captain Iain Bryce standing before him. The pirate looked like he'd had a bad day, or rather a string of them; Anders was pleased to be able to tell him they were going to get worse. "So, you have dropped the Crewman Kinden guise, have you now?"

Captain Bryce smiled and said, "May I present the *real* Captain Iain Bryce to you; I'm most humbly at your service, Sir." He took a sweeping bow and held his hand out to the man. "Right sorry for deceiving you like that. Couldn't allow a spy to remain on my ship any more than you likely would have, *Rear* Admiral, is it now?

Anders nodded and smiled; the pirate was right, he wouldn't have allowed a spy among his men either. He took the pirate's hand and shook it firmly.

Iain held the appliance requisition up to the rear admiral as he walked past him. "Is there anything better than a right good cup of joe?"

"A civilized pirate," said the rear admiral, as if that was the oddest thing he had ever heard. "I would have thought your drink would be stronger."

"It can be," said Iain, smiling slightly.

"Would you care for something now?" asked the rear admiral. He pressed a button on his desk; a portion of the wall shifted to expose a glass-shelved bar with decanters of liquor and empty glasses.

Iain snapped his fingers, "Ooh, missed that one, I'm slipping. I will take a whiskey, if you are offering. Single malt, if you've got it."

"I am. You have expensive tastes," said the rear admiral with a bit of amusement. He moved to the bar, poured a scotch for himself and a whiskey for the pirate. "You did cost me a star and my ship."

"I sincerely apologize for that. My beef was with the president and his second, not you," said Captain Bryce honestly.

The rear admiral half shrugged and passed the pirate the glass of amber liquid. "Thomas isn't nearly as jovially tempered as his father, Timothy, was, and the fleet sdmiral... let's just say I am not certain he has ever laughed at a joke." He took his seat behind the desk and opened the humidor to offer the captain a cigar as well.

Iain frowned and shook his head.

Anders took one out for himself, bit the end of it, spit it into the rubbish bin by the foot of the desk, lit it with the lighter, and took several long puffs from it, before he said, "I think they will both be pleased with me again, now, though."

"How did you know the woman was one of my crew?" asked Iain, not particularly enjoying the smell of the cigar, though they usually didn't bother him.

"After the fleet admiral finished browbeating me, he made me study your ident photos until I had your faces permanently etched into my brain. The woman has changed her hair a little, and is a bit thinner, but I recognized her immediately," answered the rear admiral.

Feeling a sudden sense of urgency, Iain said, "You said you wanted to make an exchange. You will release my security master and the colonists now you have me?"

Anders pretended to consider the question for a moment then he shook his head and said, "I think he will be even happier with me for giving him you as well as four of your crew."

"I told you already, the three men are Ansian colonists. Take me and Oakley but allow them to return to their families," said Iain, now starting to get heated.

"Yes, yes, because they're sick and dying. They looked healthy to me," said Anders.

"The men with Master Oakley were immune to the illness, which is why we sent them with her."

"I am guessing you are immune as well," said the rear admiral smugly. He smiled and blew a heavy cloud of smoke at the pirate captain's face. He thought he actually did look a bit green about the gills.

"Two of my crew ain't though. Let the colonists return to the planet with the medicine and I promise Master Oakley and I will go without fight," pleaded Iain.

The conviction in the pirate's voice had Anders actually considering saying yes. His smile broadened "I'd heard you were a persuasive sot. Tell me, how did these colonists get sick in the first place?"

"A spider. Something in its bite has caused an infection to spread. It's already killed a third of them. My quartermaster and weapons master have also contracted it," said Iain.

"A spider, you say?" said the rear admiral, he looked like he was waiting for the punchline of this joke.

Iain started to say more but found he couldn't, his throat was suddenly dry. He brought his hand up to his chest and pushed on it because it was suddenly very tight, a different feeling from his heartburn. He realized he was hot, beads of sweat were dripping down his forehead and cheeks, and he was lightheaded. He needed to sit down, lie down, anything down. For a brief moment he thought Anders had drugged him then he saw a line of black scabs on the back of his hand and realized it wasn't that.

The glass slipped from the captain's hand and smashed to the floor, spilling the liquor all over the carpet, then the room began to spin and he too was falling. It seemed forever to reach the floor but when he finally did he found it pleasantly cold. He didn't get to enjoy it long, as, without any modesty, he proceeded to vomit thick mucus onto that floor.

Anders laughed heartily at the display, thinking the man was only acting. He clapped and said, "Bravo, bravo. What do you do for a second act, Bryce?"

Iain wanted to say something flippant back but his body was now being wracked with shivers so severe he thought his bones would break if they didn't stop.

Anton started around his desk, still laughing.

The combox on the corner of the desk came alive with a frantic voice. "Commander, six men have just fallen into some sort of convulsions."

All the laughter now gone, the rear admiral turned to the man reeling on his floor, "What the hell have you done?"

The pirate had fallen unconscious.

"That pesky thing called honor..."
— *Iain D. Bryce*

While Captain Bryce was gone, Dr. Carter had determined the spider's potent venom, which included the digestive juices it used to break down its food, had caused the initial illness in the school director. It had an unexpected byproduct in the form of a contagious virus, the spores the scabs released when they broke open had mutated into a separate microbe, which mimicked the original spider bite's digestive juices, breaking down its victim's organs and, in essence, cooking them from the inside out.

Armed with this knowledge, and the spider Iain brought back, she was able to generate a vaccine and an antidote from the venom. She had synthesized enough to cure all the colonists, Jaime, Hayden and Digger, who had also contracted the virus since the captain left for the outpost. She was also able to make an inoculation against future outbreaks, which would allow the colonists to form groups to go in and exterminate any remaining spiders. This should have made them all happy but the captain, Eve and the colonists hadn't returned yet.

After three more days of waiting, with no sign of them, Dr. Carter had Kyle contact the outpost and learned of the outbreak there. She explained to the rear admiral what the illness was doing to his crew. She offered to bring him the vaccine if he gave her his gentleman's promise to release the captain, Eve and the colonists.

Having no choice, Anders agreed.

Captain Bryce waited for the colonists shuttle to depart before turning from the cold window. They were distraught with him when he refused to go with them. He insisted on staying because he'd given Anders his word he would.

Though cured, he was still weak. He was leaning on the glass of the awards case to keep from falling over, the coldness of it felt good on his still slightly fevered skin, as he watched the ship disappear into the jumpgate. Once it was gone he turned to face the rear admiral and held out his hands for the proverbial irons to be attached, "I'm yours."

Anton Anders was beyond flabbergasted. Part of him was jumping up and down at being able to give the pirate over to the Fleet Admiral, for real this time, knowing he would get his former rank back if not the promotion he'd expected, but his conscience wouldn't allow it. "I owe you the lives of my men, Bryce."

"You gave me back mine and released my security master and the colonist's, you owe me nothing."

"Respect… from a pirate?" He shook his head, partly in disbelief at what he was about to do. "I can't give you back your life only to see you hanged… I will release you, this time. I consider us even, Bryce. Know this: the next time I promise I won't be so considerate."

Black Passions

"The doing of a new evil does not
negate the guilt from the old evil."
— *Old Semai' Proverb*

Phoenix Enclave's hauls over the last few weeks had been extremely profitable. They had hit three supply convoys and a surveying ship before retiring for a bit of rest and relaxation on the First BrimTier planet, Ryger. They had been on-planet for six days, the grunts had long since spent their shares on wine and women in one of the many establishments for such on the planet and were now working on getting the ship ready for departure.

Jaime and Hayden spent part of their time off-ship purchasing weapons and ammo to replenish the stock, and a new laser cannon to replace the one that had gotten destroyed in a recent altercation with the CRF. Digger and Norris' idea of fun was scouring the junk and parts yards for a coupling coil, guide wires, fylon material and a shaft for the space-sails which had been broken for two weeks. The mast had twisted, ripping the sail fabric, during the same altercation. Mitch and Yard busied themselves replacing their food supplies and spending the colonists' shares for the next deliveries. The women on the crew spent theirs in one of the many shops on clothes and bling. Iain found himself alone, which actually suited him fine. Most of his time was spent on the soft red and black sand beach. He made the mistake of leaving that quiet and relaxing place for a bar and a drink.

The captain felt every muscle in his body tighten back up when the stupid slapstick comedy playing on the DTV behind the bar was interrupted with a special report about the finishing school on Tarnis Prime. He watched the camera pan the campus, showing all the destruction. The newscaster was telling the camera that pirates had raided the school. Some of the maintenance staff was shown sorting through piles of debris to see if anything was salvageable, then the scene changed to an older teacher, being interviewed by the reporter.

"Luckily, it's holiday, so most of the students weren't present," said the woman, who had a bruised eye and one arm in a sling but seemed to be in good spirits. When asked if she knew which pirates it was, she looked directly, and defiantly, at the camera and spat, "The black pirate. He made sure we knew who he was while he was beating us."

"That would be Victor Black, Chad, the infamous captain of the Blue Raven. They haven't accounted for all the students that remained at the school over the holiday so it is unknown if any were taken; or if they are still alive.

"The Confederational Regime Forces have asked that anyone with information come forward as soon as possible. On your screen below you'll find the frequency to contact the CRF. Anyone giving information can remain anonymous. They're also urging any who see the pirates not to attempt to capture or hinder them in any way, please leave it to the appropriate authorities. This is Trace Givens, of SPN5 News, reporting live from Tarnis Prime, back to you Chad."

Iain didn't stay to hear the newscaster, Chad, close out the segment. He was again walking the beach, but not to enjoy the view. He was trying to convince himself Caitlyn was at home for the break. There was no way he knew of to confirm this without the president finding out. He reached the end of the beach and climbed the large stones piled up to act as a barrier against higher waves from the ocean with little or no effort and stood on top of the wall looking down at his ship sitting majestically on the sandbar below.

He still caught his breath every time he looked at her. The aptly named ship's reddish black exterior and the ever-pumping, orange-yellow metallic epoxy flowing through the MVS system looked even more like flames in the dying sunlight against the dark colored sand. Her captain drew in a breath and blew it out slowly. Aboard Phoenix was the only place he truly felt himself, the only place he trusted, and the only place he didn't have to wonder whether he mattered.

He watched the activity below him for a moment. They would be leaving the next day so the doings would remain steady until all was in place. His crew was moving on, around and over the ship, like ants. Some were helping Digger and Norris with the repairs to the spacesails, which were spread out to their full glory, making the ship look even more impressive. Some were with Hayden on the top of the ship, helping get the new laser cannon in place and properly installed while Jaime operated the hoist and jib. Yard was busy supervising the loading of the supplies, Iain could hear him shouting at a grunt not to chase a pig that was reluctant to board.

He sighed again; they were all oblivious to his anxiety. He slowly worked his way down this side of the rock barrier and ignored the calls of his crew wanting his opinion on this or that. He climbed the loading ramp and went directly to his cabin.

Iain tried, without much luck, to get some sleep. He hadn't had any to speak of in three days now; being on solid ground had prevented it before and thoughts of

Caitlyn were doing it now. He had just given up when Kyle's voice came from his combadge. He said, "Go," a little nastier than intended.

"I have Dylan Nason on link for you, Captain."

Iain's heart stopped for a moment. He told the pilot to put him through and walked over to the monitor. A distraught Dylan was waiting for him. "Speak!"

"Cap... Captain Bryce, I know I should not be doing this... but I... I didn't know where else to turn. Caitlyn gave me the impression that you and... well, she thinks highly of..."

"Is she alright?" interrupted Iain impatiently.

"The school was..."

"Attacked. I know." Iain sank slowly into the seat before the monitor and his heart sank into his stomach.

"Caitlyn refused to come home when father asked. To be honest, I don't know if she stayed at the school or not. She may have gone with one of her friends... I've tried to reach her for two days and haven't gotten an answer. I'm worried..."

"If Captain Black has her your father will get a ransom call."

"But... you know he won't pay it... and I can't afford another... They won't be as kind to her as you were, will they?" What exactly the boy meant by this was clearly all over his face.

"No, Dylan, they likely won't."

"Can you help me find her, Captain Bryce? I will find a way to pay you for your time, somehow."

"Anything you do can get you shot, including nothing."
    –   Anonymous.

"If the president hasn't gotten a ransom request yet, then either Captain Black doesn't have her, or he doesn't know who she is, yet," said Jaime.

"He isn't likely to try to learn any of the women's real identities, he doesn't typically ransom hostages." said Hayden.

"Isn't he less likely to harm them if he finds out one, or more, is valuable?" asked Eve. The look Hayden gave her told her the answer to this.

"How long does Black usually take to sell off his hostages?" asked Robyn.

"He loses money every day he has to feed them, so he would dispose of them as quick as possible."

Iain interjected, "I will hold to whatever you all decide but make it right quick." It had already been four days since the attack on the school. "I promised Dylan an answer by end of day."

Jaime looked to each and tallied their vote, even Hayden, though reluctantly, voted to do all they could to find out if Caitlyn was one of the girls taken.

"Alright." Iain was trying not to sound too pleased, because it would raise questions he didn't want to answer just then. He looked at Hayden and asked, "What's the best way to approach Black and find out if he even still has the girls taken from the school?"

"Let me do it. If he has her and thinks she's worth something to you, it could go badly for her, sir."

"Point taken." Iain called up to Kyle and asked him to find and connect them with Black's ship.

The captain of the Blue Raven, Victor Black, looked just as hard as Hayden remembered. Some of his wrinkles were deeper and he was tanned the color of worn leather but he smiled quick enough when he saw his ex-security master. "Hell, Fabris, you son of a bitch, 'ave you been fuckin' profitable?"

"Adequately. Hear you went back to school?"

"Yeah. All over the goddamn news, ain't it."

The man's sick smile made Hayden uneasy. There were many reasons he had chosen to jump-ship and join Captain Bryce; the treatment, and his condoning of the treatment by his crew, of prisoners while Hayden was in his service was only one. Black hadn't appreciated him talking against it when he was one of his crew; he knew the black pirate would take it even less kindly as a rival. He had to find a subtle way to find out if the girl was on board. A crazy idea popped into his head. "The newscaster suggested some of the students were still there?"

"Why the fuckin' curiosity? Longin' for the days of old, are ya Fabris?" asked Black, squinting his eyes, his suspicions obviously raised.

"I have a proposition for you."

"I'm listenin'."

"We recently ran across a slavemonger looking for fresh workers, he and I've had dealings in the past. I was just wondering if you wanted in?"

"Your fuckin' sanctimonious captain goes along with that, do he? I thought he was above all that shit?"

"He needs not know."

"That's the Hayden I remember. Details?"

"I'd rather discuss it in person, this ship has too many… sympathizers… Can I have your coordinates?"

Black got a dark look in his eyes, "I'll meet you."

Trying to hide his disappointment, Hayden quickly said, "Place and time."

"You're near Ryger, yes? There is a brothel I find pleasantly entertainin' in the red light district, called the Crimson Belle. Meet me tomorrow at noon," said Black then the comlink went dead.

Hayden looked at Captain Bryce and said, "You've got your in."

"So what is the plan?" asked Eve.

"I just implied I have a side business going. If he has the girls, and I can get him to agree, we may be able to buy them off him," said Hayden.

"Do you think he will fall for that?" asked Eve.

"His biggest market is in the sex trade. These girls are likely all coddled and soft. Most of them will not have held up well to the treatment he has likely already shown them so there is no way they would make it in a brothel. If they are not of marketable value then he will consider them only good for one purpose..." The look in Hayden's eyes told them what that purpose was. "You will need... samples... to show him you're a serious buyer, Captain." He glanced quickly at Eve and Robyn.

"Are you suggesting we pretend to be whores?" asked Eve.

"Just long enough to make the deal," said Hayden.

"We can find some on-planet that are willing..." started Jaime.

"I'll do it.," said Robyn, quickly.

"As will I. We'll need to look the part," said Eve, then her and Robyn went to see what they had in their respective wardrobes.

The others quickly dispersed as well to make what preparations they could.

Iain was working out an appropriate disguise in his mind when Hayden called to him. He stopped and waited for him to catch up.

"What will you do if she is…"

"We'll cross that bridge when we come to it," said Iain curtly, he didn't want to think about that just now.

"Sir, what *are* your feelings for the girl?" asked Hayden. If the captain was truly in love with her he would stop at nothing to get her back.

"I don't truly know."

"You'll need to. If he does have her, and this rouse doesn't work, you may be in for a fucking brutal fight. One that could end in another pirate captain being dead…" Hayden gave the captain a piercing look to set the thought in his mind then turned around.

"DAMN IT!" shouted Iain, making a man walking on the gangway below jump.

"Everyone has a dark side which he rarely lets show, for fear it will howl."
– *Pastor Maxwell Bryce*

Hayden put on the uniform he had worn while in Black's service, hoping it would help to put the always-jumpy man at ease and went to meet the others in the hanger.

Robyn and Eve were already there, both wearing silk dresses that had once been nice but were now in shreds and their hair was disheveled, meant to look like they had been being living in captivity for a few weeks. They had made themselves up with the captain's make-up to look like they had been mistreated as well. It would fool anyone that didn't know what they were up to.

Jaime came into the hanger moments later, dressed quite flamboyantly in loose purple pantaloons and a gray and purple striped shirt and he had his shoulder length brown hair pulled back and tied with a purple ribbon. He was directing a hovercraft that had seen better days. He winked at the look on the weapons master's face then motioned up to the shuttle hatch.

Hayden caught his breath as a strange man stepped from the sandpiper. He waddled like a top-heavy barrel, using a cane to keep upright. The handle of the twisted wooden stick was in the shape of an old boot, with laces, eye grommets, tread and even a tack sticking out of the hole worn in the bottom carved into it. He had a bushy reddish brown mustache flaring out from the sides of a bulbous nose and thick eyebrows, the hair on his head, what there was of it, was a wispy mix of red and gray.

The iris of his right eye was all white, like a cataract had destroyed it, and the other was a deep green. He was wearing a waist length, jacket with different colored patches all over it, which made him look even fatter, if it was possible, over a ruffled tan tunic, a purple bandana around his neck, to cover up the distinctive tattoo, and a pair of brown pants then went inside black boots. A half smoked cigar, chewed near flat at its base, was clenched between his teeth, when he smiled Hayden saw only half his teeth were white, the other half, on the side the cigar was clenched on, were stained yellowish.

"Nice touch, Captain," said Hayden.

"Eh um, 'ello laddy, me name's Skeeta' Boots and I'm in da' bi'ness a' en'ataiment. Dese loverlies is bein' trained to servicize me clients," said the man as he touched a button on a device he held in his free hand.

Both of the ladies suddenly arched their backs and screamed in pain.

"What the hell?" screamed Hayden, realism was one thing.

Eve stood straight up and smiled, "We're acting, you fool."

"We ready then?" asked Captain Bryce, in his regular voice, which seemed foreign coming from the mouth it was now coming out of.

"What's the plan?" asked Hayden.

"You drop me, Jaime and the ladies off early so we can get into place. We'll be in one of the private rooms out back. When you're satisfied Black is interested, you bring him back to *see the merchandise* and we make a deal with him."

"The superior man understands what is right; the inferior man understands what will sell."

— Confucius

Hayden was accosted by pungent incense and smell of stale beer as he stepped through the door of The Crimson Belle. He looked around and saw burgundy lace curtains covering the windows, erotic artwork hanging on the velvet walls and lit candles on near every flat surface. He knew immediately this wasn't a place he wanted to be, resentment toward Iain Bryce began to form in his heart. He didn't like this one bit.

Not more than two seconds through the door he was approached by a large, heavily made up, woman in a red leather corset and a leopard print leather skirt that did nothing to hide the rolls of fat beneath. Her peppered hair was pulled up loosely in a bun on top of her head, held up by a large crimson bow. She had a golden ring in her left nostril, a chain hung from it across her left cheek to a ring in her left ear and another hung from it, disappearing under her skirt. He knew where without needing to see it; for all the thought was intriguing who had that piercing ruined it. She barely came to his shoulders but she was easily as wide as he was and was nothing he would have been interested in even if he didn't have Eve.

The madam eyed him up and down then smiled wickedly. She pressed her body hard against his and her hands freely explored his tight pants. She smelled of liquor, sex and something that made his head fuzzy as he breathed it in. For all he wanted to push her away at once he played along. She reeled off the services her establishment offered, he told her he only wanted to start.

She was about to tell him if that was all he wanted to find another establishment when she saw the patch of the black pirate, a tiny skeleton dancing on the edge of a broadsword, on Hayden's vest. She called out to the girl behind the bar to fetch him whatever he wanted, on the house, then said, with a long held wink, "If you change your mind you only need holler, Sweeting."

Once the woman was back guarding the door Hayden was free to look around. He took the mug of dark ale gruffly from the waif behind the bar and sat with his back to her. She seemed offended for a moment then shrugged and went back to flirting with the man playing the piano.

He took in the room once then, on the second pass, focused on the people in it. He stopped on a couple sitting at a round booth in the corner, a thin woman sitting on the lap of a bearded man, her whispering in his ear. For all he couldn't hear them he imagined she was trying to complete the transaction. Curiosity got the best of him as he found himself watched them; he quickly looked away when he realized the girl, as she spread her legs and he saw equipment that didn't belong, was actually a guy.

His eyes stopped on six girls that didn't look old enough to be out of pigtails, sitting in a row on a padded bench across from him, waiting for their next score. One winked at him and began to touch herself in an attempt to get him aroused. He pretended not to notice as he scanning the rest of the room. He jumped when he heard the voice of the man he had been waiting for come booming from the foyer. He set down his only half-drank ale, stood and walked across the room.

Captain Black teased at the chain that disappeared under the madam's skirt while he nibbled her ear. She moaned and rolled her eyes then shook slightly as he pulled away. She swooned and fell to the stool she had been sitting on, smiling strangely. Black smiled sickly back then he saw Hayden. "How the hell you been, Fabris?" Black shouted loud enough to make everyone in the place look.

"Captain Black. I'm fucking great, how are you, ya' grizzly old son of a bitch!"

The two men clasped forearms and went to a table hidden from the others.

"Wha' exactly we talkin' here, Fabris?" asked the black pirate once they had sat down.

"As I said, I've been working with a man to… augment my income. I'm hoping to purchase my own ship and break away from Bryce."

"Won't take to kindly to that, will 'e?" asked Captain Black as he lit a thin cigarette and expelled thick gray smoke from his ample nostrils.

"He doesn't know. But yeah, he won't be happy since a third of the crew will be joining me."

"I've never met 'im, is 'e really as fuckin' half-hearted as 'e's been portrayed?"

"He doesn't take to pirating well, thinks he can be a fucking hero and a crook."

"I 'eard his fuckin' balls hang low as well, take it you find 'im a weak shit too?"

"Shit! Any would be after you, Black!"

Captain Black laughed heartily at that and slapped Hayden hard on the upper arm, "You know, I always did prefer a struggler!"

"Speaking of, you had your fun with any yet?"

"Been awful busy but we did find one bitch most entertainin' for a few hours. Don't fuckin' think you'll be wantin' 'er though; my crew was most harsh with 'er."

Hayden had to look away so he wouldn't bring attention to how much that statement had turned his stomach. He knew Captain Black had intended it as a jab; he'd always made it clear he wanted no part of the gang rapes. He smiled as wickedly as he could muster and said, "Times change. How many you got?"

"None 'ere to your likin'?"

"A little too roadworn for me," said Hayden.

"Did always prefer your ass sweet, didn't ya," said the pirate. He paused and looked around to be sure none were listening before leaning closer and whispering, "I 'ave ten, well, nine, not countin' the used up toy. How much does your backer pay for a fuckin' healthy bitch?"

"If they're virgins more but a pretty enough piece of ass, or least a well turned, can go for upwards of five thousand," said Hayden.

"How do we proceed?" asked Black.

"My contact is in a room out back with some recent acquisitions he's been training, care to see him?"

"Lead the way."

The weapons master stepped through the black curtain into a long dimly lit corridor that had several doors opening off it. The sounds of people getting off in various ways could be heard from behind most of them. He stopped Captain Black at the second door on the right and softly knocked on it. When he heard permission to enter he pushed the door open. He was momentarily shocked at what he saw.

A large round bed, covered in blood red sheets, was set against one wall and a black iron gate like structure was standing in the center of the room. Chained to this was Eve, half-naked, Robyn was cowering in the corner, chained to a metal ring in the wall, and Iain was in a chair behind the metal gate, leaning back on the rear legs, which looked ready to give.

"Agin?" Iain, as Skeeter, asked.

"Please, no more," cried Eve, very convincingly.

"Ya 'ill perform den?" asked the fat man.

"Yes... Yes... I promise..."

Skeeter picked up a device setting on the table beside him and pushed a green button. The shackles around her wrists and ankles released and she fell to the floor with a painful thump. She lay were she landed, shaking, for a few seconds then arched her back and screamed.

Hayden watched Black's eyes go to the device in Skeeter's pudgy hand and saw he'd made the connection that it was controlling the woman's pain.

"Perform!" Skeeter shouted in a strained voice.

Eve began to crawl toward the two men that just entered the room. She used Hayden's pants to pull herself up, unbuckled his belt and his pants then began to run her hands under the fabric. This wasn't his idea of fun but having her hands on him did make his body respond. He moaned and closed his eyes, wondering how far she was willing to take it. He wasn't sure if he was glad Captain Black interrupted or not.

"Name's Victor Black, captain of the Blue Raven, where can I get one of them?" asked the black pirate with obvious desire, pointing to the device the fat man was holding.

"Skeeta' Boots at yer service. I only deal in exchanges, wha'cha be offering?"

Iain, fully engrossed in his Skeeter Boots persona, and Captain Black spent the next hour exchanging stories of their past indiscretions, each more gruesome than the last. Hayden couldn't believe Iain's imagination. He hoped that was all it was – if it wasn't, he made Black look an angel. The women were both chained to the wall now so he couldn't speak to them, without raising Black's suspicion, so he said, "I'm gonna get a drink."

Both nodded and waved him away as if they couldn't care less.

Hayden knew Captain Bryce was the consummate actor; the theatrics he felt went along with pirating was proof enough of that. He was always amazed at how deep into character he could get; each one so completely different from the others. He had to admit he was jealous of the captain's command of any situation; his only real asset was his brawn. He walked back into the bar and asked the girl working it for another ale. He didn't drink any of it. He wondered where Jaime was. He was about to leave to look for him when Black stepped from behind the curtain.

"Quite a fuckin' card, that one! I tried recruitin' 'im but I get the idea he enjoys his job too fuckin' much. I don't blame 'im," said Black, obviously impressed. "I'm gonna fetch the merchandise, you wanna come with or stay here?"

"I'll stay. I think I'll let that woman finish what she was about to start," said Hayden, smiling a very realistically wicked smile.

Black nodded to him and, after teasing the madam again for a bit, left the building.

The black pirate was back less than an hour later, alone. He found Hayden and Skeeter sitting at a booth in the corner and strode over.

Skeeter blew a ring of smoke from his fresher cigar at the man and said with a smile, "'Ello, Cap'n Black, are ya ready now?"

"I am. Can you walk?"

"No need," said Skeeter. He put two pudgy fingers into his mouth and whistled shrilly.

Jaime came running from behind the back curtain and dashed outside. Skeeter rose then and motioned them to follow him as he wobbled to the door. He threw a gold coin to the Madam with a wink as he walked by. Black looked at Hayden who only shrugged.

Outside was the small hovercraft Jaime had loaded into the shuttle earlier. It was barely big enough for Iain with the fat suit of Skeeter on. It dropped about two feet, hovering barely six inches off the ground, when he sat down on it. Once comfortable, he motioned Black to show him the way.

The craft sputtered and spit as it followed behind the men on foot, as if unhappy with its occupant. Skeeter cursed at it a few times then it backfired loudly and sped off at a much faster rate of speed than he apparently wanted it too, making Black laugh and the other two shake their heads.

The black pirate took them to a warehouse on the edge of town, guarded by several of his men. They all saluted their captain when he came into view. More than one's jaw dropped seeing Hayden, remembering him. Many sniggered loudly at the ridiculous man in purple pantaloons and then even more at the sight of the man behind him on a pathetic hovercraft.

Captain Black waited for the thing to stop fully then watched, in utter delight, as the man with all the jewels tried to help the bulging man exit it gracefully. He laughed aloud as Skeeter pushed the jeweled man away gruffly, knocking him to the ground.

Deep in his own part, Jaime rolled onto his hands and knees and crawled toward Skeeter, begging for his master's forgiveness.

Skeeter grumbled about not being worth the effort, "Get off'n yer ass a'ready ya right pathetic piece of shit, knew I shud'na taken ya in, ya insolent ass." Skeeter turned to Hayden then and said, "Masta' Fabris, you shud stay out here as well, da' less contact with the loverlies. Don't need ya getting' ideers," he said, placing a very fat finger to the right side of his nose and tapping it.

It took several tries for Skeeter to get through the tight door and several seconds to get his breath back once he was. He was bent over, holding his side. Finally, he stood, took a deep breath and turned to Black, telling him to lead the way.

Captain Bryce locating several guards while pretending to huff and puff with his head back. Part of his condition wasn't an act; the synthetic skin that made up Skeeter's body was heavy and hot. He counted ten in plain sight and knew probably close to as many were hidden. Too many for he, Jaime and Hayden to take alone, he would have to play along a little longer.

Black wasn't waiting for him so he had to all but run to keep up, one legged, relying on the cane to keep up appearances. Finally, in his strained Skeeter voice, he shouted for Black to slow down. "If I die fore we's able ta' complete da' transaction neever of us 'ill be 'appy."

This made Black laugh heartily, but he did stop and wait.

Almost breathing normally, Skeeter followed the black pirate through a wider doorway into a room with a large cage at the back. Sitting in the cage was nine girls. His heart sank and then sped up when he saw Caitlyn was one of them. She looked disheveled but didn't appear harmed. "Might I?" asked Skeeter, taking out a thick monocle and pinching it between his cheek and eyebrow, on the side of his good eye.

Black smiled and signaled for a guard to unlock the cage.

The girls began to cower and whimper, unsure what was happening.

Iain made like he was examining them, touching various parts of their bodies and making comments about their shape, teeth or skin. He winked at Caitlyn when he reached her but she was fooled by his disguise and spit in his bad eye. This actually made his smile, he knew then she was alright. "Righ' spunky, dat one, ain't she," he said, as he walked out of the cage. "'Ow ya wanna work dis? I kin give ya da' money fer all up funt, or we kin take 'em ta' da' auction an see what we gets?"

"How much are you offering?"

"Well now… Da' first tree 'er wurf tree thou apiece, I 'ill give ya twenty-five 'undred each fer da next five and five 'undred fer da' last one," the last one being Caitlyn.

Both she and Black looked flabbergasted.

"But she's the fucking prettiest in the bunch."

"Righ', see, she'd take too long fer'n me ta train."

"That's…" Black was counting on his fingers, trying to figure what Skeeter was offering.

"Tirty two tousand," said Skeeter, pointing at his temple. "Mind fer numbers."

"Fabris said you'd go as high as five each."

"At auction, day might'n fetch dat, an day might'n not…You'ud take yer chances." He pretended to be refiguring, then said, "I kin maybe go thirty five thou total and weave ya wiv da' righ' spunky one ta' do as ya' please. Dat's be'er dan four thou each."

"If you take the spunky ass bitch and leave me that fuckin' control device and a collar, ya got a fuckin' deal," said Black quickly, trying to hide that he believed he was really getting the better deal.

Iain had hoped the man would be interested in the device. He pretended to be thinking it over. "Maybe..." He pulled out an old style adding machine and punched the keypad, mumbling under his breath, as he entered figures into it, "could be profi'ble..." Skeeter turned back to Black then and said, "Seein' as dis is r first dealin' I 'ill go dis one fer ya... da' next'n I 'ill no be so righ' easily turned."

Black nodded as if the point was well taken and asked how long it would take him to get credits.

Skeeter pushed the comlink on his shirt.

Jaime came running in with a large black leather bag in his bejeweled fists. He pretended he was getting pulled over by the weight of it as he bowed and held it for his boss.

With a sour expression on his face, Skeeter opened it and rummaged around inside. He removed two sacks, a collar and the control device. He handed the bags and collar to Black and said, "The trainee wears dis."

Black let out a girlish yelp and dropped it as a sharp shock bit his fingers. He was smiling as he picked it up.

Skeeter winked his white eye at the black pirate and held the controller out to him.

"Can I contact you if we find more *merchandise*?"

"Do it true Masta Fabris, fer now. I musta be movin' my location righ' often so da' aut'orities canno' fine me," said Skeeter.

Captain Black nodded.

"Well den, chain da' loverlies up, if'n ya please, Black. And a righ' Goo' day to ya den," Skeeter said to the pirate as he motioned his servant boy.

Black followed behind him with the chained girls in tow. He passed the end of the leash to the fat man and watched him slowly move away from the warehouse.

Iain started to let himself breathe, thinking they were about free and clear. He looked behind him and saw Caitlyn had recognized Hayden and Jaime and that she looked about to say something, which would ruin it. He grit his teeth, he said, "Move yer arses," and yanked hard on the chain. This caused the first three, which included Caitlyn, to fall to the ground hard. When they got back up they all looked ready to cry but they'd gotten the hint.

Iain was waiting outside sickbay while the girls were being treated; wanting to be sure none had taken injury during their stay with the black pirate. Though he was worried about all of them his biggest concern was Caitlyn, of course. She was the only one that hadn't come out of the exam room, which worried him; he hoped he hadn't hurt her. He was about to go in to see what the hold-up was when Hayden stopped him.

"What is it?"

"I didn't like deceiving Black, Captain Bryce."

"Thought you didn't care for him or his ways."

"I don't, it's just... Why did you give him that device? You do know he will use it on other prisoners?"

"I made sure the batteries only had enough charge to zap once or twice more. Black will likely waste that showing his crew the new toy."

"Then he will think I cheated him..."

"No, he'll think Skeeter Boots cheated him," said Iain, not liking where this was going.

Hayden looked about to say more then apparently changed his mind and stomped away.

Iain watched him go. He knew then his problems with the man were just beginning. He shook his head and stepped through the doors into the sickbay.

Robyn started to clean Caitlyn's skinned knees; she was being gentle but Caitlyn was still tense. She knew this was because the last time she'd seen her was in Iain's cabin after a night of sex. She was about to explain when the captain stepped in. He was still in the Skeeter disguise so it took both of them a moment to relax.

"Can we have a minute alone?"

"Yes, Captain," said Robyn.

Iain pulled off the fake balding headpiece, the huge nose, bushy eyebrows and mustache so his own face now showed, though he looked funny in the fat suit and a white and green eye. He shook out his matted hair and said, "Had to be sure we weren't being followed before I could change. You alright?"

"How… " Was all Caitlyn could manage to say.

Iain smiled and said, "Your brother." He stepped over to the sink, removed the contact lenses from his eyes and peeled off the rest of the synthetic fat suit. All he had was a pair of black boxer shorts when he was done, he said, "Right bet I lost fifty pounds in that thing."

Caitlyn giggled at the silly look on Iain's face and said, "I'm sorry I almost blew it."

"I'm sorry I had to hurt you." Iain reached out gently touch the skinned knee closest to him. He had meant it in more ways than just that; the look on her face told him she had caught the dual meaning. "Are you okay? I mean… Black didn't…"

"No. I think I was… What happened to Claudia?"

Iain figured Claudia must be the girl Black and his crew had *enjoyed*. "I'm sorry."

"How much... I'll get you the money back..." she started, her throat hitching.

"No biggie, I have paid a hell a lot more for far less," said Iain smiling.

She jumped off the table and threw herself into his arms, crying hard into his chest.

Iain hugged her tight and stroked her hair, waiting for her to get it all out. When she was done he pushed her away from him a little and looked into her eyes. The smell of her filled his nose, the feeling of her body under the thin gown she had on was hard to ignore and he had little doubt she could tell this through his thin boxers. "Caitlyn," he said with longing.

Their lips met and this time there was no stopping their passion.

Winds of Change

"The cynic complains about the direction
of the wind; the romantic hopes it will
change; the practical adjusts the sails."
—   *Admiral Walter Flint*

Captain Bryce was relaxing in his office with his feet up on his desk, a digital tablet with recent news from Earth on his lap, a cup of half drank coffee on the corner of his desk and his eyes closed. This was the first time he had relaxed in close to three days.

With Dirk Riley's enclave gone they had been able to invade the open territory without fear of retribution. The pirate council had yet to assign it to anyone, so it was fair game. The news had reported sightings of Butch Herrick's and Victor Black's ships in the sector as well, also taking advantage of the opportunity. He had no idea how they had fared but Phoenix's coffers were more full than usual for it.

They were currently on their way to the party planet, Desana, for a real break, not just to re-supply. He and his crew preferred Ryger but they had spent too much time there lately.

The captain hadn't intended to stay at his desk so long but, in spite of himself, he started to doze off. Just as his body had fully relaxed the combox buzzed loudly. "Jesus!"

He jumped, nearly falling out of his chair. This knocked the coffee cup off the corner of the desk and the digital tablet from his lap. The coffee spread across the floor and the screen of the tablet cracked. "Shit, shit, shit!" he said as he grabbed a towel. It was too late; it had already soaked into the carpet, making him curse even more colorfully. He reached for the combox to ask Yard to send a grunt in to take the carpet out and clean it when it buzzed again; reminding him what had caused the incident in the first place.

"Go already," he snapped.

"Captain Bryce, Leftenant Commander Jared Way is on the link for you," said Kassie's voice timidly.

"Sorry Kas, didn't mean to snap, just surprised me, is all," said Iain quickly. "Put him through and ask Master Yardley to send a hand in here, if you please."

"Yes sir."

Iain hadn't spoken to Jared since he'd zinged him on the planet Sunnen, trying to escape from Admiral Flint. He had wanted to call and explain why he had done it but wasn't sure just what to say so he had left it alone. After all, what was one more CRF officer that hated him. He took a deep breath and held it as he pushed the receive button.

"Hello, Iain," said Jared a little flatly.

"Hey, Jared," said Iain. Without meaning to, his eyes went to the side of the CRF man's head. It was still a little pink but didn't look scarred.

Jared saw his eyes go to the spot. He turned his head and said, "It's healing quite nicely, thank you."

"I'm sorry 'bout that, I didn't know any other…"

"I know, Iain, the situation was unavoidable. The last few months have been unbearable as it was… with the questions of what, if anything, you said that might give up your location. It would've been far worse if they knew I was there as a friend rather than a hostage."

"You still consider me a friend, then? Not the nicest way to say thanks."

Jared only shrugged.

Iain put a finger up to him as the door alarm told him the grunt he had requested had just arrived. He said enter, waved the man in and pointed to the stained carpet.

The grunt nodded, rolled it up and left.

Once he was alone again the captain looked back at the monitor. "How's Senator Oakley? I need to thank him for his efforts on my behalf as well."

"He's better. It took him a bit to get over the death of Riley. He wouldn't allow himself to believe it until the body was recovered. Eve never told him of losing the baby, and she asked me to keep it quiet as well. Just as well, since I don't think he'd take it well." Jared looked away as if preoccupied.

"Eve will tell him in her own time," said Iain.

"Yeah..."

"You're acting right peculiar, Jared," said Iain, he hadn't been around the man a lot but he knew he wasn't one for idle conversation.

"You're quick, I keep forgetting that. I'm lately having an attack of conscience."

"Meaning?"

"I'm beginning to question my loyalty."

"I'm a right bad influence, am I?" teased Iain.

"In a way, yeah. I've had time to think, is all."

"How can I be of service to your conscience? I ain't gonna turn myself in to ease it," said the pirate, hoping the man wasn't suggesting that.

"Actually, Iain... I was kind of hoping you could use a new shipmate? I've got weapons experience, some knowledge of science and a lot of CRF routes and edicts?"

Iain was surprised beyond words and that was not an easy thing. He started to say something flippant, but changed his mind. "You understand what you are asking, Jared? You likely won't be able to return to your CRF position, or the CRF at all, if you change your mind."

"I do. I have been uncomfortable here for several years, your appearance only made the reality of it too hard to ignore any longer. What say, want me on your crew?"

"You on my crew would be a boon, Jared. I have no officer positions open just now, only grunts. And, I could only offer you three quarters of a share. That's better than my other grunts get but it's a far sight less than you could earn in the CRF."

"I have a fair amount saved up, and few needs," answered Jared.

Having no good argument against it, and kind of liking the idea, Iain said, "We are en-route to Desana. We will be there about two weeks. Maybe take a leave of absence and join up with us there. We can discuss it in greater detail, and you can fly with us for a bit, before you fully cut ties to the forces, if you like."

"Thank you, Iain... sorry, Captain Bryce," said Jared, suggesting he didn't need any more time to think on it. He smiled and saluted with a bent finger to his forehead before cutting the link.

"Whoa!" said Iain as he sat back.

"If it jams, force it; if it breaks,
it needed replacing anyway."
– Anonymous

"Shouldn't that have been a decision for all of us?" spat Hayden, after the captain told the officers of their soon-to-be guest.

"Captain Bryce always has final say in his crew, Hayden." Eve snapped back.

"You and Jaime usually screen them first though, *Eve*," Hayden slammed back at her.

"I've known Jared for years, he is a good soldier and I approve of him," said Eve.

"Yeah, I bet you do," Hayden grumbled under his breath, drawing upset and disapproving looks from Jaime and Yard who were sitting on either side of him. "He's a soldier, he's fucking CRF! How do we know he's not the same sort as Gideon?"

Jaime and Eve both barked at that, with just cause.

"Alright, the lot of you," snapped Iain, before it came to blows. "Jared proved himself our ally when he helped find me on Sunnen, Hayden. He right well could'a handed me over to Flint but he didn't. I may not trust him as much as I do all of you, but I do trust him."

"He's a high ranking CRF officer, *Captain*. He won't be happy taking a lowly fucking grunt position." Hayden said curtly, slamming his fist down on the table, spilling coffee and making most of them jump. "I don't think he will like pushing a broom."

"He understands what position he'll be in and is fine with it," said Iain sternly.

"Until he gets here…"

"Hayden, what is going on with you?" Eve asked.

Hayden and the captain's relationship had never really mended after telling Iain that Eve was pregnant. Her losing the baby, and then the captain using his past position with Captain Black to get Caitlyn away from him had only made it worse. More and more anything Iain said or did seemed to irk the man. His conduct was getting more aggravated daily, and more public. It was spilling into his and Eve's relationship, because she sided with Iain more often than Hayden felt she should. Jared's joining them now was apparently the final straw.

"I just don't like the way things have been fucking handled lately," said Hayden, pushing his chair back and standing up.

"We'll discuss this after the meeting. Sit down," started Captain Bryce.

Hayden was now walking stiffly toward the door.

"Master Fabris, you haven't been dismissed," said Mitch, hoping to stop him.

"Kiss my ass," said Hayden as he stepped out the door.

Eve looked at Iain with concern, "May I go?"

Captain Bryce waved her away and grumbled, "Dismissed!"

Jaime held back, once the others had left he said, "You okay?"

"No, I am not, Jay! He's being right *blatantly* insubordinate now and I'm getting fucking sick of it."

"Do you want me to speak to him?" asked Jaime.

"No, I'll go. He needs to know I ain't gonna put up with it any longer."

"If you kick a stone in anger you
will hurt your own foot"
–   Korean Proverb

Iain found Hayden and Eve in their cabin, or more precisely heard them. He pushed the door alarm button and waited. It slid open to a red faced Eve, who gave him a look that said she was at her wit's end.

He smiled reassuringly at her, "Bad timing?"

"Nope, I'm done here, Sir!" Eve stormed out.

"Good goddamn riddance, Bitch," barked Hayden as he picked up a heavy glass paperweight and chucked it across the room. It smashed into the wall, leaving a deep divot, only inches from the captain's head. The weapons master looked surprised and sorry, for a moment, then he got an impudent look on his face. "What the hell do *you* want?"

"Alright, Hayden, I could set your ass before the crew for breaking two articles already, wanna go for a third?" Iain was sick of pussy footing around.

"Do what you must, I care not!"

"I can't allow this to continue any longer, Hayden; it is beginning to affect the crew. I don't want to have to reprimand you but you are right fast leaving me no other option." The captain's usually calm voice was quickly rising. He took a deep breath, not wanting to go this route if he could avoid it. "Maybe you should take a break from us for a bit, go off and get yourself in order?"

"*You planned this*," shouted the weapon's master.

"Planned what?" asked Iain, spreading his arms out and squinting.

"Jared! You, Jaime and Eve have been planning him joining up since helping the Colum colonists, I *ain't* stupid. Now you can get rid of my *insubordinate* ass."

"Don't be ridiculous, Man! I had no idea Jared was gonna call, neither did Jaime or Eve. And I told him he was not, I repeat NOT, coming in as an officer. Jeez,

Hayden, you know me better than that," said Iain, hoping to get through whatever was clouding the man's mind.

"I thought I did once."

"What the fuck does that mean?" growled Iain. He didn't like where this was going. "I recommend you not say any more Hayden, before we both regret it."

"Don't give me any of your goddamn fucking charity, Bryce. I can't fucking afford it," said Hayden. He started to pass the captain to leave.

Iain wasn't nearly as big as Hayden but he was now mad enough that it didn't matter. He grabbed the weapons master's arm, swung him around, forcefully slammed him into the wall and used his left elbow in the crook of the man's throat to hold him in place. With the index finger of his right hand only inches from the man's nose, Iain spat through clenched teeth, "I've had right about enough of your goddamn fucking attitude, Fabris. *I am your captain* and I *will* be treated as such. You're gonna set on your ass a few days in the brig. See if that brings you to your fucking senses, though believe me, I'd love to do more to you right now!"

Hayden twisted Iain's arm back and pushed him away. "You'll do nothing to me!" He was out the door before Iain could stop him.

The captain punched his combadge and shouted for Eve to find the man and detain him by any force necessary then he straightened his shirt and left the couple's cabin.

Jaime met Iain in the corridor. The captain was messaging his arm, the same one he'd fractured not so long ago, that and the look on his face, made him uncertain if he wanted to ask the question this brought to mind.

Iain answered that question without him having to. "Yes, he laid hands on me, Jay!"

Eve's voice came over Iain's com then, telling him Hayden was in the hanger. Iain looked at Jaime and saw the same thought in the other's eyes. They reached the hanger bay at the same time as Dr. Carter, who had a tranquilizer ready. They found the man cornered by three grunts with rifles trained on him. Eve was on her knees before him, begging him to apologize before it was too late. The man guffawed and spit on the deck, the wet mass landed just in front of where the captain's right foot came to rest.

Captain Bryce stepped over the glob and motioned Eve to step away. "Hayden Fabris, you have broken civil order, ignored captain's orders, laid hands on a superior and have now been caught trying to steal a ship with the intention of deserting. Five articles broken, Man! You know the punishment for any one of these, by itself. You could face being marooned. If you apologize now, I'll go easy on you."

Hayden didn't respond; he only sat with his face down, shaking in anger.

"Unless we change direction, we are likely to end up where we are going"
– Old Chinese Proverb

Captain Bryce had smashed all the coffee cups in his office and was heading for the mess to get another when Eve appeared beside him. He wanted to ignore her but knew his bad attitude wasn't her fault. He waited for her to speak, unsure what he might say if he did first.

"May I speak plainly, Sir?" Eve asked quietly.

"Go."

"Giving Hayden time to think doesn't seem to be helping. I am really scared for him, Iain."

She was right, Hayden had been in the brig for four days and he still refused to apologize or ask for mercy. He wouldn't have anything to do with anyone, not even Eve. He spouted every swear known to man, and a few he had made up, whenever anyone came near him. He punched his combadge hard and said, "Jay, call a meeting, *now!*"

"We need to do something, besides giving him a time-out, to show the crew this is unacceptable behavior, Sir. Even if he apologizes tomorrow," said Yard.

"We're talking about Hayden, Yard," said Robyn.

Captain Bryce said nothing.

"It will set a precedence with the crew if we don't. We can't afford that; mutiny could be the least of our worries if they decide to test us," continued Yard.

"The Hayden I know would not have done these things," said Eve.

"Yet, he did," said Jaime; he was of two minds in regards to how to handle the man.

"I hate to say it but Yard is right, Sir," said Robyn, quietly. "The crew doesn't need to know he broke so many articles at once. They essentially only know about him attempting to steal a ship to desert. Perhaps we can punish him for just those?" Like Eve, she wanted to allow the man to keep some dignity.

Captain Bryce said nothing.

"He will learn nothing if we go easy on him and if the crew found out later that we did… They need to see they can't get away with breaking even one article." said Digger.

Captain Bryce still hadn't said anything; he just sat staring out the window.

All eyes turned to Jaime, he was the closest to the captain, at the table, physically, sitting in the chair next to him, and emotionally, as his best friend, and was far less likely to get berated for speaking to him. Jaime didn't look especially happy about that at the moment. "What are you thinking, Iain?" asked the man.

Iain turned his face to them. He rested his eyes briefly on each of their faces, stopping on Jaime, making more than one cringe and want to shrink into their chairs. His usually bright blue-gray eyes were almost solid gray, his jaw was clenched tight enough to show every muscle around it, his shoulders were tight enough to make the veins on the sides of his neck stand out and the tattoo on the right side of his neck pulse with the heated blood pumping under it. "If we punish all of his crimes together that would mean marooning him... So, yeah, let's just dump his ass on a dead planet and leave him to die? Who should have the honor of closing the ramp on him? Digger, You want it? Or you, Yard? *You* wanna fucking do it, Yard?"

Everyone shrank back. None of them had ever seen the captain this mad; they weren't sure if saying the wrong thing could set him on them.

"If we do each crime by itself the man will have no skin left to him, since the severity of two of his crimes should get him the gauntlet. I have seen the after-effects of a man going through that once... I would not want to see having to do it twice... even giving days between to recover… Right bit kinder to maroon him," the last words ended in almost a whisper.

Jaime knew Iain didn't want to do anything so drastic to any of the crew, but most certainly not to one of his officers, he didn't want to himself, but something did have to be done. "None of us wants to send him through the gauntlet, even once, or maroon him, Captain. He does need to be given a harsher punishment than just the brig.

"I think we all agree this is an unusual situation. He has already done the brig, so may I suggest docking his share of the next hit and have him flogged. Instead of the ten hits we would give for breaking one major article, double or triple that." Jaime felt sick to his stomach as the words left his mouth; as quartermaster, it would be him giving the man those hits. "We can explain to the crew that, though his crimes were severe, since these were his first offenses, he is going to be shown leniency."

Iain brought his gaze back to Jaime. He looked ready to say something venomous then, awakening from his malevolent thoughts, he slowly nodded. "You're right, as always, Quartermaster. Call a meeting of all the crew in the hold for this evening at six. Eve, send five grunts, amply geared, to fetch Hayden at half 'til. You may go with or not, whatever. He'll be given a chance to repent, per the articles, if he refuses we will dock him and he'll receive forty lashes, less one, on bare back. He attempts any further disruption after this he will be marooned." Captain Bryce was standing up as he finished saying this, he added, "Dismissed," dejectedly as he went through the door.

Jaime couldn't get his mind to relax nor could he find his center; it felt like he was falling off the edge of a cliff. Finally giving up, he opened his eyes and stood. He grabbed a fresh tunic and pulled it over his shoulders. He slid the door of his dojo open and was only a little surprised to see Iain coming up the hall toward him. He stepped back inside and waited for him. His saw that his demeanor was no less rigid than when he had left the meeting two hours earlier.

The two sat quietly for several minutes then finally Iain asked, "Did I provoke him in some way, Jaime?"

"I wasn't in the cabin with you but I witnessed his behavior after. I know you enough to know nothing you said or did could have, or should have, made him that mad. Like Eve said, something has changed in him. I have had a feeling he no longer wanted to be with us for a while. He was spoiling for a fight while you were gone."

"Yeah… while I was gone,' said Iain under his breath. "I fear punishing him will make him worse but I can't have the rest of the crew thinking this is acceptable either."

"Don't let this shake you, Iain. He stepped out of line. He would want any of *us* punished if the tables were turned," said Jaime.

Iain sighed and looked at his friend, "I've seen the crew looking at me sideways, Jay, like they think the head injury changed *me*... while I was gone. Even Digger and Yard have made comments. They think *I* was deserting then, which makes me more than a right bit ambiguous if I punish Hayden for attempting to do it now, don't it?"

"You weren't deserting," said Jaime pointedly. "I won't deny the thought crossed some of our minds, Iain, but it didn't stay more than a few seconds. We all knew what shooting Riley meant to you. It was frustrating because none of us could tell you that you did what any of us would have. I know I wished it had been me, and I think Hayden wished it were him."

Iain said nothing, only nodded. He appreciated his friend's strong belief in him but, to be honest, he wasn't entirely sure he *had* planned to come back. The hours after shooting Riley were still in a fog. He started to speak again when his com buzzed, "Go."

"Captain Bryce, Jared Way is off the larboard bow, should I open the bay?" said Kyle.

"Shit! Forgot he was coming?"

"Fighting for your principles is easier
than living up to them."
–   Old Chinese Proverb

Iain met Jared in the hanger. The look of pleasure
the now former CRF officer had on his face made him
want to either be sick or punch his lights out.

Jared saw the sour look on Iain's face and asked,
"You changed your mind?"

"No, just a change of situation. You may right well
wish you hadn't asked to join us by the end of this day,
Mr. Way."

Jared waited for Iain to explain the cryptic remark
but the man turned and walked out without another word.
Suddenly feeling a bit apprehensive, the new pirate
followed the captain to the conference room where the
other officers, with the exception of Hayden, were
waiting. He saw similar looks on their faces. The air in
the room was thick and less than welcome. He wondered
if Hayden not being there was because the man didn't
want him to join them.

"Welcome aboard, Jared," said Eve, trying to put a
friendly smile on her face.

The others said the same, looking in any direction other than him or each other.

Iain seemed to shake off a little of his funk as he said, "I don't need to read the articles to you again, since they haven't changed, so let's skip to the end. Jared Way, do you accept the terms of joining Phoenix Enclave?"

Jared asked, "Before I do, what's the matter?"

Yard and Digger started to say he didn't need to know, Jaime and Iain both said he deserved to know if he was going to join them. The rest all nodded to this.

"Come with us," said the captain.

They led Jared to the gangway that ran around the cargo hold. He saw what he guessed was the entire crew standing around the perimeter and a metal pole now set in the center. That pole had chains ending in shackles attached to it. He realized they were about to punish a crewmate for breaking one of the articles. He hadn't expected to see this side of the pirate life quite so fast. He had seen CRF soldiers being punished before but no one took it as seriously as this crew seemed to be. He knew Iain valued all of his crew, which was part of why he wanted to join them, but he couldn't imagine a grunt having this much affect. He was about to ask Jaime which one, and what they had done, when a group of security grunts entered with the accused. He realized why Hayden hadn't been in the meeting then.

He looked at Iain but the captain's eyes were fixed on the opposite wall, Jaime too was looking away. All but Eve had their heads and eyes down, staring at their feet. The crew below began to whisper as Hayden was led into the bay. He looked ready to chew nails as he eyes went to the officers standing on the gangway above him. Jared was glad there were five men with charged rifles at his back when he locked eyes with him.

Jaime walked along the gangway, down the stairs and took up a position beside the pole. The flogger was clutched in his right hand; ten strips of leather cording, stung together, each with a small metal tip. He snapped it once in the air, making several people flinch, then looked at the captain to give the word.

Captain Bryce nodded to the quartermaster.

Jaime called out, "Eyes forward, mouths shut, ears open!"

Iain cleared his throat. "Hayden Fabris, you stand accused of breaking five articles: disrupting civil order, failure to follow orders, laying hands on a superior, and attempting to steal a ship with the intention of deserting. As these are your first offenses we are prepared to show leniency. Your punishment for the first offense was time in the brig; the second will be to forfeit your share of our next haul, the third, fourth and fifth require more severe punishment; for these you will receive forty lashes, less one, on bare back. You have one chance to explain your actions, if we find your reason just you will be spared the flogging. What say you?"

Hayden slowly brought his head up but he only smiled sickly.

"Speak, Man, don't make us do this," Jaime said beside him, through clenched teeth, just loud enough for Hayden to hear.

Hayden ignored Jaime, spit on the deck and held his hands up to be chained to the pole.

"Very well," said Iain plainly. "Issue punishment."

Jaime locked the shackles on the pole around the big man's wrists and released the other three sets from his body then walked around him and ripped the back of his tunic off. Lines from an ancient act, like this one, long since healed over, crisscrossed the man's back. Murmurs went through the grunts at the sight of them.

The captain called for silence.

Jaime tried to focus his mind as he whipped the straps at his friend's back, gritting his teeth with every swing.

Hayden took the first ten without crying out, seemed oblivious to the next ten, began to grit his own teeth, to keep from making any sound, the ten after that, the final nine had him slumped in the shackles and groaning in pain. The skin on his back, the back of his neck and the tops of his shoulders was shredded and bloody, his chest and face was covered with sweat, his bottom lip was split open where he had bitten it to keep from making a sound, his wrists were peeled raw and bloody from straining against the metal cuffs and his head was lulling from side to side, only half conscious.

The medical assistance, Harris, and five of the security grunts removed Hayden from the pole and took him to sickbay to get his wounds tended. Dr. Carter left the gangway and followed them.

"Let this stand as a lesson to what you will get if you break an article on this ship. Dismissed," said the quartermaster, somehow managing to keep his voice steady. He slowly walked back up the catwalk and stopping between Iain and Jared, looking a little green about the gills.

Eve, Yard, Digger and Mitch all looked a bit ill also. They left the captain, Jaime and Jared on the gangway; no one feeling particularly sociable at the moment.

Jared wasn't sure exactly how to take what he had just witnessed. The CRF used laser whips, there was no blood, it was meant more as a psychological punishment. He was as white as a ghost as he turned to Iain and said, "That wasn't because of me, was it?"

Iain didn't answer at first, his mind still set on the image he had used to keep from seeing what was before him. "No it wasn't. Guessing you no longer wanna join us now though." He turned and walked off the gangway, not waiting for an answer.

"What did he do?" Jared asked Jaime.

Jaime didn't answer, instead he asked, "You want a drink?"

It took Jaime a while to find the words to answer Jared's question, when he finished he looked as drained as the mug before him. Jared remembered Hayden had been a little odd when they had helped the Colum colony but he hadn't known him well enough to know if it was just the way he was or not. He sat back and drew a deep breath. "That must've been hard for Iain."

"It was the very last thing Iain wanted to do, but had he no choice. He doesn't enjoy having to punish a crewman for breaking only one article; Hayden making him dole punishment for five at once was punishment to the captain. And that was the first time he's ever had to punish an officer… It Seems you are getting to see a lot of firsts from the captain," said Jaime. He realized how sardonic he sounded then and said, "In most enclaves Hayden only broke two crimes. If he were still in Black's crew, only one. Iain's not a cruel man, Jared. He is strict, at times, and expects us all to live up to his high moral code. Most of us strive to, and enjoy doing it. Hayden asked for what he got, by all rights, he really should've gotten more."

"And my timing sucks. Maybe I shouldn't have come."

"None of us would blame you if you have changed your mind. Being a normal pirate is not easy, our form of it is… unconventional."

"What will Iain do now? Will Hayden be able to go back to being… himself?"

"Some grunts have been able to, some rebel more and are eventually released or finally do desert. As to Hayden, I really don't know."

"It isn't holding on that makes one strong."
— *Jaimes A. Cable*

They reached Desana the next day and almost everyone was more than happy to be given shore leave. Few wanted to be on Phoenix just now, the air was thick with tension. Jared took the pirate oath and formally signed the articles then he, Eve and Mitch headed to the casinos. Yard, Digger and Norris went to the kitchen and restaurant equipment shop, in search of a new cooler for the galley. Their old one still didn't work right; it hadn't since shutting it down when the fuel was all but gone. Jaime was meeting Kohzu, to sell off the trinkets they took in their most recent haul. Kyle and Kassie were heading to some thrill rides at the amusement park. Iain was sitting alone, in his office, trying to get his mind around recent events.

The captain was about to pour himself a third cup of coffee, planning to add a healthy shot of whiskey to this one, when his door alarm buzzed. He said, "Enter," without really hearing himself. He turned to find Robyn standing in the doorway with a smile on her face. He gave her a look that said he didn't want it.

She didn't back down. "I'm prescribing you a day of fun off-ship, Iain."

"Not now, Robyn," Iain said flatly, as he poured that healthy shot of whiskey into his cup.

"Stewing is only going to make you sick," chided the doctor. "I have the authority to make this an order."

"Enough, Robyn! I'm not in the fucking mood!"

"Ok, Iain. I will be in the market if you want me," said Robyn, sweetly.

Iain knew Robyn was right, but he couldn't allow himself to enjoy himself right then. Knowing it was probably a mistake, but needing to do it anyway, he slowly walked to the infirmary. Two grunts, near as big as Hayden, were standing on either side of the doors; both saluted the captain as he walked past. He nodded to them and closed the doors behind him.

Hayden was on the bed in the far corner, his face turned toward the wall, on his stomach. The scars on his back and shoulders were still red and raised even after days of Bethany applying antiseptic. His back was still glistening from her last application and a strong medicinal smell hung heavy in the air.

Iain pulled a stool over, sat down beside the bed and cleared his throat to get the man's attention.

Hayden slowly turned to face the room, clenching his teeth and wincing in pain as he moved the tender skin on his neck. When he saw who it was he sighed angrily and snarled, "Come to gloat, have you?"

Iain sighed. "I didn't come here to argue. Believe me, this wasn't what I wanted."

"I'm not in the mood to pacify your emotions today, *Captain*," said the man through clenched teeth, in anger and pain.

"Can't we talk about this?" asked Iain, trying not to sound like he was begging.

"I don't see as there is much to discuss," the large man said in an irritated voice.

"Is this about the baby?" asked Iain.

"Don't fucking go there, Bryce," growled the man.

"If we are to stay shipmates, Hayden, we need to get this aired."

"You offered me a chance to take my leave, that offer still stand?" asked Hayden.

"It does."

"Dr. Carter says I'll be released tomorrow, I will be going then. If you have nothing else, I'm very tired." Hayden's head was facing the wall again as the last word came out.

"That's it then?" asked Iain.

Hayden didn't respond.

"Opportunities come in many forms."
— *Kohzu Wu*

Iain was standing on the cliff overlooking Phoenix, watching Hayden leave his ship, with a mix of emotions. He'd known it would come to this, deep down, and was okay with it. He truly hoped the man found peace. He turned and started away from it himself. He was enjoying the warm breeze on his face and neck as he rounded the last row of trees and came to the road to town. He was surprised to see both of his pilots running toward him. He stopped and waited to hear whatever was causing them such anxiety.

"Captain… Captain Bryce…" shouted Kassie, waving a yellow poster at him.

"What is it, Girl?" asked Iain, laughing himself at the huge smile on the girl's face.

"Captain!" said Kyle, as excited as his sister was, as he handed him the poster he was holding.

It was for an auction to be held on Penta, a merchant planet in the First BrimTier, in a month. The list of items up included everything from ships, private sales and confiscated by the CRF, to miscellaneous parts and, what had excited the twins: slaves. A holograph in the center of the poster showed a group of people linked together like they were members of a chain gang. The third and forth from the left of the group were two colored people; the man slightly slouched, the woman looking forlorn. Iain recognized them as the twins' parents immediately. He knew they had been saving up to purchase their parent's freedom for quite some time, now it seemed they would have their chance. The captain smiled and said, "We'll need to ask Mr. Wu to get invitations."

Life aboard Phoenix over the next four weeks was much more relaxed. Iain was back to his jovial self, Eve had gotten over some of her recent funk and Jared was fitting in quite well. Though he hadn't been formally offered the position, he was filling in as weapons master in the meetings, having more experience than any other grunt aboard. This meeting was for more than just normal pirating business though.

"Kohzu was only able to get us four tickets. I'll go as Skeeter Boots, since he is linked with such. Jaime will come as my servant boy. Jared, I want you in on this and Dr. Carter, to check out the merchandise."

"We want to be there too, Captain," said Kyle and Kassie in unison. Though they were both fully entitled to be in the meetings they usually had no desire to be. Usually they didn't have so much interest.

"No. If your parents recognize you they might cause a scene. It needs to look like we are there to buy slaves, not parents."

"You could disguise us."

"These meat auctions can get right graphic like and I don't want anything to go wrong." The twins started to argue but Iain was ready for them. "Don't test me, I'm not so easily bent anymore. If I even *think* either of you have left this ship, I will string your asses up to her hull!"

Both said they would obey him under their breath.

Iain dismissed them and started toward his cabin, feeling more like himself than he had in ages. He was looking forward to an off-ship adventure; and Skeeter was fun to play. He reached his office door just as Robyn came from hers. Their eyes connected, she smiled at him, he smiled back, then she walked to his side and the two entered his cabin in each other's arms.

"What makes vanity in others insupportable is that it wounds our own."
— François de la Rochefoucauld

Jared was waiting in the hanger for the captain, Jaime and Dr. Carter, ready for his first real pirating job. He was amused when Jaime stepped into the bay, dressed far more flamboyant than usual, with wide pantaloons in bright purple, a white shirt, a gaudy ring on each finger and a dangling chain ending with a green stone in his left earlobe. The bedazzled quartermaster smiled, winked and blew him a kiss as he walked past. Jared watched him directing a hovercraft that had seen better days and floated a little bit askew onto the shuttle. He didn't get a chance to inquire on it because his attention was drawn to the doors to see Robyn enter.

The doctor was wearing a white smock and had her medical bag but she looked nothing like herself. A red curly wig covered her blonde hair and thick glasses exaggerated her blue eyes to near ugliness. He smiled and nodded at the change.

His jaw dropped when the last of their party stepped in… or more like waddled. If Jared met the man walking toward him on the street he would have never known it was Iain – the transformation was that complete and realistic. He had heard reports of the man's skill in disguise but this was his first real experience with it. He smiled and said, "Impressive."

Iain had the same overall appearance as he had as Skeeter when he, Jaime and Hayden had gone to free Caitlyn from Captain Black, except he was wearing a deep purple silk shirt under the patchwork jacket and he had a frayed straw hat sitting on his head. The captain winked his white eye at Jared, removed that hat to expose the balding head with wisps of gray hair, and bowed, then slapped the hat back on top of his head and stuck a fat hand out to him. "Ello, Skeeta' Boots at'n yer service, Sonny. We 'ave only tirty tousand credits ta' spend chil'en, let's no be bringin' 'ome too much junk, ya 'ear me," said Iain as Skeeter Boots, flashing the odd half smile of his character.

They climbed aboard the sandpiper, which had been disguised to look like a ship more appropriate for a man such as Skeeter and started for the planet.

Kohzu Wu had come through with flying colors; the passcode he gave them to get into the closed auction was spot on and the ground security directed their shuttle quickly to a landing spot among several hundred other craft. Iain pointed at a black shuttle opposite them and said in his own voice, "Good thing I changed, that's one of Captain Black's shuttles."

An auction hand met them at the bottom of the ramp with paperwork to fill out in case of purchase and explained the auction policies. Skeeter handed him the four invitations. The man handed each a tag to show they were approved to attend and a paddle with the number 389 printed on it in big black ink. The captain thanked him and handed him fifty credits. The man smiled and wished them good luck.

The crowd was a mix of people, from all stations of life. Some looked like this was the first auction they had ever been to; others looked comfortable and had already staked out places in the buyer section, which was filling up quickly. Iain managed to get himself on the hovercraft without it spilling him and they too moved into the crowd to find a good spot for themselves.

It looked like they were going to end quite a ways back. Jared noticed the auction hand that had registered them waving for them to come to the front, he tensed, thinking they had been found out. Captain Bryce put a fat hand on his arm and winked the white eye at him.

The attendant had marked them off a spot in the front row, four nicely cushioned chairs and a small table had been set up for them; the number 389 set in each corner. Skeeter thanked the man again and handed him another fifty credits. The attendant bowed, wished them good luck again and went back to registering buyers.

"You never cease to amaze..." said Jared shaking his head in disbelief and awe.

"Those reports are never as colorful as they should be," said Iain, smiling.

"How did you know he would do that?"

"Instinct."

Jared nodded in admiration.

They had arrived with plenty of time; the auction for the slaves was set to begin at one o'clock and it was only eleven. Iain was also interested in another object on the list: the Gray Hawk, deceased pirate captain Dirk Riley's, ship, was to be sold at noon.

The hot sun was making Iain's life miserable as they waited. Robyn was worried the captain was at risk of heat stroke. She sent Jared and Jaime to find him something cold and wet. She was trying to inject a chilled saline solution into his veins to reduce his body temperature and fight dehydration but she was having a hard time getting past the synthetic fat that made up the costume of his arm. She had just moved to his leg, which didn't have as thick a covering on it, when a voice bellowed from behind them. This made her jump and stab his thigh much more forcefully than intended.

"Skeeter Boots, ya son of a bitch, s'that you?" said the voice of Captain Black. The man himself stepped up and stuck his hand out.

In trying to recover from the sudden needle thrust, Iain forgot to use Skeeter Boots' voice, "How are you, Black?"

Captain Black looked at him funny, then he saw the needle in the hand of the woman beside him and smiled, apparently thinking it was a pleasure drug. "Not as good as you, by the looks."

Iain went along with it, pretending to be high on the effects. "Yeah, all's good! Wha' ya 'ear afta'?"

"Sellin' off fuckin' hostages. I tried reachin' you, wantin' to do business again, but 'ad no luck," said Black, the suspicion thick in his voice.

"Oh, 'ell, I 'ad ta' release Masta' Fabris, wasn't workin' out, ya see," said Skeeter as if preoccupied, hoping Black would take the hint and go away.

"Funny you should say, he 'ad a similar story."

Iain choked on his tongue and had to bend over to keep from swallowing it.

Jared and Jaime were just coming into the section at that moment.

Jaime quickly went to Iain's side. He put one hand on his shoulder and began to pat him on the center of his back with the other. He called for Jared to open one of the bottles of water quickly. "I've begged him not to do that shit when it's so hot!" Jaime said in the lisp of his character, pointing at the needle in Robyn's hand.

Iain grabbed the water from Jared, sloshing some of it onto the stunned grunt, and drank half of it down in one gulp. This was partly to allow himself time to regain his composure and partly because he needed the liquid. He thanked Jaime and Jared and looked back at Black, "E's 'ear t'day, den is 'e?"

"Aye. Spoke to 'im not more'n ten minutes ago," said Black

"Tis a free auction. S'pose 'e is 'ear ta sell off merchandise as well?"

"Nope, here to buy a ship!" spouted Black. He seemed happy he knew something Skeeter didn't.

"Good for 'im. Left dat Bryce fella' den, did 'e?"

"About fuckin' time you ask me. That man makes me sick," said Black as if he, for one, was surprised it had lasted as long as it had.

Jaime put a hand on Jared's shoulder, seeing him tense up. Their acting weapons master wasn't used to the theatrics.

The auctioneer drew their attention away before Iain could respond. The man looked like he would be more comfortable on a farm, wearing blue coveralls and a checkered doo rag on his head. He began to go over the auction terms.

Black wished them luck, though it didn't sound even remotely sincere, and went to his section, only two over. He looked at them sideways every few sales as if curious of what they were there to purchase.

Iain finished the other half of the first bottle of water and almost half the second one. He informed Jaime and Jared that Black said Hayden was there and told them to keep an eye out for their former shipmate; the last thing they needed was for him to decide he was going to expose them in some misguided attempt to get back at the captain for every wrong he felt he'd done him.

The first section of sales included several single seat crafts and a few hovercrafts. Iain would've liked to bid on one of two starlings but not knowing how much the Cambridges might go for, he didn't dare.

Movement to their right caught Iain's eye. He saw Hayden moving up the row in their general direction. The captain motioned to Jaime who grabbed Jared's attention.

As if the situation wasn't tense enough, they saw Black was coming toward them from his section.

Hayden had a hard time hiding his surprise at seeing them there. He stumbled over addressing Iain as Skeeter at first. "How've ya been… *Skeeter*?"

"Isn't this a happy fuckin' reunion?" asked Black.

" 'Owdy, Masta' Fabris, I bin well, an' you?"

"Been better."

"Eard ya left Bryce's service, bet dat makes yer life a right bit be'er." Iain didn't much like zinging himself but with Black there, he had to keep up the act.

"It wasn't a very hard decision, let me tell you. Captain Bryce is an asshole that thinks his shit don't stink, and his crew is not but one step above vermin," said Hayden, glaring at Jared as he spit on the ground before Iain.

Again, Jared started to tense, and again Jaime touched his arm to stop him.

"Ell den, a good ting ya didn't let his stink rub off on ya den, ain't it," spat Iain, if he didn't know better, which at that moment he didn't, he would have thought Hayden was serious.

"Yup, no longer have to answer to Bryce's fucking *infantile* commands. I am starting my own Enclave."

"So, ye're plannin' ta' purchase Riley's ship 'en, 'er ya?" Iain said, trying to change the subject before the sun was not the only thing making him hot under the collar.

"Yeah, thought it would be *right* fuckin' inspired, seeing as *Captain* Bryce made it so *right* conveniently available."

"No shit! Bryce did shoot him, then? I didn't think he had it in him," said Captain Black.

"Maybe da man s'not so soft as 'e is bin made out ta' be, den," said Skeeter, trying not to get too put off.

"That remains to be seen. If you'll excuse me, I am not liking the air here." Hayden turned from his former captains and started to walk away.

Captain Black gave Skeeter a look of surprise then turned and followed Hayden.

Jared and Robyn both started to speak. Iain put a hand up and hissed for them to keep quiet. He was ready to burst as it was, anything they said right now would likely set him off.

He watched Hayden intently as he began to bid against two others for the ship pictured on the large poster that was being held up for viewing. Iain wished he knew what was going through the man's mind, he wished he knew if he'd keep secret his true identity, and, a little guiltily, he wished he didn't get the ship.

Hayden did though, for one hundred fifty thousand credits. He smiled and waved a quick middle finger at Iain then turned to Black.

Iain felt like he was going to go off like a rocket and take half the people around him with him. It was a good thing he didn't have his pistol on him just then. He didn't wish Hayden any harm but he hoped the pirate council gave him a territory on the other side of the Tier. He was about to tell the others he needed fresher air, looking quite peaked even through the make-up, when he saw Black and Hayden coming toward them again. "What now?" he grumbled.

It was little consolation but Hayden didn't look like he wanted to be back in front of the captain either, "I haven't seen you biddin' on anythin', nothin' to your likin'?" asked the black pirate.

"Thought you might be after one of the starlings," said Hayden, without really thinking about it – Skeeter wouldn't fit in one.

Black and Iain both looked at him oddly then Iain said, "Nope, I's afta' new en'atainas."

"Ah, slaves. Didn't see any that looked good enough for you," said Black sniggering.

"Clients wiv unusual tastes," answered Skeeter with a wink.

The auctioneer was back onstage now and was calling for their attention. A group of about forty people, aged between fifteen and close to sixty, of every sex and a few of foreign heritage, were led onto the stage. He said anyone interested in bidding on them could send up a representative to inspect the bodies.

Skeeter turned to his doctor and told her to go to it.

Hayden and Black both watched her walk onto the stage and work her way down the line. She stopped every few people so it wasn't obvious whom she was really interested in.

Hayden realized, as Robyn got closer to a colored couple, what his previous captain was doing, those must be Kyle and Kassie's parents. He knew Captain Black was intent on getting in the way of anything Skeeter was up to, just to be an asshole. Part of him knew he should stop Black, the twins had never done him any harm, but a bigger part of him was looking forward to seeing Iain sweating more than the fat suit was already making him. His former captain was trying to act like their presence was nothing unusual but his shifting eyes told the real story. He set his feet and prepared to watch the scene unfolding before him with great pleasure.

Iain was clearly agitated now, which was making Jaime nervous. Something told him one, or both, men intended to start something. He motioned Jared to step back and whispered, "Be ready, this goes poorly we may need to incapacitate Black or Hayden."

Jared nodded.

Finally the group that included the Cambridges was brought onto the stage. Skeeter hissed for silence. The auctioneer told the crowd each person's strengths then said they were to be sold in a lot, all eight at once, with a starting bid of twenty thousand credits, which was offered almost at once, the bidding climbing quickly to forty thousand.

"Shit!" said Iain, he had intended this to be under his breath. The thirty thousand he had on him would have been more than enough if it had been just the two of them.

Jared and Jaime both tensed this time but Black only laughed.

Hayden mouthed to Captain Bryce, 'not enough on you?' A strange smile came over Hayden's face then; surprising them all. He put his card up and said loudly, "Sixty thousand."

"Sold to 262."

Captain Black was looking suspicious.

Iain was speechless. His heart was in his boots and his stomach instantly twisted into a knot. He started to ask his former shipmate what his intentions were, hoping the purchase had not been out of spite, when Black pulled Hayden away. He slammed the empty water bottle down hard enough for it to embed near an inch into the soft ground beneath the hovercraft, and said, "What the hell's he playing at?"

"No man can think clearly when
his fists are clenched."
   –   George Jean Nathan

They stayed at the auction for the next hour as the rest of the slaves were sold off, waiting for Hayden to appear and explain himself. He didn't. Jaime and Jared did a quick walk through but couldn't find him and they noticed Black and his crew had cleared out also.

The suit Captain Bryce was wearing was really affecting him now and his agitated state was making the situation even worse. Sweat was pouring from every place possible, which was causing the spirit gum holding the fake bits of skin on his face to bubble and the edges curl.

"You have to get out of the sun," said Robyn, truly worried for his health.

Iain wanted to argue but he knew she was right.

They made their way back to the shuttle quickly. Once inside, Robyn helped Iain remove the suit and made him drink some more water before she'd let him stand. As soon as she did, he did. He grabbed a laser pistol from the holster hanging over the arm of the pilot seat, set it to kill and started for the door of the shuttle, not caring that all he had on at that moment was a pair of black boxer shorts.

Jared and Jaime both called for him to stop.

"I'm gonna find Hayden, ring his bloody fucking neck and get the Cambridges!"

"But, Black will see you," said Robyn.

"I don't give two shits if he does, I promised Kyle and Kassie I'd get 'em their parents and one way or another I am right fucking going to!"

"Black doesn't know me, Iain. Hayden's likely at the cashier paying for them and the Gray Hawk, I'll try to catch him there," offered Jared.

Iain started to say no, then he nodded and said, "Alright. Jaime, go too. If Black's with him say you want to make an offer on behalf of Skeeter for them."

Both men said, "Aye, aye, Captain," in unison and Jaime punched the bay door open.

Their simultaneous intake of breath made Iain turn quickly. He had his laser pistol up and aimed at the head of the man standing in the opening in a split second.

Hayden slowly walked up the ramp with Kyle and Kassie's parents in tow. "Tell Kyle and Kassie they're a gift from me," said Hayden.

Dr. Carter saw the skin on their wrists and necks were raw from the shackles. She motioned them to one of the seats and began to put a salve on the cuts.

Jaime motioned Jared to follow him into the helm section, leaving Iain and Hayden alone in the center of the shuttle.

"Thank you, Hayden. I will repay you, in full." said Iain.

"No need." He started to turn away, then added, "This brings us square, Bryce, I owe you nothing!"

"Hayden..."

"No! I want nothing more to do with any of you. I can't promise the next time I see you, either as yourself or another, I will be as fucking benevolent." Without another word, the former weapons master walked down the ramp and disappeared into the crowd.

Bait and Switch

"If you want to test a man's
character give him power."
—   Old Chinese Proverb

Jared hit the small rubber ball with his racket and watched it soar through the air, bounce off the back wall and rebound toward Iain. The captain ran to the center of the court and hit it back. It bounced in the center of a red line that went around the perimeter of the room about three feet off the floor, the so-called sweet zone, and whizzed back toward Jared. He twisted around and barely caught the edge. He did manage to keep it in the air, running into the wall to stop his momentum. Iain jumped for the ball but missed it entirely, landing hard on his stomach with a loud exhale of breath.

The captain stayed in that prostrate position. He slammed his racket into the floor and said, "Damn it!"

"I was champion of my squad three years running, Sir," said the former CRFer as he offered Iain his hand.

"Yeah, well, that's that ain't it," spat Iain. He shook his head sharply at the offered hand and pushed himself up. He threw the racket, sideways, into the corner, where it spun and clanged loudly before coming to rest on its side. He stomped to the door, threw it open hard enough to crack the window and exited the court.

Jaime, who had been watching the game from behind that window, jumped when it cracked. He watched Iain go then looked at Jared and made a weird face.

"Should I have let him win?"

"That would have only made it worse," said Jaime passing him a towel. "He'll get over it. He gets this way sometimes; don't take it personally."

It was hard not to. Jared had been with the enclave for nearly five months and was still getting mixed signals from the crew. He had thought the captain was glad to have him but in the last days even he had been less than encouraging. He wondered what he had done to change Iain's feelings about him.

"You want to get a beer?" asked Jaime.

Jared shrugged.

The two pirates walked to the bar across from the gym. Jared pulled the door open and stopped, it was pitch black inside. He looked back at Jaime just as the man pushed him inside. He stumbled over his own feet in the dark then was all but blinded as the lights suddenly came on full. He found the captain, all of the officers and several of the crew in the bar room. "What the hell's going on?"

"Phoenix is right heavy with grunts just now. We can't afford to keep any on that can't pull their weight. You suck royally as a grunt so I'm afraid I've got no recourse but to relieve you of duty," said the captain flatly.

Jared was stunned. He looked back at Jaime. The large man was standing in the alcove before the door, as if blocking his exit.

"We can't let you live knowing what you know of us off-ship so I see only one course of action," said Iain as he reached into his jacket.

"Iain, no!" said Jared.

"I'm gonna have to offer you the position of weapons master, for real," finished the captain. He pulled his hand out and showed the man he was holding a patch up with two laser rifles crossed behind a grinning skull and rendition of their ship's namesake.

It took a few seconds for what the captain had just said and what he was holding out to him to register. Jared opened his mouth but couldn't think of anything to say.

Iain could no longer keep a straight face. "I right recommend you think long and hard on this offer before accepting it, Mr. Way. It isn't offered, nor should it be taken, lightly. It'll mean more off world adventures, a higher level of responsibility and spending more time with me and him," pointing at Jaime. "Before you is your guns staff and your fellow officers. They, for reasons I can't right fully comprehend, have already approved of your promotion."

Jared opened and closed his mouth several times but still didn't say anything, in complete and utter shock.

"By God, we've rendered him speechless!" said Captain Bryce, chuckling softly. "Quick, Master Cable, make sure he hasn't swallowed his tongue."

All in the room, but Jared, burst into laughter.

"Assholes!" Jared said quickly, "I thought you were mad at me for beating you just now."

"Nah, I could've beat you if I'd really wanted to. You always make the same backhanded twist to hit the ball on the rebound, a strike to the wall an inch further away and you would have been overextended and down on your ass."

"Asshole!" Jared sputtered again.

"So?" asked Jaime, "What say you?"

"I accept, I guess, as long as you promise to never do this again."

"I'm sorry but we can't promise that, if another opportunity should present itself. We're all right pleased to have you as an officer, Jared," said Iain, holding his hand out to the man, who shook it a little firmer than usual. The captain pointed to a chair in the back of the bar with a medieval looking torture device beside it.

Jared smiled, knowing what it was immediately. He had wanted to get the enclave tattoo, to prove his commitment, from day one but Iain had refused, saying he wanted to be sure he truly wanted this life first. It appeared he had decided he was ready for that as well. He was a little shocked, and a little pleased, to find Eve was going to be giving it to him.

Halfway through the inking, Iain and Jaime pulled chairs over and sat across from the new weapons master, more than obviously up to something. They didn't say anything at first, just watched the two squirm under their stares for a bit.

Jared tried to ignore them and in a real sense had no trouble doing it. He wasn't disliking the experience but he wasn't exactly enjoying it either. It didn't help that Eve kept asking him if he was okay or if he needed a break. He kept saying he was fine but knew it was probably obvious he just didn't want her to know how much it really did hurt. When the security master stopped to clean her needle and change ink colors, the two men staring at them finally spoke.

"I remember my first tat," said Jaime, pointing to his right shoulder blade, where a red dragon rearing on its hind legs, with claws bared, spitting fire, was, signifying the CRI fighter squad, Dragon Troop. "I had an ugly man doing mine; wasn't the littlest sympathetic of the pain and suffering he was inflicting. I thought he was going to etch it into my bones."

"Yeah, my first was a right burly fellow as well, 'course mine was at Cape Benwick, and wasn't one I particularly wanted either," said Iain, rubbing at the inside of his left forearm where a patch of raised reddish skin was still visible. That tattoo was gone now, he'd had it laser etched off because he didn't want the memory of it, though he doubted he would ever forget it, or the looks of disapproval it had gotten him. It had been a five-digit number used to identify him as an inmate of the prison camp. "You know, I hear tell it can be a right sexual experience... with the right person doing it."

The needle jumped a little and stopped only an inch from Jared's arm. Eve and Jared both looked up at the captain and she actually blushed, something neither man believed they'd ever seen her do before.

The captain smiled and, feeling egged on by their reactions, said, "Course, you do realize now, Weapons master Way, that as you're an officer now you can't sleep in with the grunts."

"What are you suggesting, sir?" said Eve quickly.

"We, meaning all us officers, just want you both to know we approve," said Iain with a wink then he tapped Jaime's arm and the two walked back to the bar.

Eve waited a moment to be sure they weren't coming back before she looked at Jared and blushed again. "Better finish this."

Jared only swallowed hard and nodded.

Over the next hour the others began to wander out of the bar, leaving the two alone.

When Eve had finished the tattoo, she rubbed Jared's arm down with a cleaner and an antiseptic then pointed to a mirror behind her. "How does it look?"

Jared stood and looked at his left triceps, he flexed it a couple times. She had inked it in a way so when the muscles of his arm flexed the skull appeared to be laughing. He smiled at it proudly and whistled through his teeth. He added, with sarcasm, "My Da would've loved that."

"Didn't like tattoos, I take it?" asked Eve as she was putting away her equipment.

"Or pirates," answered the new weapons master. He placed the gauze pad Eve handed him over the image that was red and raised but looked really good and asked, "When did you learn to tattoo?"

"Just sort of picked it up after watching Jaime get his. I've been doing it for about five years now; when the captain gives the okay."

"He's a very cautious man, isn't he?"

"He has to be, not all that join truly know what we're about. Some grunts don't like the unusual code of ethics, or the fact that we give a portion of the hauls to the colonists, or that Captain Bryce is so selective with hits. He wants to be sure their level of commitment first. I'll give you though he's been especially cautious in your case.

"He wanted to be sure you weren't just enamored by us. We get ourselves into trouble faster than the others because we rub the CRF's faces in our hits. I think he wanted to be sure you were truly finished with them first, that you wouldn't feel any loyalty to them. Our world is fast, cruel and can be painful; it takes a certain type to be able to live on the edge of a sword, between right and wrong, and not get cut. He wanted to make sure you truly understood that and still thought you wanted this life," finished Eve.

"I think that's partly what drew me to you all. Just a year ago I would've said I despise all pirates and all they stand for, now I know my view was one sided. I still don't particularly like the stealing part but the adventure of it, and seeing the faces of the colonists we've helped, is beyond words. I honestly don't think I could do this any other way.

"I know not all the pirates are bad, though I don't think I would've been quick to even speak to any other pirate without a gun on them. Captain Black is bad enough but Dirk Riley scared the crap out of me. I know it bothered Iain to do it but I'm glad he's dead." Jared realized what he'd said then, "I'm sorry, Eve."

Eve still blamed herself for what had happened that day, if she'd obeyed Captain Bryce's orders to stay on Phoenix she wouldn't have lost her baby and Iain wouldn't have been hurt. "It doesn't hurt so bad now," she said, meaning both the physical and mental wounds. "Is it a completely crazy idea?"

"What?" asked Jared.

"You and me?"

Jared wasn't sure how to answer. They had gone out a couple times when they were at boot camp, but when she made leftenant commander before him they had to end it – it's against CRF rules for an officer to date beneath their rank. She was placed in Vice Admiral Wallace's unit and they hadn't seen each other again, until she stepped from the pirate ship on Colum.

He had to admit being near her again was part of the appeal of joining them but he was also drawn to Iain Bryce, intrigued by the enigma of a man. He wanted to know all that had gone into making him who and what he was. He felt they were kindred spirits of sorts. He hadn't lied when he contacted Iain six months ago to say he wanted to join them. He had been questioning his allegiance to the CRF for several years. He had thought he would resign his post and go back to university, then he found this new life choice before him.

He was game to rekindle their relationship but there was a wrinkle they, and she, was forgetting here – Hayden Fabris.

"Things between us had been strained for a while; even before we found out I was pregnant. He'd been saving to buy a ship of his own for near five years, before leaving Black to join us. I never told Iain because I didn't think it my place. He'd planned to break away when he had enough saved, on friendly terms. I have no doubt Iain would've been more than happy and encouraging to him, had he been given the chance.

"He wanted me to go with him, as quartermaster, but I told him my loyalty was to Iain and Phoenix first. He thought me being pregnant would change that but it only made it stronger. I told him I wouldn't consider having, or raising, a child anywhere else. I think that's what really sent him off his pins.

"He was jealous of my relationship with Iain, and Jaime. He accused me of being in love with them both. I do love them, like brothers, and the others, to a lesser degree. I was on this crew for four years before Hayden joined and I've gone through so much with all of them. They are my real family."

Jared felt a little guilty asking the next question, but he wouldn't begin anything with her until he knew the answer, "What are your feelings for Hayden now?"

"Part of me will always be his, I can't say otherwise and be honest with you, or myself, but we aren't the same people. He took it too far for us to have any hope of rekindling anything."

"Then, in answer to your question, no, it's not a completely crazy idea."

Eve smiled at Jared and asked if he liked roller coasters. He thought she meant it as a metaphor for their relationship but she meant the real thing in the theme park on the opposite side of town. The two started in that direction, meeting up with Iain, Robyn, Jaime and Bethany on the way.

"I paint objects as I think them,
not as I see them."
   –   Pablo Picasso

Iain and Jaime were giving Jared funny looks as they watched some grunts loading a crate that stood about five feet tall and four feet wide but was only six inches deep into the hold. It was an oil painting they had purchased, legitimately, from a gallery on Avonlea. It was for the director of one of their colonies. The funny looks were trying to get Jared to tell them what happened with he and Eve after they left them in the amusement park last night. Jared was ignoring them, only giving them a shit-eating grin.

Tolimon was another of their colonies that didn't need their help much but they checked in with them from time to time. The planet hadn't needed terraforming. It had its own atmosphere and with only a little work it was able to support most plants and animals native to Earth. It's director, Wesley Warren, was a wealthy man, but he wasn't like most of them, Captain Bryce could tolerate this one – most of the time.

Director Warren was an insufferable sot but he did have good merits. He had voluntarily chosen to go with the colonists to this planet twenty years ago. He had given up a lucrative position in a business conglomerate and a chance at a seat on the CRP because, like Iain, he didn't feel the people with less should be shunned.

The man did have ulterior motives, it hadn't been all for the sake of the colonists. As the richest man on the planet, and the only one with the desire and drive to be, he quickly became the people's leader. He designed and laid out the cities, set up the infrastructure, and wrote many of their laws. He was a decent director, for the most part. He made sure all were treated fair and had all they needed to have a comfortable life.

Warren did have eccentricities, as any rich man does. His main one was his obsession with art. He was an avid collector of all forms and of antique furniture. He often asked them to pick up a new piece he had acquired to add to his collections. He paid them for the service so Iain usually didn't mind.

The trip to Tolimon went smoothly but their luck ended there. They hadn't been able to raise anyone on the planet since they had entered orbit above it.

"Still no word from below?" asked the captain as he stepped in behind Kyle; Jaime, Jared, Eve and Robyn right behind him. They had been circling the planet for more than a day at this point.

"No, Sir." answered the pilot.

"One final attempt, then we will go down, invite or not. Jaime, do the honors," said the captain as he leaned on the bulkhead.

"Phoenix to Director Warren," said Jaime.

Only static answered.

"Phoenix to anyone on Tolimon?"

"Hello?" asked a very frightened sounding voice.

"Who is this?" asked Jaime, looking quizzically at the others.

"I'm Douglas Roth, is this Captain Bryce?"

"Where's the director?"

"Director Warren has been taken to the Pit."

The Pit was an abandoned mineshaft that had been shut down when the roof of the main access tunnel collapsed, trapping and killing several men inside.

Iain took the mike and said, "Why and by whom?"

"I can't, he's coming!" said Douglas.

"Who's coming?" There was no answer.

"Do you want us to land, Sir?" asked Kyle.

"No, we'll take a small group down, hopefully this is just a prank," his tone told them how much he believed this. "Jaime, Jared, Eve, get yourselves suited and ready, Dr. Carter, I want you on standby," said the captain as he left the bridge.

"The difference between genius and stupidity is that genius has its limits."
— Anonymous

Iain told them to keep their weapons handy but uncharged as they started for the doors of the director's office. Jaime touched his arm and pointed to a spot on the horizon that had once been the city's gardens. It was now a blackened patch of ground. They saw piles of rubble where homes had been and a row of what looked to be wooden crosses along the main road. Iain motioned them back to the shuttle and told Jaime to take them closer.

Five crosses lined the road, four with bodies on them. The first had been a woman, lashed to the structure by a hemp cord, she looked about two weeks dead; the others were men, two in near as bad condition, the other was still alive. Iain and Jaime knew him, the director's assistant, Tarren Smyth. Iain motioned Jaime and Jared to cut the man down.

"Captain Bryce? Is it really you? I tried to fight them," said Tarren, his voice dry and cracking.

"Easy, Man," said Iain, "Jared get some water." When the man had drunk his fill Iain asked, "What's happened?"

"Some men came. As is our way, we welcomed them. They looked strong so we offered them work, housing, clothes and food but they wanted more." He fell silent and closed his eyes.

Iain shook him gently and he opened them again.

"Captain Bryce?" he asked, then he started again, "Their leader forced his way into the director's home and set up there. The director was taken away when he tried to send the man away… They've burned homes of any that tried to stop them, each time one of us steps out of line they are taken and put on these…" the man pointed to the large wood cross they had just removed him from.

"Alright, Tarren, we're gonna send you up to Phoenix so Dr. Carter can treat you."

The captain, quartermaster and weapons master returned about an hour later, dressed as miners. They used some of the ore lying next to the road to streak their faces so they looked as if they'd just come from the mines. Iain had decided they would start at the local tavern. News and gossip typically came easily to tongues loosened by spirits.

The local tavern, The Soggy Boot, had always been a tidy establishment, now it was a shambles. Most of the barstools, chairs and tables were broken and piled up in the corner, several of the overhead lights hung lop-sided, their bulbs shattered, throwing parts of the room into shadows and the large mirror, behind the bar, was cracked in several places, being held together with duct tape.

Captain Bryce recognized the man behind the bar, though he couldn't come up with his name just then, he knew he was the owner. He was in his early fifties and had been healthy the last time Phoenix was here, now he had a black eye, a large scab on his lower lip, making it stick out, and was walking as if he had bruises under his clothes. He looked at them as they entered but he didn't seem to recognize them.

The captain said, "Three beers."

The man brought them and quickly went back to the other end of the bar.

Iain used what was left of the mirror to look around without being obvious about it. Three tables in the back had people at them, looking like they wanted nothing to do with anyone, two men were standing at the other end of the bar, both staring at their mugs, three were sitting at the bar beside them, talking in hushed tones, and three were playing pool, being obnoxious.

A slip of a girl with dark hair in a braid over her shoulder and big brown eyes came from the back room of the tavern and stopped at one of the tables in the back, taking the men's order. As the pirates watched, one of the three at the pool table strode over and put his arms around her waist, pulling her away and kissing her roughly on the neck. She started to struggle then stopped when the other two came up behind her.

The barkeep looked up quickly and started to move then stopped, lowered his head and went back to cleaning the mugs, wincing at her squeals.

Jared harrumphed and started to go to the girl's aid. Iain stopped him with a shake of his head and a sour face. It was killing him to listen to her screams as well but they were there to gather intel and they needed to stay out of trouble to do that. Hopefully the worse she would get was violated.

The act was over quickly at least.

The men came back into the main room after only a few minutes, buttoning up their pants and laughing raucously as they went back to playing pool. The girl stumbled back into the room moments later, pulling her clothes back into place. She looked around then burst into tears and ran out of the room.

The barkeep threw his towel down on the bar and followed her.

After a few seconds they came back out. The girl was still sniffling but she went back to taking the order of the men at the first table, none of which would meet her eyes now.

Iain called the barkeep over and motioned toward the three men, "Who are they?"

He didn't want to answer at first, shaking his head briskly, then he took closer at the man, "Captain Bryce? They's with the overlord."

"Overlord?" asked Jaime, not liking the sound of that.

"He have a real name?" asked Iain.

"Yeah, Terrance Lockheed. He showed up a couple months back. About a week ago he overthrew the director and said he was now boss of this planet. He's building an army, he says. Recruiting men from the outer villages with promises of women and lots of credits."

"What's he building an army for?" asked Jared.

"Don't rightly know. Something 'bout planning to hit some bank somewhere. He don't much like to answer questi…" The barkeep got a weird look on his face and turned around, pretending to be straightening the bottles lined up on the bar.

Movement in the mirror caught the captain's eye; he looked up to see the overlord's men staring at them, none of them looking especially happy. Through clenched teeth, he told his men to let them do whatever they wanted, seeing those men starting toward them.

One of them stepped behind each pirate and the larger one, the one that started the attack on the girl, said, "Who are you all?"

"We're from the Price Mine, just got off workin' a thirty day stint. Got us a couple days off," said the captain, holding his glass up to the others.

"I never seen you in here before," said the one on the right.

"We live in Brukner, only in town to visit a friend," said the captain quickly.

"Any of you play pool? None of these pussies will play with us anymore," said the big one, laughing wickedly.

"I've played a bit in the past, it's been a right little while though. What game you playing," asked Iain, shrugging dispassionately as he set his mug down.

"Twelve ball, Best two outta three?"

Iain nodded and walked over to the rack on the wall. He took his time selecting a stick, picking up each and looking down the length, trying to find one that was usable. Nearly all of them were either bent or warped. He found one that was straight enough to play half decent with and stepped up to the table. "Who goes first?"

"You can," said the big man.

"Good 'nough. What are the stakes?"

The overlord's men looked at each other, then the big one said, "How's about your life, what that be worth to ya'?" They all broke into exaggerated laughter.

"What if I win?" asked Captain Bryce undaunted.

"Uh?" said the man, obviously not expecting it. "You can take one of theirs," he said, laughing again. The other two started to as well then realized what he had said and stopped, glaring at him. He pulled them aside and whispered something to them, which made them both laugh again.

Iain wasn't lying, it had been awhile since he had last played but he had no doubt he could beat these oafs. He would fake otherwise to begin with, in hopes of getting information.

Twelve Ball was a version of pool popular in pubs on the smaller colonies because it was easier to keep score of and follow along with when drinking heavily. The balls, numbered one to twelve, were to be hit in numerical order into one of six pockets around the table. If one went in out of order or failed to go into a pocket the player's round ended. The player who sunk the most balls was the winner. It was most often played head to head. It wasn't Iain's favorite version of the game but it was simple enough to win – or lose.

The big man stepped up to the table and waited for one of his friends to rack the balls. He placed the grayish cue ball before him and sent it across the table to break.

Iain walked around the table slowly, twice, leaning down in various places, trying to find the best angle to hit ball one from, rubbing a block of chalk over the end of his stick as he did. When he found the angle he liked, he leaned down and hit the cue ball toward the number one ball. That ball jumped a little, rolled into the left wall, bounced once, rolled into the end wall then slowly toward the right side center pocket, coming to a halt just an inch before the drop.

"Oh, bad luck, Mate!" said the big man, obviously not meaning it. He leaned over and finished the ball's intended conclusion then stepped around the table to set up his next shot. "My name's Carl, that's Nash," pointing at the bald one, "And, Geoff's the quiet one," motioning to the shortest of them, who waved stupidly.

"I'm Iain, and my friends are Jaime and Jared."

"Iain and Jaime? Them's awful girly names, ain't they," said the big man through a thick laugh, winking at his two cronies who laughed a little back. "You say you work in the mines?"

"Mm hm, getting' right tired of working me self to death in them though. Bet I must near cough up a ton a' ore dust near every night."

"There are other ways of makin' a livin'."

"Like workin' for this boss a' yours?" asked Iain, leaning against the wall as Carl went through the balls.

Carl looked up and nodded.

"What kinda things are expected?"

"Not much, he needs muscle is all," said Carl as another ball went in a pocket.

"For what?" asked Iain, getting out of the man's way.

"A big job off-world is all I know," said Carl as two more of the balls disappeared.

The man was hitting the balls easily into the pockets around the table. He looked like he was going to clear it when the grayish cue ball followed the five into the right corner pocket. The man cursed colorfully and slammed his fist into the wall, but did step back so Iain could take his place.

Iain shrugged. He pulled the cue ball out of the pocket, placed it at the left back corner, leaned over and, without even looking, sent the next ball into the right corner pocket. The last six went into various pockets around the table seconds later.

Carl was flabbergasted for a moment then he scoffed and said, "You was bound to get a couple."

Iain nodded for Geoff to rack the balls up again.

Iain sunk the first two quickly as he asked, "If a person *was* interested, how does one go 'bout joinin' your overlord?"

The look on Carl's face suddenly wasn't so congenial, telling the captain he wouldn't be as talkative if he thought he might lose. Iain hated looking foolish but for the colonist's sake he messed up the next shot. The number three ball should've been an easy sink but he rammed his stick into the maroon felt, sending it spinning off mark. He cursed to imply it had been accidental.

Carl laughed and finished the shot, "You may not live to find out."

Iain laughed at the joke and waited for Nash to rack the balls again then he broke them for the final game. Carl pocketed the first three balls quickly, making Iain nervous; he needed a chance to play. Hoping to cause a reaction, but not get himself killed, he quickly spit out, "I hear tell the overlord's a criminal."

The man stumbled forward and sent the fourth ball careening off line, missing the pocket he was aiming at by almost two inches. He looked up at Iain, who had an innocent look his face, and said, "Does that matter?"

The pirate captain stepped up and finished the man's shot. "S'pose not," he said then sunk the next four effortlessly.

Seeing the nine ball was blocked by the eleven and twelve, and no easy way to get it out without one of the others going into the pocket, out of order, first, Carl smiled and said tersely, "Tell ya' what, ya clear this table and I'll set up a meetin' for ya'."

Iain slowly walked around the table, twice, scratching his chin as he checked the different angles then, choosing one that looked like it couldn't possibly work; he leaned over and slowly nudged the cue ball.

That ball spun as it rolled, softly tapped the nine ball, which barely kissed the twelve ball, then continued to the center pocket; falling effortlessly. Meanwhile, the twelve rolled sideways into eleven and the two slowly rolled towards ten. The three balls fell in the right corner pocket in sequential order, making two loud clicks as the balls came together. Iain stood up, leaned on the slightly warped stick and said arrogantly, "So, when's the meeting!"

"Be here tomorrow at noon."

Iain nodded.

Without another word Carl dragged Nash and Geoff out of the bar.

After they were out, Jaime asked, "What now?"

"Now we see about the director," answered Iain.

The barkeep came up to them and said, "Either you're really brave or you're an idiot."

Jaime and Jared looked at each other and quickly said, "An idiot!" at the same time.

The captain put his hand over his heart and swooned as if he'd been mortally wounded, then nodded and said, "You are all probably right. Any idea the director's situation?"

The barkeep went to the door, looked out into the street in both directions then turned back and answered, "He, his wife and son were taken to the Pit. We've been supplyin' meals for them so I believe they're still alive, though I know not if they are well."

"Any idea how many cronies this overlord has in his service?" asked Jared.

"I believe they've not more than fifty."

"What of the local police?" asked Jaime.

"Some's joined the overlord, some's been put to death, some's just biding their time."

"How do we get in touch with the latter?" asked the captain.

"I will try for you, how do I let you know?"

"We'll be back here tomorrow," said the captain, pushing his half full mug away from him.

The door to the bar opened then and the barkeep jumped. He relaxed when he saw they weren't a threat. He quickly nodded to Iain and went to wait on the newly arrived customers.

"Let's go," said Captain Bryce. He tossed a couple credits on the bar and motioned his men out with him.

"Yes, risk taking is inherently failure-prone. Otherwise, it would be called sure-thing-taking."
   –   Tim McMahon

The three pirates slowly made their way up the steep slope to the base of the Tower Mine entrance. The road would've been a much easier traverse but they didn't dare take it in case some of the overlord's men were moving about it. They crawled to the edge of the ridge across from the opening, hid in the underbrush and watched the entrance. They saw nothing out of place, it still looked abandoned. Iain was about to send one of them to take a closer look when two men stepped out of the darkness.

"I don't wanna kill 'em outright yet, in case more show up. Set your pistols to stun only. Once inside, we split up. I want to find the director and his family but we can't free them yet, for all I'm sure they'll wish it, just make sure they're alright."

The guards hadn't moved, other than to pass a cigarette back and forth. Iain signaled Jaime to take out the one on the left and Jared the one on the right. Both men squeezed their trigger at the same time, dropping both men at the same time. They waited a few seconds to be sure no one else was alerted to them falling before breaking their cover and running to the entrance. Jaime and Jared took the feet of the man they had shot and dragged their bodies to a shed beside the entrance.

They entered to long unused mine tunnel and found a few yards in it split into three shafts. Jaime took the one on the left, Jared took the right and Iain stayed straight.

Iain and Jaime found their ways anything but easy, having to maneuver over and around sharp rocks that had fallen from the walls and timbers that had been used to shore up the sides. Once he got past the initial blockages, Jared found himself walking along a fairly open shaft.

The new weapons master was listening to what he thought was the echo of dripping water but soon realized were voices. He came to a large opening where the tunnel broke into three others. He pressed himself against the cold, rough wall, slowly inching his way out. An area had been caged off across the back of the cavern. Inside it was two men, one in his fifties, the other but a teenager, and a woman, who was crying. The men were trying to console her but she wouldn't stop. It didn't take much for Jared to figure out this was the director; exactly as Iain and Jaime had described him. He was about to step out when he saw movement to his right.

"Shut that bitch up, or I will!" someone shouted; the words echoing down the passage.

The woman quieted a little but didn't stop.

"Please, let my wife and son go. I'll give you anything you want, I'm a wealthy man. Just tell me what you want?"

The guard spit in the director's face and laughed then started toward where Jared was hiding.

The weapons master checked that his pistol was still set on stun then stepped away from the wall and fired it, completely surprising the man. He made sure he was still alive then dragged him to the back of the cavern and tied him up with some rope hanging over a broken ore cart, abandoned when it went off the tracks.

The woman did stop crying then, all three were now looking at him expectantly.

"Quick, there are two more," said the director.

Jared didn't say anything to them, only punched his combadge and called for the captain.

Iain was about halfway through a tight cleft when his combadge beeped; his arms were pinned to his side so he couldn't reach it. "Brilliant! Why didn't I say yes to the voice activated ones?" he asked a small spider sitting on a web above him. It jumped at being blown on. He cringed and closed his eyes and mouth, thinking it might fall on him. After a few seconds he opened one eye and saw it was still attached to its web. He nodded at it and began to work his way back to a spot where he could reach the button. "Go."

"I've found the director, Captain," said Jared.

"The third guard?" asked Iain as he tried to pull a cobweb out of his hair and only got the sticky strands wrapped around his fingers for his effort.

"Stunned and tied up, sir."

"Marvelous, I'll be right along," said the captain. He looked back the way he'd come, at all the obstacles he was going to have to climb back over, and sighed.

Jaime reached the passageway Jared had taken at the same time as the captain; both were covered with cobwebs, mud and ore dust and had skinned palms. They both guffawed as they started up Jared's path, at finding it so easy going.

They could hear the director begging Jared to unlock the cage before they had walked more than a few feet. Not wanting to shout down the corridor, which would have echoed, Iain punched his com, startling Jared and the director, and said, "Mr. Warren, kindly hold off your tongue; we don't want anyone to know we're here, thank you."

The director turned his angry glare on the captain as he came into the passage, "This man has said we must remain here. I demand you release us, at once, Captain Bryce."

"Director Warren," said Iain very patiently, "We can't right now, the overlord will know. I've arranged a meeting with him and will assess his threat then take him out. You need to stay here and say nothing about us in order for this to work. Understand?"

The director looked like he was going to argue but then nodded.

"Now, what can you tell me of him?"

The recon they could do in the planet mostly finished, the pirates climbed into the shuttle.

The captain commed Phoenix as they left orbit. "Kyle, we're just leaving Tolimon. Ask Mitch to see what he can learn of a man named Terrance Lockheed, been calling himself the overlord, and have him meet us in my office. And have Robyn meet us in the hanger bay. The quartermaster and I have minor injuries to be attended to."

"Aye, aye, sir."

"What of the director, Captain?" asked Eve.

"He's not especially happy about his situation but he's healthy. I told him to sit tight and we'd get him free as soon as able."

"He won't like that much, Sir."

"So be it. How is Mr. Smyth doing?"

"Dr. Carter says he'll live but he has a long road ahead of him. He was dehydrated and hadn't had any food in four days. He says he's been living off what he could catch of rainwater," answered Eve.

"Not fun."

Two beeps through his com badge let him know the statement was heard and the security master was in concurrence of the sentiment.

Captain Bryce was still drying his hair when Jaime, Jared and Mitch came in. He tossed the towel away, went to the coffee pot and poured out three cups, Mitch had sworn off the stuff months ago, made him too jittery. He handed one to Jaime and one to Jared then took his and sat down behind his desk. He put his hand out for the man to begin when ready.

"This Terrance Lockheed is a right nasty piece of work, Sir; he makes Captain Black look like a puppy dog. He has escaped from every prison they have tried to put him in and has over five hundred murders attributed to his name. You remember the horrid massacre on Lafayette five years back? That church that burned with fifty colonists inside?" All three nodded, remembering the graphic photos the digital papers had shown. "Yeah, well, he's the one that ordered it done. *Nasty* piece of work, this one," Mitch said; obviously vexed. "I don't know what your options of strike are, I found no weaknesses."

"I can think of two, right quick," said Iain quite shrewdly. "Pride and greed."

"We should forgive our enemies, but only after they have been taken out and shot."
 — Anonymous

Rear Admiral Anton Anders disliked it this far out-space, the term used loosely by the CRF for the entire region of space beyond the First BrimTier boundary, which they considered dead space. He had never liked being stationary; he missed his battlecruiser, Archimedes, and his crew. He knew he would not see them again anytime soon. He was constantly reminded in messages from Earthside that he had let the pirate, Iain Bryce, go, not once but twice. He didn't feel guilty for the second time, he had truly felt it was the right thing to do after he had essentially saved his current crew. He had vowed he would never do it again, no matter what the pirate did or the circumstances it was done in.

At that moment he was lost in thought of just what he would do the next time he had the pirate before him; smiling with the pleasure of it and squeezing his hand as if it was around the man's throat now. He was pouring himself a scotch as the combox on his desk buzzed. This made him jump and slosh some of the amber liquor over the edge of his glass. "Damn it, this had better be good!"

"Commander Anders, we have intercepted some com waves I believe you'll want to hear."

"I'll be up shortly."

Anton stomped onto the bridge, thinking this was another jab from Earth forces. He didn't need it today.

"First we got this one, which sounded suspicious, Sir," said the helmsman as he turned the dial on the unit up. Two men could be heard speaking to each other, the echoes after the words made it sound like they were in a tunnel or cave.

Anders' mood perked up instantly, he didn't recognize the first voice but the second one made his heart jump. "Oh, good, good."

"There's more, Sir. We began to check this same frequency every few minutes after and got another." They heard the pirate captain telling someone to hold their tongue, rather harshly.

Rear Admiral Anders nodded, "Where are they?"

The man at the helm smiled as he started the next exert, and they heard Iain telling two of his crew they were leaving Tolimon and returning to the ship.

"This place, Tolimon, any idea what it is?"

"It's a planet two sectors from here, in this Tier, Sir," answered the helmsman.

"Excellent. Enter the course into the computer of my battleskip and have two garrison geared and ready to depart within the hour."

"Yes sir."

"You can win a fight without fighting,
but it is tougher to do, and the enemy
may not cooperate."
— Anonymous

Captain Bryce told Jared to outfit fifteen grunts with weapons and for Eve to take them down in the second sandpiper but to stay aboard until she got word they were needed and she wasn't to contact them before. He, Jaime and Jared climbed into the other to make their meeting with the overlord.

The barkeep had fresh bruises when they walked into the bar. Jared started to ask who had given him them when the man nodded toward the back room and shook his head just as Carl and Geoff stepped into the room.

They seemed a little surprised to see them.

"Still interested then?" asked Carl.

"Thought we would go hear what your overlord is offering, got to be a right sight better than them mines."

"Alright, I got a hovercraft outside," said Carl. He shoved Geoff toward the door and started out it himself.

Jaime and Jared were right behind them. The captain held back a moment, wanting to find out the barkeep's luck with finding them help on the planet.

The man shrugged and mouthed 'not many'.

Iain tapped the top of bar twice, "Keep asking."

The front of the director's once beautiful estate was wrecked and the conditions inside weren't much better. The foyer was largely untouched but the sofas in the parlor were shredded and the artwork; many they had brought the director themselves, were either sliced up or had graffiti on them. The destruction made the pirates sick to their stomach. They hid it well though.

It was several minutes before Carl returned with the man who was calling himself the overlord. He was bald and had a tattoo of an eagle flying over a mountain range with the letters TRL underneath on the right side of his scalp. He kept his head turned slightly so this mark was visible to all in the room, obviously proud of it. Iain immediately didn't like the man. He'd seen crazy men before, Dirk Riley and the pirate he'd gotten Phoenix from, Eugene Boscoe, were both off their rockers; and he'd seen evil men, Victor Black and Vice President Nikolas, but this man had a look even beyond them, this man would be capable of anything, without warning.

The overlord was wearing an antique breastplate shaped like a muscular torso, complete with nipples, abdominal muscles and bellybutton, over a black t-shirt. Guards covered his upper arms, elbows and legs from upper thigh to knee, black leather gloves with the fingers cut off were on his hands, and his left hand was resting on the grip of a large laser pistol, which was fully charged.

He looked over the men before him and said in an accusatory tone, tilting his head a little and raising an eyebrow, "Carl says you've been working in the mines? I had them gone through quite thoroughly and don't remember anyone like the three of you being described." He looked at the captain hard and said, "Have we met?"

"Doubt it. Been workin' deep in, clearin' out one of the spokes for the next blastin'," said Iain.

The man nodded as if that was feasible. "You all look like you can handle yourselves well enough. Any of you afraid to die?"

"We've come right close more than once," said Iain. Jared and Jaime; both nodded. "Everyone has to die someday, may as well go with a blast!"

The man laughed and asked, "Do you have family on this planet?"

"Not a lick," said all three men in unison.

"Very good. We are having a meeting tonight to go over the final plan. Carl here will find you a room and get you geared up for the assault."

Iain's eyes went to the clock on the wall; he was a little surprised to see it was undamaged. He needed to com Eve. "We need to report back to the mine in an hour, let us tell 'em we ain't coming back, won't you?"

Terrance looked like he wanted to say no to this but he smiled instead and said, "The meeting is at eight, don't be late."

The three pirates started back to town, wanting to check in again with the bar keep. The road before them was suddenly flooded with bright lights. Iain thought at first that the overlord had remembered where he knew him from. He couldn't be so lucky. A squad of CRF soldiers with fully charged rifles came into the light and surrounded them.

"We's just on our way back to Brukner, Sirs, it's the next town over," said Iain, holding his hands up to show he was no threat. "We work in them mines there, just out having drinks at the local pub." He added, hoping they would take them as colonists. That hope was dashed when their commanding officer stepped into the light. "Brilliant!" said the captain, thick with sarcasm.

"Why go out on a limb? Because that is where the fruit is?"
— Frank Scully

Three chairs were set before the desk in the rear admiral's office. Jaime and Jared sat in the side ones, leaving the center one for Captain Bryce. Iain didn't sit in his; he was pacing behind them as Jaime filled Jared in on their first run in with the CRF officer.

"Anders lost a star and was reassigned here, deep in out-space, because he took Gideon Welch, who we now know is Gideon Brody, a CRIA agent, to the vice president thinking he was Iain," said Jaime.

Jared nodded. He had heard of the man. He now remembered he had seen him with Vice President Nikolas when he had gone to Earth with Senator Oakley once. "Brody and Anders were both the butt of many jokes after," said Jared

Jaime continued, "He let Iain go after the epidemic that hit Ansi was accidently spread to this station. He said he couldn't watch Iain's life be taken after he had shared the cure with him and his men."

"Meaning he will redouble his effort to take us now," said Jared.

"Yeah, I right doubt we'll get away so easily this time," said Iain, just as the door behind him opened.

"On that you're correct, Mr. Bryce," said Anders, sounding even more pretentious than usual.

The rear admiral walked to the side wall, pushed a panel to expose the bar and asked the men if they wanted anything, all three refused. He shrugged, poured himself a scotch and went to his desk. "I recognize Master Cable," said the rear admiral quite cordially, nodding to

Jaime, who nodded back, "But you are new to the crew, yes?" he asked, looking at Jared

"Rear Admiral Anton Anders, may I introduce my weapons master of six months, Jared Way," said Iain, quite proudly, which made Jared smile.

"What of Master Fabris?" Anders asked. The look that came to their faces made Anton curious; it didn't last long, recognizing the name of the man before him, "As in former Leftenant Commander, Jared Way?"

Jared nodded a little slowly, Iain smiled proudly.

"Cable here, Ms. Oakley, Crewman Kinden, and now Mr. Way? You are one for collecting our best, aren't you? Tell me Bryce, what is it that makes a person willing to go against all they've known for you?" asked Anders rhetorically, and more than a little incredulously.

Iain flashed his trademark smile; he had a feeling the man before him was finding himself closely fitting that account, though he was trying to fight it.

"What are you up to on the planet below?" asked Anders, over the top of his glass.

"How did you know we were below?"

"Intercepted messages."

Iain nodded. He made a mental note to ask Digger to check the com scramblers were still working when they returned to Phoenix. He thought about holding his tongue but was almost certain he could convince the rear admiral to help them; the CRF should be interested in capturing this overlord as well. He stood up straight, squared his shoulders, crossed his arms over his chest, locked his blue-gray eyes on the rear admiral's hazel ones and said, "A man, named Terrance Lockheed, calls himself the overlord, has taken up shop on the planet. He has imprisoned Tolimon's director and family in an abandoned mineshaft, burned homes and killed any not willing to accept his rule. We've been acting as miners trying to infiltrate the man's gang in hopes of deposing him."

The rear admiral had a hard time looking away from that steady, confident gaze. He did finally, feeling like he had to or he would lose himself. He smirked, halfheartedly and tried to force out a sincere sounding laugh. "Still telling whoppers, ay? I'm pleased you have not lost your flair for theatrics. I am guessing you are the overlord in this story?"

"I may be a right lot of things, Rear Admiral, but you know full well that ain't what we're about," said Iain candidly.

"Yes, that's right, the civilized pirates," replied the rear admiral a little too curtly.

Iain could tell the man knew he was right and could see his hard shell of dislike cracking. Iain pushed on; hoping he could wrench a few of those cracks into chasms, "Have your men look into Mr. Lockheed's past, you'll find he's right far more dangerous than me and mine to allow free."

Anton looked at the pirate sideways for several seconds then he leaned forward, pushed the button on his combox and asked for a background check to be run on the man.

Iain leaned between the chairs, one hand on the back of each, as they waited for a response. It was only minutes.

The man repeated, almost verbatim, what Mitch had said but he added that Lockheed was near the top of the CRF most wanted list.

The rear admiral looked up at the pirate captain and said, still a little suspicious, "How do I know this man is truly there?"

"Your intercepted messages. If I'm not mistaken, I had just called up to my ship to ask my procurement master to look into Mr. Lockheed's background. I would have no reason to pull that name out of the big black if I had no idea anyone, other than my crew, was listening."

Anders wanted to argue but couldn't; reluctantly nodding in concurrence. He stood and walked to the window that looked out over the moon below them. He clasped his hands behind his back and curled his thick fingers together, opening and closing them several times.

The captain looked from Jaime to Jared, winked and mouthed, 'wait for it.'

Anders swore under his breath, not believing he was about to do what he swore he'd never do again. The CRF man turned back to the pirates and said, "What is your plan to take this man down?"

"He is planning a hit off world; a bank somewhere. We had planned to have one of our shuttles intercept Lockheed and capture him."

"Alright, Bryce, how can I help?"

"Never ceases to amaze." Jared shook his head.

"Absolutely correct, Mr. Way, absolutely correct," said the rear admiral.

Iain and Jaime were only smiling.

Eve jumped a little when the captain's voice came over the shuttles com. She grumbled, "Captain, where the hell have you been?" before she realized it.

"Master Oakley, right watch your tone, you're not speaking to Jared here," said the captain, amused at her audacity.

"Sorry, Captain," said Eve quickly, "You had me worried, you were supposed to check in three hours ago."

"We'll be landing shortly, with Rear Admiral Anders and his men," said Captain Bryce, knowing what her face would look like without even seeing it.

"Okay?"

Eve lowered the ramp of the shuttle and waited for Iain, Jaime, Jared and Anton Anders to step in. The rear admiral had a look halfway between amusement and bemusement on his face. Eve looked at each of them, ending on the captain. She looked like she wanted to ask a question but wasn't sure how to word it.

Anticipating what she wanted to know, Iain said, "Anders picked up our conversations of earlier today and came to fetch us for prosecution."

He sounded far calmer than Eve thought he should, given who it was beside him.

"I explained the situation we found here to Rear Admiral Anders; he has rightly agreed that Lockheed is a bigger threat than us. He is gonna help us take the man out, and will get to collect his bounty, in exchange for us going free." He flashed the knowing half-smile he was famous for at her.

Eve shrugged, having become used to the captain making enemies into allies. "How do we proceed?"

"Commander Anders has a full garrison on his shuttle, which he's putting under your command, Master Oakley. Jaime, Jared, and I are gonna continue to the meeting as planned. When I give you the signal go to the Pit and fetch the director and family. More guards may have been put on since our earlier incursion, so be ready. You have permission to use whatever force is necessary." The captain turned then, about to leave his security master and the rear admiral to work out the finer details.

"Bryce," said Anders suddenly, making all but Iain jump. He had a look halfway between pleasure at being able to help and disbelief that he was helping a pirate as he pulled three devices out of his pocket. He handed them to the pirate captain and said, "These may come in handy."

Captain Bryce looked down at three square units resting in the palm of his hand. He recognized them immediately – personal electromagnetic interrupters. He looked at the rear admiral with pleasure and said, "What are you doin' with these?"

"Something we confiscated from another pirate, and… I forgot to turn in. I thought they might come in handy one day; seems this may be that day. If I'm going to help you it may as well be all the way."

"Good enough!" said Iain. He gave the man an appreciative nod then left the shuttlecraft.

"You will turn over new leaf only when you learn we must all write on scratched-out pages."
—   Mignon McLaughlin

Anton turned to Eve and asked, "Well, Madam Pirate, how do you wish to proceed?"

"If you please, I ask that you address me as Master Oakley and I will address you as Rear Admiral Anders, we have both earned the right," said Eve.

"Very well, Master Oakley, what do you wish of me?" replied the rear admiral, a little amused.

"I want you and your men to stay put. I need people I can trust behind me, people who'll do as I command without question," said the woman pointedly.

"I know I told Bryce I'd bend to your will but on this I'm insisting. If I'm to allow you to leave this planet without chains about your body I, at least, will be with you, Master Oakley."

Thinking it was probably best to keep him close so he couldn't try anything, Eve nodded and said, "Alright, but if you step so much as a toe out of line I will shoot you and say it was the overlord's men, understand?"

The rear admiral nodded and only smiled.

Phoenix's security master, Rear Admiral Anders and fifteen pirate grunts slowly worked their way up the same hill Captain Bryce had used the day before to scope out the mineshaft entrance. The captain said the director was being kept in the center shaft; otherwise they were flying blind.

A man was walking back and forth across the tunnel opening with a laser rifle held firmly in his hands, no other guards were visible. Eve motioned Anders back and told one of the grunts to get himself in place with his rifle ready, the rest would backtrack and approach from the road.

The overlord's guard saw the large group of people just as they broke the final bend in the road. He didn't have a chance to alert anyone of their presence because the bullet hit the man square in the temple. Eve ordered the body removed, told two other grunts to take up watch and started into the shaft.

"That was a fine shot," said Anders; unable to hide how impressed he was with the grunt's shooting ability.

This made Eve smile in secret triumph; she had trained that grunt herself.

Within minutes the pirates were swarming the mineshaft. They took out three more guards, the final one had his rifle to the director's head when Eve and Anders stepped into the opening between spokes in the mine.

"Now, now, Son, you really don't want to do that," said the rear admiral, in his most condescending tone.

Eve rolled her eyes and said, "Fuck the niceties," as she brought her gun up and took the man between the eyes before he even had a chance to answer.

"What did you think you are doing, Master Oakley, he could have shot me!?" spat the director indignantly. "Where's your captain? Where is Captain Bryce? I'd like a word or two with him, *let me tell you*. This is absolutely unheard of; it's downright atrocious…"

"Director Warren," started Eve, seeing him getting very wound.

"…to be treated this way by strangers is one thing, I would expect different, better, of Captain Bryce. He should know better! He left us here to rot and die and I want to know why…"

"Director…"

"What made him think this was an acceptable way to treat me…us? Bring him here at once!"

"Director Warren, *shut up*. We are here to get you out of here."

"Well, *well*, do it then. Now, if you please," said the pompous man. "Take me to my home, I must see what those heathens have done to it," said the director abruptly, trying to straighten and clean his dirty attire, his wife and son doing the same as they stepped beside him.

"You cannot return to your home yet; we're taking you to our shuttle. When we're given the all clear then you may." Eve could see the man was about to say that wasn't acceptable so she motioned a grunt forward and said, "Shoot him dead if he says another word."

The director said no more but he was sniffing quite indignantly.

Rear Admiral Anders fell into step beside the female pirate; "Your captain actually likes this man?"

"No, but he is better than most."

Eve inventoried the weapons they'd recovered from the guards and ordered several grunts to carry them back to the shuttle then waited for the last of her men to come out of the shaft with the director and his family and fell into step behind them.

Anton wasn't especially comfortable watching the pirates taking the weapons, knowing it was wrong on many levels, but he said nothing, only put a disapproving look on his face. He waited for the security master to walk back in his direction.

"That was a clean operation all around, Master Oakley. You should have stayed in the CRF. I wouldn't be a bit surprised if you might even have made rear admiral by now."

Eve gave him a look that said not only did she not want his opinion and wondered why he felt the need to compliment her at all and said, "We need to get back to the shuttles to be ready for Captain Bryce's signal."

Anders walked beside her most of the way back but didn't say anything, deep in thought, which suited Eve fine; then he apparently found a question he couldn't answer on his own, or keep quiet any longer.

"Can you tell me what is it about Iain Bryce?" he asked, just loud enough for her to hear.

Eve shrugged. Her father had asked her that same question, as had others, but she'd never been able to put it into words, just a feeling of rightness. She tried to explain and was only a little surprised when he only nodded in agreement.

"Whether he's right or wrong in his actions, in the way he goes about achieving his goal, you can't help but admire his tenacity. He makes you *want* to believe he is right," said the rear admiral, very insightfully.

"That pretty well sums it up," said Eve as they reached the shuttle.

> "It's impossible to make a plan fool-proof because fools are ingenious."
> — *Admiral Walter Flint*

Iain, Jaime and Jared felt extremely uncomfortable waiting with the overlord's cronies for him to make his announcement. They were standing in what had been the director's gallery, a long hall that connected the east and west wings of his estate. Landscapes and portraits, by long dead artists, that had once been beautiful hung on the walls around them.

A minute to the hour Carl appeared at the end of the long room and held his hands up to quiet them.

Terrance stepped on the dais and held a fisted hand over his head, pumping it. A cheer went through the room. Once it quieted, he said, "We are ready for the siege. We have received the plans and will be handing out placements at the end of this meeting. We have three shuttles waiting to take us to the First Tier planet, Minara. We will be departing in one hour and arriving in waves, the first will take out the front guards, second will take the lobby hostage and the final will take the vaults." Another loud cheer interrupted further instructions. Terrance held his hand up again, to silence them.

Jaime flinched at the mention of his home world.

Iain had only been to Minara a few times, visiting the quartermaster's sister, but he knew there was only one depository on the planet, and Jaime's father was the head of it. He pushed the button on his combadge "Eve, don't speak, just beep once if you can hear me." One beep sounded. It drew dirty looks from the men around them. Iain waited for them to return their attention to Lockheed before whispering, "The overlord is readying to leave the planet heading for Minara in three shuttles in about an hour. I want you and Anders to intercept them. Please remind him we'll be aboard one of 'em so he shouldn't blast 'em away! Least not 'til he knows which one we're on." Another beep sounded. Again a few dirty looks were thrown at them but no one seemed aware of his impending mutiny.

Jaime and Jared were assigned to shuttle number two and Iain number three, the one with Terrance, Carl and Geoff. Something told Iain this wasn't good. He put an innocent look on his face as he was directed to a seat, the three men sitting down around him. He tried to look in awe of their leader, like the others, but knew it wasn't believable by the look they gave him back.

"Tell me why you look familiar?" asked Terrance.

"I have that kinda' face?" said Iain, trying to sound more dumb than sarcastic.

"No, you have a distinctive face, like mine. I can see in your eyes that you don't like taking orders; you enjoy giving them."

"I 'ave ad ta' be spoken to lots by the mine master for talkin' back, that whatcha mean?"

The man brought out an ident reader much like the CRF use to identify people. He held it out to the man across from him without saying anything.

Iain smiled smugly and said, "I am pirate captain, Iain Bryce."

Geoff was staring at Iain as if seeing him for the first time. "You're the one who left the vice president on the desert planet and killed the pirate, Dirk Riley... You got big brass ones, ain't ya?" said Geoff, in awe.

Both Carl and Terrance shot ugly looks at the man who quickly shut his mouth.

The overlord turned his piercing gaze back to Iain. "Why would a pirate, such as you, be interested in joining my employ? Not finding much treasure lately?"

Iain remembered telling his procurement master that the ways to get to the man were either to question his pride or appeal to his greed; he chose to test his pride first. "I've heard stories; wanted to see how good you are, to be sure I'm better."

"You what?" the man growled.

Carl and Geoff both backed away then, thinking the two might fight. Not entirely sure who would win.

"I'm one of the best lock pickers, and safe crackers out there, once got a ZF1200 open in less than a minute," said Iain, shrugging nonchalantly. This was one of the hardest safes to crack, no one had *publicly* admitted to being able to get into one in less than three minutes. "I've often thought of trying a bigger, and a right bit more fiscally rewarding, application for my brilliant abilities. When I heard what you were planning. thought I'd invite myself along. I didn't think you'd mind the competition."

"You think you can open the vault quicker than me, do ya? We'll have to see, won't we?"

Iain looked at the two men beside him and gave them a satisfied look, "Right sounds like a challenge to me, don't it boys?"

Geoff nodded quickly; Carl wasn't as enthusiastic, seeing how upset Terrance was. Geoff was too busy staring at Iain, as if he was a god, to notice.

"You got one. We each take a vault and see who can get in first."

Iain reached his hand out to take the overlord's to seal the challenge. He thought briefly of calling Anders off, feeling his own pride being tested, but didn't get to think on it long.

"Two shuttles and six starlings just dropped from jump, they've got us surrounded," said the pilot of their shuttle.

"Outrun them!" shouted Terrance, still locked in a staring contest with Iain.

"We can't. Their guns are hot."

"Surrender or we'll take you out," came a voice over the shipwide speakers.

Not wanting to, but having no choice, the overlord looked away from the pirate captain and ordered Carl to get them outfitted with guns and for all to be ready to fire on any CRF that step foot in the shuttle.

Captain Bryce was surprised when Carl handed him a rifle then quickly moved to stand with Terrance, leaving him and Geoff alone. He seized the meager opportunity. "Geoff, you help me you can join my crew."

"What about Terrance?"

"With me you'll be... well, you'll still be a criminal, but not like this," shrugged Iain, realizing it was a pretty lame offer.

"Stealing for the poor you mean? Yeah, might be good for a bit. What do you want me to do?" asked Geoff, still in awe of the man beside him.

"Don't fire on the CRF men."

"I thought you didn't like the CRF?"

"Most yeah, but these guys are on my side." Iain had to bite his tongue not to laugh at how moronic that statement had sounded even to his ears.

"Wow."

Iain fought the urge to bash the man beside him in the brain right there. He really didn't want Geoff as a crewman, the man was a complete dolt, but he needed an advantage and just now he was the only thing he had, feeble as it was.

The ship shifted as a docking tunnel was attached to the hull then the hatch was released.

Captain Bryce told Geoff to shut down his rifle, when he saw the light blink off he hit the button on the EMI Anders gave him. He watched the other's rifle charge lights go out then heard the ship's engines die. The pilot shouted that the CRF must have hit them with an EMP because shuttle two was dead as well. As if punctuating this, the hatch opened and a man in full body armor stepped through with a large rifle in hand.

Terrance ordered his cronies to charge him but no one moved, except to drop their rifles and raise their hands without being told. He turned to look at them and found Captain Bryce's fully charged rifle in his face. "You? You were in on this?"

Iain only smiled, shrugged and nodded.

Rear Admiral Anders brought his rifle to bear as well, but it wasn't aimed at Terrance.

"Lower the rifle, Anders," said Iain.

Anders had a look halfway between amusement and longing on his face as he smiled and said, "I think it's you that needs to lower yours, Pirate." Then, to drive home the point, ten CRF soldiers took up positions behind him with their rifles aimed at Iain's chest.

Iain was beyond flabbergasted; he had apparently misread Ander's from the start. That thought didn't sit well for the pirate who'd always prided himself, and was envied for, his ability to read people's intentions, that thought bothered him more than being taken prisoner. He dropped his rifle and put his hands up.

A message came through the officer's comlink at that moment telling him the other two shuttles had been taken successfully as well. The rear admiral ordered them all to be led to the brig, for the shuttles to be grappled and towed back to the outpost then turned and left.

"Laws control the lesser man. Right conduct controls the greater one."
— Chinese Proverb

Iain was fuming as the soldiers directed him down the hall at gunpoint. The layout this ship was different than Phoenix so he couldn't tell where they were taking him. He knew it wasn't the brig. He was stopped at a door on the central deck, which slid open to a guestroom; Eve, Jaime, Jared and the grunts were all inside.

"Did Anders betray us," asked Jared.

"Could be. S'pose we'll find out when he decides to grace us with a visit."

It was near two hours before the lock on the door released and the rear admiral stepped in with a satisfied smile on his face. Jared started toward him but Iain put a hand up to stop him. He turned his well-practiced glare on the rear admiral.

"Mind telling me the meaning of this, Anders?"

"Captain Bryce, you look right ready to have an aneurysm, should I fetch my medic? Wouldn't want you to collapse before me again," said the rear admiral, fighting back a laugh.

He had a look on his face that was so completely exultant that it was all Iain could do not to jump him and strangle the life out of him.

"Relax, Bryce," said Anders, realizing he had reached the end of the amusement rope. "I didn't want Lockheed to know I was helping in case he thought to use it as leverage to reduce his sentence. I don't wish to lose more stars on account of you, if you don't mind."

Captain Bryce hoped he was being forthright, "So we aren't prisoners?"

"No, we're about to set down on Toliman," said Anders, smiling cunningly. "I must admit, I did seriously think, for the briefest of moments, of keeping you though."

Iain smiled back and tried to laugh off his reaction, not liking that the man had been able to play him so well. "Had me right good, Anders; got a flair for theatrics yourself, have you?"

Anton smiled and titled his head in answer to that. "I just thought I'd see how deep *your* pride runs."

Iain nodded to the rear admiral and bowed to him in true respect, the man was now an equal in the pirate's eyes. "What of my shuttles?" he asked.

"You will get them back as well. May I have the EMI devices back?"

"I was hoping they might be a reward for helping you capture Lockheed. After all, you will be getting a substantial enough prize for that," said Captain Bryce.

Anton looked hard at the pirate then said, "I suppose they are more useful to you. Very well, but if you're found with them you didn't get them from me."

Iain smiled and put his hand over his heart

The rear admiral motioned them out then walked them to the hanger.

After the first shuttle was out and Jaime was warming the second, Captain Bryce turned to the CRF officer and said, "I 'spose you're gonna give me your spiel about next time we meet not being as right accommodating now, are ya?"

"It would seem required, given who we are, but as the last encounters have shown, I can no longer say it and mean it. Instead, I'll say, well see when next we meet, yes?"

"Sounds like a plan," said Captain Bryce. He put his hand out to the man. "I owe *you* one now, Anders. Feel free to call it in anytime, long as it's not to use me to get your rank back."

"That you will not have to worry about. For all I never would've believed this just two days ago; I have found assisting you… educational. I can honestly say I hope you are never captured because it would be a far less interested big black without you flying in it," said Anders, then he smiled and added, "Now, get the hell off my ship before I change my mind."

A Pound of Flesh

"It's for that moment when pleasure
and pain become indistinguishable."
—   *Tessa Stanney*

Iain, Jaime and Jared had been playing poker in the aft lounge for nearly six hours. They were all getting a little slaphappy, and more than slightly drunk. Jared's stack of ceramic chips was increasing, Jaime's was hovering and Iain's was shrinking, very fast. They were currently playing Jaime's favorite version of the card game, called Texas Hold 'Em.

Iain's cards were the king and ace of diamonds, he was first to bet this round; he only had fifty thousand left so he slid the puny stack to the center of the table, going all in. Jared folded; his deuce of spades and seven of clubs wasn't worth even the twenty thousand he already had in as small blind. Jaime called; placing another ten thousand in to go with the forty thousand blind he had already paid.

Iain flipped his cards over then Jaime flipped his, two queens, of spades and clubs.

Harris, Robyn's medical assistant, was dealing; he whistled loudly. This got a very irate look from the captain, who suddenly found himself very sober. He discarded the top card and took the next three, laying them in a row on the table for all to see, the queen of diamonds, eight of diamonds and deuce of clubs.

"Ooh, another diamond and it's yours, Iain," said Jared, trying to will him some luck.

Iain looked at him sternly and said, "Don't jinx it!"

Harris discarded another card and turned up the next card: a six of diamonds. Iain pumped his arm, he had a diamond flush, five cards of the same suit; the only thing Jaime could beat him with was the queen of hearts.

Eve stepped through the hatch at that moment and stepped up to the table behind Jared, rubbing his back. She drew in a breath when she saw the cards and that the captain was on the verge of busting out. She started to speak but he looked at her sternly and held up a finger.

"Any card deck but the queen of hearts, if you please, Harris," said Iain, leaning forward and staring at the deck as if he could will it to flip what he wanted.

Jaime looked from Eve to Jared, smiling, then to his captain and said, "You gonna space me if this is?"

Harris hesitated, holding the river card, the final and deciding card, in his hand.

"Just turn the card, Man!" said Iain impatiently.

He did and they all caught their breath; it was the queen of hearts, giving Jaime four of a kind.

Iain grunted painfully, stood up and said, "Good show, Jaime." He pulled the left side of his shirt open and grumbled, "Go ahead, take your pound of flesh," then he chugged the last bit of whiskey down and added, I'm retiring to my cabin to sulk."

"Sorry, Captain Bryce," said Harris. He only got a low growl in response. He shrugged and said, "Master Oakley, do you want me to deal you in?"

Captain Bryce was usually lucky at cards, he'd won the ship they were on in a poker game, but lately he couldn't catch a break. He was now down ten thousand credits. He slid down the ladder outside the lounge and disappeared into his cabin in silence, glad that he hadn't run into anyone en route.

He was just about to strip out of his clothes and climb into his bed when the com unit buzzed. He gave an exaggerated sigh, tossed his hands up in defeat and flicked the switch. He expected to see Kassie's face and wasn't able to hide his surprise when instead he saw a man he hadn't seen in near fifteen years.

The man on the monitor before the captain had a slight graying at the temples of his short auburn hair, was wearing wire rimmed glasses, and had a few more wrinkles than when Iain had last seen him. "What can I do for you, Mr. Tobias?"

Zachary Tobias was the manservant for a woman he was involved with as a teenager – Tessa Stanney. She was one of the wealthiest people in the universe; she all but owned Ewie, a planet in the Inner Tier. She had been a headstrong and beautiful woman of forty-four that knew what she wanted, which, at that time, was Iain Bryce.

"The mistress has passed away," said the man.

Iain remembered him as always being blunt. He wasn't sure what to say, wondering why he needed to be told this. "Right sorry to hear but not gonna miss her. Pardon my callousness, what's it got to do with me?"

"You are named in her will, Mr. Bryce. The reading will be at her estate in two weeks."

"Why would she have left me anything, we didn't exactly end things on good terms," said Iain. The thought of her leaving him anything turned his stomach. She had a sadistic streak and had likely held a grudge all these years. It was probably a large and steaming pile of horse shit. The only thing Tessa had ever given Iain, willingly, was an addiction to the drug called beads, a stimulant that enhanced any experience, especially sexual, that took two years to kick and had nearly killed him; one he still got the powerful urge to experience on occasion.

"I cannot answer that, Mr. Bryce, only tell you of her final wishes," said Zachary as if he really couldn't care either way.

"I'm not sure I can make it in that time, is there any way you could tell me what it was?" asked Iain.

"It's sealed and won't be read until all parties are present. Can I mark you as planning to attend?" asked Zachary.

Iain didn't know what to say, he needed time to think, being at the estate would drag out things he had tried hard to forget, "Do you need an answer right now?" he asked, sounding a bit like the irreverent seventeen year old boy he'd been when he'd last seen the man.

"I have two others to contact, let me know by the end of the day, if possible. The barrister says any not present must forfeit their bequest," said Zachary.

"I'll give you my answer within a few hours," said Iain as he cut the connection.

Iain shook his head, set it back against the glass case behind him, closed his eyes, and unconsciously began to rub at his left forearm, the place where the five-digit number had been tattooed on his skin. He wasn't ashamed of his past, it had made him the man he was today, in many ways it had shown him what he was and wasn't willing to put up with, but he didn't need reminding of this particular bit of it.

He'd been barely fifteen when he was taken to Cape Benwick Correctional Camp to serve a six-month stint for an unprovoked assault on a CRF officer. That number had been assigned to him for tracking purposes. It was during his stay there he became acquainted with Tessa Stanney.

Tessa had inherited a large portion of her wealth from her father, who was a shipping baron. She also inherited his keen business sense so she invested that bequest in several lucrative business ventures, which added to that wealth. She had estates on several planets throughout the Inner Tier, including one on Earth, but she preferred the one on Ewie, partly because there she had access to cheap, free, labor.

Iain heard talk of her fine estates and how she allowed the workers to use the pools and horses when they were finished nearly as soon as he step foot in the facility so he hadn't thought twice when he was asked if he was interested in joining a work crew.

Most of the time the work crews had dealt with the manservant so when he got his first glimpse of the lady herself sunbathing on her terrace he'd been more than a touch stupefied. She was about as well turned as any woman he'd ever seen and stirred more than a few urges in the young boy's brain and body. It was during this same outing Tessa first laid eyes on the spry boy that was already quite well built, strikingly handsome and very comfortable with himself.

She had called him out of the gardening crew to come to her room to fix the stuck flue of her fireplace. A sweaty and dirty job she'd watched him doing quite intently. She made it more than obvious she was as interested as he was. When he was done she took him to her bed without even allowing him to clean up. It wasn't long after this the mistress was requesting him for other *special* services.

The other inmates of the prison camp were jealous of him; knowing the mistress wouldn't take kindly to anyone messing with her toy kept them from bothering him. Tessa wasn't his first sexual partner; that was a girl on his home world when he was twelve, and there had been others in between, but she was many firsts for him. As his stint on Benwick neared its end, she asked him to come live with her as her lover. For the boy of a mere fifteen, who didn't have many other career options, other than the life of crime he had begun, the life she offered was a dream come true.

Tessa had been a beautiful woman then; she had long blondish brown hair that fell in waves of curls past her shoulders, strong features and dark brown eyes. She knew she was beautiful too, and knew how to use that beauty to get what she wanted. She also knew how to please a man. He had thought he had won the lottery. In the beginning it had been an amicable experience, the first six months full time on the estate had been heaven, the next year was bearable enough – the last six months were torture, literally.

She lavished him with gifts of clothing, expensive toys, food, liquor, any number of recreational drugs, and anything else his heart desired and most of the time he was left to himself and allowed to enjoy the estate alone while she was away on business, which was quite often in his first year at the estate. It wasn't exactly hard to take, being left alone on the hundred acre estate; he had gardens to explore, dozens of horses to ride, over several miles of trails, several different pools to swim in, a fully equipped fitness room to build his body and stamina up, game rooms to enjoy, a library full of very good books, servants to wait on him hand and foot and a huge house to shelter him. A right hell of a sight better than what he would've been facing if he returned to his home planet of Beta Four where he technically had no home.

Iain wasn't stupid and it wasn't that he didn't want to go to school so much as the schools on his home world weren't much for teaching. Tessa taught him how to read, how to speak more grammatically, though she couldn't break him of his habit of using *right* as an adverb, science, mathematics, which helped him immensely in calculations for navigation in his next life choice, and etiquette expected a young aristocrat out in polite society. That was something he supposed, to this day, he was thankful of. She had made him into a proper young man; teaching him how to walk, think, speak, dance, and a lot of the gentlemanly habits he still had today. That was the first time he had felt like he was more than the piece of shit he had been told he was all his life.

He had to do very little for her in exchange for this life of opulence, in truth. She liked having him as escort when she had to make an appearance at a public function – having a handsome and much younger man on her arm was a good status symbol – and she liked him sharing her bed.

At first he hadn't minded her attentions or, to be honest, the sex. After a year of this life it began to sour though. He rarely saw anything but the estate on Ewie and he was bored. He wanted to explore the universe but she wanted him at her beck and call. The hundreds of things he had to keep him entertained couldn't curb his building wanderlust but he stayed because he had no money of his own or a way to get off-world. He soon wished he had left when he first got the urge to.

Once Tessa thought he was hers she began to push him to do things to settle up for her generosity. She had always had strange tastes in sexual pleasure but it wasn't until a year into the relationship that he learned she was a sadomasochist. To be truthful it excited him at first. She preferred playing the part of the receiver, getting excited and climaxing from the pain he would inflict on her. She wasn't afraid to try anything. Occasionally she played master; he didn't find the excessive pain nearly as pleasurable as she did inflicting it. There wasn't much the two of them hadn't tried by the end of his second year.

She began to bring other women to their bed, women with almost as sick desires as she had. Sometimes she wanted to watch him with them, sometimes she made him watch her with them, but most of the time they were together with them. He was finding himself sickened by anything to do with sex and began to have a hard time performing. Even for a sexually crazed mind of a teenage boy, it was too much.

He told her, several times, he wasn't comfortable anymore but she would only scoff and tell him to stop acting like a simpleton. She expected him to indulge her desires without question, reminding him he owed all he had to her. He soon learned it wasn't a good idea to refuse her, he thought the pain she inflicted while they were playing her sex games was bad, but it was nothing compared to her anger. Her temper was dreadful and painful; he had more than a few scars to prove that.

She would make him beg for mercy and force him to full tears before she would finally stop, then leave him in the implements until he was so twisted and sore he would be out of use for days, which was a painful reprieve but a reprieve all the same. The final straw broke when she asked him to do the one thing he wasn't willing to do, even high on beads.

The last time he saw Tessa was a day in late June, sixteen years ago. She was entertaining friends, in this case a group of parliament spouses, at an intimate party on Ewie, a little too much for his liking. She had introduced him to her guests and paraded him around, showing them how she'd primped and pampered her little criminal boy. He endured it, knowing he'd pay dearly for it later if he didn't. He had hoped her peep show would be over quickly and he could wander off and entertain himself the rest of the night but this time was different. She told her guests of their sexual exploits and his prowess in bed, and to his complete surprise, asked if any of the guests wished to give him a try.

He had laughed uneasily, thinking she was only joking. As he watched hands rising and looks of desire come across the faces before him he realized she was serious and they were eager. She was offering him to her friends, and most weren't women. That was one thing he had always refused to do, no matter how much pain and suffering she inflicted. He said he was having no part of this and told her, in front of her guests, that this time she had crossed the line. She had simply smiled, turned and left him in the room alone with her guests.

He stormed into the woman's bedroom. The white-washed walls, scarlet lace curtains, huge bed with black silk sheets, silver tiger skin carpets and the fireplace with a white marble mantle and surround all suddenly looked very ugly to him. A bottle of champagne was chilling in a silver bucket of ice in front of the lit fire. A dish of chocolate covered cherries and strawberries was beside it and dozens of candles were around the room, giving off sweet scents. Tessa was on the chaise lounge before the fire, dressed in a pink gossamer robe; the belt tied loosely so if flared open every time she moved.

"What the hell was that about?" he barked. His hair was bedraggled, his blue-gray eyes were on fire and his full pouty lips were pinched so tight they were nearly gone. The royal blue silk shirt she had bought him, special for this night, was ripped half off, done by one of the over-zealous guests, several fingernail marks ran across the left side of his chest where another tried to hold him down and the zipper and crotch of his black leather pants was ripped where a third had tried to pull them off him.

"Now, now, Iain, Dear, calm yourself or you'll get stress wrinkles," Tessa replied in her sultry voice.

"I don't give a right royal load of shit," spat Iain. He slammed the door hard enough to splinter the hinges.

"How many times do I have to tell you to stop using that word? It makes you sound like a philistine," she said very portentously, shaking her head angrily.

"You *right* mean this *right* fucking word, Tessa? Guess maybe I am *right* dim-witted, ain't I? I told you I would *never* do that. Are you a *philistine*?" he screamed, as he motioned toward the doors.

"Don't be so juvenile, Iain! You will enjoy it like all the rest have. Stop pretending this is all so disgusting to you. What do you think I have been priming you for?"

"I will never do that, not for anything or anyone!" shouted Iain, "I ain't your fucking sex toy to be shared, Woman!"

"You always did have a high opinion of yourself," said the woman under her breath. She poured a second glass of bubbly and held it out to him.

"Why? Because I won't be your slut?" shouted Iain. He hit the glass out of her hand, it smashed against the mantle, making her and the flames both flare up dangerously.

"Don't you *ever* raise your hand to me again!" she growled menacingly. She was a little surprised that the man before her didn't even flinch, others would have been groveling at her feet at this point. This actually turned her on. In a softer tone she said, "Stop being such a petulant little boy. You can't deny you've enjoyed yourself."

"Parts yes, in the beginning, but this is it!" barked Iain. He walked to the oak wardrobe, began to pull out clothes and stuff them into an empty cloth potato bag.

"What are you doing?"

"What the fuck does it look like I'm doing?"

"You cannot leave!" growled the woman, starting toward him.

"Try to stop me, Bitch!"

"I own you, Iain Bryce, *you belong to me*!" spat the woman venomously. She grabbed the bag from his hand and tipped in over, spilling the clothes on the floor.

"I belong to no one, Woman, and never will." He tore the rest of his shirt off, grabbed a t-shirt he had not stuffed in the bag yet and pulled it over his head.

"I bought and paid for you, Iain Bryce, you would be nothing but a stupid, petty criminal with crappy teeth without me."

Iain quickly turned to Tessa, threw the handful of clothes he had picked up from the floor at the woman and said through clenched teeth, "I had my dignity, that no one will ever buy and can never fucking take from me again!" He ripped the rest of the leather pants off and slammed them to the floor, kicked off his boots, grabbed a pair of brown slacks pulled them on, then grabbed the boots, and said, "I want nothing else from you."

"Where do you think you will go? I'll speak to them, you won't be welcome anywhere."

"*You think I want* them *to welcome me*?" Iain shouted at the top of his lungs, pointing at the doors that came from the room where the party was still going.

"Iain... Darling, calm down," she said as if speaking to a child, "I sprung this on you too quickly, we can discuss this; it doesn't have to happen tonight."

"IT WILL *NEVER* HAPPEN, TESSA!" shouted Iain. His hands had formed fists beside him and he was shaking violently. "I feel right fucking *vile* having *your* disgusting hands on me." he growled through clenched teeth.

"Come, have a drink and some berries, we can discuss this in the morning," entreated the woman, realizing he was serious.

"You only want me to stay so *they* won't see me leave. God, Tessa, you are so fucking pathetic!"

Tessa took the last few steps between them and grabbed his arm, digging her long nails into it and drawing blood, "I will not let you leave me like this."

"I've given you the last pound of my flesh, Bitch!" said Iain.

The look of hatred in his eyes made the woman let go of his arm and fall back a step.

Before she could say anything Zachary Tobias, entered the room and said, "Mistress, the guests are questioning where their entertainment is."

"You can be their fucking entertainment, Mr. Tobias. I'm getting the fuck out of here!" spat Iain. He went through the open door and walked past the guests who were looking at him with anticipation at first and uncertainty after.

"Iain... *IAIN BRYCE*... Get your ass back here!"

Iain shook himself out of the memory violently; there wasn't much that could make him feel dirty but that woman had found most all of them. What could she have possibly left him? Whatever it was he doubted he wanted it. A part of him was curious. They were only a week from Ewie and had no particular place to be just then. There was no saying he had to accept whatever this bequest was. His mind made up, Iain called Mr. Tobias and told him to expect him.

"Woman remember the first kiss;
men remember the last."
–   Unknown

Jared and Jaime were both excited to see where they were going; they'd heard stories of the wild parties Mistress Tessa Stanney threw. He told them some of what the woman had expected of him and some of what finally ended it, so they wouldn't be completely surprised if anything offhanded was said, leaving out the more embarrassing bits. The thought that Iain had been a part of that world was beyond entertaining to them. Of course Iain didn't see it the same, threatening to space them when they had finally made one too many jabs.

The palatial estate that appeared before them was beyond enormous. It had three gardens, two outdoor pools and one indoor, and six guesthouses. The servant quarters alone was as big as most mansions. The main house was beyond massive, sprawling across the valley like a giant cat soaking up the sun. It could've housed many of their colonies easily; in some cases more than one.

The buildings of the estate were gleaming white with golden roofs, the stables were red with black roofs, and the barns were weathered brown. The grounds were lush and well cared for and the gardens were in full bloom. It all looked perfect.

Jaime set the shuttle down on the landing deck, beside three other ships, and they walked to the main doors. It was barely seconds after Iain rang the bell before the door opened.

"Welcome back, Mr. Bryce," said Zachary Tobias. The manservant was wearing a navy blue pinstriped tuxedo with full tails and had a tray with glasses of champagne perched on his left hand. He seemed taken aback to see the other two but he didn't refuse their entry. He led them to the room where the last party Iain had attended had been held and told them to help themselves to the buffet, which had every possible luxury – from caviar to truffles.

Three other men, each about Iain's age, were in the room but no one was speaking, each eyeing the others as if gauging whether one of them was higher on Tessa's list than they. Jaime and Jared were eyed as they entered the room as well, which Iain found amusing, and satisfying, the others obviously thought they were once hers as well.

One of the other men was about Iain's size with light skin, like porcelain, brown eyes and hair so blonde it was nearly transparent. The second was dark skinned and stout in stature, with tightly kinked dark hair. The last was an effeminate man who walked with a swing to his hips. Jared joked Iain must have driven her to that one, the look Iain gave him told him it wasn't much appreciated.

The quartermaster and weapons master enjoyed looking around; the former's parents were considered the richest family on Minara but this was opulent even to him, the latter was from a middle class background, the only place he had ever see the stuff around him was in museums. They were a both stunned that most of the artwork and sculptures around the room were of a sexual nature.

After about an hour, Mr. Tobias returned and told them the barrister was ready to proceed and motioned them to follow him into the study.

The study was actually a library. Tall shelves filled with books ran the full length of the back wall and dark wood paneling, soft lights and woven tapestries of waterfalls and woodland scenes gave it all a very comfortable feeling. It was the only room Iain had ever felt comfortable in, the same even now.

A trestle table had been brought into the room, set off center across the back corner, and five chairs had been arranged before it. A somber looking man was sitting behind it. He had thin gray hair, dark eyes behind round wire-rimmed glasses, and was dressed in dark robes. An open briefcase and five stacks of papers were sitting before him. He had a serious expression on his face and he looked hard at each man as they entered, trying to relay this seriousness to them. He didn't look like he particularly wanted to be there, any more than Iain, but was likely being paid handsomely to be.

The barrister looked oddly at Mr. Tobias as he closed the door, "There are only supposed to be four men." The manservant walked over and whispered into the man's ear, likely explaining the other two were with Iain. He nodded as if he really didn't care as he began to look at the papers. "Let's begin. Raise your hand when I call your name. Hawking, Chet?"

The light haired and skinned man raised his hand and smiled, not as disarming as Iain's but there was a confidence behind it.

The barrister nodded. "Rameriez, Hector?"

The colored man raised his hand to this.

Again, the barrister only nodded. "Ponch, Quinn?"

The feminine one smiled and put his hand up.

The barrister's eyes shifted to Iain then and said, "So you must be Iain Bryce?"

Iain nodded; there was no smile on his face.

"Good, we are ready to begin."

"Who's the last chair for?" asked Quinn.

The barrister looked at him sharply. "Please refrain from speaking until the entire document has been read. Understand?" He didn't continue until all had nodded, Iain being the last to.

No one was paying attention as the man read through the legal mumbo jumbo. Finally he came to the part that pertained to them; all but Iain sat up straighter, in anticipation. Iain actually slumped further, wishing he could dissolve into the chair he was sitting in.

"If you wish, you may leave after your portion has been completed. When we are finished, you will need to sign these forms, listing your bequest, confirming that you understand and accept them. Any contestation will be handled in private."

Chet was given five million credits, two cases of expensive champagne and three of the purebred horses, apparently the ones he had favored during his time on the estate. Hector received two million credits, the extensive wine collection and the antique grand piano in the parlor. Quinn was given three million credits and the mistresses' jewelry and clothing wardrobe. Iain got the books on the shelves around them and the closet full of clothes he had left behind when he left.

The other three, Jaime and Jared were shocked Iain wasn't given any credits. Iain wasn't. Taking even a dime from the woman would have proven he had been bought and paid for by her. He was happy to have the books, they were the only things in this place that he ever felt any affinity for anyway.

Hector and Chet looked back at the barrister. They asked, in almost perfect unison, obviously expected more for themselves, about the rest of the property. "All but

Mr. Bryce is dismissed." The other three men looked back curiously but Mr. Tobias closed the door behind them. The barrister looked oddly at Jaime and Jared. "This is for your ears only, Mr. Bryce."

"They stay or I don't," said Iain. Jaime and Jared took a chair on either side of the captain.

The man shrugged and said, "The mistress asked you be included in a final bequest."

Mr. Tobias nodded to the barrister then walked to a door on the opposite wall. He opened it and motioned to someone beyond. A young man, nearly a spitting image of Iain, stepped through it. The pirates looked at each other, confused and surprised.

"This is Ryar. He was given the remainder of the estate. This is Iain Bryce, and friends of his."

"And this pertains to me right exactly how?" asked Iain. He was sure this was Tessa's sick way of rubbing his nose in what he could've had if he had cooperated.

The new man looked from Jared to Jaime to Iain before he sat down hard in the fourth chair. "Get on with."

"Mistress Tessa wished you, Mr. Bryce, to know *you* were her favorite and all of this was meant for you, until Ryar came. She thought of giving it to you jointly, but she knew you'd refuse."

"She was right!" snapped Iain.

"That's why she chose to bequest it to Ryar. She has left it to him to decide whether you should receive anything more."

"Why should it be his place to decide this?" asked a befuddled Iain.

"Ryan's surname is listed as Stanney on his ident records but, legally, it should have been Bryce."

"Excuse me?" asked Iain and Jaime in unison.

"Ryar is your son, Mr. Bryce."

"The fuck he is," said Iain quickly.

Ryar stood up then, knocking his chair over, "I knew it was gonna be like this! Mum said you were an arrogant fucking bastard!" He stormed out the door he had come in through, slamming it behind him.

Mr. Tobias waited to see if the boy came back then said, "The mistress didn't realize she was with child when you left, Mr. Bryce. In her stubbornness, she never contacted you to inform you of her condition."

"But we always used precautions. How... He can't be," said Iain in total disbelief. The conviction was quickly waning. "It matters not. He's old enough to be on his own, what does this got to do with me?"

"The boy has been coddled his entire life, Mr. Bryce, he has no idea what the real world is about. Mistress Tessa was hoping you could teach him to be strong and self-sufficient. She said you were always so severe in your self-preservation," said Mr. Tobias.

"I can't teach the boy a thing like that! A lot of experiences he's never had made me this way," said Iain, looking from Zachary to the barrister and back, waiting for one to tell him this was a sick joke. When neither did he guffawed and said, "Brilliant, right fucking brilliant!" He asked Zachary to pack the books and Jaime and Jared to bring them to the shuttle then walked through the same door Ryar had exited.

"Memory is the diary that we all carry about with us."
   —   Oscar Wilde

It surprised Iain that he still remembered where everything in Tessa's home was. It suddenly felt like he had never left; each room he walked past brought out a new and horrible memory. He was having a hard time breathing. The main house had over a hundred places Ryar could be hold up. He knew where he had always gone when he wanted to be alone, so he went there first. There was a huge oak tree in the back garden that had been his secret place. Tessa hated it and had wanted it cut down. She thought it was hideous, with all of its knots and twisted limbs, but Iain loved it, it had character. It was the perfect shape for climbing and had a wide branch, about twenty feet up, which was an excellent place to sit, without your butt falling asleep. He had spent hours in that tree, sometimes hiding from her, but mostly imagining his life off-planet and out from under her thumb. He wondered if it was still there. He wouldn't have been surprised if it was the first thing to go after he left.

Iain stepped out the door off the huge kitchen and smiled. He walked up to the tree, put his hand on the trunk and lovingly rubbed the crusty, rough bark. "Hi, old friend. Bet ya thought you would never see me again, huh?" he said. He was only a little surprised to see feet dangling from the very branch he'd always used when he looked up at it.

He wondered if he would still be able to climb the thing, he wasn't nearly as limber as he once was. He jumped to grip a burl about eight feet off the ground, placed the ball of his feet on the trunk and pulled himself up. It wasn't nearly as graceful as it once had been but he reached the center of the tree only a little winded.

Ryar sighed loudly as he heard someone climbing up the tree. He started to climb down the other side of it.

"Wait... Ryar," said Iain.

"How did you know where to find me?"

"This is where I always went when I was in need of solace. It just made sense."

"I've taken care of myself for the last ten years, I don't need your help now," said the boy, sniffling a little.

Despite how much he might want to deny it the boy was acting a lot like him, especially when he was that age. Iain smiled and said, "Of course you can, you come from strong stock."

"My *mother* was weak and sick."

"Your mother may have been a right lot of things, Ryar, but weak was not one of them," said Iain, never expecting he would defend her.

"Then why did you leave?"

"That's between Tessa and me. Just know that had I known about you, things would have been... might have been ... different."

"You would have stayed?"

"No." Iain couldn't lie, "but I would have made sure you knew who I was."

"I do," grumbled the boy, "My mother told me all about you. You're a pirate. You think by snuggling up to me you can steal my inheritance, don't you?" asked Ryar sarcastically. "You heard the barrister; it's up to me. I can choose to give you nothing."

"Believe me, I want nothing from Tessa, least of all this estate; and I expect none, and will accept none of it, from you," said Iain.

"You broke her, you know?"

"I doubt that," said Iain sardonically.

"I never saw her happy. Mr. Tobias said she was, when you were here."

"If it makes you feel better to believe that and blame me, so be it. I have places to be," said Iain as he turned his back on the boy.

"Why did you come looking for me?"

"I was gonna ask if you wanted to see my ship, Phoenix, but I guess you have made up your mind to stay bitter," Iain said plainly. He was halfway down the tree and about to jump down the rest of the way when Ryar called out.

"I... I would... please."

Iain didn't look back, but a smile creased his lips, "Very well, follow me."

"Never let your guard down."
—   Old *Semai'* proverb

The shuttle rose from the landing dock of the Stanney estate for what Iain hoped would be the last time. He had no idea what he had expected from this visit to his past but a son was certainly the farthest thing from his mind. He couldn't have said when he first heard just what that meant but after spending time with Ryar, before they left, seeing how much alike they were; he found himself warming to the idea. He now had someone he could show his world to, and pass his legacy on to if or more likely when he was no longer able. He smiled, in spite of himself as he watched Ryer looking out the portal window in awe. He found he was glad he had decided to make this trip.

Ryar's eyes were as big as they could get as he watched the huge estate, the city it was in, the continent it was on, and finally the whole planet disappear below them. He did not look away until they were well out into space. "Are you all pirates?" he asked in the eager way boys do.

"Yes," answered Iain, he was in the pilot seat, Jaime was beside him and Jared was in the back with Ryar. "This is Jaime Cable, my quartermaster," he added, nodding toward Jaime, who waved his hand at the boy.

"Hello. What is a quartermaster?"

"Second in command," answered Jaime.

"And, that man beside you is Jared Way. He's the weapons master." There was no need to explain that position.

"Cool! And you are?"

"He's the captain," answered Jared.

"No way? Really?"

"Yes. Phoenix is my ship. She has a current crew of forty two, of which we are three."

"Whoa," said Ryar, barely able to contain his disbelief. "Do you really rob people? Have you ever killed anyone?"

Jared and Jaime looked at each other with a strange look, wondering how Iain wanted to answer that.

"We do rob people but not in the way other pirates do, we give a fair portion of our spoils to some of the colonists of the Second BrimTier. And yeah, we have *had* to kill people, but not because we wanted to. We do our best not to. You ever been off your world?"

"No, Ma always said I didn't need anything she couldn't give me."

"Sounds like Tessa," said Iain under his breath.

"You can drive this thing?" asked Ryar, leaning into the cockpit.

"It's called piloting or flying. Wanna try?"

"Can I?"

Iain set the autopilot, waved Jaime to move to the back of the ship then motioned Ryar forward. He waiting for him to strap himself in the seat then squatted beside him and pointed at the gages for altitude, yaw, pitch and roll, fuel storage, controls for environmentals, com system, forward and aft thrusters, boost and hyperdrive engines and autopilot controls then showed him how to hold the throttle and wheel. He told him to let her fly on her own and just get a feel for the stick first.

Ryar had a smile that went from ear to ear as he felt the wheel vibrating under his hands. He looked around at all the gages. He was about to ask about one that was flashing red when the ship suddenly shifted and they were thrown back in their seats. "Did I do... did I hit something?"

"No. We just dropped from jump, that's what we call leaving hyperspace," said Iain as he pointed to a ship drifting gracefully before them. "And, that's Phoenix."

If it was possible, Ryar's eyes got even bigger than before, then he jumped a foot when a female voice spoke through a speaker beside him.

"Welcome home, Sirs," said Kassie.

Iain leaned over the boy and pushed the button to answer her. "Thanks, Kas, it's good to be. Open the bay doors, if you please."

"Yes, Captain Bryce."

Ryar looked at him funny and said, "A girl pilot's your ship?"

"Ain't none better! Actually, I have two pilots, twin brother and sister. That was Kassie, you'll meet her when we..." Iain wasn't able to finish the statement as the sandpiper suddenly veered sideways and began to spin erratically, "What the hell?"

"Captain, a CRF cruiser just dropped from jump off starboard!"

Captain Bryce pulled Ryar from the seat without so much as a word and jumped into it. He punched the thrust engine, it fired instantly but they didn't move. "Fuck! They've got us grappled. Kassie, get the hell outa' here."

"But, Captain?"

"Do it, Kassie…"

Three starlings appeared before them, heading for Phoenix. They were too late, the pirate ship disappeared into a jumpgate with a blast of blinding light.

"What do we do?" asked Jaime, jumping back into the copilot seat.

The shuttlecraft was slowly drifting backwards as the starlings, which had been heading for Phoenix just moments before, took up position around them, guns red and hot. Iain Bryce looked at his son then said rather flatly, "We surrender, Quartermaster."

"When in a firefight, kill as many as you can; the one you miss today may not miss tomorrow."
    —   Anonymous

The shuttle came to rest on the deck of the hanger inside the battlecruiser gently enough but the people inside it were frazzled.

Iain couldn't believe he had let himself get so complacent. Jaime and Jared tried to console him by reminding him they hadn't been watching the scanners either but he would hear none of it. The only one not saying anything was Ryar, he appeared in shock. He wanted to reassure the boy they were going to be alright but he didn't know that they were. He hoped this was either Vice Admiral Hunt, who'd released them in the past, or Admiral Wallace, who was *sympathetic* to their cause and would at least make their imprisonment comfortable, but of course, that was too much to ask. They found Admiral Flint waiting with a group of fifty men, all with charged laser rifles trained on them. The triumphant look on Flint's face was perfect, and made Iain sick.

"Welcome aboard my battlecruiser, Prometheus, Captain Bryce. I am Admiral Walter Flint. May I assume you have your memory back?"

Iain said nothing.

The admiral recognized Jaime, "Master Cable," he said with a polite nod. He looked past the unknown face beside him, guessing he was only a grunt, and stopped on

Jared. He recognized him from the hospital on Sunnen. "Having your men impersonate CRF officers now as well? Another charge we can add to your docket, Bryce."

Jared spat quickly. "I *was* a CRF officer then… "

"Hold your tongue, Master Way," said Iain.

"Sorry, Captain," Jared said and shut his mouth.

"The Fleet Admiral won't be happy we lost the rest of your crew but the four of you will be consolation. He will be especially pleased to see you, *Captain*." The three upper level pirates stood firm and set, the younger one shuffled and shifted in place but said nothing. "Take them to the brig," said the man, pointed to the lower ranked pirates, then waved the captain to follow him.

They walked into the admiral's dayroom. Three black leather sofas were set in a horseshoe around a large coffee table. A video screen was recessed into the wall at the end of the seating arrangement. On the screen, larger than life, was Vice President Nicholas' face, with a look that closely mirrored Flint's.

"Mr. Bryce, it is *truly* a pleasure to see you again. I'll much enjoy watching you brought to justice, though I fear you won't find the experience quite so pleasant."

Iain set his jaw and said nothing.

"No comment, ay? No worries, you'll speak plenty later, I'm willing to bet," said the man then he turned his attention to the admiral, "Excellent job, Admiral Flint.

We'll be awaiting your arrival. Be prepared to present yourself and your officers to the parliament at a dinner in your honor, and make room on your sash for the medal you'll be receiving."

"Thank you, Fleet Admiral, but holding the man in front of me is award enough for me."

"Modesty is all well and good, Admiral Flint, but the pirates' prizes will likely make your retirement fund much more comfortable, I'm willing to wager."

Flint smiled and nodded.

The two exchanged pleasantries for another few minutes then the signal was cut. During which Iain stood completely still, not even changing his facial expression. He was, in fact, so tuned out that it took a moment to realize the admiral had spoken to him.

"Tell me who the fourth man with you is so we can be sure to get it correct when your capture is announced over DTV?" said the admiral, as if they were simply having a personable conversation.

Iain said nothing.

"Very well, you interested in a drink then?" the admiral asked, jovially.

Iain said nothing.

"Oh, come now, I know you are a man of some couth. Other officers that have attempted to hold you have told me of the hours of interesting conversations they have had with you. Have a drink and entertain me for a bit," said Flint, irritation that he wasn't playing along creeping into his voice.

Iain said nothing.

"If you are not going to be civil then neither will I," spat Flint as he stumped over to a combox and called for the guards to take him to the brig.

Iain had expected to be taken to the same cell as his men but he was shown to an empty one. He asked where the others were but only got sick smiles in answer. When he was sure they were gone, he called out for his officers but neither answered. He didn't dare call to Ryar and risk any listening, he didn't want them to know his name so they couldn't do him harm, but he wanted to very badly. Wouldn't it be just about par to learn he had a son and lose him all in a single day. In frustration, he screamed, "Son of a bitch!" as he slammed his fist into the wall, bloodying his knuckles.

"Defeat may serve as well as victory
to shake the soul and let the glory out."
 — Edwin Markham

"We've reached Earth. President Nason and Vice President Nicholas are eager to see you, do you wish to clean yourself up first?" asked the admiral, referring to the pirate captain's five o'clock shadow and lack of shower for three days.

Part of Iain wanted to say yes, he hated being dirty almost as much as he hated being a prisoner, but he wasn't going to let the man, or any man, see how much that filth was bothering him. "They will take me as I am," the pirate answered smugly.

"So be it," said the admiral, his obvious disgust said more than words could. He told the guards to release the laser bars and directed Captain Bryce to walk in front of him.

The pirate captain was taken to Earth in a shuttle. He was less than happy to find his men and Ryar not aboard. He was getting anxious to know their status but he bit his tongue and tried to act perfectly content. Once on the ground he was led into a complex and onto an elevator. He rode it down many stories then was taken down several halls to a cell where he finally learned of their fate.

Jaime, Jared and Ryar were chained to the back wall. They didn't look harmed but they didn't look happy either. He moved his hand in front of him and asked Jaime, using sign language, if they were alright. A quick blink from the quartermaster told him they were. Before the captain could ask anything else, the guard pushed him to a chair set up across from his crewmen and told him to sit down. It looked like any other chair except it was metal, which made him a little nervous. Iain had heard of the Nikolas' obsession with torture.

Within minutes, the vice president stepped through the door. He smiled nefariously at the pirates. "Hello, Bryce, you can't *possibly* imagine how much I have wished for this day. I will finally have my pound of flesh!" said the man enthusiastically. He turned his attention to the three on the wall, "I recognize Cable." His eyes squinted as he looked at the man chained beside the former dragon trooper. He looked familiar, Gerard wondered if he was another of his former officers that Iain had brainwashed. "I don't believe I have ever met the other two." He looked back at the captain and asked, "Tell me who they are, won't you?"

"They're hostages," said Iain quickly.

"Really?" Gerard motioned to someone in the hall.

A soldier entered with an ident device in his hands. He forced the weapons master's index finger into the device and waited, then turned to vice president and said, "Jared William Way, Leftenant Commander, stationed on Colum Province. The docket states he went AWOL eight months ago."

"Thought so." Gerard clicked his tongue at Captain Bryce and said, "That's one lie. Do I need to do the same to the boy?"

"I couldn't care less what that fucking device tells you, they are hostages," said Iain through clenched teeth.

Gerard motioned for the soldier to continue.

Ryar tried to fight him off but his finger was finally forced into the device.

"Ryar Daniel Stanney of the planet Ewie, listed as a student, Sir."

"Stanney? Any relation to Tessa Stanney?" asked the vice president. Ryar didn't say anything; a look of defiance had come to his face. Gerard saw a look of pride come over the pirate's then, which confounded him. "We got word Mistress Stanney had died. Let me guess, Bryce heard also and thought he would rob the estate and took you, expecting someone would be willing to pay for your safe return?"

None of them spoke.

An extremely amused look played across the vice president's face as he said, "It matters not, I believe you *are* likely a hostage. Release the boy and take him to my office."

"What are you gonna do with me?" asked Ryar, looking over at the captain, his big eyes filled with fear.

"Leave the boy alone!" said Captain Bryce gruffly. He started to stand up. "I'm the one you want, Nikolas."

With a signal from the vice president the pirate was slammed back into the chair then jabbed in the right shoulder with a taser that was held in place for quite some time. Iain ground his teeth, but didn't cry out. The electrical charge sped through his muscles, making him go limp but he managed to stay in the chair.

"Tisk, tisk, let's have no more of that now," said Nikolas, looking very pleased to have provoked the man. "Tell me why you care so much for his safety if he's only a hostage?"

Iain looked briefly at Ryar then back to Mr. Nikolas and spat, "Eat shit, asshole!"

Again Captain Bryce was hit, this time with two tasers, this time they weren't taken away for several minutes. He slid from the chair and flopped on the floor, but still they didn't remove the devices.

Nikolas motioned for him to be lifted up and set back in the chair then the he stepped over, grabbed a handful of his hair and yanked his head back hard.

Iain hadn't gotten the use of his muscles back yet so all he could do was look at the hated man.

Gerard smiled and said, "Got anything else to say, have you? No? No matter, we will find out all we need from him," pointing to the boy, who was now off the wall, being held between two guards. He released Iain's hair and pulled a handkerchief out of his pocket. He wiped his hand with it, then made an ugly face as he added, "I can't allow you before the president smelling as you do, can I? Take them to the quadrangle."

Ryar was pushed toward the door; he looked back at Iain then followed the guards out of the room. The other two were released from the wall and the pirates were led out as well, with Jaime helping the captain to walk since the muscles of his legs were still in spasm.

"I have no fear! What is in store for me shall find me self-reliant, undismayed."
—   Reverend Jack Appleton

The quadrangle was a cross between an arena and an auditorium. An area for CRP was portioned off directly before them, a viewer box was set into the wall below this, and rows of seats, enough to hold more than two thousand people, ran the back and both sides. The captain guessed there was probably close to three hundred people there now.

He looked at the faces watching them, hoping to see his crew, more hoping he wouldn't, he hoped they were as far from here as they could get and wouldn't be stupid enough to come after them. He looked at the viewers' box and watched the president walk in and sit in the very center chair. The vice president was right beside him, leaning over and whispering in his ear. He stepped away when Dylan and Caitlyn walked in. They sat in the front corner of the box then his son was brought in and set in a seat in the back corner. None of them looked like they particularly wanted to be there. Ryar and Dylan were staring at them, Caitlyn was looking down at her hands. They were too far away for him to signal to them. He hoped they knew enough to hold their tongues, no matter what Nikolas did to them; he didn't need the man getting any other ideas.

Unsure what was about to occur, Iain looked at his men and said, "I don't expect either of you to take any more than right humanly possible, understand? If the chance arises, I'm ordering you both to save yourselves."

Both said in unison, "If we go, we go together."

The captain said, "Idiots!" the admiration in his voice was strong.

The pirates squared their shoulders and faced their captors stoically and proudly; ready for whatever they intended to throw at them.

Vice President Nikolas stood and said loudly, "Remove your clothes."

This surprised Jared but Iain and Jaime had partly expected it. They'd made the man strip naked when they had marooned him, in front of the president's daughter, and he intended now to do the same to them. They did so, without hesitation, Jared followed suit, albeit a little slower. Mr. Nikolas seemed irritated at their lack of modesty. They watched him motion to someone then they were hit with streams of water from large hoses. They stumbled a bit from the unexpected surge but quickly regained their footing. Jaime and Iain began to rub themselves down, working their hands through their hair as if this was a simple shower. Catching on, Jared quickly followed suit.

The force of the water hitting their naked skin obviously stung a little, by the redness left behind when the hard streams were moved, but it didn't debase them as the vice president had hoped. Gerard frowned and signaled for the onslaught to end. The three looked like drowned rats but were still standing defiantly. The vice president ordered them back to their cell.

"What more do you plan to do to them?" President Nason asked when they were behind the closed doors of his office. He wasn't against Iain Bryce being humiliated but he didn't want to prolong his life either; the longer he lived the better chance his crew had to attempt a rescue.

"Just give me a few more hours. I've recently learned a thing that may break Bryce."

The president smiled at the thought of that.

Thomas knew Caitlyn and the pirate captain had become intimate and that it was consensual. He knew Dylan had gone behind his back last summer and paid the pirate Caitlyn's ransom when he had taken her hostage en route to Tarnis Prime. The captain of the Calypso had given report that his son and the pirate had spent a fair amount of time together before the pirate left. Then, only a few months ago, Dylan had contacted Bryce regarding Caitlyn and an unfortunate incident with another pirate captain, Victor Black. He was glad his daughter was returned safe, both times, but it was the principle of how and who had rescued her. The fact that the pirate had further undermined the already tense relationship with his daughter was a bit bothersome but to have come between him and his son was outright underhanded. Captain Iain Bryce was making him look bad in more ways than he liked.

Feeling the hatred boiling inside of him again, President Nason asked the vice president for details.

In answer, Gerard motioned to someone outside the room, a man stepped in and gave the president a wicked smile.

"What do you think they've done with Ryar?" asked Jared.

"I really can't think on that just now," said the captain, plainly.

"And Phoenix?" asked Jared. The tone of his voice revealed how anxious he was.

"I hope they're lightyears from here," grumbled Iain.

Jared started to say something more but a look from Jaime stopped him.

They were back in the cell and were now wearing orange jumpsuits. Jaime and Jared were again chained to the wall, the captain was left loose. He was pacing the small room, leaving a distinct path in the dirt on the floor.

He knew his being left loose was to try to weaken his men's bond to him, if they thought they weren't worth as much as him they might be willing to speak against him to save themselves, which, in turn was supposed to build his anxiety. He used a similar strategy in the first stages of a siege. Knowing this, he tried not to let it bother him. It was getting harder the longer he was left waiting. He could have picked the locks holding his men to the wall but what good would it do them. They had no idea where Ryar was or really even where they were. "Why don't they right get it over with already?"

"Excuse me, Captain, I, for one, am not in a particular hurry," said Jaime.

"I don't want that either, Jay… just this incessant waiting."

Jaime knew it was Ryar Iain was really anxious about. He couldn't imagine how the man must feel to learn he had a son and then get him arrested, and potentially killed, in less than a week. "He'll be okay, Iain, he's made of good stock."

"Yeah, thanks." said the captain gruffly; though still pacing, the speed had slowed down some.

"We often hate another because we see something in them we lack."
— *Pastor Maxwell Bryce*

Iain was on nearly his five hundredth turn about the cell when the door opened and the vice president stepped in again. It was all he could do to hold himself from jumping the man and killing him with his bare hands then and there but he knew Nikolas wasn't alone and he'd likely die before he even touched flesh so he only turned to face the hated man and waited for whatever new torture he was going to attempt.

He watched a soldier bring the metal chair back in and again was told to sit in it. This time his ankles were attached to the legs and his wrists to the arms of the chair with cuffs. He looked at the vice president's face and saw a strange look in the man's eyes. For one of the few times in his life, Iain was worried.

Gerard looked at the men on the wall and said, "I know both of you were once highly decorated officers. Show me you still have integrity. I promise we will show you mercy if you assist us in taking down Iain Bryce."

Jaime said, "Never," instantly.

Jared took only a second longer, "Not a chance."

The vice president didn't look at all surprised. He signaled and another metal chair was brought in then. He smiled at how disconcerted the pirates appeared but said nothing, only motioned to someone outside the room.

A guard forcefully pushed Ryar into the room. The boy's head was down, as if not willing to meet their eyes.

Iain stiffened. He had hoped the vice president would have released Ryar. He should have, if he believed he truly was just a hostage. His being here meant Nikolas either suspected otherwise or had figured out who he really was. Ryar didn't know anything about them so he was really of no threat to them. He guessed Nikolas intended to threaten the boy with harm to make him speak. When the boy was pushed into the second chair and shackled in as well, the captain realized that was apparently to be the case. "Your issue is with me, Nikolas, let the boy go and I won't fight whatever you wish to do with me."

"How very gallant of you," said Gerard scathingly. "No, I will leave him right where he is. You see, I learned something recently that I found quite interesting. I'm wondering if anyone else might be interested to know this side of you."

Iain wasn't worried about Jaime and Jared hearing whatever the vice president thought might cause him discomfort and though he didn't want his son exposed to whatever Nikolas was planning, eventually he would need to learn what his father was all about so he could decide if he wanted to be a part of his world. He smiled up at the vice president; he was about to tell him the attempt was for naught when Caitlyn and Dylan walked into the room and stood in the corner. That changed things a bit.

Dylan was glaring at the vice president. Caitlyn was looking at the floor.

Gerard looked at the president's offspring and asked, "Have either of you ever heard of Mistress Tessa Stanney?" Dylan gave him a disapproving look, Caitlyn looked like she would be sick, telling him they had.

"We checked into Tessa Stanney's death, wanting to be sure it wasn't caused by violent means and learned her throat had been cut and she had been stabbed multiple times, suggesting that very thing. You wouldn't happen to know anything about that, would you, Bryce?"

Iain hadn't thought to ask the manservant how Tessa had died; he really hadn't cared. He did feel bad it was so violent, for Ryar's sake. He gave Nikolas an equally hard look back and said, "Nope."

Gerard smiled and indicated the boy sitting in the chair. "This is Ryar Stanney, the mistress' son. He had one of his mother's diaries on him. It made for interesting reading. You wouldn't mind if I summarize a few of its more... interesting passages, would you?" He didn't get any reaction from the pirates. He turned to the Nason siblings and said, "Did you know that Bryce was one of her lovers? In fact, he was one of her favorites."

The only one this bothered was Caitlyn. She looked into Iain's eyes, hoping to see it wasn't true. She looked away quickly, with tears in hers.

Feeling invigorated by the girl's reaction, Gerard plowed on, "I am sure you have all heard stories of the lady's rather, how should I say it, aberrant sexual tastes? She was an extremely masochistic lover, was she not, *Iain*? The diary tells of some of the *poses* the two of you enacted, and *instruments* you used on each other." The man said this as if it sickened him but the glint in his eyes showed he was actually excited by it. "She writes, in graphic detail, of a room with bondage apparatus. She said *Iain* enjoyed this room immensely."

Iain knew the man was hoping to humiliate him with this disclosure. There were a lot of things in his past Dylan and Caitlyn wouldn't understand and didn't need to hear. He grit his teeth and tried to shut the man's voice out of his head.

"Every room in the house was a stage for sick exploits, and much of the grounds, as well, weren't they? She tells of orgies of oral gratification, masturbation and sodomy."

Caitlyn was clearly uncomfortable. She looked like she was ready to run out of the room. Her brother's hand on her shoulder kept her from moving.

Dylan wasn't enjoying this either, his own jaw was clenched tight. He didn't intend to give the vice president the satisfaction of having broken them.

Iain was finding it harder to keep quiet as he watched their faces lose shades of color.

"Mistress Tessa wrote that your most *favorite* activity was her infamous orgies."

"That's a lie!" spat Iain, finally at his wit's end.

Gerard smiled. He didn't consider it a complete victory yet. This recount hadn't bothered the pirate's men but he had disturbed the president's children. Juiced by this, he turned to Caitlyn and asked, "Tell us, Ms. Nason, was he rough with you or do you like it that way?"

"Don't fucking speak to her like that," said Iain under his breath.

"Or has he been *nothing but kind* to you," repeating her words to her father when the pirates had used her as a shield to escape capture at the Ky'istra challenge. "He is probably afraid if you saw the *real* Iain Bryce you'd run away screaming. He's so proud of his image, aren't you though, Bryce?" None of them particularly reacted to that. He turned the page in the diary and smiled. "Ah, this was something that surprised me. She says here, that they used pleasure drugs, beads, and whips, tasers and hot wax played significant roles." He looked at Iain and saw what he took as confirmation in his eyes, "No, can't deny that, can you? Ryar, can tell you a bit about that too, can't you?"

"Leave him alone! *He is innocent,*" said Iain in a voice so sinister that even Jaime was taken aback.

"*Innocent,* you say? I doubt you would defend him if you knew what he has told me of you," said Gerard.

Ryar appeared surprised by this remark.

Iain gave the vice president a look to say he didn't understand the cryptic remark.

"Tell me, Bryce, who is Ryar Stanney to you?"

"A hostage," the pirate captain growled.

"Really? Then he means nothing more than credits to you, does he?" asked the man. He grabbed a handful of Ryar's hair and pulled his head upward. The boy's body lifted out of the chair, if he hadn't still been cuffed to it the piece of furniture would have fallen over. Nikolas placed the end of a laser pistol under his chin, charged it full with a flick of a finger and said, "His death would only be a loss of those credit then and you wouldn't care what became of him after, yes?"

Captain Bryce was straining in his chair now, three guards quickly took up stances around him with taser wands positioned inches from him. "Leave him be!"

"Why, Bryce?"

"*Leave him be!*"

"WHY, BRYCE? TELL ME WHY?

"He is just a kid!"

"*Just* a kid, you say?" Nickolas pulled Ryar's hair tighter, making him yelp.

"*HE'S MY SON!*"

There was a fast intake of breath from the corner, "He can't be. Your aren't old enough to be his father. He goes to school with me," said Dylan.

"What?" Iain croaked, his head snapping around to Dylan.

"Oh, he had you fooled! I almost wish he'd had a chance to continue his charade a bit longer. *You thought you had an spawn...*" said the man, putting out his lower lip like he was sad, the look of condescension in the vice president's eyes was perfect. "Your blood *does* run through his veins, Bryce, but not in the way you think."

"Ryar?" Iain's mind raced. Dylan was about twenty two, give or take a year. If Ryar was the same age, he would've only been eleven years old when Ryar was conceived. He remembered his father had left him and his mother about that time and stayed away for a couple of years, and she wouldn't tell him where his father was. It was then she had started drinking heavily, and blaming him for driving his father away. When the man returned he had changed, and had begun to beat his mother and him on a daily basis, often within inches of their lives.

Iain still had vivid nightmares of the numbers 75896 floating before his eyes, every time his father's arm came at him to hit him. When the man returned that number was tattooed on the underside of his left forearm, in deep black ink; he remembered wondering what it had meant at the time. Only four years later he had a similar number, 95246, in his case, tattooed on his own forearm. The ident number Cape Benwick Correctional Camp had given him. He had never made the connection before – if his father had spent those missing years at Cape Benwick that would mean he could've been available for a work crew on Ewie... Iain looked at the boy who had said he was his son, and asked, "Ryar?"

"I see you puzzling it out, *Bryce*." Gerard looked from Iain to Ryar and asked, "Do you wish to tell him or shall I?"

Ryar's eyes came to rest on Iain's, eyes that were just like Iain's and Iain's father's – the look in them was beyond crazy, beyond hatred, beyond evil. "My father *was* Iain Bryce; I just didn't say which one. It doesn't matter; I hate you both. *Mother* sent me away when you came, I was barely four and she didn't want you to see me. She didn't think you would find her sexy if she had a boy tagging along. She sent me to a school that might as well've been a prison. I was beaten and raped regularly, by students and teachers both. When I did hear from *mother* it was to tell me how much better than our father *you* were. She recognized you as soon as she saw you, even without knowing your name, and thought it a *right* brilliant joke to say she'd had you as well your father. It excited her I think, but then you left too, didn't you.

"*Mother* took several lovers after you, but she never kept any of them for more than a few months; like I said, I think you broke her. I was fifteen when she finally allowed me to come home. She was different by then, she looked at me different. I think, at first, she thought I was you or him, our *father*. I was so starved for affection, of any kind, that… I… I… let her do things to me…" the boy shivered in his chair, as if trying to knock something off him that he didn't like. The look of hatred in Ryar's eyes when he looked up at Iain then was almost physical. "She told me to do it the way you did and wanted to call me Iain; you can't *imagine* how much I hate that name. I didn't want her dead but I am not sorry that she is."

Iain shook his head slowly.

"*You ruined my life*, so now I am ruining yours. Look at the girl, do you think she could ever look at you with innocent eyes again?" spat Ryar.

Iain's eyes unconsciously went to Caitlyn in time to see her look away. He felt his heart clench at that moment, there had been a day he thought they were better off if she hated him, a part of him still did, but not like this.

Dylan put his hand on his sister's shoulders again but this time Caitlyn pulled away.

She walked up to the vice president and slapped him hard across the face then ran out of the room.

"My father will hear about this," said Dylan as he followed her out.

Gerard laughed heartily. He motioned for Ryar to be released then the two of them and the guards left the room, leaving the captain shackled to the chair.

Captain Bryce's head was down, his eyes were closed, his jaw was clenched tight and he was pulling on the bands holding him to the chair so hard they were cutting deep into his wrists.

"There was no way for you to know," said Jaime empathetically.

"Oh, I think a part of me knew… part of me knew from the start. Tessa had made comments that I'd taken as just her sadistic and sarcastic jabs, I now see was sick references to my father and Ryar."

"It couldn't have been easy to learn like that…" started Jaime.

"Don't try to psychoanalyze me, Quartermaster, believe me, my mind is not a place you would right like to be just now," growled the captain.

"So, what now?" asked Jared.

"Now, I would guess we will be getting a right bullocks of a trial," said Iain smugly. He looked up at Jared and added, "I'm sorry, Master Way, you, as yet, have done nothing to deserve what you're about to get."

"Maybe not in a physical sense, Iain, but I have in my heart. So, I'm with you to the end."

"But, it was such a short run," said a sardonic Captain Bryce.

"I have read reports that say you've gotten out of stickier situations than this, I have faith you'll get us out yet," said Jared with such certainty.

Iain smiled. Sounding more like his wiseass self, he said, "Yeah, well, if only I could reach my lock pick set. Of all the bizarre things I learned from Tessa, how to fold myself in half was not one of 'em." He was sniggering as the last words came out.

They all laughed for several minutes, drawing the attention of the guards who looked at them as if they were insane, which made them only laugh harder.

"Fear is faith that it won't work out."
   —   Sister Mary Tricky

Eve fidgeted with one of the captain's pens while she waited for her father to come to the monitor. His assistant was quite put out that she insisted on speaking to him even though he said he was in a meeting. She hadn't spoken to him in eight months, not since Hayden left and Jared joined them; she wished it were on better terms now.

He looked older than she remembered when he stepped in front of the screen. "Hi, Daddy."

"I can't help," said Markus quickly, before she was able to ask.

"Why not?"

"There will be too many eyes on me. They know you're with Bryce, and that I have also lost Leftenant Commander Way to him. The coincidence is too great. I'm on shaky ground as it is," said the man, dejectedly.

"I can't force you to help and I *do* understand; just remember, part of what they will be charging them with was because of you," referring to killing Dirk Riley. "You know what Nikolas will do to them..."

"Yes and I will be expected to vote in favor of it, Evie. I can't risk going openly against him." The look of concern on his daughter's face was so striking. He had never been able to say no to the girl before. "I'll see what I can do but I make no promises."

"Thank you, Daddy."

"Are *you* alright? You look tired, Evie." With Captain Bryce, the quartermaster and weapons master in custody she would be acting captain. He knew she had never particularly liked leadership.

"I'm not the most comfortable trying to fill Captain Bryce's large shoes, but Robyn is helping me."

"Not that I condone Jared's joining you, but he is useful and is well practiced in such."

"He was one of the ones taken," said Eve.

"The reports said they had the top three?"

"Hayden is no longer a member of our Enclave. Eve said quickly, and, without stopping, added, "Will you let me know anything you can as soon as you can. We've been trying to get to Earth but the spaceways are crammed and CRF are out in full force."

She said the first so fast Markus wasn't sure he had heard her right but the second was what concerned him, "*Do not come to Earth*, Eve. They are hoping you will do that."

"I know. I haven't been out of the CRF that long."

Jared being one of captives actually gave Markus a possible excuse to go see them. "I'll try to get in to see them."

"Thank you, Daddy... Thank you... I love you."

Markus was stunned; she hadn't said those words in five years. "I love you too, Darling."

Eve took a moment to get her thoughts together before leaving Iain's office. She walked the few steps to the ladder, climbed to the top deck of the ship and walked into the conference room, where the others were waiting. They all looked up when she walked in and more than one let out deep breaths when she smiled at them. "He's going to try to see them before the trial…"

"Is he going to help us get them out?" asked Mitch.

"He says there is no way too."

"We've all seen pirate trials before, they are rarely just, let alone fair, which means they will hang," said Mitch.

"We can't get through the borders, and I don't think Captain Bryce would want us to try. He knew what it meant to get caught and has been ready for the day it happened," said Yard.

"I still can't figure out how they knew where we were," said Digger.

"I'm betting this *Mistress Tessa* the news is going on about was involved," said Yard.

"I wouldn't put it past her, but she's dead," said Eve. She was aware of some of the things the woman was famous for. "Let's wait and see what my father can learn and go from there."

The pirates were finally released from the room they had been held in for most of their time on Earth and taken to another cell with cots. Jaime couldn't sleep, Iain was drifting in and out but Jared had managed to completely. Iain came fully awake when a voice he recognized sounded down the hall, he looked at Jaime and both said at the same time, "Markus?"

Senator Oakley appeared in front of the cell with a guard beside him. "Jared Way was one of the garrison stationed with me on Colum. He went AWOL eight months ago. I need to have a word with him."

The guard gave the senator a look that said he wasn't certain he should. He was in no position to deny the request though. He nodded, swiped the card in the device that operated the laser bars, motioned the senator inside, then turned the bars back on.

Markus kicked the edge of the cot Jared was asleep on, "That's right, wake up you worthless piece of crap."

Jared came awake with a start. He looked like he wasn't sure just where he was, surprised to see Markus looming over him. "Wha... what... Sir?"

"Did you truly believe you were going to get away with defecting and joining these *pirates*? I've lost all respect for you," said the senator loudly. He put up his finger to quiet them as he stepped to the opening and looked out. Seeing no sign of life he turned back and asked, "How are you?"

"We've been better," said Iain.

"Yeah, I suppose. Eve wanted me to check on you. She is trying to find a way to retrieve you but I told her to stay away. The vice president has increased the CRF's coverage of the planet. He is taking no chances."

"Right good thing that, catching them would really make his day," said Iain sarcastically.

"Yes, well… She wanted me to try to help but… I've heard most of what you'll be charged with and doubt many of the senate will be in your favor."

"Senator Oakley, none of us expects you to do anything other than rule against us. Deep down Eve knows you can't risk yourself. She knows I've been ready for this day," said Iain.

"Yes. Still. I'll see what I can do; there are some that may be swayed."

"Markus, no! We will take what we get," said Iain forcefully.

"You've always been a stubborn bastard."

"That he has," said Jaime. He squinted his eyes at his captain and added, "He's right though."

The senator stepped to the cell door and shouted for the guard to let him out. He grumbled, "Ungrateful bastard," as he walked out.

"There is no man so wholly good who, were he to submit his thoughts and actions to the law, would not deserve being hanged at least ten times in his life."
— Michel Eyguem de Montaigne

The next morning ten guards appeared at the entrance of the cell.

The pirates were ordered to stand and face the wall with their hands before them in clear view, the three did as ordered and the laser bars were dropped. One of the guards stepped in and clasped a band around each man's throat, explaining to them that they emit sonic waves that will prevent them from speaking. They were led out of the cell, taken to the quadrangle and led to a dais that was hovering a few feet off the ground before the spectator box. A smaller dais, also hovering, slightly to the right of theirs, had a single chair on it – the witness box.

All of the Confederational Regime parliament was seated before them; some had looks of disgust on their faces other looked bored. The president and vice were the only ones in the spectators box but neither had happy looks on their faces. All the major space news stations had camera crews set up, ready to relay the proceedings to any that couldn't be there in person and wanted to see *justice* given.

Iain glanced around, as best he could, without drawing attention, he couldn't see Dylan, Caitlyn or Ryar anywhere. It was just as well, he might well have tried to get to Ryar to kill him, and he didn't want Caitlyn there anyway. The stadium was packed full though, he thought offhandedly how many colonies he could help with what they would have collected in admission fees. He brought his eyes back to his men and looked from one to the other, 'Whatever happens, it's been a right grand honor pirating with ya both,' both men mouthed the same back then they looked straight ahead and waited.

Gerard's heart was beating fast and he felt like he was flying. He was looking forward to this; even the mood of the president wouldn't sour it for him. Thomas hadn't thought it necessary to expose his daughter to the degradation that was Iain Bryce's past, even if it might change her opinion of him, that wasn't how he thought it should've been handled. Gerard didn't care, he wanted his pound of flesh.

He stood and called for silence then stepped to the edge of the box and turned to face the senatorial body. "Venerable men and women of the Confederational Regime parliament: President Nason and I want to thank you for making the trip. I know many of you came a great distance, on short notice, for this, however, as I'm sure you too will feel, the president and I felt it was of the utmost importance we handle this tribunal quickly. These men have managed to slip through our fingers on too many occasions in the past.

"We have before us today three BrimTier pirates from the enclave known as Phoenix: captain, Iain Bryce, his quartermaster, Jaimes Cable and Jared Way, whom we believe to be currently acting as his weapons master. They stand accused of numerous atrocities against the Confederational Regime and the people of all three Tiers. We are confident once you've heard all the witnesses you, like us, will wish to expedite the necessary course of action.

"First, I will read the charges against each, present witnesses to the crimes then allow you to deliberate. We hope the trial will go swiftly and without incident so that you can return to your homes quickly. We are also ready to hand down punishment immediately, if you feel it prudent." Gerard hoped he hadn't sounded quite as eager to have that very thing happen as it did to his own ears. He paused to let that statement dissolve from their minds before finishing his opening remarks, "Madam Foreperson, please say when you are ready to begin."

A stout woman of about sixty with purplish gray curly hair stood and scanned the group around her then motioned for the trial to begin.

"I, Confederational Regime vice president and Fleet Admiral, Gerard Nikolas, will be presenting the case. I will begin with the charges against Jared William Way, a former leftenant commander stationed on Colum. He is charged with deserting his post, insubordination, theft of wages, dissemination of military secrets, attacking a supply convoy attempting to deliver supplies to a colony, conspiracy to commit murder, accomplice in the murder of Dirk Riley, aiding and abetting, and various crimes of piracy; including: theft, rape, brutality and murder." Gerard looked down at the man, seeing the look of anxiety on his face made him smile.

"Jaimes Aaron Cable is accused of theft of wages after his separation from Dragon Troop, dissemination of military secrets, conspiracy to commit murder and as an accomplice in the murder of Dirk Riley. He's also accused of crimes of piracy including: theft, terrorism, kidnapping, brutality, rape and murder. He was recently convicted of the assault and battery of fifty patrons in a bar on Berem and was sentenced to ten years in Belgorian Prison, while there he assaulted nine men and escaped from the prison." Gerard paused again. He looked at the group of officials before him, wanting to make sure they all had sufficiently digested what he said before beginning on his final quarry.

"The pirate captain, Iain Daniel Bryce's, list is quite extensive. His begins nearly twenty years ago with multiple counts of petty theft then escalates to assault and battery of a CRF soldier and finally to the murder of his own father. He is being charged with escaping from Belgorian Prison, from his twenty year sentence for the murder of his father, repeated sexual deviance, theft of the ship he pirates from, coercing CRF officers into dereliction of duty, thievery, extortion, brutality, kidnapping, terrorism, depraved indifference and violence to innocents, aiding in a prison break, the previous mentioned escape of Jaimes Cable, evading arrest, numerous times, multiple murders, including most recently, Dirk Riley. He is accused of raping Tessa Stanney, multiple times, and is suspected in the recent brutal killing of the lady, and in multiple, malicious and brutal rapes of the president's daughter, Caitlyn Nason."

Angry murmurs swept through the audience and the senate at the last two statements.

Gerard smiled satisfactorily and waited for the groans of disgust to end before continuing. "They will be allowed a brief rebuttal at the end of this hearing. May I call the first witness to the stand?"

"You may," said the forewoman.

Iain wanted to laugh; the vice president was parading around the box like a peacock strutting for a mate – making a complete ass of himself. He knew this whole show was nothing but a overblown Charade.

The name of the first witness made Iain groan even though no sound came out due to the neckband. He barely recognized the man that slowly walked out of the audience to take a seat on the other floating dais, the last two decades hadn't been kind to him. He smiled wickedly as he passed them, showing the crowd what few teeth he had left in his mouth.

In a lot of ways John Viescass was the one that started Iain down the path he was now on. Last he knew he was in Serson Prison for murdering a shopkeeper after robbing him, which Iain had assisted in. Iain had testified against John then, for his freedom; how ironic that John would now be testifying for the CRF against him.

After swearing him in, which was a farce in itself, Iain doubted he could say anything that wasn't a lie, he heard Nikolas ask him to tell them, in his own words, what he was like as a boy.

"Bryce was always eager to join in any robbery or beatin's. Especially if they was gonna be weapons used. He had a mean streak that went deep. Nothin' alive had a chance 'round him. He drove his mum to drinkin', druggin' and whorin', and beat and verbally abused both his parents. I watched him near beat his father to death when he told him he wanted him out and then did kill him not long after."

Again the crowd murmured angrily. Iain and Jaime only shook their heads, both knowing the real story, Jared only looked forlorn.

"You say Bryce had a mean streak? Can you explain this in more detail?"

"Yeah, like I was saying, anythin' alive was fair game to him. I watched him mutilate dogs, cats and even a pigeon, to death, more than once. Sometimes he'd keep 'em barely alive to see how long it'd take them to die, like starvin' them to death, and the like."

John had described his own childhood enjoyment. In point of fact, Iain had saved more than one of the boy's victims and told him they had died.

"Thank you, Mr. Viescass. Now, I would like to call Zachary Tobias."

The manservant for the late mistress walked to the stand and recounted the acts he'd been witness to while Iain was living at the estate, including abuses he had inflicted on Tessa, coloring everything to make it sound as if it had been against the woman's wishes. Any wounds he inflicted on the woman was entirely by her request, and, technically, she had raped him since he was underage at the time of their first encounters. The howls of outrage from the audience told Iain it wouldn't have mattered if he tried to defend himself; they wouldn't have listened anyway.

The next witnesses told of the men's terrorism of them as victims of their piracy. Admiral Flint testified of

Jared helping the captain to escape from Sunnen. Gideon Brody told of some of the sieges he had been on while acting as a member of the crew. The vidfeed from the bar on Berem was played and some of the men involved in the brawl told how Jaime had attacked them, without provocation. Inmates from Belgorian Prison, during both Iain and Jaime's stints, testified to violence they were a part of while there, claiming it was they that tried to rape them, instead of the other way around. Four members of Dirk Riley's crew gave details of how Iain had shot Riley, who was unarmed and had already surrendered, conveniently leaving out that he'd run Eve through with a knife just moments before, and how Jaime and Jared had assisted in the disposal of his body, leaving him floating in the asteroid cluster, then took them all hostage and stole their ship, profiting from its sale.

It all looked very grim for them, the audience was already screaming for their blood and wanted them to be hanged, Iain couldn't imagine how it could get any worse when he heard Rear Admiral Anton Anders being called to the stand.

The man had helped them their last encounter and said he counted them an ally of sorts, but the rear admiral had lost a star because of Iain's trickery; what better chance to not only get it back but put himself back on the fleet admiral's favored list. He would certainly have a brighter future in that arena. Iain lowered his head and prayed it would all be over with soon.

"Vice Admiral Anders, oh, sorry, *Rear* Admiral Anders, tell us of your history with the accused before us," said Gerard, feeling more than pleased with how things were going.

"I know little of the one named Jared Way, other than his impeccable record of service to the CRF before defecting, so I can say nothing against him. I hold no animosity toward the other two; in fact, they actually helped my crew in our last two encounters."

Iain's head came up so quickly he nearly stumbled backward off the dais.

"They what? I seem to recall the pirate captain tricked you into turning in one of our own agents as him, causing you to lose a level of rank?"

"I lost the rank due to my own incompetence...."

"Did they offer you something to say this..." sputtered Gerard, upset the man was actually attempting to aid the pirates.

"Are you accusing the rear admiral of wrong-doing, Mr. Nikolas?" asked the forewoman. He shook his head. "Please allow the man to speak then."

The rear admiral continued, "As I was saying, your honors, they assisted in the capture of criminal overlord, Terrance Lockheed, who was terrorizing the colony of Tolimon. These men risked their lives and should receive special civilian accommodations, in my opinion. "

"Dismissed! *Dismissed*!" shouted Gerard, not wanting him to say anything else.

The forewoman nodded so Anton stepped out of the box and slowly started up the aisle, smiling at the three accused as he passed.

Gerard was fuming, but he quickly regained his coolness and smiled as he called his next witness: Moira Saunders, retinue for the president's daughter, and a one-time hostage of Phoenix Enclave. He had coached her on just what to say so he knew he was safe with her. "Please tell us of your experience with the pirates below, Ms. Saunders."

Iain suddenly wished he'd been nicer to her; she hadn't liked his attempts to seduce her ward much. Any help Anders might have given them would likely be quickly negated here.

"We were aboard a bluejay transport heading to Tarnis Prime. The ship's engines died, dumping us from hyperspace. Two of those men there, and some of their crew," pointing to the pirates, "boarded and stripped the ship of anything worth taking."

"Tell us what they did with any that weren't worth keeping for ransom," said Gerard, smiling down on them.

"They put them in escape pods with enough food to get them by until the CRF could find them and pick them up," she said defiantly.

"No, no, they had them killed…"

"No, sir, you are mistaken. I've spoken to several that were aboard the bluejay that day and I assure you they are alive and well," she said smiling.

"Very well, we will assume that to be the case since we have no one here that can verify that. Tell us of his treatment of you and your ward, Caitlyn Nason."

"The pirates were very courteous to us. We were fed full and satisfying meals, given the use of one of their guest rooms and allowed access to almost any part of the ship we wished. I actually enjoyed it more than the bluejay, to be perfectly honest."

"Damn it, he's gotten to her too. I wish to add witness tampering and bribery to the charges."

"Sir, the pirates have been under guard the whole time here, how could they have?" asked the foreperson.

"This is… this is ridiculous. Very well, very well, I wish to call my next witness. Eugene Boscoe."

Iain had just started to breathe again, he'd seen the looks on the faces of many of the CRP soften after Moira's testimony, which also gave him hope with Caitlyn, but he doubted Boscoe would be good.

Murmurs of repulsion went through the audience at the mere sight of the ex-pirate. Eugene Boscoe wasn't a handsome man any time, the current state of his hair and the layers of grime on his face now made him look even worse. He had been one step away from crazy before he had spent years in solitary confinement. Today he had a strange perpetual half sneer on his face and his eyes wouldn't alight on anything for long.

"Mr. Boscoe, tell us how you know the accused."

"The who?"

"The pirate captain, Iain Bryce?"

"Oh, him. We've 'ad run-ins o'r da yers tryin' to hit da same ships," said the man.

"The ship he currently claims as his was once yours, correct? Tell us how Bryce came to have it?" asked Vice President Nikolas.

"We was playin' p'ker an' he cheated. I tink he drugged me an' when I weren't lookin' switched 'er cards."

"So he cheated and swapped your cards, you say?" Mr. Nikolas paraphrased so all could understand the man's broken English.

"I 'ad two eights an' two acers when I looked away aways, an' when I looked back, I 'ad two eights and two fours an 'e had four acers."

"He swapped your *aces* for his fours, meaning he cheated. Essentially he stole the ship from you."

"Well not 'xactly, I 'ad put da ship up as I is a 'lil short on creds at the time, so if'n the hand was played right'n he would'ved won it, far 'n square."

"But if he cheated then he stole your ship!"

"I got no proof of it," said the man as he shrugged.

Gerard was getting very hot now; he had thought his witnesses were solid. "Dismissed!" he cried quickly.

"Do you have any other witnesses?" asked the foreperson.

Gerard did, but he no longer trusted what they would say so he fiercely shook his head.

The foreperson turned her attention to the three men standing accused. She sked for the collar around the pirate captain's neck to be shut off so he could speak. "Are you able to speak for all three of you?"

Iain had to clear his throat several times, the sonic waves had been tickling his voice box long enough to make it numb. "Yes," he croaked out and, after a bit of a cough, he added, "I am."

"What do you say to these charges?"

"President Nason, *Mr. Nikolas*, Madam Foreperson and CRP members, we cannot and will not insult your intelligence by attempting to refute or deny the charges before us. We *are,* admittedly, BrimTier pirates, that lifestyle comes with a certain expectation of criminal behavior. We do, however, deny ever participating in brutality, terrorism or rape. *I would defy any to find one that can honestly say otherwise!*" Iain looked directly at the vice president. "In any case, we are guilty of enough of the charges before you and will accept anything you find appropriate as punishment for *those* charges."

Many of the senators looked impressed at how well the pirate captain spoke, especially after listening to Boscoe's broken English and that he did not try to deny many of the wrongdoings. They had all sat in judgement on trials where the accused all but sold their mother's soul in claiming their innocence. The foreperson looked back at some of them before turning back to the pirates.

"We are ready to deliberate, please take these men back to their cell. We will contact the president when we are come to a decision."

"In reality, hope is the worst of all
evils, for it prolongs man's torment."
  —   Friedrick Nietzsche

Markus stepped into his stateroom. He had just come from the CRP conference and was unsure what to do. He had no doubt the radio was being monitored so he had no idea how could he get word to Eve. Even if he could, did he really want to? If they knew what was about to happen they wouldn't let the entire CRF body stop them from coming, would they?

He had to look at this objectively. He felt a little guilty that a part of him, deep down, wanted this. They were pirates – they had robbed, terrorized, pillaged and killed, and apparently Iain Bryce had raped Caitlyn Nason. He was capable of anything if he felt the need, wasn't he?

He started to pour himself a stiff drink when the combox on his bedside table buzzed, making him jump. "Please, don't let it be Eve." He pushed the receive button. It wasn't. It was a man he never thought he'd be speaking to after what Nikolas had said.

"Senator Oakley, I may be out of line here, if I am I'm sorry for this intrusion, but…" said Dylan Nason.

The president's son looked beside himself and his sister was pacing behind him, wringing her hands and not even trying to hide her tears. Markus thought they must be looking to learn the pirates' fate; probably wanting to make the girl feel better, knowing her violator was being dealt with. "I can't tell you of the decision…"

"No. You misunderstand the reason for my call, Senator. Besides, I probably already know… Your daughter is Eve Oakley, a member of Captain Bryce's enclave, right?" asked Dylan.

Markus said nothing, not certain why the boy would need to hear him confirm this.

"I wish to stop it and am wondering if you'd be willing to help?"

Markus was taken up short and choked on an ice cube, "You… you what?"

Caitlyn stopped, faced the monitor and said, pleadingly, "We can't let them kill him."

"I don't know what I can do… I told Eve…"

Dylan quickly spoke over him, "I *have* a way to get them off Earth and to safety but I need your help."

"I… well… alright," said Markus, caught between his duty to the Confederational Regime and his duty to his daughter.

"I need to get word to Phoenix?" said the president's son.

"I can't contact them, It'll be noticed if I send a message outside of Earth's atmosphere," said Markus, hoping he sounded more sincere to them than he did to his own ears.

"I can. I have a signal scrambler on my ship."

"They're just beyond the First Tier, sector fifteen."

Dylan nodded, "Do you want me to give your daughter any message?"

"Tell her… if this doesn't work, I am *truly* sorry."

The crew of Phoenix was stunned numb as they watched the ridiculous trial playing out before them. They had patched into a digital signal from Earth so they could watch the farcical proceedings. It made it worse in a lot of ways, knowing they could do nothing but watch. Some of the testimony had helped, but not enough. They knew their shipmates were about to be put to death and were absolutely sick over it.

Mitch and Digger had stormed out of the room after the men from the bar on Berem had testified against Jaime, Yard left just before now vice admiral, Flint, came on, saying he didn't want to know the outcome, Kyle was in the helm room with Kassie, neither of them even wanted to hear the trial, the ladies hadn't moved from the monitor. They couldn't bring themselves to stop watching. They were only half listening though, as the newswoman recapping the charges and some of the worst of the testimony as they paced, both ready to scream. They both did so and jumped when the com buzzed.

Eve guffawed and shook her head at Robyn as she pushed the button on the box and told Kyle to speak.

"Ma'am, I have Dylan Nason on link for you!?"

"Oh, um… well… put him through."

The young man that appeared on the monitor before the two lady pirates was trying to smile but it was obviously forced, "Ms. Oakley? Your father sends his regards… Um, Captain Bryce, Master Cable and Jared Way have been sentenced to death by lasernoose…"

Eve nodded and Robyn sank into a chair, both already knowing inside that was to be their sentence.

"I was wondering… I don't know if this will work and will likely be beside them if it doesn't," said Dylan as if just realizing this himself. He shook his head and continued, "I may have a way to get them free…"

Eve jumped, "What? How?"

"I can't give you all the details, I have yet to work them out myself, but if I can make this work can you meet us on Ryger in two days?" asked Dylan.

"Yes. How will we know if you have succeeded?"

"It will be all over the news," said the president's son bluntly.

The same look was mirrored in Eve, Robyn and Caitlyn's faces – a look of hope.

"Courage: the art of being the only one
who knows you are frightened to death."
— Old *Semai'* Proverb

The pirates were pacing the room in a neat row, listening to the guards taking bets on which would beg for mercy, cry like a babe, and shit or piss themselves first, before and after the noose went around their necks, who would die first and whose head would leave their body first. Most all of them were choosing the captain. Their roaring laughter and disgusting sound effects only made the men's anxiety worse.

"If I do, somehow, live through this, I'm gonna come back and kill them," grumbled Jared.

"From your mouth to God's ears, Master Way," said Iain.

No sooner had the captain said those words, one of the very guards appeared at the door. He sniggered as he said, "S'been decided, you're ta be 'anged."

The second guard, a little more composed but smiling just as wickedly, said, "Against the wall, arms in front, you know the routine by now."

The three were once more taken to the quadrangle and once more directed to the raised dais. They did so, a little slower than before, their eyes lingering behind them. A large structure, similar to a gallows of old, was being erected between them and the audience, and the newscasters and camera crews were being resituated to have the best view of the bodies as they swung. The vice president and president were back in the spectators box, looking very pleased, and the senators were all back in their seats behind it.

Iain tried to relay some courage to his men, but he didn't have much of it himself. He was only half aware as the foreperson stood and made her announcement.

"Iain Daniel Bryce, Jaimes Aaron Cable, Jared William Way, you have been found guilty of all counts presented before this senate. Pursuant to this decision, you are to be hanged from the neck by lasernoose until you are dead."

The audience went wild but the pirates couldn't tell if it was in happiness or anger, it all sounded muffled and distant.

Iain *had* known this day would come, it was a given in their profession. He had always said he was ready for it, and had fooled himself into thinking he was. Now he found his legs weak, his stomach twisted, his heart and head pounding and he had an overwhelming desire to cry. He tried to stand stoic and nonchalant. Jaime and Jared didn't look to be much better. He wished he could find a way to save them. He tried to get his eyes to clear and focus but the scene in front of him wasn't anything he wished to see. The dais had rotated, so they were now facing the means of their death.

The large post and beam structure stood twenty feet off the ground with a stage under it. Three rope-like lasernooses, glowing a slight orange-yellow in the lights of the stadium, hung from the top beam over a panel in the floor. The base was lit with white chaser lights to show the viewers where it would slide open to allow their feet to dangle free and their bodies to drop when those lasernooses had finally cut through the bones.

A group of guards was advancing on the pirates, to take them to that scaffold.

A part of Iain wanted desperately to run, even knowing he would likely be shot dead on the spot, and in the back. That would be less painful and less demeaning than what he was facing. He remembered the cameras and knew his crew on Phoenix and many of the colonies they supported were probably watching. He could also feel the president and vice president's eyes on him. He would be damned if he was going to let them see how distressed he was. He decided if he *was* going to die he'd do it with dignity, or at least the appearance of.

The guards had now reached the pirates.

Two stood behind Jaime, two in front of Jared, the others took up positions around them, blocking Iain in the center like a trapped rat. His legs felt three times heavier than they should, and his boots felt full of cement, it was all he could do to put one foot in front of the other, doing it out of habit at this point. His head was cloudy as all the things he wished he'd done and all the things he wished he hadn't flashed before his eyes, making him a little bit dizzy. He had a case of heartburn he wouldn't wish on his worst enemy – well then again yeah, he would Gerard Nikolas.

It seemed like forever before they reached the bottom of the ramp up to the scaffold, and, at the same time they found himself there suddenly. They were led up the platform and each was stopped below a dangling noose then the loop was placed around each of their necks.

Iain looked from Jaime to Jared and was proud to see they looked as set as he was. He gave each a quick nod and they returned it, then they faced forward. He felt a slight stinging buzz from the noose where it came into contact with his skin. It tickled the hairs on the back of his neck and made it itch but he refused to scratch. His heart was pounding so rapidly he wondered if he was even going to live to feel the hot noose close; a part of him hoped he didn't. He heard his compatriots; breathing increase and prayed to whatever God might be listening that he, or she, make this quick for them.

Iain watched the president stand to speak to the parliament, newscasters and the audience and heard him ask if they had any last words. He thought for a moment, what did he want his last words in this life to be? He looked at each of his men then back at the president. Clearly and boldly, he said, "You think this is the end but you are wrong. Another will step up because ours *is* a just cause. Never cease to amaze and stay the course!"

The pirate captain was pleased to see an odd look come to the face of the president and vice president and could see the newscasters frantically repeating what he had said so they could be included in stories that likely would be told and retold for a long time to come. His triumph was short-lived as he watched the president motion for the lasernooses to be tightened.

The pirates took a deep, and final breath, as the ropes tightened, stopping just as they reached skin, then there was nothing under their feet and they were falling.

Several of the people sitting in the audience and thousands of voices across the known universe screamed in unison.

"Have faith
– you will be taught how to fly,"
    –   *Pastor Maxwell Bryce*

Something unexpected happened then.

The lasernooses did close around their necks and the floor did open and they did fall, feet dangling free, but instead of cutting off their air supply and their heads, the ropes released and they dropped, rather quickly, and painfully, through the opening, down ten feet to a pitch-black room below the staging.

The pirates were pulled to their feet roughly and a male voice said, "Come with us."

A little dazed and confused, they were led down several dark passageways. They had no idea where they were going or who was taking them there but at least they weren't dead. They could hear people in the quadrangle screaming and feet pounding on the floor above their heads and knew guards were trying to find them.

Finally they entered a lit enough section of corridor to illuminate their escorts. None looked to be more than twenty-five. "Who are you?" Iain demanded.

"We're with Dylan Nason," said the man.

Before Iain could ask for more information, the man himself appeared; walking toward them at a fast pace.

Dylan had a big ass grin on his face and a very mischievous look in his eyes. He was holding a device that looked very much like the one that ran the shock-collar Iain had given to Victor Black to get Caitlyn back. Iain wondered, for a moment, if the man had decided he had harmed his sister and wanted to dole out his own punishment.

The young man smiled innocently and said, "This is your rescue, Captain Bryce." He waved the device over the bands around their wrists and they clicked and released.

"What the hell you doing?" barked Iain. "Are you a complete dolt? Your father will *kill* you for this."

"As far as he knows I'm heading for Tarnis Prime, escorting my sister back to school," said Dylan, rather proud of himself. "Of course, if you would rather…"

All three men smiled and shook their heads.

Iain nodded sideways at the apparently ingenious plan. He rubbed at his neck and added, "Lead the way."

The group of ten escorts, Dylan, Iain, Jaime and Jared quickly boarded a shuttle waiting at the dock outside the quadrangle. Within minutes they had launched and were docking with a battleskip just outside Earth's atmosphere. Soon as they exited the shuttle Iain was bodily attacked by Caitlyn. She was covering his face with kisses. It took both he and Dylan to call her off.

"Captain Bryce, we've hollowed out three torpedo tubes. It won't be comfortable but you need to get in them and wait until we're outside of the Tier. The CRF are searching all ships leaving Earth…"

"We will be fine, show us the way, Mr. Nason."

The young man hadn't lied, the torpedo tubes were barely big enough; in fact Iain and Jaime had to lay sideways with their knees bent, but their comfort was small enough sacrifice. He also was right about the ship being searched. They had no more than gotten into the tubes when a squad of CRF troopers boarded the ship.

Iain could hear someone pounding around on the walls and decking then a knocking on the tube he was in. He had to force himself not to scream at the loud echoes that rang through it for several minutes after. Over the ringing in his ears he heard someone say loudly that their captain wouldn't be pleased if they dented the weapon's casing, causing it to go off course in a battle. This apparently was enough to make the soldier cease his attempts.

They were left in the coffin-like hiding places for about another hour, then they were freed and led up to the conference room where a large buffet of nearly every food imaginable had been set up for them. They ate and drank heartily.

Iain was staring at the flashing points of lights of the hyperspace conduit out the window of the cabin he was given. He was so completely at peace that he jumped when the door alarm buzzed. He said, "Enter."

Jaime and Jared did, with huge smiles on their faces.

"That was a little too close for comfort," said Jared, with deep emotions.

"Jaime and I are used to this, well, as much as one can be, we wouldn't be upset if you've decided this is too much for you, Jared," said Iain.

"Are you kidding me? I've never felt more alive!"

The captain and first mate smiled, feeling the same. That adrenaline rush was quickly wearing off though. The men wished the captain good night and left to find their beds.

Caitlyn stepped in as they were leaving, "Do you want to be alone?" she asked tentatively.

"I owe your brother and, if I'm not mistaken, you, our lives, Lady," said Iain, taking her hands in his and kissing the back of each.

"Did you honestly think I would, or could, let that happen to you?" asked Caitlyn.

"I wasn't sure, after what you'd learned about me."

"It just makes you… you," said Caitlyn.

They quickly found their way to the bed and Iain used the last bit of his own adrenaline rush to thank her properly.

"I have a firm grasp on reality! I can reach out and strangle it at any time!"
— Author Unknown

The next morning found Iain at his desk, in his office on Phoenix, with a cup of coffee before him, his eyes closed and his heart filled with peace. He had honestly thought he would never be in this place again. He had just about reached his escape when the door alarm buzzed, completely breaking that reverie. Not really wanting to come back to reality just yet but knowing he would have to sooner or later, he mumbled a quick enter.

Jaime stepped into the room and pointed to the coffee pot. Iain nodded and held his own cup up so the quartermaster could refill it. The man then sat in the other chair and sighed heavily, as he waited for his cup to cool off. It was several minutes before he spoke.

"What are you going to do about Ryar?"

Iain hadn't been sure what Jaime was going to say but that was the last subject he wanted to discuss just then. He put his hands over his face, rubbed it roughly and said, "There's a right fucking harsh welcome back to reality!"

"I know you don't want to talk about him, Iain, but you need to."

Iain sighed, "I don't give two shits about Ryar."

"I know the thought of having a son was…"

"I don't have a son!" spat Iain, starting to stand.

"You *thought* he was your son though, Iain, you can't tell me the thought of it wasn't pleasant."

"Before I learned he hated me with the burning fire of two fucking suns, yeah," said Iain sarcastically. He sank back in the chair; knowing, deep down, he did need to get this aired. "Okay, yeah, having a son might have been fun. Robyn can't have kids and, the Lord knows, Caitlyn and I will never amount to anything. This is no life for a kid and I sure the fuck ain't no role-model."

"You're a great role-model, Iain. Take away the criminal part and you're strong, caring, respectful and loyal. As to the life, a child can adapt... We were all happy to hear of Ryar, especially after learning Eve lost her baby. I think we were looking forward to some young blood," said Jaime, taking a sip of his coffee.

"Well that's neither here nor there now, isn't it?"

"He's still your half-brother," said Jaime.

"And?"

"Right. So back to my initial question, what are you going to do about Ryar?"

"Right long as he leaves me and mine alone, I will leave him alone," said Iain.

Parting Words

"I have no clue of how my story will
end, but that's alright. When you set
out on a journey and night covers the
road, you do not conclude that the
road has vanished. How else could
we have discovered the stars?"
–   Unknown

Hi ya'all! Captain Iain Bryce here. I have reached
the final page of this journal, so I'll use it to conclude my
ever jumble of thoughts. As you have read, my exploits
have been rich and varied, some good, some not so. Most
of it I wouldn't have changed.

We almost lost Jaime, did lose Hayden, but gained
a fine friend and shipmate in Jared Way. We made bigger
enemies of the president and vice president, allies of
Caitlyn and Dylan Nason and have some odd bedfellows
in Markus Oakley and Anton Anders. We lost a child,

Eve and Hayden's unborn baby, well two if you count the son I never actually had, gained parents, freeing our pilot's mum and dad, killed a scumbag pirate, lost my memory, got to role-play, a bunch of us got real sick, and three of us almost got our necks stretched but we had a right bloody blast!

If I've entertained you in the least, or you're right morbid enough to want to hear more of my sorted and sordid life, please read the next installment titled *Times of a BrimTier Pirate*.

Signing off for now!

Captain Iain D. Bryce ☠

Lisa J. Comstock